The Secret Kids

To Maya

With love,

Bernadette Richards

אוצרין

The Secret Kids

Bernadette Richards

To order additional copies of this book, contact:
Xlibris LLC
1-888-795-4274
www.Xlibris.com
Orders@Xlibris.com
671126

CONTENTS

Fondly dedicated to
my mother, my sister, and to Marie, Charley and Therese, who listened.
Also dedicated to the Real Secret Kids, with all my love.

Chapter 1

Secrets

A young girl of about fourteen was sitting in a cab, in front of a grim looking boarding school somewhere in London. It was late at night, pouring rain, and her spirits matched the dreary weather. Her name was Christine Philips, and other than that, there was not much to tell about her. She had blonde hair and gray eyes, and was of slight build. She did not know where she was going, or what was going to happen to her, but she knew that she was being sent away from the only home she had ever remembered.

She had been a trouble maker, and she knew it. Though she had almost taken pride in the chaos she had caused, she had never thought that she would be sent away. She had not been happy at the school, for she had a prideful streak, and everything about the school seemed degrading and lowly to her. She felt even more disgusted by the careless way in which she was being disposed of.

She tried to remember when she had come to this school, but all she could remember was being taught how to read and write by teachers; teachers doing all the things that parents might have done. She knew that she was an orphan, but if she ever asked anyone at the school who her parents had been, or how she had arrived there, they would say that children should be seen and not heard, or they would get very flustered, or they would just not answer at all.

The only thing she knew about her family, was her secret. The biggest secret of her life.

She had discovered her secret not long ago. It had been an accident, an over-heard remark. But she loved her secret. It was something she owned, all by herself, and no one would ever get it out of her.

Just as she was thinking these thoughts, the door of the cab opened, and the Dean of the school climbed in beside her. He was a fat man, and inclined to be mean. Apparently he was assigned to take her wherever she was going.

He tapped the cabby on the shoulder, and the cab rolled slowly into motion, while the windshield wipers flapped back and forth, back and forth, incessantly, so that Christine could see at least a few feet ahead, through the driving rain.

The Dean wrapped himself up in his large fur coat, and turning away from Christine, completely ignored her. Christine felt rather annoyed at his rudeness, but she knew she would have been more annoyed if he had tried to make small talk, so she settled herself to look out the window. That only made her more worried and curious about where she was going. When she could bear the suspense no longer, she reached over and tugged on the Dean's coat. From somewhere inside him, there came a growl, and then his round, sour face emerged.

"What do you want?" he grumbled.

"Excuse me, but where am I going?" she asked.

"Away," he said.

"But *where?*" she persisted.

"To a town near the Irish Sea, if you must know, called Manchester," he snapped.

"Manchester!?" cried Christine, sitting up straight and turning very white.

"Yes, Manchester," said the Dean, "Now get some sleep, we won't get there for a long time. So be quiet, and go to sleep."

But Christine could not sleep. At least now she had something to think about; but what a horribly different thing to think about. She knew where Manchester was, not only that, she knew who lived there. It seemed as though her so well kept, precious secret, was finally going to surface.

* * *

The blazing African sun shone down on the bare black shoulders of a young boy, who stood in a small flat boat in the swamps. His skin was dark and his disorderly hair was black, but his eyes were a softer brown color. He held a long stick in one hand, which he used to steer himself. He was staring down into the muddy water, and his thoughts seemed far away. He was just about to return to the shore, when the rushes next to him moved. He froze. Out of the reeds came the gnarled, black back of an animal, which he knew only too well. He looked closely, trying to get a glimpse of the thing's head, but it doubled back, and retreated into the reeds on the other side of his boat. He sighed. For such a long time he had been waiting to find a crocodile, and not just any crocodile, but one that would make him rich beyond his wildest dreams, or so he assumed. And now one had just passed by and he had missed a chance to see if it was The One. He sighed again, and passed his hands over his eyes.

Just at that moment, when he was least expecting it, a large black tail, with hideous scales, flopped itself onto his boat. The little vessel rocked and swayed dangerously. The boy tried to keep his balance as the crocodile swam under his boat, but at the same time he kept a sharp eye out, endeavoring to get a view of its head as it came out of the water. Suddenly, the ugly head appeared right in front of him, and he gave a gasp. For there, just as he had hoped, right at the top of its long snout, was a bright yellow mark. He gave a cry of joy, but just then, the crocodile flashed its tail once again, and the boy's cry of joy turned to a scream as he lost his balance and tumbled backwards into the dark, murky water.

* * *

On the cellar stairs in a poor orphanage, a little girl sat crying. She could not have been over eight years old, and she was small for her age. Her large brown eyes and timid expression gave her a very mousy look. Her face was smeared with dirt and tears, and she had the look of one who was in complete despair.

Every few seconds she would feel her teeth, as if she was afraid they were going to fall out. She was crying because some other children had been mean to her, and because she knew that she would have to go to the dentist that day. And because of her secret, she knew that going to the dentist was almost the same as being murdered, at least for her.

She had lost quite a few teeth lately, and she did not think she could bear to lose another.

Suddenly, she bit her lip and made a resolve. She would not go to the dentist. She would run away, to a place where children could keep their own teeth if they wanted to. She leapt up, ran up the cellar stairs, and with one stealthy look into the children's playroom, crept into the large garden. It was a cold day, and her teeth began to chatter, which frightened her, for in her innocence she thought that if her teeth chattered, they were more likely to fall out.

She made sure that no one was around, and ran over to the large, ivy covered wall which surrounded the orphanage. She climbed into a tree which stood next to the wall, and when she got high enough, she slipped on to it. Then she shut her eyes, set her teeth, and jumped.

* * *

A girl lay on a hospital bed, in a big convent hospital in New York. One could look at that girl for hours, and still not form an opinion of her. She was not very tall, although she seemed at least fourteen, and she seemed very happy, with a cheerful smile that she flashed at anyone she saw. She was not what would be styled 'beautiful'; at least she wore no make-up, and did not have bright blond hair; but she had a charm about her which made you take it for granted that she was very pretty. And really she was.

Her delft blue eyes twinkled and snapped, and they seemed to forever be plotting some mischief. Her hair was very long and trailed all over her bed, and it was a dark brown, almost black, which made her pale skin look white.

Her personality did not reflect that of a girl who has been bedridden for a long time, and yet her pale features and bandaged legs seemed to contradict her sunny smile and clever wit.

On that certain sunny summer morning, she was engrossed in a book, as usual, and she had just come to a most interesting part, when the door of her room opened, and a friendly nun came in.

"Good morning Sally," Sister said, walking across the room to open the curtains.

"Good morning," said Sally, flashing her smile, "what's up?"

"Plenty," said the Sister. "You are moving."

"What?" cried Sally, sitting up in bed. "Why?"

"Well," said the Sister, coming closer to the bed and lowering her voice, "that man keeps coming and asking about you. We have decided that it is too dangerous for you to stay here. Besides," she added with a smile, "you are draining a considerable amount of resources, considering you are staying here indefinitely."

"I thought you were a charitable institution," Sally teased.

Sister smiled and fluffed the pillows.

"So I have to leave?" asked Sally.

"Yes," said Sister, "for your own safety. But we don't know where to send you."

Sally laughed. "Oh, I can handle that."

She reached over her bed and grabbed a large atlas.

"Now. Will you please hand me that pin, Sister?"

The nun handed Sally a large straight pin which was lying on her end table.

"What do you need a pin for, Sally?" she asked.

"So I can decide where I'm going."

Sally closed her eyes, and held the pin high in the air, over a page in her atlas which had a world map. She brought the pin down, and then she looked to see where it had landed.

"No dice. I landed in the middle of the ocean."

Sister laughed. "Here, let me try."

She took the pin, turned the page, and closing her eyes, she brought it down.

"Hey! You did have better luck than me," cried Sally, "you landed in England. Well, then, it's off to England."

"Wait a minute!" said Sister, "you can't just run off to England."

"Why not?" asked Sally.

"Because you would be leaving the country, and you don't know anybody in England, and, and well ... you know what I'm saying."

"No, I don't know," said Sally. "Why should I not leave the country? I mean, you are sending me away anyway, and as for not knowing anybody, well, I don't know anybody here either, except for you and the other Sisters."

The nun looked at her warmly. "It takes money to go places, Sally."

She knew Sally only too well, and she knew that she was always dreaming up fantastic adventures.

Sister looked Sally squarely in the eye for a minute. "Where in England did my pin land?" she finally asked.

Sally grinned. She lifted the pin out of the book, and looked hard at the little dot where it had landed.

"It's a little town, near the Irish Sea, called, Manchester. Ever heard of it?"

"Yes, indeed!" said Sister, looking surprised. "Our order has a house there. In fact, I think Father Thomas has a friend in Manchester, who is a doctor. Perhaps God guided my pin. I'll go ask Mother Superior about it. Then I'll feel better about letting you go."

"That's great," cried Sally. "Imagine, I had thought that this was going to be just an ordinary day, and now I am going off to start a new life."

"We shall miss you, Sally," said the Sister. "You always make ordinary life seem extraordinary. But it will be good to know that you are safe."

Sally laughed. "You know me; I'm never safe, as long as I smell adventure, with or without legs."

Sister smiled, and left Sally to her dreams.

When she had gone, Sally began to picture far off countries, and daring adventures. She had a vague idea of the name "Sally Keenan" in big lights over some theater, or on the cover of a book. She was just imagining what a book about her would be like, when she clapped her hand to her head and gasped.

"Oh no!" she cried, for she had suddenly remembered the one reason she might not be able to go. "My secret!" she muttered.

* * *

"So what's new with you, Skinny?" a rather ugly teenaged boy asked his companion as they entered a bedroom.

"Nothing really," his friend answered, and flopped himself down on the bed.

It was a hot summer day in Kansas. The two boys had a long boring afternoon ahead of them. Skinny was spending the night at his friend's house. Skinny usually lodged at a boarding house run by a young widow.

The boys made an odd pair. Mike was big and burly, and when he used his imagination at all, it was only to think about food and football. Skinny was his opposite in every way.

He was a slim boy, which was the reason for his nickname. He was about seventeen years old, and handsome. He had keen gray-blue eyes and sandy hair, grown rather long, and he was tall. He had a confident air and a steady glance, which most people could not stand for long. No matter where he was or who he was with, he always seemed above them, as if there was something that told him he deserved better.

"Did you see that cute girl looking at you today?" Mike asked, trying to get a conversation started, though he knew that Skinny was in a quiet mood and that he would not say anything that would make sense.

"Girl?" asked Skinny, starting as if he had been shaken out of a dream. "Girl? No, I didn't see any girls today."

Mike rolled his eyes, "What do you mean you didn't see any girls today? Every girl we passed on the way home made goo-goo eyes at you, and you never even noticed!"

"Oh," said Skinny carelessly, "I guess I really don't care about girls."

"Well, see what you think of this," said Mike, reaching over to his desk and grabbing a picture of a girl who resembled him.

Skinny looked at the picture and shrugged. "She is all right. Who is she?"

"My cousin. She lives over in England and goes to some creepy boarding school, that she says is run by an evil stepmother."

Skinny sat up. "Hey? Does she go to a girl's school called Miss Skinner's Academy, right smack in the middle of London?"

Mike looked at Skinny in surprise. "Why do you suddenly care so much? Yeah, I think her school is in London. She just wrote me a letter, here it is."

He pulled open a drawer and produced a letter written in neat, orderly handwriting.

"She doesn't say anything interesting," he said, "except that there was a trouble-maker who just got kicked out."

"Really?" asked Skinny, attempting to lapse back into his careless mood. "Where did they send her?" he asked, flopping back onto Mike's pillows.

"That's what's funny, they didn't send her anywhere, they just kicked her out, and she has to fend for herself."

"Poor thing," muttered Skinny.

"Oh, don't feel too sorry for her, my cousin said that she was a brat anyway."

"What do you mean?" asked Skinny, looking vaguely interested again.

"Oh, she was all high-and-mighty. She was always acting like she was queen of the world," said Mike, who had tired of the conversation and thought Skinny weirder than ever for caring so much about some random British girl that he had never met.

Skinny meanwhile, was talking to himself. "I wonder if it could be..." he muttered.

"What could be?" asked Mike, "do you know this Christine?"

Skinny leaped to his feet. "Christine!?! Is that the girl who was thrown out?"

"Sure," said Mike, "but what does it matter?"

"It matters plenty!" cried Skinny, vaulting over Mike and running out the door.

"Hey! Where are you going?" cried Mike, following him to the front door.

"I'm going to England!" cried Skinny, as he ran down the street.

Chapter 2

Chance Meetings

"So this is England. It looks pretty much the same as New York, at least the convent does," thought Sally to herself. "There was that same statue of the Sacred Heart of Jesus at the entrance." She paused in her thought. "That always makes me feel better."

She lay on her bed looking out through the window. She had to admit that a large expanse of grass with a forest behind it and a little creek flowing out from the forest, was a marked improvement from the dirty, crowded streets of New York, but she felt that all her hopes for a great adventure were dashed. Her spirits were unusually low. This convent was just as boring as the other she had been in.

She was just wondering if real adventure even existed anymore, when the door opened and a smiling nun came in. She had beside her a black boy who looked about Sally's age.

"Miss Sally, I hope that you do not mind having to share your room with another guest just for a few hours." said the Sister timidly. "There is nowhere else to put him until we can find a room for him."

"Sure, the more the merrier," said Sally cheerfully.

"Thank you."

The Sister hurried out.

Sally surveyed the boy in front of her. She liked the look of him, but she saw that there was something strange about him. She thought maybe it was that his eyes were a lighter brown than his black hair and skin, which made him look as if he were faded. At the moment he was looking at her with unconcealed curiosity, and his gaze was far from polite.

"Hi," said Sally. "Do you speak English?"

"Indeed I do," said the boy, using a surprisingly British accent.

"Boy, that's swell. I've been just aching for another kid to talk to."

"I said I speak English," said the boy stiffly, "I do not speak what you speak, which is American."

Sally laughed. "Do I? Well I never knew it. Are English and American very different?"

"Indeed," he replied, and then he turned, climbed into the other bed, and seemed to consider the conversation over.

"Were you born here in England?" Sally asked, determined to make friends with this iceberg of a boy.

He turned around. "No. Of course not. Do I look English?"

"No," said Sally, "but you sound English with all those 'Indeeds' and stuff. If you aren't English, than how come you are in an English convent?"

"You are not English, and you are here," said the boy.

"I am here because I am sick," said Sally importantly. "And anyone knows the good Sisters take care of the sick."

"Well, I am sick, too," he cried, sticking his nose in the air.

Sally looked the boy over from top to bottom. "You don't look sick."

"That's all you know," he said, and he pulled up his shirt sleeve.

Sally saw that running down from his shoulder to his wrist were four deep ugly cuts, which seemed to have just started healing.

Sally let out a low whistle. "Wow, that looks awful. Did it hurt bad?"

"Yeah, it sure did," said the boy.

Sally looked up at him sharply. "Yeah? What kind of cultured talk is that?"

The boy blushed. "Well... alright. I might as well tell you now. I was faking it. I speak American just as much as you do."

Sally laughed. "Now this is much better. I think you are the right kind of friend for me. That was a pretty good joke. I really thought you were serious."

"I'm glad you're not mad," he said. "Why are you here?"

"My legs," said Sally shortly, "They have been 'out of order' for a long time."

"That's rough. What's your name? Did the nun call you Sally?"

"Yeah, my name is Sally. What's yours?"

"Clarence."

Sally laughed. "No really. What's your name?"

"It really is Clarence. No kidding this time."

Sally scratched her head. "You talk like an American, you look African, and your name doesn't make any sense at all."

"Just forget about it and call me Clarence," said Clarence.

"Okay," said Sally. "How did you get those cuts on your arm?"

"A crocodile," answered Clarence simply.

Sally sat up straight. "Are you joking again?"

"No!" cried Clarence indignantly, "I really was attacked by a crocodile."

"That's exciting," said Sally, "How did it happen?"

"I fell out of my boat."

"That wasn't very bright."

Clarence stiffened. "Well, I bet that if you even saw a crocodile you would faint, even if you didn't have it tip your boat over. I mean, anybody would get rattled, especially if it was a crocodile that you knew could make you rich beyond your wildest dreams if you found a hidden treasure—" he checked himself suddenly and went very red.

"Go on," said Sally eagerly. "What about hidden treasure?"

Clarence turned away. "None of your business," he growled. "It's a secret."

"Oh," muttered Sally. "So you have a secret, too."

Clarence looked up. "Do you have one?"

Sally grinned. "None of your business," she said.

Clarence shrugged. "I don't care anyway."

"Oh, yes you do," Sally grinned. "You care a heap more than you let on."

"I don't care about anything you have to say," said Clarence, his nose returning to its lofty heights. "You are just a girl."

"I'm a better person than you, anyway," returned Sally indignantly. "I have the nerve to admit that I was curious."

"Look who's talking about nerve," cried Clarence. "You have never even seen a crocodile!"

"Well if I did see one, I sure wouldn't fall out of my boat and right into its mouth, like, like …. like a dukalouf!"

"A *Dukalouf*!?!" yelled Clarence, standing up on his bed.

A novice passing by in the corridor was startled to see Clarence standing on his bed. She clapped her hand to her mouth and scuttled off.

"Yes, a dukalouf!" cried Sally, "And if I could use my legs, I would thrash the tar out of you!"

"I could lick you and your whole family," Clarence scoffed in typical American fashion.

"I don't have a family. I am an orphan," said Sally proudly. "I take care of myself."

"I'm an orphan too, and I take better care of myself than anybody else ever could!" cried Clarence.

"No you don't!" retorted Sally, "you let yourself get eaten by crocodiles!"

"If that crocodile had eaten me, I would not be here now!" yelled Clarence.

"I wish you weren't here now, you little kid!" cried Sally, in her most dignified and grown-up way.

"Don't put on airs that you don't fit in *Little Girl*!" said Clarence in his most insulting voice.

"Don't make witty remarks that you don't even understand, you little guttersnipe!" rejoined Sally even more caustically.

"You're a baby," said Clarence, being at a loss for a better insult.

"I'm older than you are!" cried Sally rashly, wondering whether she was or not.

"Do you really think so?" asked Clarence sarcastically, though there was a hint of doubt in his voice.

"Yes, I do," said Sally. "When were you born?"

Clarence rose to his full height. "Eleven years ago. And I will be twelve years on September tenth."

More Sisters began congregating in the hall, peeking into the room, and wringing their hands.

Sally laughed triumphantly. "Then I am older than you!" she cried, waving an accusing finger in his direction. "I was born fourteen years ago, and I shall be fifteen on August seventh, which is just a week away!"

"Well, you might be older than me," said Clarence desperately, "but I'll bet I'm more mature than you."

"That's ridiculous," said Sally. "Girls mature faster than boys, Sister always says so."

"Well, if that's true, then you must be a pretty poor exception for a girl!" Clarence struck this final blow.

Just as the Novice Mistress was rounding the corner, Clarence threw himself triumphantly down on his bed and promptly fell asleep. The nuns in the corridor breathed a sigh of relief to hear the yelling stop and the Novice Mistress crept silently away.

Sally sat fuming for a few seconds. She had to admit that this dreadful boy had kept up with her rather well, and his retorts had been clever and quick. Sally assumed that from a neutral point of view, their fight would have been just silly. Her unquenchable sense of humor had a short fight with her anger, and then she actually found herself laughing at the stupid things that had been said just a moment before in all earnestness.

She glanced over at the sleeping form of the boy and shrugged. It was not easy for her to hold a grudge, and now she felt almost sorry that as soon as he was better, she would probably never see this entertaining boy again.

Sally Keenan had never been more mistaken.

* * *

Christine opened her eyes and shook the sleep out of her head. She had been sleeping all night in the cab as it bumped and jostled its way to Manchester, and now she saw the early morning sun was shining bright and cheery down on the picturesque countryside. The town of Manchester could be seen rising up in the distance; they seemed to have stopped on the outskirts. They were in front of a rather cheerful looking convent which lay about a mile distant from the town.

"A convent?" Christine thought out loud, ignoring the Dean, who still sat sullenly staring into space as if he had not moved since the night before.

"Yes, a convent," he said, tonelessly.

"Are we stopping here for directions?" asked Christine.

"No."

"Then what are we doing?"

"You shall see," said the Dean, and then he finally showed some signs of life. He climbed out, removed her dilapidated carpet bag from the trunk, and said curtly: "Get out."

Christine was somewhat taken aback by this suddenness, but she scrambled out obediently. As soon as her feet touched the ground, the Dean clapped her on the back, mumbled something about making her own way in the world, and then leaped back into the cab.

"Back to the boarding school cabby," he cried, and the next thing Christine knew, she was standing alone in the middle of a country road, watching the cab disappear on the horizon, in the direction of London.

"Wait a minute!" she cried, and chased after it for a few yards until she realized this was hopeless.

"You can't just abandon me! It's against the law! I think," she yelled, as the cab went out of sight. Then with a sigh she retraced her steps back to where her bag lay in the middle of the road, a forlorn heap. She kicked it savagely, and then hopped around on one foot groaning and holding on to her toe. Then she sat down beside her bag and gave way to her angry tears.

When she had finished her cry, she decided that something must be done. She looked around. The countryside sparkled after being washed clean by the rain, and the warm sun made every blade of grass shine. Christine felt better. The world looked so cheery in the morning light. And, after all, she was her own master now. No one could tell her what to do, because she was on her own. She sighed, almost happily. Maybe being abandoned wasn't so terrible after all.

When she had completed her survey of the land, she turned toward the convent. It was cheerful and kind-looking, with bright curtains on the windows and flowers lining the path up to the front steps. There was the sound of some beautiful kind of music rising up, and she could hear singing.

She picked up her carpet bag, and took a deep breath, as if to say that even though she had accepted the adventure that had befallen her, she was still a bit scared, meeting it face to face. But she ran up the front steps and faced the large doors.

She put on her most dignified and adult airs, dusted off her clothes, fluffed her disorderly hair, took another deep breath, and went in. She entered straight and proud, and walked up to a sort of reception desk. A pretty nun waited there, all fresh and starchy in her habit.

"Hello," said Christine. "Do you have any vacancies?"

The nun looked up in surprise. She saw before her, a young girl who acted like she was a princess even though she looked disheveled and sleepy, and was dressed as a school girl.

"Vacancies?" she asked. "I'm sorry, but this isn't a hotel."

"Oh, I know," said Christine. Then she decided to tell the truth and let pride go, for the time being. "Well, you see," she said, somewhat shamefacedly, "I have just been abandoned and I don't have any money with me, and even though I'm not sick, I was hoping you could help me out, just for one night, please?"

The Sister smiled. "Well, you know," she said, "you could be a bit of a help to me. You see, there is a crippled girl here from America, and she wanted a companion to talk to. We put a little injured African boy in with her while we found a place to put him, but the two fought like cats and dogs. We would move the boy, but she says she likes him, even though we hear shouting and name-calling coming from the room every ten minutes."

"So where do I come in?" asked Christine, who had been desperately trying to keep up. The Sister talked rapidly.

"Well you see, if I put you in with the girl, then she can talk to you, and we can stop the war that has been disturbing our quiet convent. All right?"

"All right," said Christine, though she would rather not spend her day entertaining some cripple. Christine imagined she was probably a boring country dunce who had never even heard of the important things in life, like cute boys and lipstick and gossip.

She followed the nun down a long hospital corridor, and tried to act as dignified as she could, even though her no-longer-shiny black shoes made her slip on the glossy floors. She found that if she wanted to stay on her feet, then she would have to walk in a gait that was similar to the goose-step, and then all dignity went out the window. The nun turned down another long corridor, to Christine's discomfort, and finally stopped at the second-to-last door on the left.

Christine was determined to be as dignified and proper as was humanly possible in front of this girl who wanted to be entertained. As they reached the door to her room, Christine dusted off her clothes, folded her hands, and put her nose in the air once again. She entered the room, in the utmost style of etiquette, but as she opened her mouth to introduce herself, three things happened at once.

She saw a boy a little younger than herself, standing again on his bed, and heatedly disagreeing with something that had just been said, (regarding him and his whole family). The second thing that happened was that Christine happened to glance at the crippled girl who sat in her bed glaring at the boy, and with that glance Christine got the biggest shock of her life. The girl who sat among her pillows, her black hair trailing all over her nightgown, was the most beautiful girl Christine had ever seen! All at once she felt embarrassed, for she knew that her school girl appearance was far from elegant and she wished to seem grand and graceful in front of this girl. Christine found herself spell bound.

The third thing that happened cut short her thoughts, for with a last desperate effort to show Sally how strong his feelings were, Clarence snatched up a copy of the Liturgy of the Hours, which lay by his bed, and let it fly at Sally's head. Sally ducked, as did the nun, and the well aimed book sailed over their heads and right into the face of the unprepared Christine.

* * *

Skinny woke up with a start. The train had stopped. He looked out the window at the English countryside.

"Well, it beats Kansas," he muttered.

He was almost alone in the car, for they were at a country station and most of the passengers had already disembarked. When the porter had asked him where he was going, he had said, "Wherever you'll take me."

This had caused some confusion among some of the railway officials, but they had found his money to be good, and so now they just contented themselves with spying on him in shifts. He flagged down the one that was at the door of the car and asked him where they were.

"On the borders of Manchester, Laddie," said the good natured porter. "All you have to do is go through this little wood on our right, and you'll know you're near town when you see St. Joseph's, which is outside of the main town. Are ye thinkin' of gettin' off then?"

"Maybe," said Skinny. "I can get off where ever I want."

"Why, Laddie," asked the porter, "are you just going for a joy ride then?"

"No," answered Skinny, "I'm looking for someone."

"And who might it be that is so important that you squander all yer money ta find 'em? Might it not be a Lassie?"

Skinny gave him a wry smile. "Yes, it's a girl that I'm looking for, if that's what you're trying to ask me in that demented form of English. And as for the money, I have plenty more."

"Do ya now?" asked the porter, "I care not about yer money, but do be tellin' an old chap like me, who is the lass that yer fancy is favorin' so kindly?"

"That is none of your business," said Skinny amiably, "and I think that I will get off now, if you don't mind."

He grabbed his small suitcase, and stood up. As he turned to go out, he patted the crestfallen porter on the back.

"Don't worry," he laughed, "if ever I find the girl I'm looking for, I promise I'll tell you."

The porter cheered up at this statement, and he absolutely beamed when Skinny slipped a ten pound note into his hand.

"Good bye, Laddie" he called. "I'll be hopin' ya find yer lass. And don't forget that when the going gets tough, the best thing ta do is pray. The Good Sisters of St. Joseph will tell you all about that."

"Thanks," said Skinny thoughtfully. "I'll remember that." But he wondered, 'Sisters?'

He climbed down the steps, and began walking alongside the train, which would be in the station for a few minutes more. He was just passing one of the empty freight cars, when he heard, or thought he heard, a tiny sneeze. He stopped and listened, and heard a tiny sigh, coming from inside one of the musty old cars.

He walked toward it, and just as he reached the somewhat open entrance, a little girl, very dirty, rather beat-up, and extremely sad looking, leaped from the car he was heading toward. When she saw him, her already big eyes got even bigger, and she spun round and tried to run. She had not gone two steps, when Skinny's long arms had reached out, grabbed her by her small shoulders, and turned her round to face him.

"Hi," said Skinny, smiling down at the terrified child. "Who are you?" The little girl opened her mouth as if to speak, then shut it again and started trembling. Skinny let go of her when he saw how really scared she was.

"Don't worry; I don't bite," he said kindly. "Would you like to walk with me?"

The little child nodded, and placed her hand somewhat timidly in his. Skinny smiled.

They walked alongside the train until the last car, and then, crossing the tracks, they entered the wood that the porter had pointed out to Skinny. For a few minutes they walked in silence, but Skinny could feel that gradually the little girl was less and less frightened. Finally she looked up at him inquiringly.

"Who are you?" she whispered. She had a European accent.

"My name is Skinny, or, that's what I'm called, and I guess you can call me that," said Skinny. "What about you?"

"My name is Becky," said the child.

"Well, Becky, are you in the habit of riding around in cattle cars, or is this a special occasion?"

At this, the child almost smiled. "I just ran away." she said, and looked up at Skinny as if she expected him to faint from surprise.

"Oh," he grinned, "where are you going now?"

"I don't know," she answered, and Skinny could see the tears well up in her big brown eyes.

"Well, why don't you stay with me for a while?" asked Skinny. He didn't really want a little girl tag-along; she probably would hinder him in his search; but he felt that he couldn't leave her alone in the world. And she was rather cute.

As for Becky, when he had suggested she stay with him, her sadness had fallen off like a cloak, and she let out a little squeal of delight.

"Oh, could I? Really?" she cried, her eyes now shining.

"Sure, although I don't know why you would want to," said Skinny, somewhat taken aback by her eagerness.

"Oh, I want to, all right," said the ecstatic child, squeezing his hand as hard as she could.

They walked for a few more minutes in silence. Then Becky looked up at Skinny, as if she hadn't noticed what he looked like before, and wrinkled her nose suspiciously.

"Why are you here in England?" she asked.

Skinny was getting somewhat tired of telling his strange story to everyone he met, but he assumed Becky would have to know, so he prepared himself for a lot of questions.

"I'm looking for someone," he stated, and acted as though that were enough information for her.

"Who?" asked the undaunted Becky.

"A girl," Skinny replied.

"A little girl, like me?" persisted Becky.

Skinny un-stiffened a little. "Yes," he said quietly. "Yes, I think she is a little girl like you now."

"Then maybe it's me you're looking for," said Becky hopefully.

Skinny smiled.

"No," he said, "the girl I'm looking for has blond hair, and a pointy nose, and I've been told lately she is snooty."

"Oh," said Becky. "What's the girl's name?"

"Christine," Skinny admitted, staring off absently through the trees.

Becky sighed. "You know, you don't talk very much, and what you do say hardly makes sense." She put on a baby pout.

Skinny started like one wakened from a dream. "Oh!" he stammered, trying to recall what she had said. "Well, how about you do the talking and I'll listen."

Becky shrugged. "Okay, but I don't really know what you like to talk about —"

She stopped short and put her finger in her mouth with a look of horror.

"What's wrong?" asked Skinny, baffled and concerned by the terror in her eyes.

"I ... I ... I just lost a tooth!" said Becky, and then to Skinny's surprise, she staggered and fell into his arms, unconscious.

* * *

"What an extraordinary day!" said the Sister who sat at the reception desk of St. Joseph's Convent. She did not make this statement to anyone in particular, just to the whole world. She was exasperated, amused, confused, and tired all at once.

She had just come from Sally Keenan's room, where she had left a most unhappy trio of children. She had been surprised at how sad Sally had been when Clarence had been moved to another room, and she had heard Sally telling the self-conscious, and disconcerted Christine that she had never met a more fascinating boy.

Clarence had been most unwilling to go to his room, for though he told everyone in the convent he came across that he hated her, he had secretly confided to the Sister that he really thought Sally was not bad, for a girl.

In addition, the nun had left Christine with her pride very bent out of shape; and her nose too, thanks to the Liturgy of the Hours. Sally was now giving Christine a quick course in all the more imaginative subjects in life, which had been somewhat neglected at the boarding school.

Sister had just settled back into her ordinary, everyday mood, when another extraordinary thing happened. A teenage boy, holding in his arms a little unconscious girl, came bursting in the front doors, leaving them swinging so that they looked as if they would fly right off their hinges. He came skidding across the slippery floors until he screeched to a stop right as he bumped into her desk.

"Hi," he said in a surprisingly calm way, despite his sudden entrance, "How are you?"

"Well I... that is to say, why well, um…. oh... I'm fine! How are you?" stammered the Sister, looking stupidly from the boy's serene face, to the unconscious child in his arms, then back to him.

"I'm fine, thanks," he said, and then added when he saw her looking questioningly at Becky, "well I guess maybe I'm not fine, I mean I'm okay - it's this kid that's got the problem, if you know what I mean."

The Sister smiled vacantly. She began to think that if things went on this way for much longer she would have to be transferred to a mental hospital.

"I gather that you want us to do something for this child," she said, trying to act normal.

"Sure," agreed Skinny. "I don't know what's wrong with her. We were walking along as nice as you please, and then she lost a tooth. It must have been painful, because she keeled over into a dead faint, and I had no idea what to do, until I saw that we were near you kind Sisters, whom I've heard of even in the States, so I picked her up, and hauled her over here. Can you do anything for her?"

"I suppose," said the nun, "We can give her a bed until she resumes consciousness, but first I'll have to get permission from Mother Superior."

"Okay," said Skinny. "Then you might as well find a bed for both of us."

The Sister looked up in surprise. "Do you intend to stay here too?" she asked helplessly.

"Sure," said Skinny. "I haven't anywhere better to go."

The Sister looked blank. "Why is it that all of the sudden everybody thinks this is a free hotel?" she asked herself.

"I intend to pay," said Skinny. "And I'll take care of this little girl's bill too."

"Well, we aren't usually set up that way," sighed the nun. "What's your name?"

"Skinny Conklin."

"That's an odd name," said the Sister, suspiciously.

"Let's not get personal," Skinny said in annoyance.

"Well then, Skinny Conklin," repeated the nun, "and what's the child's name?"

"Becky."

"Becky what?" prompted the nun.

"I don't know," admitted Skinny.

The nun looked up at him. "You don't even know her last name?" she asked in surprise.

Skinny shrugged. "We've only known each other for about fifteen minutes."

The poor Sister buried her face in her hands. "I give up."

Skinny shrugged again. "Well, is her room ready?" he asked.

She looked up. "All right," she sighed, "I'll go see what I can do." After she had checked with her Superior, she had Skinny follow her down the clean halls, still carrying the unconscious Becky. She stopped in front of a door.

"I'll take care of the little girl," she said, lifting Becky out of Skinny's arms. "Here is a room you can use. Since you're not sick or poor, I'm putting you in with another boy. I hope you don't mind."

Skinny said he didn't, and thanked the nun for her hospitality. He watched her carry Becky all the way down the hall and go in the last door on the left. Then he sighed and entered the room.

As he walked in the door, a paper airplane swooped by his face, and as it landed at his feet, a boy with dark black skin climbed out of his bed and ran over to pick it up. When he saw Skinny, he frowned.

"Did that no good Sally girl send you over here to keep me company?" he asked suspiciously. "'Cause if she did, you'd better scram, and tell her I don't need no help from no stinking girl."

Skinny smiled. "No, she didn't. Who is Sally?"

"Some dumb girl," said Clarence complacently. "Who are you?"

"My name is Skinny, or that's what you can call me," said Skinny. "Who are you?"

"Clarence. I have to get back in bed before Sister sees me."

Skinny smiled again. "You make good planes," he said. "But if you use heavier paper, they'll fly straighter."

Clarence turned around. "Do you know a lot about paper airplanes?" he asked hopefully.

"I guess," Skinny replied modestly.

"Great!" cried Clarence joyfully, "You'll be much better company than any old girl."

"What's wrong with girls?" asked Skinny as he vaulted lightly onto his bed.

"Well it might not be all girls, but there are two of them in a bedroom down the hall, and they could talk and annoy the pants right off a fellow. Here, let's make a plane."

As Skinny began to fold the paper, he asked Clarence about the two girls down the hall.

Clarence wasn't too thrilled at the idea of spending the afternoon talking about girls, but he answered Skinny's questions as best he could.

"What do they look like?" asked Skinny as they finished the first plane.

"Pretty much like what girls are supposed to look like," answered Clarence. "One has eyes that glitter like a snakes', only they're blue, and lots of dark brown hair, and a tongue as long as my arm that sticks out at you when you say something mean."

"That couldn't be her," said Skinny aside to himself.

"What do you mean?" asked Clarence.

"Nothing," said Skinny, "what does the other girl look like?"

"Well, I didn't see much of her," said Clarence. "They sent me out of the room as soon as she got there, but I don't think I would have liked to stay, she seemed kind of snooty."

Skinny stiffened just the slightest bit. "What does she look like?" he asked quietly.

"She has normal eyes," said Clarence shortly.

"What else?" asked Skinny impatiently.

"Well, she has some hair," said Clarence, waving his hand vaguely over the back of his head to illustrate this fascinating statement.

"Is that all?" persisted Skinny.

"Pretty much," said Clarence. "There's that and the fact that she's always got her nose in the air, and calls me a 'little boy.' She's pretty dumb."

Skinny wasn't listening any more. Clarence would have kept talking, but Skinny interrupted. "What room did you say she was in?" he demanded.

"The second-to-last one down this hallway," replied Clarence in surprise, "but why do you want to go see ..."

"I'll be right back!" said Skinny, and disappeared out the door.

He crept down the hall, trying to be inconspicuous. When he came to the door he stopped and listened. He heard a voice talking that sounded as if it belonged to a young girl, but he knew it was not the girl he was looking for. This voice was prattling on and on, about how to write a good story. He guessed that this was the girl, Sally, that Clarence had told him about. He wondered if she would ever stop talking, and if he would be able to recognize the voice he was waiting for.

The door was open just the slightest bit, and finally his impatience got the better of him and he crouched down to look in. But he pushed the door too far, and it squeaked on its hinges.

Immediately Sally's voice stopped. He heard her say, "What was that?" and then, a voice that made his heart seem to stop beating, answered that she had not heard anything.

He risked one quick look in, and he could hardly move. He had not been expecting to see such pretty girls, since he had only heard Clarence's description of them, but when he saw Christine, tears came to his eyes. He stood up fast and bit his lip. When he turned around he jumped, for Becky was standing before him in a nightgown.

"Are you still looking for that girl?" she asked, somewhat impatiently.

He dragged her away from the door and smiled.

"No," he said, "I've found her."

Chapter 3

The Council

Clarence was confused. It seemed that everyone he ran into was weird. He wondered why Skinny was so interested in Christine. He also wondered what Sally's secret was. He wondered if her secret was more interesting than his. He hoped it wasn't.

He thought he would try again to ask what her secret was, so he scrambled out of bed, put on his robe and headed for the door. As he reached it, he heard earnest voices just outside. He stopped with his hand on the knob and listened. He quickly recognized one of the voices as Skinny's, and the other seemed to be the voice of a small child, and it sounded like a girl. Skinny was making the other voice promise not to do something or tell somebody something.

Clarence heard him say that if she found out who he was that it would be very, very bad. Clarence wondered who Skinny meant by "she." He heard the little girl make her promise, and he heard Skinny sigh with relief. Then he heard Sally's voice come from far down the hall, calling out to Christine instructions to see what the noise in the corridor had been.

Apparently Clarence hadn't been the only one who had heard Sally, for Skinny came swooping in the door fast, dragging a tiny brown-haired girl with him, and shut it tight. The three waited listening, until they heard Christine go back into her room, probably to tell Sally that there was nobody out there.

Skinny started breathing again. He turned around from where he had plastered his face to the door, and jumped to see Clarence right behind him.

Becky whispered, "who's that?"

"This is Clarence, Becky," said Skinny, looking annoyed. "And just what are you doing eavesdropping, young man?"

"I was out of bed, and you two just happened to be at the door," said Clarence defensively. "What were you talking about?"

"None of your business. Where were you going?" asked Skinny.

"To find out what Sally's secret is."

Skinny looked down at him. "Sally's got a secret?" he asked, mildly surprised.

"Yep, and so do I," said Clarence proudly.

"Me too," whispered Becky, who was still holding Skinny's hand.

"That's interesting," mused Skinny, "I wonder if Christine has a secret."

"She does," said Becky.

Skinny looked at her in surprise. "How would you know?"

"I listened to her and Sally talking because my room is right next to theirs."

"Do you know what their secrets are?" Clarence asked.

"No," said Becky, "But I could ask them."

"I think we should all swap secrets," said Clarence, "especially because my secret is one we have to do something about, and I can't do it alone."

"That's the same with my secret!" cried Becky happily, then she looked up at Skinny, who had been wrapped in thought while they talked.

"Do you have a secret, Skinny?" she asked innocently.

"Of course he does," said Clarence. "That's obvious by the way he talks."

"Yes, indeed," said Becky. "He doesn't make sense."

"What do you mean?" asked Skinny indignantly. "I always make sense."

"Don't try to change the subject," said Clarence. "We both know you have a secret."

"Well, perhaps I do," said Skinny impatiently. "What does it matter?"

"It matters plenty," said Clarence. "Come over to my bed and I'll tell you all about my great idea."

* * *

Christine opened her eyes sleepily. It was night, and she lay in her bed trying to fall back to sleep. She had been awakened by a bad dream, and now the bright moonlight streaming in the window kept her awake. She stared at Sally, who was peacefully sleeping in her bed just a few feet away, and wondered what she was dreaming about.

Suddenly, Sally sat bolt upright, so fast that Christine almost jumped out of her skin.

"What was that?" Sally asked, looking around the moonlit room.

"What was what?" asked Christine, who was fast getting annoyed by Sally's sharp sense of hearing things that, as far as she knew, were not there.

"There is somebody, or something, outside our door," said Sally quietly.

"It's probably nothing," whispered Christine but she felt a shiver go up her spine.

"Go see," hissed Sally. "It might be someone dangerous."

"If it is, then I'm not going to go see," Christine whispered indignantly.

"Maybe it's a ghost," persisted Sally, grinning mischievously.

"Well, I'm not going to go see," insisted Christine fearfully.

"I would go myself, but I can't use my legs," said Sally, with mock sadness.

"That's what you said earlier," returned Christine, "when you thought somebody had tried to get in, and it was nothing. I think your ears are broken too, Sally. I knew that …"

Sally interrupted with a gasp, and this time Christine heard the noise too.

The door to their room squeaked open and a ghostly figure stood in the doorway. Christine gave a little scream, and ducked under her blankets, but Sally only laughed.

"Don't be scared Christine," she said. "It's only that little girl who's in the room next door to us."

Becky shut the door and pattered over to Sally's bed.

"Hi," said Sally kindly, for she saw tear stains on Becky's cheeks. "What's wrong?"

"I had a nightmare," said Becky. "Would you girls mind if I stayed in here with you for a little?"

"No, of course not!" said Sally. "Your room must be lonely; come get in bed with me."

Christine had come out from under her covers, and looked suspiciously at Becky, as if she still thought Becky was a ghost.

"How did you hurt your legs?" Becky asked as she crawled under Sally's blankets.

"It was a disease," said Sally. "Why are you here? You don't look sick."

"I was walking in the woods with Skinny--"

"Who is Skinny?" interrupted Christine.

"A boy I met when I ran away from the orphanage."

"Is he cute?" asked Christine eagerly at the same time that Sally asked, "ran away?"

"I don't know, I thought only kittens could be cute."

Sally laughed. "Well then, did Skinny bring you here?" she asked.

"Yes, and now he's in the room down the hall with Clarence."

"The poor chap," chuckled Sally. "Clarence is probably driving him bananas."

"No, he's not," said Becky. "They're busy working on our plan, but they sent me to bed."

"What plan?" asked Sally.

"Oh, Clarence has some plan to figure out what your secrets are, and Skinny wants to form a club or something."

"Why does he want to ... " began Sally, but just then their door flew open and Christine dove back under her covers with a screech. Clarence walked in and sat down at the foot of her bed.

"Hi," he said. "What's going on?"

"Nothing," said Sally. "Why are you here?"

"We heard you girls talking so we figured we'd come join the party."

"We're not having a party," snapped Christine.

"Why did you say 'we'?" Sally asked Clarence. "Is there someone else with you?"

For answer, Clarence hopped over to the door and loudly whispered, "You can come in Skinny, they're decent."

When Skinny came in the room, Christine's heart did a summersault. She knew she had never seen anyone so handsome.

"Hi," Skinny said in his confident, almost arrogant way.

"Hi," replied Sally. "My name's Sally Keenan, you already know Becky, and that is Christine Philips."

"Well, hello everybody... and we all know Clarence," said Skinny. Clarence nodded.

Sally told Skinny to turn on the lights and shut the door. He sat down on the only chair in the room, and Clarence returned to the foot of Christine's bed.

"Well now that the introductions are out of the way, let's get down to business," said Clarence.

"What business?" asked Christine.

"Before we decide to go through with our plan, I have to ask you a question," said Clarence, looking at Christine. "Do you have a secret?"

"Yes...." said Christine hesitantly, "I don't know exactly what you mean by secret, but I do know something that nobody else knows."

"Great!" cried Clarence, "then our company has been formed!"

"What do you mean?" asked Sally.

"Why don't you let me explain?" interrupted Skinny. "You see, it struck me that it is a funny coincidence that the five of us kids, all from different parts of the world, and with very different lives, should all suddenly be thrown together by chance. Even more strange is that we find ourselves together here in a convent hospital, when only two of us are really sick. Could there be some connection?"

"You mean that we were put in each other's way for a reason?" asked Sally.

"Yeah," said Clarence, "so me and Skinny started thinking ... do us five have anything in common?"

"We five, Clarence," corrected Christine, "not us five."

"Who cares?" Clarence scoffed.

"And," Skinny continued, "we hit upon the mysterious secrets that we all have hidden from the rest of the world."

"It is a funny coincidence," admitted Christine.

"Pretty strange."

"I think it's creepy," said Becky.

"I think it's great!" cried Sally. "It's a real adventure! Now let's swap secrets!"

"Not here," objected Skinny. "If we get caught by the Sisters, then we'll all be in trouble. Let's set a time for tomorrow when we can all meet in secret, and we'll have a council meeting. Okay?"

"Good," said Sally. "There's a big old basement beneath the convent, and the stairs going down to it are at the end of this hall. One of the Sisters told me about it. We should meet down there."

"Nice and mysterious," said Clarence happily.

"All right," agreed Skinny, "Then we'll say two o'clock? When the Sisters go to the chapel?"

"Right," said Sally. "But I'm afraid I won't be able to get there alone."

"Then Christine can push your wheelchair. Just try not to be conspicuous. You all right with that, Christine?"

"Yes," murmured Christine quietly. She knew she could never say 'no' to that handsome boy. She wondered about the stairs. But she was excited by all this talk of secrets and basements and adventure. She also felt a little jealous of the attention Skinny was paying to Sally.

"Now that's all settled, let's go back to bed. Come on, Clarence," said Skinny, and the two boys turned off the light and tip-toed out.

"Wow," said Becky, and cuddled down into bed with Sally.

"Isn't it exciting?" whispered Christine as soon as they were gone, "and oh, Sally don't you think Skinny is cute?"

* * *

The next day, at a little past two o'clock, Christine pushed Sally's wheelchair, with both Sally and Becky in it, down the hall to a tiny door at the end. They tried to look innocent to anyone who passed by, and Christine didn't complain about Becky hitching a ride.

When they reached the basement door, Christine looked around to make sure no one was watching, and Becky opened the door. Just a few feet from the threshold, there was a long steep flight of stairs with a rickety metal railing going down into the utter blackness of the basement.

"It looks scary down there," whispered Becky, and Sally wiggled with excitement, but Christine looked perplexed.

"How am I supposed to get your wheelchair down there without killing the both of us?" she cried indignantly.

"Oh," said Sally, cocking her head like a dog, "I didn't think of that."

"Well, then you'd better think about it now," snapped Christine irritably.

Just then Skinny emerged from the darkness beneath.

"Shhh," he whispered. "What are you two squawking about?"

"We don't know how to get Sally's wheelchair down the stairs," Becky whispered quite loudly.

"Just leave it up here. I'll carry Sally down," Skinny said.

He picked Sally up easily and went back down followed by Becky. Christine parked the wheelchair sulkily outside in the hall, and then carefully descended, clinging to the rail. She thought she would have given anything to be carried by Skinny, and Sally didn't even seem to care. She wondered why he seemed to like Sally more than her.

When she reached the bottom of the stairs, she found she couldn't see a thing. She floundered around in the darkness for a minute until she found a small doorknob. She turned it, and the small door in front of her opened, revealing a big, dusty looking room that was filled with light.

She went in and shut the door behind her. A few steps led down onto the cold cement floor, and looking around she saw some kind of furnace for heating the convent, and some folded up bedsteads.

Clarence was perched high up on some storage boxes, Becky had cuddled down next to the furnace, and Skinny was setting Sally down on a large box that looked like a coffin. Christine went and sat down with Sally, and Skinny pulled an old trunk over so that they were all sitting in a small circle around the furnace.

"All right," said Skinny solemnly. "This council meeting will now come to order."

"What does that mean?" asked Becky.

"It means that it's time to swap secrets," grinned Sally. "Who'll go first?"

Suddenly everyone felt shy. For some of them, their secrets were their dearest possessions and it seemed like a sin to tell them to just anybody. Skinny seemed to be reading their minds, for after looking at them all in turn, he said, "I know some of us feel we shouldn't tell our secrets to each other because we don't really know anything about one another, so as we tell our secrets, we should also tell a little more about ourselves, just so we all feel like better friends."

"And also, so that none of us will have any worries," he continued, "we should all solemnly promise never to expose each other's secrets to anyone outside the five of us. Okay?"

Four heads nodded in agreement, and Sally said, "I think we should promise on the bible, for love of Heaven and fear of Hell. Do you guys have any religion?"

"I'm Catholic," declared Becky proudly, and Clarence said, "So am I!"

"Me too," said Christine.

"That's a good coincidence," said Sally. "I'm a Catholic myself, and it will be handy to all be of the same religion. What about you, Skinny?" They all looked inquiringly at Skinny, who blushed.

"I guess I'm not really of any religion," he said, embarrassed. "But I was baptized a Catholic, and I'm willing to be a better one than I have been."

"Good," said Sally. "I don't know about you all, but I feel much better knowing that you believe the same things I do."

"Me too," agreed Skinny. "Now, let's get down to business. Clarence, would you like to go first?"

Clarence shrugged. "Sure, I guess."

He leapt from his perch down to the floor and sat down next to Sally. "But my secret is the best."

"How do you know?" asked Sally. "You haven't heard ours yet."

"I know mine will be better than yours," Clarence assured her.

"You see, I'm an African born boy, and both my parents are dead. This is the first time I have ever left Africa. When I was little, I lived with my uncle. When he died, I stayed living in his house, until one day, when two Americans came to our village. They said they were explorers, but from the first minute I saw them, I didn't trust those two."

"Why not?" asked Christine.

"They just acted funny," said Clarence, "and it turned out that I was right. One night when I was sleeping, they came sneaking in, and tied me up and put me in a sack, and left that village fast in their jeep, taking me with them."

"Why did they kidnap you?" asked Sally.

"I found out why a few days later," Clarence answered. "I thought it was unusual that they had picked me out of all the kids in the village. The only significant thing about me, that I could think of, was that I had been all over Africa, because my parents had moved a lot. It turned out that these men wanted me to show them around."

The other children exchanged glances.

"After we had gone far from my uncle's village, I began to figure out that they were robbers or jewel thieves, and that they had come to Africa to hide the stuff they had stolen. They had never been to Africa before, so they needed a guide. I lived with them for a few months, and they treated me decently because they needed me. But they had told me that they would kill me if ever I tried to escape. I never tried. Well anyway, they thought and thought about where to hide their treasure, and finally one of them had an idea."

"What?" whispered Becky.

"They decided to hide their treasure in a coconut."

"Then it must have been a small treasure," said Christine sarcastically.

"Diamonds are small, stupid," Clarence retorted. "They had me crack open a coconut and hollow it out, and then dry the insides out real good. Then we put the treasure inside, and they glued it back together so it looked almost normal. But then we had the problem of how to tell our coconut from all the others."

"But wait," objected Skinny. "Do coconuts grow in Africa?"

"Yes, they do," answered Clarence defensively. "But we weren't just in Africa. They took me with them to an island in the Caribbean called Tobago. It's pretty close to Trinidad."

"That's a pretty far leap," said Skinny.

"And I thought you said you have never left Africa before," said Sally suspiciously.

"Well, I must have forgotten," shrugged Clarence. "But anyway, there were tons of coconuts on Tobago, so right away they had me paint an intricate yellow mark on the treasure coconut, so we would not lose it. Then they got into an argument. One of them worried that anyone who saw that special mark on a coconut would probably figure it was something special and smack it open."

"What did they do?" asked Christine.

"They had me put yellow marks on about a hundred different coconuts, but none exactly like the one on the treasure."

"That seems like a lot of work. Why didn't they just bury the treasure?" asked Sally.

"I don't know! I guess everybody buries treasure," said Clarence, "but I just did as they told me to. They argued with each other a lot."

"Well, go on," urged Skinny.

"The next step they dreamed up was to put the exact mark that was on the treasure coconut on something else too, so that they would always know which mark to look for when they wanted their treasure, if I wasn't around. They were very worried that someone else would find the mark and steal their treasure."

"They sound overly suspicious to me," said Sally.

"They sound crazy to me," said Skinny.

"Well, we put the mark in a few safe places, inside of a tavern in Trinidad, a grove of palm trees on Tobago, and even on a crocodile they had captured, right on the top of his head!"

Skinny and Sally began to team up on him. "Wouldn't that wash off?" asked Sally.

"We used airplane paint."

"A crocodile sounds unbelievable!" said Skinny.

"Well," explained Clarence, "they had done a great deal of exploring, and they had captured a crocodile. They kept it so well fed that it would hardly ever move, it was so stuffed. It also kept the crocodile pretty harmless. When he was full, he was just lazy. They had the idea of having me put the copy of the mark on its head."

"That's dumb," said Christine, "how would they be able to catch it again?"

"I don't think that they expected it to ever get away," Clarence said. "I had an awful time painting the mark on its head. But finally I was done. The next day the crocodile was missing. Now here's the important part. I have since heard that the grove of palm trees in Tobago was cut down, and the tavern in Trinidad was destroyed by a typhoon. I lost those crooks (or they lost me), in a town called Mbandaka, which was near the swamp the crocodile was in."

"What happened to those bank robbers?" asked little Becky. "You don't know where they are now?"

"They came back for their treasure about a year later and the crocodile killed them," said Clarence shortly.

"Oh, how awful," whispered Christine.

"They were pretty dumb," admitted Clarence.

"So, was that the crocodile that attacked you?" asked Sally.

"Yes," answered Clarence. "I would never have fallen out of my boat if it had been just an ordinary crocodile, but the shock of seeing the sign rattled me."

"At least we know it's still alive," said Skinny.

"Were you able to see the mark?" asked Becky.

"Not as clearly as I would have liked to," Clarence said. "The next thing I knew some real explorers who were from England found me and put me on their plane. They sent me to an English hospital. I had such a high fever for so long that I can't even remember what the mark looked like now. Then I came to this convent for a longer recuperation, and here I am, with the knowledge of where to find a treasure that would make us all millionaires. There! That's my secret!"

The other four children looked at each other in awed silence.

"Oh, my," said Becky.

Sally applauded.

"That's a good secret Clarence," said Skinny. He cleared his throat. "Who is next?"

"Me," Becky piped up.

"I am from Switzerland," she said, "and both my parents are dead. When I was really little, I lived in a small orphanage in a tiny town right below the Swiss Alps. There were only about twenty other kids aside from me, and we all loved each other a lot. We were very happy there, and I would probably still be there, but one day, the owner of the orphanage came and told the headmaster that she had discovered that one of us were heirs to big lots of money, and when our relatives died, we would be rich." Becky still spoke with a tinge of baby talk in her cute accent.

"If you had relatives, then why were you all in an orphanage?" asked Christine.

"It was also a boarding school," explained Becky. "Some of us were orphans and some weren't, but some of everybody's parents were dead. The problem was, that the owner of the school did not know which ones of us were rich. No one ever explained it to me," Becky prattled.

"So what happened?" asked Sally.

"Well, life went on normally after that, until one day a man came and said he was the guardian of one little boy I loved a lot. His name was Jack, and he had always been my bosom friend. I had even proposed to him!"

At this Skinny had a sudden fit of coughing and Sally seemed to be having trouble looking solemn.

"The man had some legal papers and the owner said she found them to be all in order, so he took Jack away. Then one day, somebody came for me. Now, I was sure I did not have any living family members, but this man who came for me said that he was an old friend of my father's and so I had to go with him. I packed my things and said goodbye to the rest of my friends. It was awful to leave them. They were the only family I ever had."

"Well," Becky continued, "the next thing I knew, I was in a strange man's car and we were driving away from the only place I had ever known as home. I was surprised that instead of going to a different city, he drove me up into the Alps. We drove for what seemed like forever, and it was night by the time we stopped. I was taken out of the car, and told that we had arrived at our destitution."

"At your what?" asked Clarence.

"I think she means destination," smiled Skinny.

"That's it. Destination," assented Becky. "Well, I was surprised when he said that, because we were way up in the mountains, with not a single house anywhere. I suddenly wondered if I had been kidnapped. I figured that the best thing to do would be to run away, but I think the man expected me to do that, because I did not get four steps away, when he grabbed me from behind and bonked me on the head. Then my eyes went out."

"Your eyes did what?" cried Christine in horror.

"I mean, I fell over and had a faint," explained little Becky.

"What happened when you woke up?" asked Sally.

"When I woke up, I was in a huge room, with a rock ceiling."

"Do you mean you were in a cave?" prompted Skinny.

"I thought I saw Jack there."

"Maybe you were dreaming," suggested Clarence.

"Well, I don't know. It seemed to be a very big cave," said Becky. "There were lots of people, and music, and big fires. And there was one man in a shiny suit like a king, and he sat up on a high platform with lots of food."

"Are you sure you were awake?" asked Clarence doubtfully. "It seems highly unlikely that a king would be living in an underground dining hall in the middle of the mountains, in modern times. Maybe you read too many books."

"Perhaps it sounds unusual to you," agreed Becky daintily. "But I'm sure I saw people and musicians, and everything. They took me over to the man who looked like a king. He was not a king, but a baron. Then this Baron said that he knew that some child at my orphanage was the heir to a hidden fortune. He had figured, if he were in charge of us ... what do they call it?"

"Have legal custody?" asked Sally.

"That he would somehow get the money. But he didn't know which of us were the ones who would get the money, and neither did we. So he had decided to kidnap some of us, one at a time."

"How could he get the legal right to you?" asked Skinny.

"I don't know," shrugged Becky. "He had been talking to the owner of the orphanage. Both the owner and the headmaster started going about in fur coats, which they never had before the Baron came. Some of my other friends were sent off to schools and orphanages all over Switzerland and even to Paris and London! After a few days, I was taken to a horrid little orphanage in London, from which I escaped - All By Myself!" She put on another pout.

"When you left the Baron's house, did you get to see whether it really was a cave or not?" asked Sally.

"No. It was dark when we left," sighed Becky. "But before I left, the Baron threatened me. He said I must corper rate with him in every way, because he had put a spell on me, and if ever I lied to him, my head would fall off."

Clarence chuckled. "Cooperate," he corrected.

"He also said," continued the solemn Becky, "that he would kill my friends if ever I tried to lie to him, and that I would know when they died, because one of my teeth would fall out."

Her eyes grew wide with fear. "The Baron is magic! Since that day, more than six of my teeth have fallen out. I can't bear to think which ones of my friends are dead."

Becky's large brown eyes filled with tears as she finished the story, and she looked so pathetic that Christine felt like crying too.

Sally was angry. She had a soft heart and could never stand to see a fellow creature in distress. She pulled Becky onto her lap.

"That's a low trick," she cried hotly. "That mean old Baron was just trying to scare you into obeying him. I'd like to get my hands on the kind of man who would tell a little girl things like that, just so he could get some stupid inheritance money! Oh, that Baron better not ever get in my way! I'd tear him to shreds!"

"Calm down, Sally," said Skinny. "Let's hope you'll never have to match wits with that Baron. He sounds like a smooth operator."

"I could outwit him any old day," muttered Sally sulkily.

"And Becky," continued Skinny, ignoring Sally's remark, "You don't need to worry about your friends. The Baron made up that ridiculous story about your teeth just to scare you. He probably told the same lie to all of the kids. Anybody your age would be losing baby teeth right and left naturally, to make way for the grown-up teeth to come in. It happened to me myself."

The other children all nodded solemnly. Becky's eyes opened wide with understanding.

"Does that mean that my friends are not dead?" she asked hopefully.

"Yes, it does," said Skinny, "and now I know why you fainted when your tooth came out on our way here."

"Yes. That tooth had been loose for a long time. I was so afraid that I might have to get it pulled. That's why I ran away."

"You never told us how you escaped," reminded Clarence. "Was it hard? Did they chase you?"

"No. Nobody cared that I was gone. The hard thing was getting up enough courage to disobey the Baron's orders. I thought my head would fall off as soon as I climbed over the fence. But it didn't, so I ran to the railroad tracks and when one train stopped, I crawled into a cold, lonely freight car and fell asleep. I stayed in that car until Skinny found me and brought me here. And I'm awful glad I have some new friends to talk to."

"Well, you have had some big adventures for such a little girl," said Skinny. "But don't worry. If there is any way we could ever rescue your friends, we would certainly try."

"Now it's somebody else's turn to tell their secret," said Sally, "and I'll go next."

"Good," agreed Skinny, "But be quick. We should get on with things. Our absence might be noticed upstairs soon."

"Okay. Here goes," said Sally. "You all know that I am an American by birth, and an orphan. I have lived in New York City my whole life. Because I don't have any living relatives, and also because of my legs, I have lived in the care of the good Sisters of St. Joseph since I was ten."

"Wow. That's a long time," said Clarence. "Is the food in convents in America better than the food in convents here?"

"Luckily it is," laughed Sally, "but I was getting pretty sick of the food before I left. Always vegetarian meals."

"So what's your secret?" asked Skinny.

"Well, New York is a big bad city, and there are a lot of criminals operating right in the heart of it. There is one bank robber and murderer who is pretty well known, his nickname is Little Joe. Have you heard of him?"

Skinny looked uncomfortable. "Yes. Even way out in Kansas I've read about him in the newspapers." He shifted uneasily.

"Right," said Sally. "He's real bad. But he is clever too, and the cops in New York are at their wits' end. His gang just keeps getting bigger. The worst part of it is, he has sworn not to rest until he sees me dead."

"What?!" cried Skinny, jumping to his feet.

"Yup," said Sally complacently. "The fact that I'm alive seems to be a constant annoyance to him, and he won't rest until I'm dead; he said so himself."

"Why does he want you dead?" asked Skinny shakily, as he sat back down.

"I don't really know," replied Sally. "But I think it was something my father did to him before he and mom died. Little Joe swore to kill me to take revenge. I'll tell you one thing. It's not easy being hunted by a professional killer all your life."

"How frightening," breathed Christine.

Becky's eyes had grown large, and even Clarence looked solemn.

"So is that your secret?" asked Skinny.

"No, I almost forgot," said Sally. "Here is my secret. I know the whereabouts of a very prominent member of Little Joe's gang. This guy was sort of an apprentice to Little Joe, because he was only a kid when he joined the gang, though now I imagine he is bigger. The police have a big reward out for him, even in Europe. And I know where to find him!"

"Where?" asked Skinny, unconsciously lowering his voice.

"Well, I don't know where to find him exactly, but if I go out to a certain spot next to the train tracks on a night when the moon is full, at exactly midnight, provided I am exactly four miles from the train station, and facing west, I'll find the exact information as to where and who that gangster is."

Skinny blew out a long breath.

"What a romantic setting!" said Christine.

"Yes, that's partly why I want to go there so much," said Sally, "it's like something out of a book."

"Sounds a bit corny to me," mused Skinny, "the midnight business and all that. I just don't buy it."

"How did you figure all these things out?" asked Clarence.

"Well, you see when I was sent to the convent, Little Joe was pretty sure he would always know where I was," Sally began, "but he still had one or two of his men check up on me about once a month. One day, outside my room, I overheard two of his men talking beneath the window. They must not have thought anybody was around, because they were talking about secrets, and one thing they said was that it was a shame that the young teenage apprentice of Little Joe's had left the gang. One of them wondered if the boy would ever come back, and the other fellow told him Little Joe knew just where to find him, because of the special spot by the railway tracks. They never found out that I had overheard them, and I have kept that secret safe for almost two years now."

"Well, that's a good secret," said Skinny, looking doubtful. "And if nobody objects, I volunteer to go next. Do you mind if I go before you, Christine?"

"Oh, yes Skinny. I mean, I don't mind, if you go next, that is, I mean, you can ... I ... go right ahead," said Christine, blushing. She wished she didn't go all to pieces when he spoke to her. It was a bit inconvenient.

Skinny smiled at her, which made her even shyer.

"Well," he began, "I'm afraid my secret is not as interesting as you all might hope. Sally, when you lived in New York, did you ever hear of a certain teenage actor and singer who was pretty popular a few years back? It was said he died in a car wreck at the height of his fame."

"I'd seen some posters and magazines of a famous singer who died. He was young, I remember. But why bring him up?"

"Because I'm him," said Skinny flatly.

"Really?" cried Sally. "Funny, you don't look like you used to."

"Well, maybe I don't, but that is my secret."

"Why did you fake a car wreck and death?" Clarence asked.

"To get rid of all the publicity, and just so I could get back to a normal life."

"I knew you must have been a movie star or something!" said Christine, with bright eyes. "But didn't your fans recognize you if they saw you on the street?"

"They might have, but after the phony wreck I moved to a tiny town in Kansas where nobody had heard of me. That's where I've been living ever since."

"Why did you come to England?" asked Sally.

"Just sightseeing," Skinny replied shortly.

"But I thought you came here because you were looking for ... " Becky began, but Skinny shot her a look that made the words die in her mouth.

"What's that, Becky?" asked Sally.

"Nothing," Becky whispered, turning red.

"I think it's time for Christine's secret," said Skinny, but something about the way he said it gave Sally the direct feeling that he was trying to distract them from what Becky had just said, or had almost said. Still, she kept her suspicions to herself and did not question him further.

"My secret is something that I have known for a very long time," said Christine, glowing with pleasure at being the center of attention at last. "My secret," she continued, lowering her voice for a more dramatic effect, "is that I have a brother."

"What?!" cried Skinny, leaping once again to his feet.

Christine was surprised by his reaction. "Yes," she said, "I have a baby brother living somewhere in this very town, and I have never seen him. Why are you so surprised, Skinny?"

"Nothing," said Skinny, sitting back down and looking collected once more. "I was just not expecting you to have such an important secret, that's all."

Christine wasn't sure if she should consider that an insult or a compliment. "Well," she resumed, "I learned my secret about a year ago.

It all started one day when I was walking past the principal's office. I overheard him talking to the Dean. The Dean was complaining about me, so I stopped to listen.

"The Principal let him rave on for a little while about the trouble I'd caused, and then it seemed as if they were discussing something they had spoken of many times before. It was all about how I could not be expelled because my tuition had been paid for already, and there was no place I could go. Then the Dean said it. He was really mad and he yelled something about how he wished my brother was dead, and all this trouble was over and done for. I almost fell over when I heard him and I began to wonder how it was that I had never been told I had a brother.

"Later that day, a man came to our school to give a lecture on science. He was an old professor. He lived in Manchester, right here where we are now. Most people thought that he was crazy, and I'd heard that his house, which doubled as his laboratory, was full of strange inventions. After he gave his talk to the students, he went into the Principal's office with the Dean, and they locked themselves in there for hours. I listened at the door. It was a highly secret meeting. I heard there were many strange things he kept in his lab. As he talked, I began to see that he was a bit absent-minded. He seemed to take great pride in the basement under his lab. Then, they spoke of a stolen little boy whom he kept as his lab assistant! Those were his exact words! It suddenly dawned on me, that he could be my brother!"

At this point Skinny rolled his eyes.

"If I did have a little brother, as the Dean had been saying earlier, perhaps my brother was being held prisoner! I didn't know what to do, so I didn't do anything. I have been carrying that secret around in my head for almost a year now, and I always figured that if ever I left that school, I would come here to Manchester and rescue my brother. It's amazing that they left me here! So that's it."

"Wow. That's a swell story," said Sally. "And I'll bet that you're right about that old professor. He seems like a crazy old chap - I'd like to meet him."

"Me, too," agreed Skinny, "And that's a very good secret, Christine. You certainly know how to use your brain, and your ears for that matter. Now," he said quite seriously, "I think we should form our company."

"Right," cried Clarence. "Me and Skinny figured, that we kids should form a sort of club, or alliance, and help each other do the things we need to do about our secrets, like find my treasure, and find Christine's brother, and Sally's gangster, and Becky's friends. Do you all agree?"

"Of course," declared Sally. "Let's all swear to stand by each other through thick and thin! Till death do us part."

"Death?" Christine asked hesitantly.

"Of course!" said Sally. "I hereby declare that 'The Company of Secret Kids' has been formed!"

"'The Company of Secret Kids,'" repeated Skinny. "I like it."

"Me too," Clarence agreed. "Now let's go start our adventures."

"Now, wait a minute!" said Skinny, "We can't just go running off into things without being prepared. We need a plan of action."

"Right," assented Sally. "Whose secret should we try to resolve first?"

"I say Christine's, because it's closest," said Clarence.

"And then mine," piped up Becky.

"Okay," said Sally. "Then it's agreed. We'll go after Christine's secret first?"

"No," said Skinny suddenly. His face had gone a sick color. The other four looked at him in surprise.

"I mean, I have another idea. I think we should go after Clarence's treasure first, because if we find it, then we'll have money to finance our other trips."

"That's a good point, but I don't think it would be very expensive to drive across town to find Christine's brother." argued Sally. "What if he's really being kept in a basement? Wouldn't that take priority over MONEY?"

"Well, there are lots of details that would have to be worked out," insisted Skinny, in a confused way. "And besides, don't you all want to see Clarence's treasure?"

After much debating, Skinny finally won the others over and they decided to try for Clarence's treasure first. Little did they know what adventures lay before the newly formed Company of Secret Kids.

Chapter 4

Off to Africa

"Do you think we'll find Clarence's treasure right away, Skinny?" Becky asked.

"Probably not. Africa is pretty big."

"How much do you think it will be worth?" asked Christine.

"That's anybody's guess," Skinny replied.

The three were on their way back to Sally's room after having had their lunch in the refectory down below.

Almost two weeks had passed since the day they all swapped secrets in the basement, and the five children had become much more used to each other's company. Christine found that by now she could actually talk to Skinny, without freezing up or turning red. Becky had stopped being overly shy; in fact she could hardly be made to shut up. Sally had devised nicknames for the others, which were fast beginning to stick. Christine was 'Chris', Clarence had become 'Clare', and Becky was sometimes 'Toothless One'. She figured she was going to have to mull over 'Skinny', which was already a nickname in itself.

Ever since they had decided to go after Clarence's treasure, the five children had all been very busy. Clarence had told them that it had been arranged by the kind Sisters and the authorities, that when he was sufficiently recovered they would fly him back to Africa, where no doubt he would want to return. The Sisters had many generous benefactors in Manchester who helped them in all their work. Skinny had assured Clarence that he should accept the arrangement, and somehow, (Skinny would figure this out later), bring his four friends along for the trip.

After much thought between the five of them, and a few ridiculous suggestions from Becky, Sally hit upon the idea of going along with Clarence as stowaways.

Though it was impossible for Sally to be hidden away because of her handicap, and Skinny was most inconvenient because of his height, they finally agreed that some stowaways might be a good solution. Accordingly, Skinny sent Becky, Christine, and Clarence to scour the convent for large baggage articles, and after much trouble, Christine found an old trunk in the basement that she could fit in, provided she did not have anything against the smell of moth balls and didn't mind getting a little cramped. Becky and Clarence were very proud of an old carpet bag they had found in a hall closet buried beneath some white linens, which was the perfect hiding place for Becky when she curled into a tight little ball.

Now as they walked down the hall on their way back to their rooms, Skinny was pondering how he should hide himself.

"Why don't you go as a dead person in a coffin?" suggested Becky, when he asked them if they had any ideas.

"That's a great idea," said Skinny sarcastically. "All my life people have mistaken me for a corpse."

"Well, it was just an idea," returned Becky, putting on the baby pout.

"You should ask Clarence if he has any ideas," volunteered Christine.

"And if he can't think of anything, then maybe it would just be all right to try coming along as you are and hope nobody stops you. It's just a small, private plane, right?"

"But what if they do stop me?" asked Skinny. "You all wouldn't be able to survive fifteen minutes in Africa with Clarence as your guide and Sally as your brains. No, I can't take any chances."

"You talk it over with Clarence," said Christine. "I have to go finish packing."

When Christine entered their room, she was surprised to see Sally standing at the door to their closet, critically eyeing the clothing she had brought from New York.

"Sally!" Christine cried in surprise, "I didn't know you could stand up on your own."

Sally jumped when she heard Christine, and clutched her nearby bed post, leaning on it heavily.

"Well, I can't," said Sally, seeming flustered, "I mean, not without something to hang on to."

"You weren't holding onto anything when I came in," objected Christine.

"Oh, yes I was. I was leaning against the wall," insisted Sally. "And besides, you should not come sneaking in on people."

"This is my room, too, you know," said Christine irritably.

"Well, all right. Did you just come back from lunch?"

"Yes."

"And has Skinny decided if he's going to be a stowaway like the rest of you?"

"No, he's talking it over with Clarence right now."

"Then let's go and help them decide," Sally said. "Boys can never make decisions on their own."

"But I have to pack," objected Christine.

"You can pack later; come on."

Sally sat herself down in her wheel chair, and without waiting for Christine to reply, she wheeled herself down the hall to the boy's room, and kicked the door open.

Ever since The Company of Secret Kids had been formed, the nuns at Saint Joseph's Convent had been forced to bend many rules to keep their five young guests happy. It was not uncommon for one to see light streaming from under the girls' bedroom door at all hours of the night, or to find the more mobile of them ransacking a closet or scrounging about in the basement. Skinny was providing the necessary funds for his own room and board as well as Becky's, and though it was known by very few, he also made sure a generous donation was made on Christine's behalf, though she never saw it.

Now the Sisters had learned to ignore Sally as she cruised down the hall to the boy's room.

When she entered, with Christine at her heels (or wheels), Skinny was finishing boring the air holes in Christine's trunk, with Clarence's help, while Becky played with their fast growing paper airplane collection.

"Hi boys, what's up?" Sally asked, while Christine inspected the job the boys were doing.

"We just finished the trunk," said Skinny triumphantly.

"Here Christine, try it out."

Christine crawled in, and Skinny snapped it shut, setting it upright.

"Got enough air?" Skinny called into one of the holes.

Christine was able to flick the latch open through a hole, and she did so. "Yes, and you needn't shout in my ear so," she said, letting herself out. "But you boys better make sure that I'm kept in an upright position."

"Don't worry, we'll make sure," said Skinny, as he helped her out. "And Clarence and I have just thought of a way that I could come along."

"You're going to come in a coffin, disguised as a corpse?" asked Sally mischievously, for she had been the first to hear Becky's idea. Clarence laughed.

"No, you moron, and why does everybody think I would make such a lovely corpse?"

"Why, you're a natural for the part," grinned Sally. "Just to look at you I'd think you'd been dead for weeks."

Clarence roared with laughter. Skinny glared at Sally, but she could tell that there were the beginnings of a smile about his lips. Though she could find many faults with him, Sally had to admit that Skinny could take a good joke, even when it was on himself.

"Okay, very funny," he said, "but now you should listen to our real idea. It's terrific."

"Okay, shoot," said Sally.

"Clarence and I thought this out step by step, and we came to the conclusion it is veritably impossible for me hide in luggage as the girls are doing, because of my size. So then we began to look at the options of me coming along openly. If we wanted to make sure I did not get left behind, I would have to go as someone who was absolutely necessary to one of you who will not be hidden.

"So, since we've decided that Sally is to come along as an old friend that Clarence cannot bear to be parted from, and who is going to Africa with him because of her health, we figured that the one person she could never do without, is her professional physician, who is an expert on her special condition."

"What does all that mean?" asked Becky.

"It means that I'm going to be Sally's doctor."

"My what?" cried Sally.

"Your doctor," repeated Skinny.

"But you can't. You don't know anything about my disease."

"Well you can tell me what to say if I have to prove myself. I'm sure you know all about it. Besides, how hard could it be?"

He knelt down and grabbed one of Sally's feet. "First, what's the disease called?"

"Appendicitis," said Sally.

"Appendicitis? That's part of your digestive system! It has nothing to do with the feet or legs, everybody knows that."

"Well it's a long Latin name like that and you wouldn't be able to pronounce it or remember it," Sally said loftily.

"Try me," offered Skinny, as he pulled Sally's shoe off, "I've got a good memory."

"No, no. It won't work, Skinny, there are lots of details and things, now let go of my foot, ouch, Skinny that hurts!"

Skinny let go of Sally's foot and looked up at her from underneath arched eyebrows.

"You do know what is wrong with your legs don't you?" he asked suspiciously.

"Of course I do," Sally snapped. "But another thing, you don't look like a doctor. You're far too young, and you look too wild and happy."

"A minute ago I looked like a corpse," smiled Skinny. "Well, you girls go on back to your room. I need to try and punch some air holes in Becky's carpet bag. I'll stop by in about twenty minutes, Sally and we can go over all the 'details and things' you mentioned, and you can show me how sourpuss doctors act. Okay?"

Sally was still unwilling, and she and Christine returned to their room.

Christine at once began packing, carefully folding and rolling things together so she could fit all her own clothes, as well as a few gifts Sally had given her, into the small bag that she had brought from the boarding school.

"Sally, what do you suppose the fashions are like in Africa nowadays?" she asked, as she rolled an old novel with the word 'Fabiola' on the cover into her school skirt and shoved it in. Sally didn't answer.

Christine glanced up. Sally was sitting on her bed, writing furiously, her face set in hard determined lines, in a small black notebook that she carried everywhere with her. She stopped for a few minutes, looked straight up at the ceiling, as if trying very hard to remember something. At last she looked down, and wrote something.

"Sally, what are you doing?" asked Christine. She stood up, and walked over behind Sally, trying to see what was in the book.

"I'm trying to remember something," said Sally, holding the book closer to her so Christine couldn't read it.

Just then their half closed door swung open and Skinny vaulted onto Christine's bed.

"Okay. Let's get down to work."

"All right," said Sally, still seeming reluctant. "I just hope this bluff works."

"It will," said Skinny, wondering if there was a double meaning to her words. "It will. By this time next week we'll be in Africa."

Chapter 5

The Adventures Begin

Christine had an itch in the dead center of her back. An itch you can't reach is always a nuisance, but when you are hiding in a big trunk breathing through air holes (even if you could make a noise) and there is no way you can possibly get your hand to your back because of the position you are in, then an itch in your back is a most consternating thing.

"Shhh. I can hear you breathing," Sally hissed into one of Christine's air holes.

"Good. If you stop hearing me breathe, that's when you worry," Christine retorted as best she could.

The two girls were already aboard the small explorer's plane that was to take them all the way to Africa. They had been put on with several of the larger baggage articles. Skinny and Clarence had gone back to the terminal for the last few things.

Because it usually carried only a few passengers, and lots of equipment, the plane was made up mostly of open floor space. This was providential to The Company of Secret Kids, because of their more concealed members.

Sally was seated comfortably by the window, in one of the large seats. Beside her was the trunk that kept complaining.

"Hey, you should see how many men they need to put gas in just one tiny plane," said Sally as she looked out her window, thoroughly enjoying the sights.

"I wish I could see," moaned Christine. "Stop telling me what I'm missing."

"Okay. Have you ever been on a plane before, Christine?"

"No."

"Oh, then you're going to have fun taking off. That's the best part of the trip."

"Is it as fun from the inside of a stinky trunk?"

Sally was about to respond that she didn't know, when Clarence and Skinny came in the door of the plane, carrying a bulky carpet-bag that was breathing heavily.

"Hi boys, when do we take off?" Sally greeted them.

"I, Ow! Don't know," said Skinny as he hit his head on the low doorway for the third time that day. He let go of his handle of the carpet-bag and Clarence dropped it.

"Ouch!" said the bag, seeming to echo Skinny.

Sally laughed. "Well, you boys better hurry, the sooner we get to Africa the better. Christine's got an itch."

"Yes, and Sally isn't being any help!" said the trunk.

"All right. Clarence, help me drag Becky over beside Christine, where Sally can keep an eye on them until take-off," said Skinny, still rubbing his head.

"Sally isn't very good at keeping an eye on people," protested the trunk.

"Shhh, somebody's coming!" hissed Clarence, and Christine had to let her protest go.

A nice looking young man entered the plane, carefully ducking under the doorway.

"Well, we're almost ready for takeoff," he said cheerfully. "For those of you who don't already know, my name is Tom Ranlyn, I'm your pilot."

"Nice to meet you," replied Sally, "and, uh, I was wondering, will there be any other passengers on this flight, sir?"

"Only one," said the pilot as he unlocked the door to the cockpit, "a Doctor Johnson, professional on African reptiles. He's going over to join the exploration party that found your friend Clarence."

"Oh. Will he be riding in here with us?" asked Sally, trying not to look at the trunk or the carpet bag at her feet.

"No. He'll be in the cockpit with me. Why do you ask?"

"Oh, just curious," Sally smiled innocently.

"She's always curious," said Clarence, looking uncomfortably from the pilot, to the luggage.

"That's fine. It's good to be curious," replied the pilot.

He stooped, and went into the cockpit. He turned around to shut the door, and smiled at them.

"Oh, by the way, I think that before we take off, you should remove the young ladies in the trunk and the carpet bag and give them proper seats. They might be getting uncomfortable."

He winked at them, and shut the door.

"Did I just hear what I thought I heard?" asked the trunk.

"Yes, you did," replied Skinny. "You can come out."

He knelt down, unlatched the trunk, and pulled Christine out. Becky wriggled out of her bag, and sat down behind Sally with a sigh of relief.

"Wouldn't you know it?" asked Skinny, as he pushed the trunk off into a corner. "All that work and worry for nothing."

"I wonder how he figured us out," mused Sally.

"It was probably your stupid curiosity," said Clarence.

"Well, it doesn't matter now," Skinny hurried to say, before Sally could make a response. "I'm just glad we are successfully on our way."

"Africa," said Sally, turning to look out the window once more. "Imagine."

She turned to Christine who had taken the seat across from her. "Lions, tigers, elephants. Adventure in the jungles. It's like something out of a book."

"I just hope it's a book with a happy ending," replied Christine. She was beginning to wonder if she would regret coming on this 'Adventure.'

* * *

It was going to be a hot day. The thing Christine hated most about Africa was the stupid heat.

She and Becky were alone at their campsite, trying to get breakfast ready. Christine also had to admit that she didn't especially like camping either.

They had been in Africa for only a little over a week now, but so much had happened that it seemed like a year.

Since they had been flying on a private plane, they didn't land at an airport, but on a private landing strip near the explorer's base. The Company of Secret Kids had found themselves in the heart of the African continent, with only one well populated village nearby. Skinny had immediately taken charge, and rented a small beat-up car from an inhabitant of the village.

Then he strapped a small canoe type boat on top of it. He and Clarence had previously arranged that they would make a methodical search for the crocodile, and they wished to get started right away.

The lake Clarence indicated was located up on a hill, about twenty miles away, and before the other kids had even started unpacking, Skinny had gone off to buy camping supplies, and told them they were leaving in the morning.

When they had arrived near the lake, they had found a nice flat piece of ground looking down at the lake from one direction and at the village in the distance in the other direction.

The boys soon had the tents put up; small triangular affairs made of poles and blankets; and the girls started experimenting with their cooking supplies. After a few rough nights, and some burnt dinners, they started to get into a routine. Once they were settled, Skinny and Clarence took turns searching the lake. Neither of them knew what he would have done if he had found the crocodile, but still they said that they were making progress, so the girls didn't object.

They had only gone back into the village once, for Sunday Mass, which was the most lively mass they had ever attended, in a little chapel with windows with no glass and extremely colorful paintings of saints and angels on the walls.

Christine had finally learned how to toast bread over a fire, but she still dropped a piece in the ashes occasionally.

"Becky, go get some soda pop from the snack box," she said over her shoulder, as she tried to rescue a smoldering fragment of her toast.

"What do you want soda pop for, if you are making toast?"

"I need to wash the dirt off this piece of bread, and Sally told me that soda-soaked toast would taste better than water-soaked toast."

"I think it would taste better if it wasn't soaked in anything at all," said Becky, as she handed Christine the soda.

"But if I didn't wash it off with something, it would be dirty," said Christine. "Although sometimes I think dirty might taste better than soggy."

"Me too," said Becky. "Maybe someday you won't drop it in the fire at all."

Just then Skinny came up the hill, lugging a large metal pail filled with water.

"Here's the water supply, Chris." He dropped it at her feet. "Oh, my back hurts."

"We can have breakfast as soon as Clarence gets back with the wood," she said.

"All right," said Skinny. "I'll go get Sally."

He left their little clearing, circled around a clump of reeds, and climbed up a little ridge. Sally was sitting in her wheelchair on a flat, hard rock plateau that she had discovered a few days before. It looked down upon the plain on her right, and out towards a rocky cliff at her left. Sally could sit backed right up against the rocky wall, partly covered by brush, and never be seen by someone who passed over the plateau.

When Skinny approached her secluded spot, she glanced up from the book she was reading. "Hi, Brother Fat. Is breakfast ready?"

When she had given nicknames to the others, Sally had not been satisfied with the name 'Skinny.' She found it too literal. After thinking it over, she had borrowed a name from one of her favorite authors, Fr. Francis Finn. He had invented it for a similarly built character. Now both Sally and Clarence called Skinny 'Brother Fat' almost always, unless it was a formal occasion, in which case they used 'Skinny'.

"Yes, but Chris dropped the toast in the ashes again," said Skinny as he took the brake off her wheelchair.

"Well, it does give the toast a unique flavor," admitted Sally, "but I think ..."

Skinny never got to hear what Sally thought, for at that moment they heard Christine calling Skinny in an alarmed voice.

"Hold it, Sally. I'll be right back."

Something in Christine's voice warned him that he should go immediately.

When he ran in to the camp, he was faced with two frightened faces.

"Clarence is gone!" Christine cried, wringing her hands, "Becky has been looking for him, and he's disappeared!"

"Are you sure he's not somewhere around?" asked Skinny.

"He really is gone," said a very white and trembling Becky, "and it looks like he was killed!"

"I'll go see," said Skinny, and ran towards where Clarence had been chopping their wood supply. There, all around the chopping block, in the somewhat moist soil, were the footprints of two grown men, maybe more, and Clarence's smaller tracks were almost totally wiped out. The hatchet he had been using was thrown aside, and there were blood stains on the handle. Christine and Becky were both in tears.

"Don't worry, girls," said Skinny, but there was a note of trepidation in his own voice. "At least we know that they didn't use the hatchet blade on him. It would appear that he was grabbed from behind, by the look of the footprints." Skinny studied the ground. "I think somebody took the hatchet from him and hit him with the handle."

"But why?" asked Christine. "Why would someone want to kidnap Clarence?"

"Probably for the same reason that he has been kidnapped before," muttered Skinny, more to himself than to the girls. "Someone must have figured out that he knows the whereabouts of the treasure. We were far too careless to appear in the village as we did. At least we know they won't kill him, not yet anyway."

"Where did they take him, Skinny?" Becky asked through her tears. Skinny looked around the clearing, carefully studying the prints.

"I think it was only two men, and they took Clarence that way." He pointed towards the plateau.

"How do you know?" cried Christine. "The footprints are all over."

"Well, you see the place where they entered this clearing was over there, behind you, because that's the direction Clarence would have had his back to. If he had seen them coming, he probably would have yelled for help. Then we can see lots of prints where a struggle must have taken place, and where they hit him with the hatchet. Then, there are the clear footprints of two men, and a smear, going out the opposite way. That smear is probably Clarence's feet. If he was unconscious, they would have dragged him away."

"It looks like they were heading straight to where Sally is!" said Becky, looking up at the plateau.

Skinny was kneeling near the tracks, studying the hatchet. When he heard Becky's words, his head jerked up and he looked at her, then up at the plateau.

"You're right!" he said, and leapt to his feet. "Girls, go back to the campsite, and stay there, no matter what. If anyone comes there, yell bloody murder. I'll be back!"

The two girls hurried to obey him, and Skinny shot up the rocky side of the plateau. A hundred thoughts raced through his head at once, and he wished he had a gun with him. And although there were more important things to worry about at that moment, he still wondered about a suspicion he'd had for weeks now....

When he reached the flat surface, the first thing he saw was Sally's wheelchair lying overturned and empty where she had been sitting. Then he looked up and saw Sally making her way gracefully over the rocks, with her heavy metal leg braces in her hand.

"Sally!" he called and raced over the ground towards her. Even in that moment of excitement his first thought was that his suspicion about Sally was confirmed. "You little faker!" he said, as he grabbed her arm and turned her around. "You can walk as well as I can."

"Skinny! Let me go!" cried Sally, struggling to wrest herself from him. "They've got Clarence, and I have to rescue him!"

"We will," said Skinny, trying to hold her still, "but we don't want to do anything rash. Let's think this out."

"Clarence could be dead by then!" yelled Sally. "Let me go. You can come with me, but we have to go now!"

"No," returned Skinny, "you go back to camp; I'll see what I can do."

"Go back to camp?" she practically screamed. "No, I'm coming! I'm the one who can do something!"

"Drat you Sally, you have to listen to me!"

Sally was overwhelmed by the thought that time was very short, and while she knew she couldn't change Skinny's mind, she absolutely had to go after Clarence. Without thinking out what she was doing, with one final wiggle, she freed her arm from Skinny's grasp and taking her metal braces in both hands, she brought them down on Skinny's head as hard as she could.

Skinny's determined look faded from his face and he fell to ground, unconscious at Sally's feet.

She was a bit taken aback, for she hadn't meant to actually knock him out, but remembering how short the time, and rather glad he was out of the way, she didn't waste a minute on examining him, and turned and ran off in the direction where she had last seen Clarence.

* * *

Sally's heart was pounding so hard she thought it might burn a hole in her shirt. The heavy braces she was carrying were becoming cumbersome, she had torn a hole in her skirt, and her long hair was getting in her way. She had been running for about ten minutes, following as best she could the trail left by Clarence's captors.

The land was uneven and rocky, and large rocks kept obstructing her view, but Sally was quick and light on her feet. It felt good to run and climb again, for up to now, she had always had to exercise in secret.

Just when she thought she had lost them, and was looking around wildly, hoping for a sign, and trying to catch her breath, she heard a voice just ahead of her.

She crept slowly toward a large rock, taller than she was, and leaned against it. The voices were just a few feet away, probably right on the other side of the same rock.

"Let rest. Need rest," said a voice with a thick accent that sounded like it belonged to an older man.

"Stop," said another voice.

Sally heard the sound of something heavy being set down on the rocks.

"Boy much weight," said the first voice, "you bear next."

The other voice grunted. Then she heard the sound of both men sitting down, and leaning up against the rock. They began to talk in a foreign language and by the sounds they were making, Sally got the impression they were proud of themselves.

Sally thought hard. She figured that these men were after Clarence's treasure, so they would probably not hurt him too soon. She wondered if she should go back to Skinny, and try a better planned rescue. She turned all the options over in her mind, and decided that now was the time to act. If these men had means of transportation, they might take Clarence far away very soon, where the rest of the company could never trace him.

"Jesus, help me," she prayed silently. "Dear Guardian Angel, protect me."

Suddenly, for no apparent reason, the unconscious face of Skinny flashed before her mind's eye. She thought of how horrible the reality was; that she had actually struck him so that he lost consciousness. This out of her own free will. With this thought, all the rash and thoughtless actions she had ever done came crowding upon her thoughts, painting a black picture of her character.

"I've got no right to pray, with that sort of crime on my soul," she thought miserably, "I don't even deserve to be successful with this rescue."

For a moment she wondered if she should even try to go on, but her doubts didn't last long. If there was one thing Sally was certain of, it was of the mercy of God, and the constant presence of her Guardian Angel. She had been taught by the Sisters that even if she had sinned, she could still pray.

She whispered an Act of Contrition and meant it with all her heart. As she finished the beautiful prayer her courage returned, and she silently resolved to do her best on the mission she had undertaken, and to make amends for her rashness if she survived.

Now that she had made the decision to act, Sally wondered what she should do. She was sure that there were only two men, the same two that she had seen go by with Clarence on the plateau. She looked around at her surroundings, thought for a moment, and put her only idea in effect. She was nothing if not bold.

Quickly she strapped one of her braces onto her right leg, lay down on her back near the large rock, and taking the other brace in her right hand, she put on an angelic face.

"Help!" she called in the most plaintive tones she could manage. "Help!"

She heard the men scramble to their feet. They came around the rock and jumped when they saw her. Sally was somewhat surprised at how big they seemed. She wondered if she had made the wrong decision. But she figured she had gone too far with her plan now to back out.

"Help me, please," she whined, "I'm lost and I can't walk."

The men looked at each other. "Is friend of boy," said one to the other, pointing back over the rock when he said 'boy.'

The other man looked annoyed. "Leave her," he said, looking at the leg braces. He turned to go back around the rock.

"But I've got money," said Sally, holding out her hand and then tapping her pocket to show what she meant.

The men looked interested. "Money?" said the older man. He said something to the other in their native tongue.

"Yes," said Sally, "and diamonds. Look."

She put her hand into her empty pocket and pretended to pull something out. She held her hand toward them, carefully keeping it turned so they couldn't see it was empty.

Both men hurried forward to see what she was holding. Just when they both leaned over her to see, Sally's right leg, with the heavy brace on it, came shooting up from where she lay, and hit the younger man full in the face with all the force she could muster.

The man fell backwards with a curse, and before the other could gather his wits about him, Sally had leapt to her feet, and raising the other brace high above her head, she brought it down on him in the same way she had felled Skinny. Though this man was bigger than Skinny, he was taken totally off guard, and staggered backwards. Luckily for Sally, he happened to run into the rock, and bashed his head on it, and tumbled off the side of a shelf into some rocks below. This kept him out of the way providentially, for the younger man was just rising to his feet, his face livid with rage. He snarled and drooled like a wolf, and sprang at Sally, pulling a knife from his belt as he leapt.

Sally jumped aside just in time, and to her surprise, the man fell flat on his face. She recovered herself quickly though, and gave him a good whack on the back of the head.

She didn't wait to see if he was fully unconscious. She snatched his knife up from where it lay next to him, and ran around the rock to where Clarence lay.

Clarence was lying with his face to the sky, his clothes torn and bloody. There was an ugly gash on his forehead, and what she could see of his arms and legs were badly scraped and bruised.

Sally tucked the knife under her arm, and somewhat clumsily dragged Clarence around the rock. She noticed that the younger man was already stirring. She realized she could never outrun him with Clarence, or fight him.

She whispered another prayer to her Guardian Angel, and almost immediately she spotted a bank of tall grasses that grew behind the rock, where the rocky terrain stopped, offering fairly good shelter.

With much difficulty, she managed to get herself and Clarence both well hidden in the tall, hot, scratchy grasses. No sooner were they concealed, then the man who had fallen appeared, bloody, bruised, and angry.

"Where?" asked the older one.

The other growled something inaudible.

"Chase?" the older one asked, looking around wearily.

"No."

"What?"

"No. We go back to master and tell. He will retrieve boy. He will take revenge. Girl will not live. Master will make sure she do not."

"Yes," panted the other, seemingly relieved at the thought that they were not going to chase. "Master Black Hawk will take revenge."

"She has written her own death," said the first with grim satisfaction. They turned and tromped off away from Sally, in the direction they had been going when Sally stopped them, away from the camp.

Sally waited silently until she couldn't hear any sound of them. Then she cautiously stood up and peered around.

"All right," she whispered to the unconscious Clarence, "let's get you back to camp."

* * *

"Do you think we'll ever see Clarence again?" asked the tearful Becky.

"Yes. Of course," Christine tried to say confidently, but she sounded so scared that Becky didn't believe her.

They had been sitting together in their camp for what seemed like hours. At first they had heard shouts coming from up on the plateau, but now everything was silent.

"Skinny has been gone a long time. Shouldn't he have brought Sally back here by now?" asked Becky, standing up and starting to pace.

"I guess so," said Christine, "but ..."

"Shhh," hissed Becky, crouching down to the ground like an animal. "I hear someone coming."

"Are you sure?" whispered Christine, standing up and starting to wring her hands.

"Yes. Somebody is walking towards us, from around that rock wall that is the back of Sally's plateau."

Christine looked around wildly. The camp was all disorganized. She had no idea if Skinny had brought a weapon with him. Now she heard too, the sound of labored breathing and slow steps, approaching steadily. The last words she had heard Skinny say now rang in her ears, "Stay at the camp no matter what. If anyone comes near you, scream bloody murder." Now Christine wondered how he expected them to keep anyone away. The steps were drawing nearer. She looked down into Becky's terrified eyes, and she suddenly realized that she, scared though she was, had to protect Becky.

She set her lips in a hard determined line. Going over to the large box that was used as their trash barrel, she pulled out two empty soda bottles. Taking one in each hand, she crept over to the rock wall that made up one side of the camp. She flattened herself against the wall and pulled Becky up against it beside her. They both listened in silence, hardly daring to breathe, while the sounds of the intruder grew louder every second.

Suddenly, when she thought she could bear the suspense no longer, Christine saw the form of a man come around the corner. Her eyes seemed blurred all at once, and she couldn't think clearly. Shutting her eyes, she raised both bottles above her head and brought them down on his head as hard as she could. She heard the sound of breaking glass, and then the sound of a body falling to the ground. She opened her eyes triumphantly.

"I did it!" she cried, feeling very brave. She looked proudly at Becky, who was staring at the man's limp form with a strange expression on her face.

Christine looked down at her vanquished foe, and her cry of triumph died on her lips.

"Oh, Skinny!" she cried in horror, "Skinny, I didn't mean it!"

She knelt down and rolled him over. Becky gasped when she saw him and Christine stifled a scream. There was a gash on his head and red stained hair fell over his brow in disorderly locks. There was blood on the ground. Christine took his head on her knees and cried over it.

"Oh, Skinny," she moaned, "I didn't mean to, don't you believe me?"

"I don't think he can hear you," said Becky handing Christine a rag to stop the bleeding. "He looks like he's dead."

Christine looked up at her, her horror redoubled.

"No!" she cried, looking back at the white face in her lap, "I can't have killed him. I'm not that strong! Please God, don't let him die!" She raised her lovely face heavenward and wept.

Becky sat down beside her and bawled. They made a forlorn picture, kneeling side by side, heads thrown back, giving way to grief.

Suddenly, when they had both stopped wailing long enough to take a breath, they heard Skinny groan. Christine looked at Becky, hardly daring to hope. Then his head stirred on her lap, and Christine laughed out loud for pure joy. She looked down at Skinny, and in her schoolgirl imagination she suddenly thought the whole scene seemed right out of a romantic movie.

Skinny groaned again, and it seemed to Christine he would wake up at any moment. She bent down and kissed his bloody forehead. Becky gasped. When he felt the kiss, Skinny's eyes shot open and he looked up in shock.

His surprised blue-gray eyes looked straight into a shy pair of the exact same color. Skinny sat up as fast as he could, then winced and felt his head gently.

"What happened?" he asked dazedly. "Did I keel over?"

Christine blushed scarlet and couldn't speak. The ever helpful Becky said complacently, "Christine smacked two pop bottles open on your head."

Skinny looked in surprise at Christine, who smiled bashfully, while wishing she could strangle the ingenious Becky.

"I didn't mean to Skinny, honest!" she cried, wondering if he was angry.

"I believe you," said Skinny wearily. "It just seems hard to believe I could get knocked out cold twice in the same hour by two girls that aren't half my size. It's shameful."

"Twice?" asked Christine, "why Skinny, did someone else hit you also?"

"Yes," sighed Skinny, "only that time it was fully intentional. That Sally is a wild-cat when she's loose."

"Sally hit you?" Becky asked, "and she made you all unconscious? How did she do it from her wheelchair?"

"She's been faking it, that's how," said Skinny. "I've always suspected her, ever since she didn't know what was wrong with her legs. You don't need to feel bad, Christine, I doubt you hurt me at all. It was all the fault of that idiot with the perfectly good legs, and a great swinging arm."

"I suspected Sally too," said Christine, then she gathered her wits about her. "Skinny, we really should bandage you up."

"Don't worry," smiled Skinny, "I'm not in any danger." He looked at their tear-stained faces. "You really thought I was over the hill didn't you?"

"No," said Becky. "We knew you were right here, but we thought Christine had killed you."

"Oh shut up," growled Christine.

Skinny laughed. "It would take a lot more than that to do me in," he said, "I hope."

"Well, we still need to fix your head up," insisted Christine. "Did you bring any first-aid equipment?"

"Sure," said Skinny, getting to his feet and going over to his tent. Christine followed him, still determined to get the pleasure of bandaging his handsome head. Skinny pulled rubbing alcohol and a cloth from his pack and began wiping off his head. Becky was still kneeling where he'd lain, and was looking up at the plateau.

"Skinny, where is Sally?" she asked.

"Probably getting herself killed by cannibals, or crocodiles, or pirates. At least that's what I hope."

"No, really Skinny," said Christine, "where is she?"

"She went off after Clarence," muttered Skinny, sitting down dejectedly, "and I let her, just like any barbarian. She's probably heading straight for her death, without me to help her. She certainly has a do or die attitude."

He looked so miserable that Christine sat down beside him and put her arm around him.

"It's all her own fault," she said, taking the cloth from him and trying to stroke his brow.

"No, it's not!" he cried, standing up and pacing around the camp, feeling half angry and half guilty. "I'm responsible for the rest of you because I'm the oldest, and she's only a girl. I should have known better than to try and make her come back here. I knew she was stubborn and

I could have easily let her come with me, but I didn't. And now who knows what she's getting into? I wonder if she's all right."

Christine didn't like to see Skinny distressed, and she felt vaguely jealous at him thinking so much about Sally.

"Maybe she'll come back on her own," she suggested lamely, hoping he would settle down.

"Not unless she has Clarence with her," replied Skinny. "She would never give up. And I doubt she'd be able to ..."

Suddenly Skinny looked up and his expression changed. Becky got to her feet.

"Well, I'll be switched. Look," he said, pointing towards the edge of camp.

"What?" asked Christine, but she didn't need an answer. Through the trees, she could clearly see the slight figure dressed in blue, slowly approaching the camp, dragging behind her a limp body.

"Sally!" cried Becky joyously, running to meet her. Skinny and Christine followed.

"Hiya!" returned Sally, setting Clarence's shoulders down and catching Becky into her arms.

"Oh, Sally," gasped Becky, still amazed to see Sally walking. "I'm ever so glad to see you. Skinny said you were eaten by pirates!"

"He did not!" protested Christine, as she and Skinny joined them.

"I'm glad to see you back, you trouble maker," sighed Skinny looking her over to make sure she was all in one piece. "Another minute and I'd have set out after you." He turned his attention to Clarence.

"Why?" asked Sally complacently, "I already told you I was going after Clarence, and you probably wouldn't have been any help. By the way, I really am sorry for smacking you in the head with my braces, I won't do it again."

She spoke lightly, but something in her eyes spoke an apology that only Skinny noticed. He smiled at her, and nodded. Sally sighed, and returned the grin. She was forgiven.

"Well," said Skinny, breaking the awkward silence, "let's get him some help."

Sally looked at Clarence where he lay at her feet.

"He's in need of a few repairs," she admitted, "I don't think the fellows that bundled him off had his personal comfort in mind. I also think they must have drugged him, 'cause he's sleeping like a log."

"I'll carry him back to camp," offered Skinny, but Sally shook her head.

"Oh no," she said determinedly, "I rescued him, and I've brought him this far, so it's my right to bring him all the way back. Besides, I don't know if you're in good enough shape."

"All right," agreed Skinny, holding his head. "I've learned that trying to change your mind usually doesn't pay."

Sally smiled victoriously, though a little remorsefully, and lifted Clarence up by his arms and dragged him the last few feet into the camp. There she deigned to allow Skinny the honor of pulling the only cot they had in camp, with which the girls took turns, out of Christine's tent and placing it in the open air where the shady trees offered some protection from the heat.

When Sally and Skinny had lifted him onto it, and opened his torn collar, Sally took charge like the captain of a ship.

"Skinny," she ordered, "Go get some fresh water from the creek. Christine, you round up every clean cloth we have around here, and Becky, you sit here and tell me what's been going on, and why Skinny's head is so bashed up?"

While speaking, Sally went over to Skinny's tent and picked up the bottle of rubbing alcohol he'd been using on himself. Then she returned to Clarence's side, sat down on the edge of the cot, and started looking critically at his injuries.

When Skinny and Christine had brought her the supplies she needed, they all sat around on the ground and watched. Sally gave them a brief summary of her fight and the rescue, as well as the dialogue which she'd overheard between the two villains. Skinny was impressed at how she told the tale without giving the impression that she had been a hero. She simply told the facts, including how scared she'd been. But he could read between the lines, and started to have more respect for her.

When Sally was done, Becky told her how, just before breakfast, they had discovered the kidnapping, and that Skinny had run off and they had almost worried themselves to death back at camp. When she told how Christine had hit Skinny with the soda bottles and "made him all unconscious," Sally roared with laughter, while Christine turned red all over again.

"And you actually thought you'd killed him?" Sally asked Christine, still laughing. Then she sobered slightly, saying, "Why, when I clobbered him with my braces I never even thought how he'd feel about it."

"I know," grumbled Skinny. "You thought it would be real fun for me to wake up lying there on the rocks with an aching head and no idea where you were or what you were getting into."

"Oh, stop complaining," said Sally jovially. "I told you I was sorry, and that I wouldn't do it again. And just be thankful you didn't have to fight with those two fiends that carried him off. They were hard to handle."

"I'm surprised you got out alive," replied Skinny. "But I hope those two don't try to come back here. We'd be no match for them."

"Oh, we could take care of them alright," Sally said reassuringly, "Christine, hand me that rag will you?"

Sally took the rag from Christine, poured a generous amount of alcohol on it and started carefully wiping a gash on Clarence's forehead.

"What would you do if they did come here, Skinny?" asked Becky, "Would you beat them up?"

"Oh," mused Skinny, leaning back on his elbows, "I guess I'd first get you girls to safety. Aren't you going to object to that, Sally?"

He pulled himself up into a sitting posture. "Sally? Hey, what's wrong?"

Sally was leaning over Clarence, staring intently at the cut she had just been cleaning. Her expression showed surprise, but at the same time she looked as though she had just realized the answer to a mystery.

"Sally, what's wrong?" repeated Skinny, and he too looked at Clarence.

Sally shook herself as though coming out of a dream. "Look," she said in a strange voice, "look at his skin where I put the alcohol."

The girls and Skinny looked closely at Clarence's face and perplexed expressions came over their faces.

"What's happening?" asked Becky in a scared voice, looking up at Sally.

"His skin is coming off!" cried Christine, "how dreadful!"

She appeared to be right. All around the cut that Sally had been cleaning, there was a blotch of tan. His black skin appeared to be wiping off like paint, for Sally's cloth was stained dark brown.

"I think I get it," muttered Skinny quietly.

"Me too," said Sally, "he's been faking it."

"What?" asked Christine. "You mean he's not a dark skinned boy?"

"Not anymore than you are," answered Sally.

"The stuff he used to color himself must be only removable with alcohol," said Skinny, "because I've seen him wash his hands or face."

"Well, let's make sure," declared Sally, "hand me that bottle."

She soaked her rag in the alcohol again, and started none too gently rubbing Clarence's left arm. Almost immediately, they could see the dark color rubbing off, and white skin appearing underneath.

"Hey, he's got freckles!" cried Sally.

"Here, let me help," offered Christine, and picking up another rag, she coated it well with alcohol, sat down on the other edge of the cot and attacked his other arm.

"Now I know why Clarence was always reading the ingredients on soaps before he used them," smiled Skinny, "it would have been awkward if his skin had washed away with the dirt."

"And now I know why I always thought he looked so funny," said Sally. "I always thought it was strange his eyes were a lighter brown than his skin. Now he'll look normal."

"I guess he's not the only one who's been keeping secrets," Christine said icily.

Sally smirked.

Skinny shifted uncomfortably.

"Clarence looks funny now," remarked Becky solemnly, "he's all spotted."

Skinny grinned. "He does look a little like a dalmatian," he said, "or maybe a zebra. You girls keep hopping around and cleaning different places, so he hardly looks human."

"Well, we want to see what he looks like, so we clean off the important parts," retorted Christine, carefully wiping his nose. "I think he looks older like this, and definitely more refined, don't you think Sally?"

"I thought he was okay the other way," shrugged Sally, not quite sure what Christine was talking about.

"Hey, I think he's coming to!" said Skinny, bending over him.

"He'll be in for quite a surprise," chuckled Sally. "I imagine it would be a bit disconcerting to wake up after having been kidnapped, rescued, and changed colors all within an hour or two."

Clarence groaned. They all four stared at him, while he moved uneasily in his sleep.

"Well come on, wake up!" said Sally, giving him a gentle slap. Slowly his eyes opened, and a look of perplexity came into his half black, half white face. He blinked twice, and sighed, then he suddenly sat bolt upright, pushing Christine off the cot and onto the ground with a swiftness she didn't really appreciate, and came nose to nose with Sally, who grinned at him.

"Hi Clarence," she said cheerfully, "how'd you sleep?"

Clarence looked at her, then at Christine on the ground, then at Becky standing next to him, and last up at Skinny, towering above him with a kindly look on his face.

"What happened?" he asked, and put his hand to his head. Before anyone could answer, he pulled his hand away from his head with a speed that credited his reflexes, and stared hard at it. Three of his fingers were black, and the other two were a light tan. Clarence then looked at his arms, and felt his face, and then, blushing scarlet under what paint was left on his face, he looked guiltily at Skinny.

"I guess you guys are pretty mad at me," he said.

"No, we just want to know why you've been faking," said Sally, "are you hiding from the police?"

"No," said Clarence shutting his eyes, "oh, man, does my head hurt."

"You're pretty beat up," assented Skinny kindly. "I think explanations can wait until you've been taken care of."

"Yes," agreed Christine, rising from the ground, "and you should take a bath too, so we can see what you really look like."

"Okay, and then maybe somebody will please explain how I happen to be in our own camp, and all bashed up, when the last thing I remember was two big men carrying me off, over at the wood pile."

Sally got up and walked over to the water barrel. Clarence stared wide-eyed. "Sally, what's with you?" he asked in surprise.

"We'll explain everything," said Skinny. "When you are bandaged up, and all one color, we'll have a council meeting. Let's meet here at two o'clock this afternoon, and have a real secret meeting, just for old time's sake."

Chapter 6

More Secrets, and A Villain Enters.

At two o'clock precisely that afternoon, the five were seated in the center of their camp, to discuss the past, the present and the future.

For the past few hours, the girls had been banished to Sally's plateau, while Clarence bathed, and Skinny searched the area around the lake for any trace of the kidnappers.

When Skinny finally called the girls down from their lofty seclusion, he reported that there was no sign of anyone around their camp. Then he introduced them all to the new Clarence. At first they hardly recognized him. He was wearing the same old clothes he always wore, but his skin, dotted with many freckles, was a lighter color than even Sally's. Now his dark hair and eyes fitted him perfectly, and Christine thought he looked very handsome. One thing they all noticed was that he looked older. His bearing also was changed, and he had a shy quietness about him that had not been there before.

Skinny took charge of the council, and when he had everyone seated on the ground in a small circle, he became the master of ceremonies.

"All right," said Skinny, "this council will now come to order."

Unlike their first meeting, when everyone had been shy, they now all started talking at once.

"Quiet!" ordered Skinny, in his sternest tones, "one at a time. Let's see what we have to get accomplished. The first thing we have to do is move this camp to a hidden location. That we will do immediately after this meeting. And now I think we should tell Clarence how he was rescued."

After a somewhat confused narrative, told by all four at the same time, with many interruptions and a few fights, Clarence got a fairly accurate idea of what had taken place.

"All right," said Skinny, when they had come to the end, "now what?"

"We want to hear Clarence's life story," said Becky.

"The true one," grinned Sally.

"Okay," assented Skinny. "Clarence, go ahead."

Clarence blushed. It was the first time anyone had ever seen him look flustered.

"Well?" prompted Sally, "how about you tell us how old you really are? You can't be the twelve year old you said you were. We all know that."

"Okay," said Clarence, "I'm fifteen, almost sixteen."

"Holy cow, the guy is older than me!" cried Sally indignantly. "Man, that was some good acting, Clarence. I'd never have thought ..."

"Sally, pipe down and let him go on," interrupted Skinny. Clarence smiled and seemed to be more at ease.

"First off," he began, "I'm really an American. I was born in California. When I was nine, I was in an automobile accident with my parents, and they were both killed. Then I was put under the care of my very wealthy uncle, who loved me very much. He wrote me into his will, as heir to millions, and he always gave me whatever I wanted. I was a delicate kid, and it seemed as if I was always going to doctors, because the accident that had killed my parents had messed me up pretty bad too. It was discovered that I had a serious back injury, and if something didn't change, I would become crippled for life. The doctors said my only hope was to go to a specialist in England, who was familiar with cases like mine.

"My loving Uncle, willing to spend any kind of money to help me, immediately made arrangements for me to go to England. Because he had some trusted friends in London, and also because his health was failing too, he decided to remain in California.

"So the next thing I knew, I was living, and going to school in London. The specialist found that I was not as badly off as the American doctors had thought, and after only a short time, I was out of danger and on my way to recovery. I wanted to return to home, but even though he was fairly certain of my good health, the doctor wished to keep an eye on me for some time yet, and so I stayed in London for the next few years.

"Because there was nothing else to do, I threw myself into my studies. I became especially interested in geography, particularly the Asian and African regions, and the professor of that field at our school took me under his wing. He was soon showing me off in the social circles, having me exhibit my knowledge of the inner terrain of Africa. That eventually led to my kidnapping.

"The two jewel thieves that you already know about were then working in England. For some time they had wanted to get out of Europe, because they were in possession of stolen diamonds. They had to take the treasure somewhere far away. When they heard about me, a twelve year old kid who had no living relatives in the country and knew the layout of Africa pretty well, they thought I would be the perfect guide. So one night on my way home, I was hit on the head, shoved in a car and driven off, out of the country.

"When I woke up the next day, we had crossed the English Channel into France. From Paris, we flew to Africa. There, they painted me black to keep me from being recognized. From then on, you know what happened."

"The whole story about the coconut and crocodile is true?" asked Skinny.

"Yes."

"And the part about the crooks getting eaten, and you meeting the crocodile in the swamp?" queried Sally suspiciously.

"Yup," answered Clarence, "all of that is true, right up to the moment when I first saw you in Manchester."

"Then why did you keep faking?" expostulated Sally. "Why the whole thing about being an eleven-year-old, and an African, and all that?"

"I guess I thought you would think I was more interesting if I told you that. And it was getting a little difficult to get out of the deception after so much time had passed."

"Well, I think being African is swell," said Sally, "but the true story is even better."

"And I think," put in Christine, "that being really from America and California, where Hollywood is, is downright amazing. Did you know many movie stars?"

Clarence was about to answer that he didn't but Skinny interrupted.
"Hey Clarence," he asked, "whatever happened to your Uncle?"
Clarence sighed. "He died while I was in England."
"Then you inherited all his money?" said Sally. "Wow."
"Yes, but I heard of his death only days before I was kidnapped, so I never had time to claim my inheritance. I suppose it's somebody else's by now."

"No, it would still be in your name, and all you need to do is write your uncle's lawyer, and let them know you're alive," said Skinny, "and that will be a big help, considering we need to pay to get to away from here."

"Imagine," breathed dreamy Christine, "we have a rich member of the Company."

"That money is just as much yours as it is mine," said Clarence, "you guys are all the family I've got, and so it's your money too, especially Sally, to whom I owe my life."

Sally blushed, and an awkward silence settled over them. Skinny cleared his throat.

"And now," he said, "that we know Clarence's story, and all the mysteries are cleared up, it is time we hear the truth from our little female faker."

He turned his gaze penetratingly on Sally. She smiled innocently.
"Well, Sally?" asked Skinny, "Little Miss Crippled?"
"Okay, okay," said Sally, "you don't need to act like I'm an ex-convict. I've been planning to tell you guys my other secret for some time now."

"Well, then go ahead," said Skinny impatiently.
"Okay, here goes," said Sally, giving Skinny a withering side glance. "You already know about Little Joe the gangster, who's trying to kill me. Well, he is the reason I've been faking. It all happened one night, not long after my father was killed by Little Joe."

"Little Joe killed your father?" asked Skinny, in a strangled voice, turning pale.

Sally glanced at him curiously.
"Yes," she answered, slowly, "to take revenge on him for something, I never heard the details. My mom didn't seem too crushed by dad's death, 'cause I think they didn't got along real well, but when he was gone mom was always on the lookout for trouble, and she told me she

suspected Little Joe would try to kill her too, and maybe even me, to complete his revenge. And sure enough, one night, when I was about ten, we were out walking in the park after dark, when we heard noises as if someone was behind us, and before I could do anything, I heard a gunshot, and something hit me on the back of my head.

"I fell over and lay very still under a big bush. Turns out I wasn't noticed lying there. I thought I heard someone say something about a kid, but I felt as if I were going to faint, and I couldn't think clearly. As soon as it sounded as if they were gone I got up, and feeling dazed, went out to the main street. There were some people on the sidewalks, and the bright lights made my head ache. I didn't go two steps before I keeled over in a dead faint.

"The next day I woke up in the hospital. I learned that someone had picked me up on the streets after I had fainted, and brought me to the hospital. I never saw my mother again. When Little Joe wants to get rid of somebody, they are never found, if you know what I mean. I told the doctors what had happened the night before, and I figured that my mother was most likely dead already. I was sent to the Sisters' New York Convent House."

Skinny began pacing back and forth while he listened.

"At first the reality of losing my mother sent me into a serious fever which lasted for a few weeks, but when I recovered from that, there was really nothing the matter with me, only shock and a few bruises. But the doctors decided I should stay with the Sisters until something could be done about my welfare. Then the next day, a rough looking man showed up at the convent, and started asking about me. He said he was an uncle of mine, but one of the nuns recognized him from newspaper photos as a member of Little Joe's gang. It was decided that if I was sent to an orphanage, Little Joe would hunt me down and kill me. I had no other living relations to go to.

"It was finally decided that I should stay with the Sisters, at least until the danger had subsided. The Mother Superior told all the Sisters that I had contracted a serious disease in my legs, and wouldn't be able to leave for a long time, maybe never. This was done to slow down Little Joe's rush to get at me. Soon this message reached Little Joe's henchmen, and from then on, about once a month, one of his men would come and ask about me.

"So I stayed in that convent for over three years. It really wasn't that bad, because I made friends with all the nuns and the other people they help. Because I had to act like I couldn't walk, I started reading a lot. I must have read hundreds of books in that time, and every time there was a movie playing in the theater down the street, I got someone to take me. I also started writing stories on my own, and telling them to the other people who were sick. Then came the day when I overheard Little Joe's men talking, and I got my secret. You guys already know all about that.

"When things began to get too dangerous again, it was decided it was time for me to leave New York. I chose to go to Manchester, and one of the priests had a friend there, so they paid for my trip, and then I ran into you all. You know what happened from there."

"But why did you keep up with the crippled act?" asked Skinny.

"I suspect I am still being watched by some liaison of Little Joe's. I think I'm safer if he sees me as crippled, and no threat to him. Besides, I guess I just liked the idea of having another secret that none of you knew about. A girl can't tell all her secrets," shrugged Sally, "and it was getting awkward trying to figure out how to get out of it all."

"Well, I'm glad I won't have to push you around in your wheelchair anymore," said Skinny, and added sulkily, "and I guess you were pretty brave today, but in the future I'd appreciate it if we could work together in emergencies."

"Okay," grinned Sally, "next time somebody gets kidnapped, I promise I'll let you come along."

Christine shuddered. "Oh, let's hope we never have another situation like this," she said.

"I'm afraid our troubles are not over yet," sighed Skinny. "I didn't like the sound of those two men Sally tangled with. And we don't know who this Black Hawk fellow is that they talked about, the one who is supposed to take revenge on her. Have you ever heard of him, Clarence?"

"Vaguely, I think," said Clarence. "When I was over here before, I remember hearing about some old world pirate, who went around robbing and killing people in the area. He may be the same man. From what I remember, he wasn't a very nice sounding person."

"Yes, and they said he'd kill her," said the frightened Becky, "and he would make sure of it."

"Oh, it's okay," grinned Sally. "You know that's not the first person that's sworn to see me dead, and I'm still around. I'm used to it."

"True, but this Black Hawk sounds serious," said Skinny. "I think we should all be on the watch."

"Yes, we won't let him get Sally," said Clarence, a determined light coming into his eyes. "Not after what she's done for me."

His eyes met Sally's in a serious gaze, and she blushed.

"Oh, pshaw," grumbled Sally, "you make me sound like some kind of hero. Skinny would have done no less and probably more, if I had let him."

"Yes, only Skinny would have killed those dreadful men, and then we'd be out of danger," said Christine, who felt that Sally was getting far too much attention.

"I don't know about that," said Skinny, "but I might have to fight them yet."

"Well, if the meeting's over, than let's eat dinner," said the unruffled Sally, "I'm starved."

* * *

Late that night, when the full moon was looking down on the quiet camp, its gentle light fell upon Christine, lying awake in her tent. They had talked Skinny out of moving the camp that evening, as they were all exhausted and hungry.

Christine's sleeping bag and head were sticking out of her tent, so she could look up at the stars. Lying awake, thinking over the events of that amazing day, and what the future would be like, Christine thought she heard the faint sound of someone moving at the edge of the camp.

Immediately thinking of Black Hawk, Christine sat up and looked around fearfully. She saw Becky's head in the doorway of her tent, quietly sleeping, and on the other side of the camp, she heard the boys' peaceful breathing.

Then she glanced toward Sally's tent, and started. It was empty.

At first she thought of kidnappers, and was about to call Skinny, when she saw a white-clad figure at the top of the plateau. She quietly crawled out of her tent, and pulled on her robe, which doubled as her pillow. She tiptoed through the camp, and climbed up to the plateau.

At the top, she spotted Sally sitting on the ground, her arms wrapped round her legs, and her chin resting on her knees. As Christine crept closer, she was taken aback to see tears on Sally's cheeks, shining in the moonlight as they dropped off her nose.

Suddenly Sally heard someone behind her, and spun round, springing to her feet. She sighed when she saw who it was, and without saying a word, Christine sat down. Sally resumed her position next to her, and smiled.

"It's a nice night," she whispered, and Christine nodded.

For a few minutes they sat in silence, looking out over the grassy plains.

"Sally," Christine finally ventured shyly, "why were you crying?"

"I was thinking of my mother," came the quiet reply.

"Oh," said Christine, and was silent again.

"It's terrific to have a mom," whispered Sally.

"Is it?"

Sally looked at Christine and her expression seemed to soften. "Did you ever know yours?" she asked.

"No," sighed Christine, "but I wish I had."

"I wonder what your mom was like," continued Sally, edging closer to Christine. "Can you remember what she looked like?"

"I think she had light brown hair, and grayish, bluish eyes, and a pointy nose."

"Sounds like Skinny," said Sally.

"I guess, yes, though I never thought of it that way. She did almost look like Skinny, from the pictures I've seen. That's funny isn't it?"

"Yes."

"What did your mom look like?"

"She looked pretty much like me," answered Sally, "except she was prettier."

"You're very pretty," whispered Christine shyly. Sally looked at her again, her face mildly surprised.

"So are you," she smiled, "though I don't think about that kind of thing much."

"I think you were very brave today, Sally,"

"So were you," returned Sally with a grin. "It takes muscle to smash two pop bottles on someone's head."

They laughed together in the moonlight, and Sally put her arm around Christine.

"Let's be buddies," she said, "and always look out for each other. Okay?"

"Okay, and share secrets, and personal things?" asked Christine.

"Sure," said Sally. "I've always wanted a sister, and you would be a fine one."

"Really?" asked the flattered Christine. "You like me that much?"

"Sure."

"Then, Sally," said Christine, blushing in the moonlight. "I'll tell you something that happened today, that Becky forgot to mention."

"Hmm?"

Christine blushed again, and edged closer to Sally, to whisper in her ear.

"I kissed Skinny."

Sally rolled her eyes. She gave Christine a look of surprise, amusement, and disgust all at the same time. "Where?" she finally asked.

"On the forehead,"

"What did he do?"

"I don't think he was conscious, and he still doesn't know. You won't tell him, will you Sally?"

"Of course not, what kind of girl do you think I am?"

"Thanks," whispered Christine, giving her hand a squeeze.

"It's okay," returned Sally, giving her an understanding smile.

"Do you think he's handsome?" Christine whispered after a few minutes.

Sally opened her mouth to reply, but just then, someone spoke behind them, and they both nearly jumped out of their skin.

"What in the world do you two think you're doing, up here in the middle of the night?" Skinny asked, in a loud whisper.

Both girls started breathing again, when they saw it was him, and Sally hurriedly wiped the tear-stains from her cheeks.

"We were just talking," answered Christine, as they scrambled to their feet.

"What are you doing up?" Sally asked him.

"I thought I heard someone up here, and I guess I was right."

"Well, don't sneak up on people like that," muttered Sally as she brushed the dust from her nightgown.

"You two come to bed, before you wake Becky and Clarence up."

Sally and Christine followed Skinny meekly back into camp and returned to their tents.

"Good night," Sally called softly, as she settled herself down.

Christine smiled an answer at her from her tent, and soon the moon smiled down on a peaceful camp, and two happily sleeping girls.

* * *

When Sally woke the next morning, she could already smell breakfast burning.

She scrambled out of her blanket, and emerged from her tiny tent a few minutes later, fully dressed in her habitual light weight blue skirt and blouse. After quickly braiding her long hair and securing the end with a piece of string, she pulled aside the blanket that was hung in front of the girls' tents, and hopped over to the fire.

"There's nothing like waking up in the morning to the smell of dirty, soggy, then burnt, toast. It almost makes you want to stay in bed," she said, grinning at Skinny, who had offered to help Christine make breakfast, and was having serious trouble.

"Aw, go chase yourself around the lake," growled that eloquent young man, without looking up. "I'd like to see you try to toast this rotten piece of bread."

"That's not fair," objected the grinning Sally, "I have to eat it. That's harder than cooking it."

And ignoring any retort Skinny had to make, Sally ran down to the lake, where she saw Clarence getting the day's water supply.

"Hiya, Clarence!" she called, "Good morning!"

"Hi," returned Clarence, who had already ceased feeling shy, and seemed his old self again.

"When's breakfast?" he asked, as they started towards the camp with the water pail.

"As soon as Skinny's done burning it," said Sally. "Then I suppose he'll expect us to eat it. Blah!"

"I heard that!" came a voice from the fire pit. Sally laughed.

"Where's Christine?" she asked as she and Clarence delivered the water to the struggling Skinny.

"She took Becky for an early morning walk," answered Clarence, seeing that Skinny was in no state to answer.

"I'll go see if I can find them," and Sally sped off towards the plateau. When she gained the top, she found no trace of the other girls, and she had already started back towards the lake, when she suddenly stopped on the edge of the plateau, and stared out onto the prairie, wondering if her eyes were playing tricks.

Far in the distance, but fast coming nearer, she thought she could see a cloud of dust, and in it, what looked like a band of horsemen, about twenty in all.

"Am I seeing things?" thought Sally, but whether she was or not, the horsemen were drawing nearer at a surprising rate.

After a moment's anxious wondering about what they were planning, Sally suddenly noticed that one of the horsemen was carrying a flag. A brisk breeze had made it unfurl, and she could see it plainly. It was a blood-red flag, and in its center there was a picture of a hideous black bird, that appeared to be in the act of hunting something down, its large claws reaching menacingly toward her.

At first Sally thought she was imagining things, for nobody went around on horseback anymore, carrying standards with pictures on them, at least not in the world she had come from. Then she suddenly had a terrible realization.

She looked again at the device on the flag, and turned a sickly white. "Black Hawk," she said out loud, and pinched herself, hoping she would wake up from a bad dream. But she didn't wake up, and the terrible flag and riders drew nearer. "How did those villains get all the way back so fast when they were on foot?"

Suddenly Sally found she could move again, and move she did. With one final look at the approaching danger, she turned and sped towards the camp.

Skinny glanced up at her from next to the fire and sprang to his feet when he saw the look on her face.

"Hey, what's ... " he began, as Sally ran over to him, and started kicking dirt on the fire.

"Black Hawk," said Sally, and before he could answer, she shot off towards the lake.

Skinny stood still for a few seconds, thinking about what she'd said, and about what to do. Then he too sprang into action.

"Clarence!" he shouted, as he ran towards the tents. "Clarence, go with Sally, I'll be there in a minute!"

Clarence came running to the camp from the wood pile, where he had been sent to get the day's supply, and glancing at Skinny, who was emerging from his tent with a hunting knife, he ran towards the lake where he could see Sally standing at the water's edge.

"Sally, what's wrong?" yelled Clarence as he came to her side.

"Black Hawk is here," responded Sally, trying to keep her voice steady. "He has come for me."

"Don't worry, we'll protect you," said Clarence, wondering how he and Skinny expected to keep away enemies of unknown power and strength. "I say, where are Becky and Christine?"

"I don't know, that's why I'm down here," said Sally, starting to run along the edge of the lake.

"We have to find them!" cried Clarence, and he started after her.

Just then Sally saw Becky approaching from the other side of the lake, and Christine a little behind her.

"Hey! Becky, Christine!" yelled Sally, "come here, quick!"

The two girls ran over, and in a few words Sally told them what she had seen on the plateau.

"Oh, how dreadful!" cried Christine. "Clarence, do you think they'll come here?"

"It's a safe bet they will," answered Clarence grimly. Christine looked up at the camp fearfully.

"Where's Skinny?" she asked.

Clarence glanced up the hill. "He said he'd come in a minute."

"Do you think Black Hawk captured him?" she cried, but before Clarence could answer, they all saw Skinny dashing down the hill towards them. When he got near them, they saw a determined look that had come into his eyes.

"Sally's right," he said quietly, "there are several men approaching the camp on horseback, and they have a flag with a black bird on it. At the rate they're riding, they should be upon us in the next fifteen minutes."

"What'll we do?" cried Christine, looking fearfully back up at the camp. "Will you try to fight them Skinny?"

"I wouldn't have a chance," he replied, and then looked at Sally, as if hoping for guidance.

Sally had calmed down surprisingly, and was staring hard at the murky lake, and the banks of reeds that dotted it, her brow furrowed in thought.

"Hey," she said, looking up at Skinny, "don't you think we could hide in the lake, in among those reeds and such?"

Skinny looked at the water, and slowly nodded. "Yes, I suppose that's about the best hiding place we can find around here."

"Good, then come on!" said Sally, and waded out into the lake until she was waist deep.

"It's awfully dark water," said Christine fearfully, as she and Becky gingerly stepped into it.

"It's okay, you just need to get used to it," said Clarence, as he splashed over to Sally.

"What's the matter, Skinny?" called Sally, turning back towards the bank. "Are you afraid of a little water?"

Skinny was standing on the bank, staring back up at the camp. He turned when he heard Sally's remark, and seemed less worried to hear her joke.

"Watch it kid," he called back, "or I might just come over there and give you a dunking."

"Try and catch me!" laughed Sally, and threw herself backwards into the water, disappearing from view.

Skinny gave one final look towards the camp, and splashed into the water.

"Come on, girls, there's not much time," he said as he caught up with Christine and Becky, who were still standing hesitantly in the shallows.

They followed him deeper and deeper, till Becky had to tread water, and finally to where Christine couldn't stand up any more. Sally had emerged far from where she had gone under, and was swimming in and out of the reeds that gathered thickest at the edges of the lake.

Clarence joined her, and they soon concealed themselves well. Skinny helped Becky make her way towards the reeds, and Christine swam close beside him.

"Can you see me?" asked Sally's voice from within the reeds, when Skinny and the girls had reached them.

"No, that's good," answered Skinny, "where's Clarence?"

Clarence's head suddenly emerged from the dark water, right next to Christine. "Hey, you know if Black Hawk's men decide to search the water, we can always duck under, pull these reeds up, and breathe through them. They're hollow clear through, just like straws."

"Oh, people are always doing that in movies, when they have to hide from the villains in water," said Sally. "I've always wanted to try it."

She disappeared under water. Clarence followed her.

"Well, we'd better get hidden," Skinny told the girls. "Swim into that bank of reeds, and stay as much underwater as possible."

Christine and Becky hurried to get concealed. The reeds loomed high above their heads, as they treaded water, in and around them, looking for a good spot. Christine gave a little shriek as she felt something alive underneath her, but it was only Sally, who came to the surface looking radiant.

"It works!" she cried happily, wiping the wet hair out of her eyes. "I could have stayed under there for hours, breathing through the reed."

"You should have," hissed Skinny, swimming over to them, and pulling the reeds closer together, "that would have kept you quieter. Now, pipe down."

Sally gave him a dirty look, but held her peace.

"For the first time since we've come here, I certainly hope that crocodile isn't in this lake," she whispered to Christine, as they waited through the long and terrible moments.

"For goodness sake," said the horrified Christine, "don't even think things like that."

"Shhh," said Clarence, coming up from underwater beside them, "I think they're here."

The five waited in anxious silence, fearfully watching the hill that led up to their camp. Just when Sally was beginning to wonder if she'd dreamt the whole thing, they heard shouts coming from that direction. Then they heard the sounds of their camp being ransacked, and of angry voices.

"Gee, I'm glad I keep my bag with my precious belongings hidden," whispered Sally.

"Watch it, here they come," said Skinny, "if I go underwater, follow me, and breathe through the reeds."

"I don't think I could bring myself to go under that dark water," moaned Christine.

"Then we'll leave you up here, for Black Hawk," said Clarence mercilessly.

Just then they saw through the reeds, many fierce looking men, all armed, come running down the hill towards them. They were all dark skinned, large in stature, and many were wearing earrings. When Christine saw them, she felt she'd gladly go underwater. She had noticed that even Skinny had turned a shade paler, and Becky was trembling in every limb. Sally's face was set in a more serious expression than Christine had ever seen before, but her eyes still had their twinkle.

The men circled the lake, and started into the trees on the other side. Then, a huge man appeared at the top of their hill. Christine shuddered when she saw him.

He was the biggest man she had ever seen. His arms were as thick as Becky's waist, and he had rings on every finger, and one in his ear. His skin was dark and scarred, and a blood-red bandana was pulled low over his squinting eyes. He was smiling a terrible, cruel smile, which showed off the fact that he was missing several teeth. In one hand he held a knife, and at his side was slung a massive curved saber, that looked as though it must weigh fifty pounds.

"Look at the size of that guy," whispered Skinny, and for once his cool manner disappeared.

"That must be Black Hawk," said Sally, and she too looked pale.

"Should we go under?" whispered Becky fearfully.

"Not yet," said Skinny. "Let's wait and see what happens."

As they watched, Black Hawk came slowly down the hill, looking bigger every second.

"He looks more like an elephant than a hawk," whispered Christine, and Sally smiled slightly.

Black Hawk walked right to the edge of the lake, so that the toes of his boots got wet. He scanned the lake carefully with terrible, searching eyes, and when he looked at the reed thickets, all the occupants therein felt their blood run cold.

When he seemed satisfied with his search, Black Hawk started slowly lumbering along the banks, stopping every few minutes to peer around in all directions. After what seemed an eternity, he finally reached the point where he'd started, and there he stopped.

"I think he knows we're in here," whimpered Becky. "What if he tells his men?"

Skinny didn't answer. He was wrapped in thought, and his expression was puzzled.

"Guys," he said at length, speaking to Clarence and Sally, "what if they decide to camp here, indefinitely?"

"I know," said Sally, "I was just wondering the same thing."

"Got any ideas, Clarence?" asked Skinny.

"No."

"Well, I have a plan," said Sally.

"Let's hear it," said Clarence. "We're desperate."

"Well, when they all come over to this side of the lake, nearer our camp, I could swim over to the other side, and pop up, and start yelling and making a fuss."

"Suicide isn't a good idea," said Clarence.

"Let me finish, will you?" retorted Sally. "So anyway, I'd go over there, and they'd all come after me, and I'd run into the woods. Then you all could get into our camp, and get on their horses, and then I'd get to camp somehow, and we'd all ride away."

"A decoy plan?" mused Skinny. "Not bad, I guess. A little risky, though. What if you couldn't get to our camp, or what if they caught you?"

"They won't," scoffed Sally. "That forest is nice and dense, and I could outrun any of those big, clumsy men."

"I don't know," said Skinny, "maybe it should be somebody else as the decoy, because after all, you are the one they're after. If they caught another one of us, they might just let us go."

"But it couldn't be you," insisted Sally, "because you need to get the escape ready, or handle anybody they might have left to guard the horses. And if they caught Clarence, they'd probably just carry him off and forget about us, because he knows where the treasure is. Becky is too small, and Christine doesn't know the forest well enough. It has to be me."

"Okay," assented Skinny reluctantly. "I just hate to let you take risks like that."

"Don't worry, I can do it."

"Okay, then. When some more of his men come to this side of the lake, we'll try it."

Almost as he spoke, the main body of men appeared behind them, and circling the lake, they all surrounded Black Hawk, and seemed to be making a report.

"Now is my chance," whispered Sally, "wish me luck."

"Oh, Sally, do be careful," whispered Christine.

"Right," said Sally. "And Skinny, get these two girls on those horses fast, I'm not sure how much time I'll be able to buy. Oh, and get my little bag with my special stuff, and bring it, it's stuck in the tree above my tent."

"Okay," smiled Skinny, "and if you don't show up within fifteen minutes, I'll come get you."

Sally should have said something gracious, or something poetic, about meeting again and all that, but she didn't. She simply smiled at them all, and whispered, "Pray for me."

Then she took a deep breath, slipped quietly underwater and swam off through the reeds.

For a few agonizing minutes, they heard not a sound. Then suddenly, there was a tremendous splash, and they heard a shrill voice on the other side of the lake.

"Hey! You over there!" yelled Sally from across the water, "Hiya, you evil mud-eyed freaks! Try to catch me!"

Black Hawk turned, and his eyes lit with an evil fire.

The four children in the rushes watched as the body of men on one side of the lake all turned and charged around the water, towards the slim figure dressed in blue, who was madly dancing to and fro on the water's edge, dripping wet.

When the men started getting close, Sally turned and skipped gaily into the seclusion of the trees, still chanting insults in a sweet voice, as though she were playing tag.

When Black Hawk and his men had disappeared after Sally, Skinny motioned for the others to follow him.

They swam as quietly as they could to the nearest bank, and scrambled out. Then, trying to stay as close to the ground as possible, they crept up the hill to the camp, where they found everything in an awful mess, but thankfully deserted by the enemy. The fire had been stamped out, and all their cooking equipment thrown aside. The tents were torn down, and Skinny's bag of clothes was missing. Tied to the trees were several horses, who seemed not to notice the wet children, and went right on eating any grass within reach.

Skinny lifted Becky onto the nearest horse, and told her to stay put.

"Have you ever ridden a horse before, Christine?" he asked as he helped her up.

"Only once, on a field trip, and it was a much smaller horse," she said, trying to keep her hands from shaking.

"Well, just don't let it know you're afraid of it," instructed Skinny.

"I'll try," said Christine, through chattering teeth. "Skinny, do you think it minds that I'm all wet?"

Skinny only smiled, and hurried over to Clarence, who was just descending the tree with Sally's bag. He and Skinny looked at each other for a moment, and seemed to read each other's minds. Clarence looked down at Sally's bag in his hands and sighed.

"I only hope she lives to need it again," he muttered.

"Shhh, don't scare the girls," whispered Skinny. "Now, you'd better get on a horse, and be ready to get out of here.

"I'm not leaving without Sally," said Clarence determinedly.

"Right," said Skinny, "we'll all wait for her."

Clarence nodded, and mounted the closest horse, holding Sally's bag closely, as though he felt it were her.

Skinny hurried over to where the girl's tents had been, and found Christine's only bag, and Becky's rag doll, that Sally had made. He distributed the things to their rightful owners, showing them how to hold on to them, and still stay on the horse. Becky sniffed when she saw the rag doll, and asked Skinny if Sally would ever come back.

"Of course," he tried to say lightly, but he noticed that Christine was watching him with a worried look.

Skinny sauntered over to Clarence, and patted the horse he intended to ride. He glanced up and found Clarence staring at him, a strained expression on his white face.

"Darn it," blurted Skinny, "I'm going after her!"

Clarence smiled, and Christine started breathing again. Skinny found a loaded gun in the horse's saddle bag, and he made ready to return to the lake side.

Suddenly, Sally came crashing through the trees, and ran towards them, panting, but smiling. Skinny breathed a sigh of relief and a prayer of thanks when he saw her, but as she ran up to him, he saw that her shirt was stained with blood, and there was a cut on her forehead. Her left arm hung limp at her side, stained and bruised.

"Sally, what happened?" asked Skinny, grabbing her arm and staring hard at her.

"Nothing," said Sally brightly, "we got in a sort of scuffle back there, but I'm okay."

"You sure?" persisted Skinny, leading a horse around.

"Time to hurry!" Sally said, and gave him an understanding look which seemed to say "don't scare the girls." Then she wiped away the blood with the back of her hand, and turned toward the horse. "Let's get out of here," she said, glancing back towards the trees, whence she had come. "I'm not sure how far behind me they are."

"Right," said Skinny, "let's go."

"No, wait," said Sally, "if you leave all the other horses here, then Black Hawk's men will have a way of chasing us. Help me untie the others, and they'll follow us."

"Good thinking," said Skinny, and Clarence slid from his horse and began helping quickly.

As soon as all the horses were free to run, Sally took her bag from Clarence, and dashed over to the best horse in the group, with a silver saddle and Black Hawk's insignia stamped on its saddle bags.

"Sally, that one looks like its Black Hawk's horse," warned Skinny, "you sure you want that one?"

"Yup," answered Sally, "if it's good enough for him, then it's good enough for me."

Skinny didn't argue. "Need any help mounting?" he asked, but he knew his offer was pointless. Sally only gave him an exasperated glance, and swung into the saddle easily.

"Hurry!" she said.

Skinny smiled as he quickly mounted. They turned their horses toward the village, and shooed the others before them. Skinny dug his heels into his horse, and glanced back over his shoulder toward Sally. As he did so, he gave a cry of dismay.

Sally seemed to be having trouble getting her horse to move, for the beast was used to a rider much heavier, and behind her, approaching stealthily with his unsheathed saber gleaming in his hand, and an evil light in his eyes, was Black Hawk. Sally was oblivious of the danger so close, and Skinny's voice died in his throat, as his eyes met Black

Hawk's. Those terrible eyes froze every bone in his body. He desperately tried to turn his horse around, but before he could make a move, Clarence, riding directly in front of him, had spun his horse around with amazing speed, and shouted a warning.

"Sally! Behind you!" he yelled, barely in time. Sally turned just as Black Hawk's saber made a broad sweep toward her. She flattened herself down on the horse's back, and the deadly stroke missed her by a few inches. Then, before Black Hawk had time to recover himself, Sally pulled on the reins, and gave the horse a kick that made the huge beast rear up on his hind legs, just a few feet from Black Hawk. The evil man stepped backward to avoid the flailing legs before him, and it seemed to Skinny that a look of fear came into his eyes as he looked up at Sally, high above his head.

It was amazing that Sally remained in the saddle, but somehow she did, and as the horse's forelegs returned to the earth, she gave Black Hawk a well-aimed kick in the face with one foot. Then, without a moment's hesitation, she dug her heels into the horse's sides, and it galloped madly toward the four children, all watching in amazed horror.

As it appeared that Sally's horse had no intention of stopping, Skinny motioned for the others to follow. Clarence yelled, and Becky and Christine's horses broke into a run, while the two boys came last, perpetually looking back over their shoulders to where Black Hawk stood, unable to give chase, ominously shaking his fist at the little company.

Skinny was finally able to make his knees stop shaking, but he still felt as though someone had poured ice water down his back. He glanced over at Clarence as he galloped next to him, and felt a little better to see that Clarence's face showed more anxiety than ever before, and he seemed dreadfully shaken. Skinny would have said something reassuring to him, but before he could think of anything, Clarence stood up in the stirrups, looked over the girls to Sally in the lead, and spurred his horse toward her. Skinny followed him with his gaze, and was just in time to see Sally slump over, and start to slide out of the saddle.

Skinny hurried his horse forward, but Clarence was already at Sally's side, and caught her onto his horse as she fell. Skinny reined up next to him, and helped Clarence with her unconscious form. Christine gave a little shriek when she saw Sally's white face. At this, Sally opened her eyes and managed a weak smile.

"Never say die," she whispered.

Then her face paled, and she fainted once again.

Chapter 7

A Change of Scenery

When Sally awoke, she hadn't the faintest idea where she was. Above her, all she could see was the roof of what looked like a large tent, lit by the early morning sun.

She could smell food cooking, and it occurred to her that she was hungry. She sat up in bed, and a sharp pain went through her head. She gingerly felt her brow, and found that it was bandaged up. She saw that she was in a very nicely made, very large tent, lying on a cot, with medical supplies all around her.

As she was trying to sort out all her thoughts, and wondering if she was really awake, Becky came in the doorway on tiptoe. When she saw Sally sitting up, her face brightened so much that she looked positively angelic.

"Oh, Sally!" she cried, and running over to the cot, she threw her arms around the confused Sally, and almost knocked her out of bed.

"Whoa Becky, hold on," said Sally, trying to disengage herself. "You're like a tiny human octopus or something. Now, let me go, and tell me what the heck is going on!"

"You've been asleep for almost three days Sally, and we've all been so worried about you, and we're staying with the explorers who found Clarence, and their doctor wrapped up your head like that, and Christine thought you were dead when you fell off your horse, and Skinny has called Clarence's lawyer, and we've got the right to all his money, and we're leaving for Switzerland!"

After delivering this amazing oration, Becky skipped out the door to tell everyone else within yelling earshot, that Sally had "finally waked up," and left Sally in a more befuddled condition than before.

She was just wondering whether there was any possible way to obtain breakfast, without injuring her head, when Christine appeared at the door flap.

"Hi," said Sally, "what time is it?"

To Sally's surprise, Christine burst into tears at this inoffensive question. She rushed over to Sally, and gave her a hug, crying and laughing at the same time. Then she blushed scarlet and ran from the tent.

Sally sat staring out at what little daylight she could see, and wondering if it was possible that everyone she knew had gone stark staring mad all on the same day. She was wondering how long it takes a person to starve to death, when Skinny stuck his head in at the door.

"Hi," said Sally, "Skinny, when's breakfast?"

To her horror, Skinny's face took on a look of relieved happiness, and he took a step towards her.

"Skinny Conklin, you stay right where you are and don't move," cried Sally. "If you come over here, hug me, and then run out crying or yelling, then I'm gonna strangle the next person that comes in here! Now, for the love of anything, please tell me what's going on, and how to get some food."

"Good old Sally," smiled Skinny, "you don't realize what it's like to see you acting like yourself again."

"'Good old Sally!' Good grief!" cried Sally. "I at least expected you to show some sense; now cut out all the sentimental slop and answer my questions."

"Okay," said Skinny, and still smiling, he sat down on a crate beside her bed. "I suppose you are a little confused."

"A little!" returned Sally. "You guys almost had me eating my sheets with this practical joke."

"Well Sally, the truth is, it wasn't a joke at all," said Skinny seriously. "You see, for a few days, we four weren't sure you would make it."

Sally's face expressed a closely written paragraph of astonishment. "You're kidding, you thought I was going to die?"

"Well, Clarence and I had hope, and the medic here at the camp wasn't too worried, but Christine and Becky could not be persuaded to cheer up in the least."

"Poor guys," murmured Sally. "Imagine all that worry over somebody like me."

"Well, now you see why they were excited to see you up."

"Yeah, but it was kind of disconcerting. They both came into the tent, said 'Sally!' and then ..."

Sally was then interrupted by Clarence, who entered the tent at a dead run.

"Sally!" he cried, and rushing over to her side, he threw his arms around her.

Sally looked exasperatedly over Clarence's shoulder at the laughing Skinny, and gave him a look that plainly said "see?"

"Okay Clarence," smiled Skinny, "that's enough, now go find some breakfast for Sally."

"Yeah, and make it a big one," added Sally.

"Okay, but after that, we'll want to start getting ready to leave," said Clarence. "The plane is all ready, and so are the rest of us kids." As he left the tent, Sally turned to Skinny and sighed.

"Wow, sounds like I've missed a lot of action around here lately. Suppose you clear me up on a few facts."

"Okay," said Skinny. "Well, the first thing you should know, is that we are right now in the camp of the explorers who found Clarence originally. We brought you here when you fainted off your horse, as we were escaping Black Hawk. We've stayed with them for almost a week, and they have helped us retrieve some of our things from our wrecked camp, and they've even arranged for a plane that will fly us to Switzerland."

"Switzerland!?" cried Sally. "I thought Becky was kidding, why are we going to Switzerland?"

"Well, for a few reasons. First is for safety's sake. We have been safe here, in this camp, and Black Hawk has not even come near us, but all the authorities here say that it would be suicide to stay in Africa, for Black Hawk would track us down as soon as we were on our own again. So, we four held a council meeting, once you had been taken care of, and we decided it would be best to leave the country now, and return for the treasure later. This is possible now, for we are well off financially."

"So Clarence got his inheritance?" asked Sally.

"Yes, and that means that we will never have to stow away again. We're rich."

"Was it hard to get the lawyer to arrange to let us have use of the money?" asked Sally.

"No, we got help from the people in charge here, and Clarence's identity was proven, so the lawyer set it all up and will handle all our expenses."

"That'll really be a help, considering all the traveling we have to do," said Sally, "but continue; tell me why you all chose to go to Switzerland next."

"Well, we figured it would be a nice place to spend the winter. Time has gone by so fast, that it's going to be December by the time we get there."

"Gosh, is it really that late in the year?"

"Yes, it's been almost three months that we five have known each other. It seems longer because of all we've been through."

"It seems as if we have always known each other," said Sally. "I can hardly remember what life was like before that day in August, when me and Clarence got in a fight in my room."

"'Clarence and I', Sally, not 'me and Clarence,' Skinny corrected absently, seemingly buried in memories.

"Whatever," said Sally, "but you have to admit, it does seem like ages ago that we met."

"It sure does," mused Skinny, "and since then, we've come to Africa, made a new enemy, found out that you could walk, changed Clarence's skin color and bashed my head open twice."

"Oh, Skinny that reminds me," said Sally soberly. "I never really got a chance to apologize for hitting you with my braces."

"You did apologize, and I forgave you, so forget it."

"No, there's more to it than that," persisted Sally. "It's not so much as for that one action, as it is for my whole character. I'm no good."

"What's come over you, Sally?" asked Skinny. "What do you mean you're no good?"

"It's true," said Sally. "I've thought a lot about it, ever since the day we rescued Clarence, and while I've been here I dreamt about it. I never think about something before I do it, I just do it. And then it turns out all bad. I'm just plain stupid."

"Sally, where would Clarence be right now if you hadn't acted the way you did?" asked Skinny. "Do you think he would even still be alive?"

"Well, I guess that's so," admitted Sally, "but I bet it would have turned out okay if I had gone back to the camp, and you had tried to rescue him."

"You don't know that," said Skinny, "but anyway, it's all over and done with."

"The crime is," said Sally, "but the criminal isn't. I'm still here."

"Oh, don't turn yourself into a gangster over one little rash act," said Skinny. "It takes a lot more to be really bad, believe me, I know."

He sighed, and for a moment it seemed to Sally that he was about to tell her something, but then he appeared to change his mind, and turned back to her.

"So, don't worry about your character, Sally," he said. "You're all right."

"But Skinny, I want to ask you something," said Sally, still not convinced. "It was a bad thing to hit you, even you know that."

"Are you kidding, it hurt like anything," said Skinny with a grin.

"Now, let me finish," said Sally. "What I was saying was that what I did was bad, and none of the heroes of the books I read would have done anything like it, and I don't want to do that kind of thing anymore. The problem is that when I'm excited, I don't think through things, and I just do whatever comes into my mind. So, what I want you to do, is to be on the watch for when I do rash things, and tell me they are bad, so I'll stop doing that sort of thing. Okay?"

"Okay," smiled Skinny, "and you know Sally, you are on the right track already."

"How's that?"

"You noticed that clobbering me was bad, all by yourself."

"That's true," grinned Sally. "Well, maybe I'm not so far gone after all."

Here the conversation was cut short by the reappearance of Clarence and the two girls, announcing that breakfast was ready.

"Oh, Sally I'm so glad you're back to normal," said Christine. "The doctor here in camp says that you'll be fully recovered now and ready for the trip to Europe."

"Hallelujah," said Sally. "Now I'll go eat, and we can start for Switzerland as soon as you fellows want, and I say the sooner the better; I want to have it out with Becky's Baron."

"Oh, Sally will you?" asked Becky.

"I think that for now you've have quite enough of 'having it out' with people," said Skinny.

"You wait and see," returned Sally, climbing out of bed, and giving him an impish grin. "I've got a few tricks up my sleeve that I'm just itching to try out, next time I'm in a tight spot."

"Let's just hope you don't need them too soon," said Skinny, "we don't want to go looking for trouble."

* * *

Christine looked up from the book she was reading and stared dreamily out the window. From their room on the top story of a quaint hotel, she had a direct view of the gigantic base of a mountain in the beautiful Swiss Alps, and she loved to stare at the snow covered mountainsides, imagining herself scaling one of them fearlessly.

They had arrived in Zermatt, a little town in the Alps, only the night before, and settled themselves in the nicest hotel Skinny could find. Now that they were well off financially, the five children treated themselves liberally to all the luxuries they had ever dreamed about. The boys had already made themselves well known in the local bakery, and their room, which was a few doors down from the girls' was always well stocked with delicacies.

Christine had already decided that she liked Switzerland much better than Africa, which she had not been sad to leave. Sally had said that the Alps seemed to her like a mystery, which was waiting to be discovered, and Becky was overjoyed to be home.

Now Christine was lying on her bed by the window, eating some delicious sort of Swiss pastry she had stolen from the boys, and happily reading one of Sally's novels. Becky sat on the floor by the bedside, playing with her rag doll, and telling Christine all her memories of the orphanage where she had lived. Christine was just turning away from the window and back to her book, when Sally came storming in the open door, a determined look on her face, and a half empty laundry basket in her hand. Her long hair was disheveled, and coiled messily round her arm.

"That does it!" she said, speaking to the whole room. "I've got to do something about this horrible, dreadful, stuff!"

"What's the matter, Sally?" asked Christine patiently, knowing Sally wouldn't settle down until she'd had her fill of complaining.

"Oh, I just got my hair caught in the laundry shoot door," said Sally, "and I've decided that I'm going to do something about it."

She marched into the bathroom, and slammed the door. Christine smiled, muttered something about good old Sally, and returned to her reading. Becky laughed and said she wished she could have seen Sally's hair get caught in the laundry shoot.

Christine was absorbed in her book, but even through the realms of fairyland, she kept wondering what Sally had meant by 'do something about it.' She listened subconsciously, but all she could hear coming from the bathroom was a thin, measured, rasping sound; a sound she knew she had heard before, but couldn't quite place, for her mind was still occupied with the story.

"Hey, Chris," said Becky, staring up at the bathroom door, "do you hear scissors?"

Christine sat bolt upright. She opened her mouth to speak, but before she could, the bathroom door opened, and Sally trotted out serenely, picked up the laundry basket, and left the room. Christine and Becky watched her in stupefied silence, staring in horror at her cropped head. Sally's hair was now the same length as Skinny's, falling over the back of her neck, and just a bit above her shoulders.

As she disappeared through the door, a smug expression on her face, Christine and Becky leapt to their feet and flew to the bathroom door. There, almost hiding the tile floor from view was a mound of beautiful, wavy, dark hair. The locks still held together as though she had chopped it all off in a few strokes. Becky knelt down, and gently picked up a handful. She looked at it for a long second, and then leaving the bathroom, she laid the hair in her doll's lap.

"I'm going to give my dolly real Sally hair for her head," she told Christine.

Christine turned and smiled sadly at her. Then she gazed back at the lovely hair on the floor. She too, bent and picked up a lock.

Just then, Clarence and Skinny came in the door at a dead run. They glanced at Becky, and hurried over to Christine. She hurriedly stuck the hair she was holding into her dress pocket. Skinny's face took on a shocked expression as he came to the door and saw the hair.

"Hey, was that Sally who just went down the hall?" asked Clarence, then he glanced at the floor, and his jaw dropped.

"Why did you let her do it?" Skinny asked Christine.

"I don't know," moaned Christine.

"I thought I heard scissors," said Becky mournfully. Christine turned away, leaving the two boys in the doorway.

"I just hope she doesn't regret it later," murmured Clarence. "It would take years to grow it back, as long as it was."

"And she had asked me to keep her from doing anything rash," muttered Skinny.

"How did it happen, Chris?" asked Clarence, going over and sitting down on the bed.

While Christine was telling Clarence about the laundry shoot, Skinny stood staring at the pile of hair that had graced Sally's head only a moment before. He glanced over his shoulder, and saw that the other three were not looking at him, so he quickly bent down and slipped a section of the hair into his pocket. He straightened quickly, for he knew it would be hard to explain why he felt he wanted to keep some of Sally's hair, especially to Clarence.

"Well, what's done is done," he said, "and Clarence, we should go finish making plans. Come on."

He left the room, and hurried down the hall. As he was passing the laundry shoot, he saw the girl's laundry basket lying next to the shoot door, and the legs and feet of a girl, wearing a blue skirt, and mismatched socks, sticking out of it. He sighed, glanced exasperatedly up in the direction of the heavens, and grabbed her feet. As he pulled her out of the laundry shoot, and saw Sally's cropped head, he couldn't help wincing.

"Skinny, why'd you go and pull me up? I was trying to see if it's possible to slide down that thing. I think it'd be great fun."

Skinny stared hard at the grinning face in front of him, surrounded now by wavy curls.

"Skinny, what's the matter?" asked Sally. "You look sick."

"Sally Keenan," he said sternly, "why did you go cut off all your hair without asking any of the rest of us if we had an opinion in the matter?"

Sally looked astonished. "But, why would any of you care either way what my hair looks like?" she asked. "Even I hardly care, and I only did it to keep it out of the way."

"But Sally, what if you regret it later?" asked Skinny. "What if this is one of those rash things you asked me to warn you about doing?"

"Oh Skinny, it's not like that at all," said Sally. "My appearance isn't something important to worry about. When I told you to keep me straight, I meant about things like life and death."

"Well, I just hope you won't be sad when you wake up tomorrow with no hair," sighed Skinny.

"I've been meaning to cut my hair for years now," said Sally, "and I'm glad I finally got around to doing it. So, going back to the original point, do you think it's possible to slide down a laundry shoot?"

"I think it sounds dangerous," smiled Skinny, "and I don't recommend you try it while we're here."

"Well, okay," grinned Sally. "I guess I'll go find a broom somewhere and go back to my room to clean up the hair that I left on the bathroom floor."

She skipped down the hall, and Skinny turned toward his own room, thinking that Sally actually looked better with short hair. As he reached the door of the room, he saw Clarence, with his back to the door, nervously but carefully putting a large amount of Sally's hair in his bag that he reserved for special articles. Skinny smiled to himself, and politely turned away from the door. Then he cleared his throat loudly, and went in again. Clarence hurriedly put his bag aside, and tried to appear casual.

"Hi, Skinny," he said. "I, um, I think we should decide before too much hair passes, I mean, time passes, when and where we are going to look for Becky's Baron. Don't you think so?"

"Sure," said Skinny, flopping down on his bed. "In fact I think we should start into the Alps this coming Monday, the day after tomorrow."

"Okay, then let's start by buying the stuff we'll need."

As they went down the hall toward the girls' room, they found Sally rummaging through the maid's closet, armed with a broom, and looking for a dustpan.

"Wish I could come with you fellows," she said, when they told her where they were going, "but I've got to sweep up, clear away, and throw out, a whole lot of hair."

"You're going to throw it all away?" asked Clarence, trying to sound careless.

"Sure, what else could I do with it?" she asked, climbing up on an empty bucket, and reaching for the dustpan on a top shelf.

"You could save it," suggested Clarence, "just to show people how long your hair was."

"Who would want to know?"

Here Sally finally managed to reach the dustpan, pulled it out, lost her balance, and accidentally hit Skinny in the face as she came down.

"Well, doesn't Christine like your hair a lot?" asked Skinny as he helped her to her feet.

"I haven't been in there yet, but when I walked by, I heard them talking about putting my hair on Becky's doll. Anyway, I better go tidy up."

The boys followed her into her room, to tell Christine they would be out running errands for a while, and ask Becky what the French word for "snowshoes" was.

Sally started into the bathroom, but stopped at the door in surprise. There, where she had left her large pile of hair, were a few loose hairs scattered on the tile, but nothing more. Sally did not know how fond the others were of her, so much so that they had taken, without letting each other know, enough to make it noticeable. She shrugged, and turned away.

"It looks like I'll come with you boys after all," she said laying the broom down and scratching her head. "Hey, does anyone know what happened to my hair?"

Chapter 8

A Dance Routine

When Skinny, Sally, and Clarence returned from shopping that evening, the Company of Secret Kids held a small council meeting, and decided they would tackle the Alps early Monday morning, and try to find some sort of trace of Becky's Baron and his underground fortress. They had purchased all the warm clothing and the equipment they would need, and a good deal that they wouldn't need, but had bought anyway, because they could.

They all attended Mass at a beautiful little church the next day, and Sally continued giving Skinny what she called, "a crash course in Catechism." Once again, as happened every time they went to Mass, the other four children were deeply impressed and edified by Sally's conduct during the service. She still had her roguish ways and happy smile, but she seemed to be in a much deeper state while adoring her God. Also, she had a somewhat strange enjoyment for the Mass, for a girl her age, which proved to be contagious. Christine found herself looking at the Altar, instead of at Skinny, and she felt deeply ashamed of her vanity whenever she saw Sally's face, more beautiful than ever, after she had received Communion.

Skinny too, was being edified by Sally's conduct. Before he met up with the other kids, he had graced a church with his presence on Easter and Christmas only. When he came into Sally's clutches, he found that this was going to change. She immediately sent him to Confession in Manchester, where he made a general confession of his whole life, (and confessed things that Sally would not have believed had she heard them), and since that day, he had never again missed a Sunday Mass.

When Clarence asked Sally why she seemed to enjoy going to Church so much, Sally told him that she always came out feeling brave and heroic. She found that this feeling lasted, and grew stronger whenever she was in a tight spot. Ever since the night when Sally had lost her mother, she had prayed very much to the Blessed Mother, and so had grown close to Jesus. She always asked Him, and her cherished Guardian Angel, to assist her in all difficulties. So far it had seemed to work.

When Mass was over, they returned to the hotel to collect their things, while Skinny visited the tourist agency, and figured out the best routes to take for an all day hike at the base of the Alps.

Before the clock had struck twelve, the five happy children were on their way up into the Alps, and into one of the biggest adventures they had yet come across.

* * *

"Okay, so this map says, we follow the trail, to the top of this hill, and then turn right at the fork in the road," said Skinny, trying to hold the map still, and hoping he had it right side up, while walking up a steep, snow covered hillside.

"Okay, so when we reach a fork in the road, we'll turn right," panted Christine, just behind him. "Did you guys hear that?" she turned back to Sally, who was talking to Becky, who was happily riding up the steep hill on Clarence's back.

"Did we hear what?" Sally asked.

"We're supposed to turn right, at the fork in the road," repeated Christine.

"There's a second one?" asked Sally.

"What do you mean?" asked Skinny, coming to a full stop and hurrying down to them.

"Well, when you were carrying Becky, and were in the back, we came upon a fork in the trail," said Clarence, "and we followed Sally, who was in the lead."

"Which way did you go?" Skinny asked Sally, trying to sound calm.

"Left."

Skinny looked around. The afternoon light was beginning to fade. From the side of the hill where they stood, surrounded by rock and snow, he could make no sure guess in which direction the town lay. Terrible thoughts of how to survive all night in freezing temperatures flashed across his mind. He sat down on the snow covered ground and sighed.

"Well, that does it," he said. "I'm lost."

"At least you have the guts to admit it," said Sally hopefully. Skinny gave her a weak smile. Becky slid off Clarence's back, and Christine edged closer to Sally.

"What are we going to do?" whispered Clarence, as though he didn't want the hostile landscape around them to realize their danger.

"Never say die," said Sally cheerfully.

"Even if you have to do it?" asked Skinny.

"Skinny, stop that, you'll scare the girls," scolded Sally. "Now what we need is a scout, who will look around in all directions, and I volunteer."

"Perfect, and when you don't come back, we'll really start to panic," returned Skinny. "No Sally, one thing is sure, we have to stick together."

"Then let's all go and try to find some sort of shelter," said Sally, nothing daunted. "I mean, it's better than just sitting here till we freeze to death."

Skinny looked up at Clarence for his opinion, and Clarence shrugged. Skinny got to his feet, and handed the map to Sally.

"All right," he said, "you lead us."

Sally shrugged. "Okay then," she said, putting on a military air. "Troops, line up, and follow me."

She started up the hill, but halfway she stopped, and Skinny ran into her.

"Hey, Skinny, I've been thinking," she said.

"Will wonders never cease," ejaculated Skinny sarcastically.

"Give me a chance, will you?" returned Sally. "Anyway, what I've been thinking is, why can't we just retrace our steps back, to where I went wrong, or went left, and go right?"

"Sally, look at the map."

Sally unfolded the map and stared at it.

"How many forks in the trail do you see?" asked Skinny.

"About six."

"Well, I thought the first one we would reach would be at the top of this hill we're climbing, but it wasn't. How do you know that the one where you went wrong was the first one?"

"Well, it was the first one I noticed," suggested Sally, "but I suppose I could have missed one of these little ones, and you could have thought that one of these big ones was the one I went wrong on, but then there's the point that maybe I did just go wrong on a little one, and this one coming up would be the right one that we're looking for, but if it isn't, then we'll really be off track, and then--"

She trailed off into silence. Skinny looked at her, and smiled sadly. Sally sighed.

"I think you're right," she muttered. "We're lost."

"Well, we tried," said Clarence, who had joined them in time to hear Sally's last remark.

"And we can try again," said Sally, putting on her determined face.

"Try what?" asked Skinny.

"Well, now we don't have to worry about following the map," said Sally, cheerful once more, "so we can concentrate on trying to find some sort of shelter, and we don't even need to stay on the trail. Look on the bright side! We can't get any more lost than we are now."

"Well, okay," said Skinny, "maybe there's a cave or something around here."

"We won't find it if we stay here," said Sally. "Come on!"

She took Becky by the hand, and started up the hill. For almost a quarter of an hour, they trudged along. Finally Skinny was carrying Becky while Sally explored, and Clarence was helping Christine to make plodding steps. They watched the light lessen, and felt the air growing colder. Sally was constantly encouraging, and was never without an idea. She climbed rock piles to get better views, she slid down hills, and scrambled back up them, and when she had the breath, she sang Irish drinking songs to cheer them up.

Finally, just when they all felt that they would collapse if they moved another step, the four heard a whoop from Sally, who had climbed to the top of a steep rock wall, which made up the left side of the trail they were following.

"Whoopee!" she cried, and lost her balance. She fell backwards into a deep drift, and was pulled out by the two boys.

"Are you okay, Sally?" asked Clarence, dusting the snow from her coat.

"Who cares about me?" cried Sally joyfully. "There's a cave up there!"

The echoes of the mountain rang with the sounds of the girls screaming with joy, and Clarence turned a handspring into a snowdrift. Skinny climbed up the ridge where Sally had been, and his face read pages of relief.

"She's right," he said, climbing to the ground. "There's a cave big enough for all of us to fit in for the night, and with all our coats and blankets, and a good fire, we should make out quite comfortably."

He turned back and looked up at the ridge. "Can you climb that, Christine?" he asked.

"Yes, if somebody's behind me."

Skinny turned back to ask Becky, but as he opened his mouth, he was hit in the face with a snowball. As he cleared the snow away from his eyes with his glove, Sally's laugh rang out on the silence. Skinny turned and quietly stared at her.

"I've been meaning to do that to you all day," said Sally, "but this getting lost business drove it out of my head."

She looked at Skinny, and he looked at her. His expression was stern and disapproving.

"You know, I never did pay you back for getting us all lost, and almost killing us," he said, and as he did so, the corners of his mouth started to twitch. Sally grinned.

"I think I'd better get out of here," she said, smirking, and took a few steps backwards.

"I think I should let you have it," said Skinny, now obviously smiling. "But I'm a fair person, so I'll give you a five second head start. Go!"

Sally turned and fled. She hadn't covered ten feet, when a well aimed snowball got her in the back of the head. She spun round, ducked the next missile that came at her, and as she ducked, grabbed a handful of snow, packed it well, and threw it when Skinny bent down to collect more ammunition. She got him full in the face, and took advantage of his handicap by making another ball. She raised her arm to throw it, just as Skinny cleared his vision, but before it left her hand, a ball from Clarence struck her pitching arm, and temporarily disarmed her. This gave Skinny the chance to get her right between the eyes.

"Hey, you boys are ganging up on her!" cried Christine, "That's not fair!"

She hadn't much experience at snowballing, but she was happy that they were happy. She felt she could do anything. Becky, on the other hand, had been raised in a snowy climate, and a favorite game had always been throwing snowballs. She quickly instructed Christine on how to make the missiles, and the two of them joined in the battle. They charged at the boys, who by now had Sally on her back in a drift, and were playfully cajoling her to give up the fight.

When Christine's first ball hit Skinny on the back of the neck; though she had been aiming for his head; it made him turn round, which was just the opening Becky had been looking for, and she displayed her skill by denting his nose with a miniature snowball.

Skinny leapt to his feet and ran after the two girls, who fled screaming in terror before him. He chased them around the snowdrifts, throwing an occasional ball, carefully though, so he wouldn't hurt them, and more often getting hit himself. Clarence and Sally remained in the drift, thrashing about, each trying to be on top. For a few seconds Clarence's head would appear, snow covered and rosy cheeked, while he took a deep breath before Sally pulled him down again. After another bout, Sally would emerge, starry eyed, but still rowdy, to catch her breath.

The fight, which the children later called The Great Snow Battle of the Alps, lasted almost a whole hour, until the sun was already setting, and the fading light was making aiming at moving targets rather difficult. Then, seeing as neither side would admit defeat, the battle ended in a tie, with the last ball having been thrown by the female side. Then the happy children decided to settle down for the night, though none of them felt cold, thanks to their vigorous exercise.

Their first step, in getting settled down, was to collect enough fuel to make a fire last all night. This procedure took a long time, for they had to go quite a way to find wood they could dry out or burn. Becky tried to gather dried leaves from branches overhead, but there were mostly fir trees. Christine and Sally were immersed in finding fuel without getting lost, and carrying it back to the bottom of the ridge, where Clarence carted it up to the cave, and piled it together. By the time they had enough, it was dark out, and the cold was beginning to feel oppressive.

Climbing the ridge in the dark, with only Skinny's one flashlight, proved to be harder than it looked. When they were all finally on the top, with all the baggage they thought they would need, they settled happily into the little cave, which they found, on further exploration, to be about four feet deep, and five feet high. They lit the fire just outside the entrance, and tried to keep the smoke going in the outside direction, which wasn't difficult.

They ate the food Skinny had brought along with great appetites, and then settled down to bed. When they had snuggled down under all the blankets, with the boys facing the outside, they remained in silence for a few minutes, and tried to fall asleep. It began to seem unlikely that they ever would feel sleepy, because of the exciting events of the day, so Sally suggested they sing some Christmas Carols. December was already upon them and the great holiday was fast approaching. It was a pleasant surprise to find that everyone of the Company had a good singing voice, and knew a large repertoire of songs. For a long while they taught, learned, and sang good old songs, and told each other of Christmas memories and traditions they loved, by the cozy glow of the fire. One by one, they dropped off into a peaceful sleep, surrounded by friends and happy thoughts.

The last to fall asleep was Skinny, who felt he should stay awake to protect the others. As he began to doze, he thought of how brave and cheerful Sally had been all day, and how patient and enduring the others had been, and from the bottom of his heart, he thanked God for sending him such good and loyal friends.

* * *

Skinny awoke with "Angels we Have Heard on High" stuck in his head. That had been the song they had finished with the night before, because it was Sally's favorite, and the harmony she had sung was strong in his memory. He lay still for a few seconds longer, cherishing the memory and thinking of their narrow escape from freezing to death. He was just wondering if they would find the town today, and if everything would turn out fine, when he heard Sally's voice next to him, whispering in an urgent tone.

"Skinny!" she hissed. "Wake up, we need you!"

He opened his eyes, tried to sit up, and became very alarmed. He couldn't see a thing, except for a thin outline of light, in the shape of a door, and he could hardly move, for his hands were tied together.

"What in the world?" he asked, and tried to stand up. He found out rather suddenly that his feet were tied too. He fell over, and bashed his head against something, which must have been Sally's head, for she started howling like a wolf at a full moon.

"Stop that yowling, Sally," whispered Clarence, "they'll hear you."

"Who?" asked Skinny. "Where are we?"

"We're in the Baron's Fortress," whispered Becky, in a tone cold with fear.

Christine started crying softly.

"It looks like we're in some kind of a storage room," said Sally, "and we've just been trying to figure out an escape plan."

"We will never escape," moaned Becky. "The Baron won't let anyone escape, ever."

"Sally, Clarence, what happened?" asked Skinny. "How'd they catch us?"

"I don't really know," said Sally. "I suppose they just stumbled on our cave, while we were still asleep. I thought I smelled something funny, but I just couldn't rouse myself. We were already in here, when I woke up."

"I woke up when they were tying me up, back at our cave," said Clarence, "and I gave them a hard time, but all I got for my effort was a bloody nose."

"You did?" asked Sally. "Is it bad?"

"Not really."

"I wonder what knocked me out so hard," mused Skinny. "Well, if one of us were untied, then we could look through the door jam, and find out what things are like outside."

"I heard music outside a while ago," said Christine, "and the sounds of a lot of people having a party."

"Having a party??"

"Yes," said Becky, "the Baron is always having parties. He has many entertainers and musicians, and he eats fine food."

"Do you think we are in the underground castle that you told us about, Becky?" asked Sally.

"Yes, I suppose so," said Becky. "And they say that there is no way out of the labyrinth that is his palace, except through secret doors."

"That's what the Baron tells little children," said Clarence, "but I was conscious as they brought us in, although they didn't know it. We're really in just an ordinary winter lodge, with one front door that's tall and wide. It's not underground at all, but it's located under a snowy cliff, that appears to be a shelf of rock which hides it from view, except for the entrance which sticks out a little. If there were an avalanche the whole front entrance would probably be smashed."

"Well, that makes our escape look a little easier," said Skinny, "have any ideas, Sally?"

"I'm thinking," said Sally. "If only we could get out of this room or closet or whatever it is, and see what the place looks like; especially that main entrance that Clarence saw, then we could form a plan."

"That Baron is a sneak," said Becky, "telling me all those lies. I hate him."

"I'm not too fond of the guy myself," said Skinny. "But right now, all we should worry about is getting out of here."

"It would be terribly nice of the Baron to come let us out," said Christine sarcastically, "but I don't think he has the manners."

As if someone had heard her, the closet door was suddenly thrown open, and the five children were blinded by many lights. The rough looking man who had opened the door, knelt down and untied their feet.

"Much obliged to you, my dear fellow," said Sally, as she rubbed her sore ankles. "Now if you'll just free my hands, I shall be happy to dance with you."

The man glanced up at her, and almost smiled. Sally grinned, and got to her feet, as best as she could, since her hands were still bound. She stepped out of their small prison, while the man was untying the others, and looked around, taking in the circumstances with one glance.

They were in a corner of a very large room, about the size and shape of a small cathedral, but made up to look like the main hall of a castle. It seemed as though the whole building was devoted to this room, with only little rooms along the sides. There were many people around, coming and going through doors, with trays of food, or in strange costumes like court jesters.

In the center of this hall, there was a raised platform, facing away from Sally, and on it, a tall table. Sitting at the head of the table, in a chair that resembled a sort of throne, was a very richly dressed man in his late forties. His appearance was perfect, every hair in place, and every fold in his clothing looking as though he had told it where to go. Within easy reach of his right hand, there lay a pistol, and on either side of the platform, there were men with guns.

Sally contemplated the Baron, for that was who he was, for a few moments. Then she returned to surveying the layout of the hall. She saw the large doors that Clarence had spoken of, and she studied them closely. It was a massive wooden double door, about twelve feet high, and ten feet across. It was iron bound, and there seemed to be no easy way to open it except by brute strength. Sally nodded as she took in these details, considering every one of them, and thinking of an escape route. She turned back toward the main part of the hall, and found that the floor around the Baron's platform seemed to be a sort of stage. It was a smooth, shiny wood floor that would be ideal for dancing. There was also a bandstand, to the side of the Baron's platform, and there were eight or nine musicians, with a wide variety of instruments, as if they were called upon to play many different styles of music.

Then Sally noticed that one of the small doors on the side had a plaque on it that Becky translated as, 'Dressing Rooms.'

"This Baron seems to be quite a connoisseur of the arts," Sally said to Skinny, who had emerged from the closet and was standing beside her.

"He must hire different acts to come perform for him," said Skinny, "but who cares about that? Do you see a way out of here?"

"Just give me time, I'll think of something."

The other three kids had joined them, and they stood huddled together, hoping they wouldn't be noticed, while the man who had untied them went to the platform and stood at attention. Sally glanced again around the room, hoping to see something that would aid them in their escape.

She noticed something that she had missed during her first survey, which now caught her interest. There was a large Asian gong, hanging from an ornamented stand, against the wall near a door which appeared to be the kitchen. There was a large wooden mallet lying on top of the stand.

Just as she was observing it, a cook emerged from the steamy kitchen, and going over to the gong, picked up the hammer, and prepared to strike it. Before his blow fell, one of the Baron's body guards rushed over and snatched the hammer from his hands. He then proceeded to give the cook a long tongue lashing, in a strange language.

"Becky," said Sally urgently, "what is that guy telling the cook?" Becky listened to them for a moment, and then turned to Sally. "He's telling him that he's an idiot," she said complacently.

"I gathered that," said Sally, "but why is he calling him an idiot?" Becky listened again, and said, "because the Baron has issued an order that the dinner gong cannot be used due to a storm a few days ago, which has piled snow up on the cliff overhanging the house, and if someone makes a loud noise, then it'll start an, an ..."

"Avalanche?"

"Yes, avalanche. The entryway could get smashed."

Sally turned and stared at the gong again. Her gaze traveled from it, to the large door, then to the shiny dance floor. As she gazed from one thing to another, with her brow furrowed in thought, a grin began to light up her features.

"Perfect," she muttered.

"What's perfect?" asked Christine.

Sally turned to Skinny. "Skinny, I've got our escape plan. I'm going to--"

Suddenly, the Baron glanced down at the man who had untied them and brought them in. They spoke together for a moment. Then the Baron looked over at them, and he smiled; not a very nice smile. He motioned to his guards, and they started toward the children.

"Just follow my lead," Sally whispered to Skinny, right before the guards reached them. Skinny nodded.

The five were led to the Baron's platform, where they stood like criminals, waiting for a sentence. The Baron looked down from his lofty height, and stared at them. He seemed immensely amused to see the scared expressions on Christine and Becky's faces, but he noticed, that even through her fear, Christine held her head high.

And when he saw Sally staring boldly at him, a look of mischief dancing in her eyes, he seemed a little less sure of himself. He did look almost guilty when he saw Clarence's blood stained shirt, and his solemn eyes.

But when he came under Skinny's cold, penetrating gaze, he really seemed to shrink. He began to feel as though these weren't the average little children that he enjoyed scaring.

He gave the guard a dirty look, as if to say, "I thought you said they were children." But then he collected himself, and began speaking in English.

"Who are you, and why are you in my mountains?" he asked, speaking only to Becky and Christine and avoiding the others' eyes.

"We are the Company of Secret Kids, and as for why we are here, it's fairly obvious that we didn't intend to intrude. You kidnapped us," said Sally.

Skinny would rather she had let him answer, for he was intending to be less obtrusive, but he did notice that the Baron had seemed unnerved by Sally's proud conduct and accusations.

"Yes," Skinny said, thinking the Baron wouldn't completely understand exactly what he said, as his English was not perfect. "We have come here from far away, seeking you, and we swore before our travels began, that should we find you, we would not leave you in business. We are great warriors, and we are well known in Africa and many great men fear us. I suggest you do the same, for your own good."

This was a wild speech, and although he hardly knew what he was saying, Skinny's words had a surprising effect. His commanding tone and fierce look instilled curiosity, and even uneasiness in the Baron. The four other children, meanwhile, were gazing at Skinny in no little astonishment. Sally started grinning, while Clarence tried to look heroic, and failed.

The Baron regarded them in silence for some moments, then turned to his guards, and spoke in English for the sake of the captives.

"Send the girls to the orphanage in Sweden. Kill the boys."

Clarence stopped trying to look heroic, and Skinny turned a sickly white. Christine and Becky began to cry.

"Wait!"

The Baron, his men, and the other children all turned toward Sally, whose countenance had hardly changed. She hadn't really intended to speak, but she knew she must. She glanced around the hall again, and decided to put her escape plan into action.

"Wait," she said again, quieter now, and seeming perfectly at her ease. "I have noticed that you are a man who appreciates entertainment, so I'm going to make a request."

The Baron furrowed his brow as though his English was not good enough to follow her quick speech.

"Becky, can you translate for me?" asked Sally.

Becky turned her tear-stained face toward Sally and nodded slowly.

"Now you have to repeat what I say exactly, okay? It's a matter of life or death."

Becky nodded more confidently this time.

"Good," whispered Sally. "Now tell him that I'm an entertainer at heart, and before I get sent up the river, I'd like to do one more encore." Becky looked perplexed, but she started speaking to the Baron, as bravely as she could, and it seemed he got the message. He looked at Sally with new interest, and asked Becky something.

"He wants to know what kind of act you do," said Becky.

"I tap dance," said Sally, "and I can sing, but only in English, and a little in Irish."

Becky relayed the answer to the Baron. He nodded.

"You dance," he said to Sally, and then turned toward the boys, "then you die."

"Right, first the act, then the curtains," said Sally, trying to hide her nervousness behind her joke. "It's only fair."

One of the guards untied Sally's hands, while another pushed the other four off to the side.

Sally turned and winked at Skinny, almost imperceptibly, as she skipped into the center of the dance floor.

Clarence looked questioningly at Skinny. "What's up?" he whispered.

"I don't know, but I think I'm going to have to guess. Be ready for anything."

"Hope it works," he whispered back.

Sally turned towards the small band, and asked the English speaking leader if they could play something fast and swingy.

The leader nodded, looking slightly confused, and the band started on a popular ragtime tune. Sally had heard it before.

She stood still for a moment, in the center of the floor, and took a deep breath. She didn't look toward Skinny, but he could feel she was trying to communicate with him. Then, her foot suddenly began to tap the floor. Another second and she had started dancing. The other four Kids watched her in amazed silence. None of them had known Sally could dance, and dance so well. Her small feet flew over the wood floor, with a grace that made Christine jealous.

At first she limited herself to a small area, where she let her feet do what they wanted. Then, as the music became more animated, she started to cover more ground.

The Baron watched in amused admiration, nodding his head to the music, and seemingly lost in the contemplation of her feet. He drank from a big goblet.

Sally glanced up at him, and her face showed that her plan was working. Skinny grew tense. He knew that whatever Sally intended to do, she had to do it now. The music was getting more climactic. The Baron and his men were occupied. This was their last chance.

Almost as if she read his thoughts, Sally suddenly started dancing toward the other children and toward the Baron, quickly getting closer. She danced around the Baron's platform once, and as she passed them, still behind the Baron's back, Skinny felt the rope round his hands suddenly untied, by a deft tug. It had been done so quickly, while she passed him, that it hadn't been noticeable to the Baron and his guards.

Then Sally leapt into the air, and somersaulted back into the middle of the stage, so beautifully that every eye in the place was fixed on her. Clarence was watching in open mouthed astonishment, when he felt his hands were being untied.

"Skinny, how did you get free?" he whispered.

"Sally did it when she passed behind the Baron!"

Clarence's look of admiration doubled. "She's terrific, isn't she?"

"No time for talk," returned Skinny. "I think Sally is going to need me. Untie the girls and try to get closer to the door without the guards noticing."

"The door? But it's too heavy to ..."

"Leave that to me and Sally," whispered Skinny. "See? Here she comes."

Sally was again heading towards them, and the music was almost reaching its peak. In plain sight of everyone, Sally looked towards Skinny, as if seeing him for the first time, and with a toss of her head, motioned for him to join her.

Skinny was ready. He ran to Sally, and lifted her into the air. She pushed off his shoulders with her hands and landed gracefully on her feet, not hesitating for a moment. Then Skinny did what he would have called a 'Sallyish' sort of thing. He knew that the Baron would notice the fact that he was untied, unless his attention was distracted by something quickly. He braced himself, preparing to test a skill which he hadn't practiced in months, and hoped he could still perform. Just as Sally backed up a few steps, recovering from the lift, Skinny threw his head and shoulders backwards and executed a perfect backflip. Now it was Sally's turn to be amazed. She stood for a moment, staring in wonder and admiration, while Skinny regained his balance, and giving her a quick grin, resumed the dance.

His plan worked. The Baron was so impressed by the skill that he failed to notice where the artist had come from. Sally had anticipated Skinny's plan, though she hadn't expected something so fantastic, and she quickly recovered herself.

She danced back to the center of the floor, with Skinny behind her. Then just as the music reached its height, she danced closer to the gong. Skinny now knew for sure what she intended to do, and he played along. He followed her to the gong, and they performed another perfect lift. He grabbed her around the waist, and she pushed herself off his shoulders with strong arms.

Just as he reached the gong, Skinny had glanced over and seen that Clarence and the two girls had reached the door unnoticed, by sneaking around the back of the Baron's platform. They stood by the door, watching the other two, and wondering how they were supposed to get out.

In the air above Skinny's head, Sally looked down into his eyes. As the final note sounded, she winked, and he let go of her. It looked rather strange to those watching, for Skinny just dropped her in mid-air, and ran for the door.

Sally hit the ground gracefully as the last note rang out, and as her feet touched the floor, she turned, grasped the gong mallet in both hands, and in the motion of a batter hoping to make a home run, she hit the gong so hard, that the mallet broke in her hands, and the gong shuddered on its stand.

After she had struck it, Sally stood panting for a few seconds, facing the Baron, and wondering if her plan had failed. She looked up at the roof as the gong's noise faded away. Then she heard a faint rumbling noise above and outside the hall, which fast grew into a roar. Sally looked over at the Baron, who was staring wonderingly above his head, and grinned victoriously at him. She had started an avalanche.

"Sally, come on!" yelled Skinny as he reached the door, and even as he did so, the roof above the door started to crack.

Sally fled to the door, and as she did, shards of wood and chunks of ice began to fall around her. The Baron leaped to his feet and stood on his platform, staring around at his crumbling kingdom. His men ran in every direction, yelling angry directions in French and German.

Sally was a few feet away from the large door, when the roof above it split right down the middle, with the sound of a gunshot. Skinny pulled the others back, away from the massive door. For a few seconds, it was blocked from view entirely by falling snow, and then with another terrific splintering noise, the great door cracked, its iron bars twisted and bent by the impact of the avalanche.

"Come on!" yelled Skinny, "It's now or never!"

They ran to the door, dodging snow and wood, and Sally found a crack big enough for them to slip through, which wasn't totally blocked with snow.

Skinny came last, and just as he ducked his head through the opening, and wiggled out into the dazzling sunlight, the roof of the entrance under which they had been standing only a moment before, collapsed to the ground in a pile of splintered wood and falling snow. They ran quickly as far away as they could go as another wave of snow came sliding down and blocked the entrance completely.

"Wow, look at all that snow!" cried Sally, glancing back over her shoulder as she ran. The entrance lay completely covered at the base of the mountain, with only a few telltale pieces of wood and iron protruding from the mass.

"Come on, let's get out of the avalanche zone," said Clarence.

They half ran, half slid down the steeper part of the slope in front of the Baron's lodge, and at the bottom turned to look up at the wreckage. The top of the rock shelf under which the main part of the lodge was sheltered was now visible again, as all the snow poured down toward where the doors were buried.

"Oh, its dreadful to think of all those men trapped or smashed by the snow," said Christine, staring at the wreckage, "even if they were bad."

Sally turned pale at her words, and looked up at Skinny.

"What have I done?" she whispered, "why didn't you stop me?"

"Me and Clarence wouldn't be here now, if you hadn't done what you did."

"Clarence and I, Skinny," she answered miserably. "Still, I can't bear the thought that I might have sent some those men to their deaths."

Skinny smiled. "Sally, I thought you felt bad about knocking down the entryway to his house, but I see you've got bigger scruples. For your information not one of those men is in danger. There's sure to be a back door; didn't you see them all scrambling in that direction? And even if it's blocked, they'll be able to dig their way out by tonight. The lodge is under a rock shelf."

"And the whole main part of the hall is still standing, so I doubt they'll be too uncomfortable till they dig out," added Clarence.

"Well I'm certainly glad to hear it," murmured Sally. "I don't think I'd ever get over it if they didn't survive because of me."

"I would," said Becky. "I think it's a shame that the Baron is still around, he's mean."

"Becky, we must love our enemies," Sally reminded gently.

"But Beck has a point," said Clarence. "Now the Baron may be after us, and what with Black Hawk and Little Joe already seeking revenge, the last thing we need is another powerful enemy."

"Well, we can worry about that later," said Skinny. "Right now I think we need to keep moving. I still can't believe I'm alive."

"Oh, Skinny, I was so worried about you," said Christine dramatically. "If you hadn't made it, I would have died of a broken heart right on the spot."

Skinny smiled. Her movie star ways seemed so out of place in such situations.

"Well, we wouldn't be here, if it weren't for our fast thinking Sally," said Clarence. "She's saved my life twice now."

"Three cheers for Sally!" cried Becky.

They cheered, but Skinny said, "Quietly, quietly."

Sally grinned sheepishly and trudged on.

"Oh, go chase yourselves," she grumbled, when they had finally died down. "You four hyenas are likely to start another avalanche. I didn't do anything."

Clarence gave her a vigorous slap on the back, and she took a swing at him, which he ducked. He ran off backwards, and she started in pursuit. The other three patiently kept traveling while watching them tear around in the bright snow.

"I hope this is the way back to town," said Christine, whose teeth were beginning to chatter in the brisk morning air.

"Are we still lost?" asked Becky.

"I'm not sure," answered Skinny. "I suppose the Baron's lodge would be pretty accessible to town. I'm sure he needs supplies quite often. I think we're following some kind of road."

"Then let's hurry!" said Christine. "It may not be wise to stay here on the Baron's driveway. He might dig himself out sooner than expected."

"You're right," said Skinny, "and I also think we should leave Switzerland altogether. The Baron is dangerous, and we can continue our search for Becky's friends later."

He raised his voice to Clarence and Sally, who stood together at the top of a ridge to their left. "Hey, Clare, Sally! Come on down, we've still got to find the town!"

"No, we don't!" Sally shouted back. "Me and Clarence just found it! We can see it clearly from up here! It's only about a mile away."

"'Clarence and I,' Sally," said Skinny, as the five started toward the town, once Skinny had confirmed the direction, "not 'me and Clarence.'"

Sally grinned.

Chapter 9

In New York

"New York, New York, what a wonderful town, the Bronx is up, and the Battery's down!" sang Sally joyously, skipping out of the airplane, and down the steps onto the tarmac.

When she set foot in the airport, with the other four behind her, she set her bags down, and threw her arms out towards the doors, and the hum of traffic beyond them.

"Hello, you great, big, ugly, City!" she cried, "I'm back!"

The people around them turned and smiled at the beautiful young girl, who seemingly couldn't keep her feet on the ground.

Skinny blushed, and he and Clarence hurried to get Sally out of public view.

They were soon crammed in a taxi, with Christine and Sally sharing a seat, Becky on Skinny's lap, and Clarence squeezed in the middle, with luggage piled on all open places and in the trunk. They were on their way to a hotel. Becky and Christine stared in amazement at their first sight of America. Sally pointed out major landmarks to the others and told them stories of when she was growing up in the heart of the city.

"It's a big city, all right," said Clarence, "but I think California is prettier."

"So do I," said Sally, "although, the big cities in California are just as bad as here. I guess I just hate big cities."

"Have you been to California, Sally?" asked Christine, a little jealously, visions of Sally talking casually to handsome movie stars flashing before her mind's eye.

"Yes, once my mom took me there for a whole summer."

"What'd you think?" asked Clarence.

"I loved it there," said Sally. "The mountains and trees and beaches, and everything. Except for the palm trees, they don't fit."

"Well, they dress up the cities," said Clarence, "but other than that, California is beautiful."

"It seems as if you can stretch out more in California," said Sally. "I don't know how to explain it, but it seems like the only place on earth where I could fit. There's a lot more wilderness there, too."

"Yes, you certainly seem to have trouble fitting, in other places," muttered Christine, as she pulled her skirt out from underneath Sally. "Can't you scoot over any further?"

"If I did, I'd be in the street," retorted Sally. "Besides; you're hogging all the space, so you scoot."

"You'd have loved my grandfather's house, Sally," said Clarence, ignoring Christine's interruption. "It's pretty out of the way, and the nearest town is about a half-hour drive. The house itself stands on a cliff over the sea. There are woods behind it, and every night you can see the sun set over the ocean, and smell pine trees at the same time. It's really something."

"You know Clarence," said Skinny, "that house and property is legally yours, and it's still in your name."

"Then once all the secrets are found out," said Sally, "let's all go live there together."

"Oh, that would be lovely," said Christine, giving Skinny a sidelong glance and batting her eyelashes, a trick she had seen in movies and practiced as often as possible. She was usually ignored by the other four.

"That's fine with me," said Clarence. "It's a huge house, and would fit many more people than just us. Since I've got no living family, you guys are all to consider that house yours."

"Then Clarence, can my orphanage friends live there too?" asked Becky.

"Sure, why not?"

"Oh, I wish all our secrets were settled," said Christine, "and we could all settle down."

"I don't know," mused Sally. "I wouldn't mind a few more adventures, before I turn into an ordinary little housewife."

Skinny laughed. "I don't think anything could turn you into an ordinary little housewife," he said. "But Sally is right, we need some more action before we go into retirement."

"And don't forget why we're here in New York," Clarence added, "to figure out Sally's secret."

"Are we almost there yet?" whined Becky.

"Is that all you know how to say?" asked Clarence, remembering the weary plane flight, and Becky's incessant questions.

"No, I say other things, but only when they are apoperate," answered Becky loftily.

"Oh, 'apoperate'," said Clarence solemnly, "I understand."

"Hey gang, we're passing Flannigan's Irish Pub," said Skinny, "the best place in town to buy a drink."

"Long live the Irish!" cried Sally, "and God bless that land that my mother taught me to love."

"Do you drink, Skinny?" asked Christine, ignoring Sally's patriotic outburst.

"Of course not," Skinny retorted.

"When you were a movie star, could you have anything you wanted?" asked Becky dreamily, leaning up against Skinny, and shutting her eyes.

"Um, sure, I guess," said Skinny awkwardly.

"You know, Skinny you never tell us about your life as a pop star," said Sally, and her blue eyes fixed him in a penetrating gaze.

"I guess there's just not much to tell," said Skinny lightly, but for some reason, he couldn't bring himself to look Sally in the eye.

"You know, you really don't look like you used to," persisted Sally, "back when you were big time. If I remember rightly, your hair was lighter, and you looked pretty different."

"Well, I've grown my hair longer," said Skinny, shaking his long locks out of his eyes. "And that made the color change."

"Then how do you explain the fact that those gray green eyes you have now, were once brown?"

"Here's the hotel!" Skinny said, seeming relieved, as the cab pulled up in front of a tall building.

Christine and Becky craned their necks out the windows to see the top, staring in open-mouthed amazement at the scores of stories. Skinny glanced behind Clarence's head at Sally, and to his discomfort, found her staring at him, with a steady, almost amused gaze. Skinny felt his cheeks go red under her suspicious stare. They looked hard at each other for a few seconds, until Becky began to squirm.

"Let's get out," she suggested.

"Yes, Sally, hurry up and get out," said Christine. She reached over Sally, and opened the door. Sally fell out onto the curb, releasing Skinny from her spell.

"What's the matter with you?" Sally grumbled. Christine slid out, stepped over Sally, and stood in front of the hotel, gazing up in silent wonder.

"Is it really as tall as it looks?" asked Becky, scrambling over Clarence, and leaping out of the cab. Sally was in the act of standing up when Becky's shoes came over her head, and she quickly sat back down in the gutter.

"Sally, what are doing you in the street?" asked Clarence as he and Skinny came around the back of the cab.

"I'm inspecting the gutter systems of New York," said Sally. "What does it look like I'm doing?"

Clarence laughed, and pulled her to her feet, while Skinny began removing their bags. He paid the driver. Sally went and stood next to Christine and Becky, and grinned at their gaping mouths and tilted heads.

"You know," she said solemnly, "if you two really want a good view of New York, you just have to look up high enough, and lean back far enough, and you'll find yourself flat on your back, with a great view of the skyscrapers. That's what people call an ant's eye view. Just make sure you don't get run over by a bus."

Christine gave Sally a withering glance, but Becky innocently leaned back, and would have followed Sally's advice to the letter, if Skinny hadn't caught her.

"Let's go check in," he said, "and then we can go sightsee for a while."

They were soon busily settling into their rooms on the twenty-first floor, or at least Clarence, Skinny, and Sally were, for as soon as they had entered their room, Christine and Becky had plastered themselves to the window, looking down in horror and wonder, at the small street far below.

"The people look like ants," Becky whispered, as though she feared talking too loud would make the building collapse. Christine nodded.

Sally looked up from the bag she was unpacking, and grinned at them. She tiptoed over to them, and stood staring out at the sweeping panorama of tall buildings, glinting in the winter sun.

"Boo!" she cried suddenly, giving Becky and Christine a gentle shove from behind.

The two girls shrieked, and turned upon Sally with indignant adjectives.

"Hey girls, you ready to go sightsee?" asked Skinny, sticking his head in the door.

Becky and Christine immediately stopped their admonishing of Sally, and flew to get their coats. Skinny walked over to Sally, who still stood by the window, staring out at the view, with a dreamy expression.

"What's up?" he asked quietly.

"I was just thinking," said Sally, "that somewhere in this very city, there lives a man who has sworn to see me dead."

"Don't worry about him, Sally," said Skinny, but his own voice was edged with foreboding.

All that day, the Company of Secret Kids explored New York. They examined every aspect of the mammoth city that they could get their hands on. Becky and Christine were amazed by one wonder after another. The other three enjoyed themselves too, though the sights were not new to them, and they always had the nagging fear of running into Little Joe the Gangster every time they turned a corner.

Once, when they stopped at a curiosity shop for souvenirs, Clarence nudged Skinny, and pointed to the headlines of a newspaper that another customer was holding. They read, "Little Joe Strikes Again." Skinny looked at Clarence and nodded grimly. They glanced toward Sally, who was examining a selection of pocketknives. She looked up at them, and smiled.

They tried to look casual. Sally glanced down at the newspaper, and nodded, with a sad smile.

"She's brave," muttered Clarence. Skinny only sighed.

That night, they treated themselves to dinner at a nice restaurant, after which they took a stroll through the brightly lit streets. There was still snow on the sidewalks, and the night air was chilly. The children talked and laughed, and made plans for the rest of their trip.

"It's a nice night," said Sally, "even if it is a little cold."

"Let's walk all the way the back to our hotel," suggested Christine, "and maybe we could stop at an ice cream shop on the way."

"That's fine with me," said Clarence.

"I love to look at all the fancy buildings," said Becky, and she looked up at Skinny, whose hand she was holding. "Don't you?"

"He's been looking at his feet this whole way," said Christine, "Are you afraid of tripping Skinny?"

Skinny shook himself, as if coming out of a dream.

"Skinny what's wrong with you?" Christine asked.

"I was just daydreaming," he said, staring at the sidewalk once again.

"Well, do you think we could stop by an ice cream shop?"

"If we're near one," answered Skinny. "Where are we?"

"We're in front of the Irish pub you pointed out to us," said Clarence, "Flannigan's."

Skinny looked up in alarm. They were passing the dimly lit building even as Clarence spoke.

"Come on," he said urgently. He let Becky's hand go, and hurrying forward, placed himself next to Sally. Sally looked up at him in surprise, and she saw in his face that he was not only concerned, but seemed miserable.

"Skinny, what's wrong?" she asked, lowering her voice.

"I don't think we should walk back to hotel tonight," he said, speaking so the others could hear him, but still in almost a whisper.

"Why?" asked Christine.

Without answering her, Skinny hurried over to a parked cab that was waiting outside the pub, and after a few words with the driver, he motioned for them to get in.

Clarence helped the three girls into the cab, and turned to Skinny. "Aren't you coming?" he asked.

Skinny shook his head.

"Then I'll stay, too," said Clarence.

"No," whispered Skinny, "get the girls back to the hotel, and make sure they stay in their room."

"What's up?"

"I don't know, but I've got a pretty good guess. Just keep Sally out of sight. I've got to do something."

"When will you be back?" asked Clarence, glancing at the girls in the cab.

"I don't know, and you don't need to wait up for me. Now get out of here."

Clarence slipped into the cab, but before he shut his door, he looked Skinny in the eye, and gave him a reassuring smile. "Be careful, won't you?" he asked.

Skinny nodded.

Clarence shut his door, and the cab rolled away from the curb, and disappeared into the night. Skinny looked after it for a moment. Then he sighed, and turned toward the pub. He stared up at its sign for a while, and he began to look sick. Then he took a deep breath, and putting on a determined face, he went in.

* * *

The four children sat in the cab, silent and bewildered. Becky had fallen asleep on Christine's shoulder. Clarence stared out his window, looking at the bright buildings through the fog, and thinking up terrible possibilities. He suddenly glanced up, and saw that Sally was staring out her window too, and her face was troubled.

"Hey Chris, how about switching places with Sally?" he said, trying to keep his voice casual.

Christine looked up in surprise. "Why?" she asked.

"No reason," said Clarence with a shrug.

"You don't need to play casual with us, Clare," said Sally softly. "We all know about Little Joe."

Her words seemed to echo in the silence that followed. They glanced uneasily at each other.

"Here Sally, do switch places with me," said Christine, sliding the sleeping Becky onto Clarence's lap.

Sally gave Christine a grateful smile, and slipped over her into the middle. Clarence reached over Becky and took her hand.

"Why do you think Skinny stayed behind?" asked Christine after another heavy silence.

"He said he had to do something," said Clarence, glad to be able to share his worries with them.

"I hope he's all right," murmured Christine.

"Me, too," said Sally, in a voice as cold as death.

They rode the rest of the way in silence, broken only by Becky's measured breathing, and the sound of the cabby's radio which came dimly through the glass.

When Christine looked at Sally, she found that her eyes were closed, but her lips moved constantly, in silent prayer.

Back at Flannigan's pub, Skinny was sitting in a booth in the corner, his coat collar pulled up round his face. He wasn't bothered by the heavy smoke which hung in the place, but he looked so sick, that several times waiters asked him if he needed to step outside.

After trying to gain courage from several sodas, and a good deal of thinking, he finally stood up and sauntered over to the bar. There, just where Skinny had expected to see him, was a man in his thirties, dressed in a shabby suit. He was haggard looking, and in need of a shave. His eyes were deep blue, and his hair was wavy and black and tousled. Despite his vicious looks, he was strikingly handsome. He was surrounded by other rough looking men. In his hand was a drink, and inside his coat there was a gun.

He was talking loudly, and it seemed apparent that the liquor was affecting him.

Skinny stared hard at him for a while. He gradually got closer and closer to the tough looking group. The other occupants of the pub politely ignored them, and hardly dared to look their way. They stole glances at Skinny however, making his way boldly toward the grim set of men, and their faces expressed curiosity, foreboding and pity.

The young leader of the tough men was in the middle of a story which he seemed to think very funny. He was midway into a sentence, when he suddenly spotted Skinny, standing with his feet wide apart, and his hands behind his back, only a few feet away. His words died in his mouth.

Skinny had him fixed in one of his cold stares, which few could withstand.

"It's me," Skinny said, nodding solemnly.

The man stared at him for a moment, and suddenly the light of recognition lit in his bloodshot eyes.

When the four others arrived at the hotel, Clarence paid the driver, and picking Becky up, hurried them all up to their floor. Once the girls were in their room, and Becky had been put to bed, he gave them strict orders, as the temporary leader of the Company, to stay in the room, with the door locked, no matter what. If either of the boys needed them, they would use the secret knock that Sally had invented.

"Clare, don't you want to stay with us?" suggested Sally, "I don't think any of us will sleep much anyway, and it'll be awfully lonely in your room until Skinny comes back."

Clarence shook his head. "I bet you girls will fall asleep in no time. Besides, Skinny will look for me in our room, and he'll be alarmed if I'm not there. Good night."

The two girls carefully locked the door once Clarence was out, and shut the curtains, and then stood, holding hands, looking at each other.

"Let's not put on our nightgowns yet," said Sally after a few minutes of hesitation, "maybe Skinny will come by when he gets here."

Christine nodded, and the two girls sat on the bed, with all the lights on, while Christine kept glancing nervously at the door.

"I wish Little Joe would just show up and kill me or something!" Sally burst out after a few minutes. "It'd be better than all this waiting."

"Oh, Sally, don't say things like that," moaned Christine, wringing her hands. "Oh, why did we even come to this dreadful city?"

"If we can have it out with him, I can live in peace."

They lapsed into silence again, but their imaginations worked feverishly.

"This won't do at all," said Sally finally. "Let's pray the Rosary. That always helps, no matter what your problem is."

Christine nodded, and they pulled their beads out of their pockets. Sally's rosary was old and worn, for it had belonged to her mother, and, as she put it, she "used it more than she used her toothbrush."

Soon the girls were whispering their prayers together, still holding each other's hands, and their worries melted away. Before they reached the closing prayers, their heads lay together on the pillows, the blond hair mingling with the dark curls, and Our Lady smiled upon two peacefully sleeping girls.

Clarence was not having such a pleasant time in his room. He paced up and down, and stared out the window, and sat nervously on the edge of his bed, alternating positions every five seconds. He finally lay down on his bed, but when he closed his eyes, visions of Skinny in one desperate situation after another flashed before his imagination. Once he thought he saw Skinny reading the headlines, "Little Joe Strikes Again," while behind him, Little Joe was stealthily approaching, with a long, dreadful knife in his hand. Then, he realized that the vision was no longer imagined, but reality. Clarence tried to cry out to warn Skinny, but his voice died in his throat. He watched in horror, helpless, while Little Joe got closer and closer to the unsuspecting Skinny. Then finally, when Little Joe was almost upon him, Skinny turned round, but it was too late. Skinny crumpled to the ground at Little Joe's feet. Then, Clarence's voice returned. He cried out in horror, and Little Joe turned toward him. The terrible eyes were now fixed on him. He backed away in terror, but Little Joe was closing in on him, with murder in his eyes ...

Clarence awoke with a start. His brow was beaded with sweat, and he was trembling in every limb. He glanced at the clock. It read one o'clock.

"Golly, I must have been asleep for hours," he muttered. He got up, and went over to the window. The fog had grown thicker, and looked more like a light rain. The many lights were still brilliant, and it seemed that the city was still wide awake, even in the unearthly hours of the night.

Clarence stood looking out at the midnight world for a few minutes, still trying to shake off the terror of his nightmare. Then he remembered Sally's method of praying the Rosary whenever she was rattled, and he figured he'd try it. He pulled his beads out of his suitcase, and sat down.

He had hardly started, when he heard, or thought he heard, a faint thump, like something heavy falling over, outside his door. He stood up, and crept over to the door, pressing his ear against it and listening intently. For what seemed like a dreadfully long time, he heard no sound. Then, just when he had begun to suspect that he had imagined the whole thing, he heard a low moan. His blood froze at the sound, and every hair on his head stood straight up.

He thought feverishly for a few seconds, and made up his mind to open the door, and brave whatever terror lay on the outside. He quietly unbolted it, and turned the knob, hardly daring to breathe. As soon as the door was open, he could feel that something was leaning, or pushing against it, but not very strongly. He took a deep breath, made the sign of the cross, and flung the door open.

Chapter 10

On the Tracks

He stood for a few seconds, his eyes shut, half hidden behind the door. When nothing happened, he ventured to open his eyes. He glanced down, and gave a cry of dismay.

Across the threshold of the door, was a limp form, lying on its back, its face cut and bruised, and its clothes wet and muddy.

"Skinny!" cried Clarence, kneeling down, and gingerly touching him.

Skinny moaned again. Clarence gently took him in his arms, and brushed the long wet hair out of his eyes.

"Skinny, can you hear me?" he asked, tenderly. Skinny's eyes opened, and he looked up at Clarence, and tried to smile.

"What happened, Skinny?" asked Clarence, "was it Little Joe?"

Skinny nodded, and tried to sit up, breathing through clenched teeth.

"I'm all right," he said, but even as he spoke he winced in pain. "Get me inside."

Clarence pulled him gently to his feet, and putting his arms round him, helped him to the bed.

"Hold still, I'll get you a cloth for that bloody nose," said Clarence, and hurried into the bathroom.

A few minutes later, once Skinny had been bandaged up and was wearing clean, dry clothes, the two boys sat down to have a conference.

"So tell me what happened," said Clarence, as he opened a bandage for Skinny's cheek.

"Well, I went into the pub after you left," began Skinny, doing his best to talk through the wet rag that covered his mouth and nose, "and I found Little Joe."

"How did you know he'd be in there?" asked Clarence.

"A lucky guess," said Skinny evasively. Clarence thought he saw Skinny give him a strange look out of the corner of his eye, but he ignored it.

"Well, what happened?"

"I went up to him, and ... and," Skinny hesitated.

"Well?"

"I told him that he should stop bothering Sally Keenan."

"What did he do?" asked Clarence breathlessly.

"He told his men to stay in the pub," said Skinny, "and then he took me outside, and told me to get lost, or it'd be the worse for me."

"What did you do?"

"I told him I wouldn't go, until he understood he needed to leave Sally alone, and then ... " Skinny shut his eyes and sighed.

"I know," said Clarence, "he let you have it."

Skinny nodded.

"It's a bit strange," mused Clarence. "I imagine he'd be annoyed by you, a perfect stranger, telling him what to do, but I wouldn't think he'd beat you to a pulp over it. Unless, of course, he's very touchy about that certain subject, but still, it's like there's something missing in your story."

Again, Clarence felt Skinny looking at him in an uncertain way.

"Well, he was drunk," said Skinny, "maybe that explains it. Anyway, I'm going to get some sleep. I'm done in."

He kicked his shoes off, laid his disheveled head on the pillow, and almost instantly fell asleep. Clarence pulled the blanket over him, and lay down in his own bed, hoping the girls were sleeping soundly and not worrying.

Later that night, Clarence lay awake, thinking of what Skinny had said. Skinny was now tossing and turning in his bed, and talking in his sleep. Clarence had heard him talk in his sleep before, usually after a fright. Clarence started listening to him ramble on, hoping to find some answers.

"Yes, yes I've come back," said Skinny, "no, no, never! They're my friends! They trust me. She trusts me. I can't! Call me a traitor, I don't care. I'd be a worse traitor to them. Kill me if you must! I won't do it!"

Clarence sat up in bed, his eyes wide in amazement. Skinny threw the coverlets off the bed violently, as if he were trying to ward off someone he thought was before him. Finally, he lay back down, and buried his face in the pillow. His body shook with sobs. Clarence lay back down, but listened intently for him to speak again. Finally, Skinny stopped weeping, and lay still. Then, he gave a great sigh, and whispered something. Clarence leaned over to catch the words. Skinny looked so utterly miserable as he said them, that Clarence felt deeply sorry for him. But when he heard the words, his heart grew chill, though he knew not what they meant.

"I'll do it," Skinny whispered.

The next morning, Clarence went to the girls' room early, while Skinny was still asleep. He told them briefly what had happened, toning it down a great deal so as not to frighten them. He left out what he had heard Skinny talking about in his sleep, for he felt it was unnecessary.

Christine and Becky were terribly upset by what he told them. Sally stood, after he had finished, her hands in her pockets, her brow furrowed in thought.

"It's strange," she muttered.

"It's terrible!" cried Christine dramatically. "Oh, poor, darling, Skinny! I've got to take care of him!"

She ran to the bathroom, and hastily began collecting all Sally's emergency supplies. Becky went with her, and Sally and Clarence were left alone. Sally sat down on her bed, and Clarence joined her.

"Clare, you haven't told us everything," she said quietly.

"You're right."

"What are you leaving out?"

Clarence hesitated. He looked at Sally, and her eyes told him that she could handle anything, and it would be better if she knew the truth. He told her of the strange sidelong glances Skinny had given him during his story, and of the mysterious sleep-talking.

"Anyway, the whole thing seems mighty strange to me," he finished, "and I can't make anything of what he said, except that he must have been pretty excited."

"It makes a whole lot of sense to me," said Sally gravely, "and though I've had my suspicions for a long time, I'm not too happy to have them proved right."

"Why?" asked Clarence, "what does it all mean?"

Sally smiled sadly. "Now it's my turn to be secretive," she said. "It'll be better if you have one less thing to worry about. Let's just wait and see, maybe I'll be proved wrong after all. I hope so."

Clarence knew he could get nothing more out of her, so he went and woke Skinny. His face still bore witness to his harrowing adventure the night before, but he seemed to be his normal self again, though a bit more subdued.

When he was dressed, he went to the girls' room with Clarence, where he had to sit through a full half an hour of Christine's melodramatic sympathies.

"All right Christine, let him alone," said Sally, when Skinny was beginning to look sick again, "we've got to plan out our day."

"Right," said Clarence, "now everybody sit down, and we'll discuss our plan of action."

When they were all settled around the small table, Sally began. "We know that we should get out of here as fast as possible, for safety's sake," she said, "so once we figure out my secret tonight, we'll leave."

"Tonight!" cried Skinny, turning pale, "why so soon?"

"Because the sooner we figure out Sally's secret, the sooner we can get out of here," said Clarence, "haven't you been listening?"

Skinny seemed not to hear him, and renewed his prolonged staring off into space.

"Well, anyway," said Christine, giving Skinny a worried glance. "I agree that we should leave as soon as possible. I'm scared of that Little Joe."

"Right, and we need to move on to your secret, Christine," said Sally, "so I say we should lie low for today, and not go out too much, so as not to stir things up. Then, tonight, we make our move."

"Does it have to be tonight?" asked Skinny faintly. They looked at him in surprise. It was so unlike Skinny to stay out of the discussion, and just the fact that he let Sally take charge was alarming.

"Of course, Skinny," said Sally, "that's why we left Switzerland in such a hurry, remember? If we don't go down to the railroad tracks on the seventh of the month, then the moon won't be in the same place as at other times, and so it won't shine in exactly the right place at exactly midnight."

"I don't think it's logical at all," said Skinny, glancing out the window with a troubled expression.

"Come on, Skinny," said Sally, jabbing him with her elbow. "Wake up. We need you."

At Sally's last words, Skinny started, and glanced down at her, with a look close to terror appearing in his eyes.

"Skinny, what's the matter with you?" asked Christine. "Do you feel all right?"

"Let's call the meeting adjourned," suggested Clarence, after an ominous silence.

He stood up. "Who wants to come with me down to get the free breakfast they serve?" he asked cheerfully.

"Me, I'm hungry!" said Becky, scrambling over Christine.

"Well, nice to meet you, Hungry. My name is Clarence," he said, elegantly shaking her hand. Becky giggled.

"I guess I'll come too," said Christine, but her eyes remained on Skinny and Sally, who were staring at each other in an odd way.

"Good, then come on," said Clarence, pulling Christine to her feet. He led the two girls to the door, and glanced back. Skinny and Sally were still sitting, motionless.

He shrugged to himself, and closed the door behind them.

"Skinny," said Sally quietly, once Clarence had left, "you're trembling."

Skinny pulled himself away from her gaze, and went back to staring out the window.

"What's wrong?" Sally asked, in a kinder tone than she had ever used on Skinny before.

He opened his mouth as if to speak, but glancing at her, he seemed to change his mind. He let out a shuddering sigh, as if he was fighting back tears. Sally stood up, and walked over to the window. Skinny buried his face in his trembling hands.

"Want any breakfast?" she asked.

Skinny shook his head. After a few long seconds, he stood up, and went to the door.

"Tell Clarence I'll be in our room," he muttered, as he turned the knob.

Sally nodded.

"You going to be okay for tonight?" she asked.

Skinny bit his lip. He looked down at his feet, and then suddenly swept out the door, and hurried down the hall.

Sally stood, looking at the door for a long moment. Then she sat down on the bed, cupped her chin in her hands, and went into a brown study.

That night, out on the snowy railroad tracks, a few miles away from the city, the five children stood huddled together, watching the moon.

"What time is it?" asked Christine through chattering teeth.

"Eleven forty five," said Clarence, glancing at his watch.

"It's scary out here," whispered Becky. Sally pulled her close, and hugged her tight.

"So we need to see your moon shadow, right Sally?" asked Christine.

"Yes, and I've got to face West," said Sally. "Hey, which way's West?"

"That way," said Clarence, pointing behind them.

"Okay then, not long now," said Sally.

"So why are we doing this again?" asked Becky.

"To figure out who the young apprentice of Little Joe's is," said Sally, "and I hope whatever we figure out is worth it, and he's really the one who can stop Little Joe's vendetta against me."

They stood in silence for a few minutes, each imagining what sort of a clue they were about to uncover. Christine glanced at Skinny, and found that he was deathly pale, staring ahead doggedly, with clenched teeth, and breathing heavily. She glanced at Sally. Sally looked up at Skinny, and sighed. Then she glanced back at Christine, and smiled encouragingly.

"Just a few minutes to midnight," muttered Clarence. "Are you sure we're in the right spot, Sal?"

"I think," said Sally, but she was looking at Skinny.

"Did we measure the distance exactly four miles from the railway station?" asked Christine.

"No," said Clarence, "Sally doesn't seem too concerned about it though."

"But if we don't go to the exactly right spot under the moon, we won't find what we're looking for!" cried Becky.

"And we didn't even bring shovels," said Christine, hit with the sudden realization. "Do you even expect to find anything at all, Sally?"

"Oh yes," said Sally softly, still staring at Skinny, "and I figure we won't need shovels or the exact location on the ground either. Don't you think so, Skinny?"

Skinny did not answer. Clarence suddenly looked at Sally, and it seemed that something had just dawned upon him.

"Yes, I figure Skinny knows just what we'll find here," continued Sally. Her voice was not angry, just slightly sad, and a little weary sounding, "and that's been his problem all day. Little Joe doesn't like it when his men betray him."

"No, I don't," said a voice behind them. They turned, and Christine gave a little shriek. Even in the moonlight she could see his face well, and from the pictures she had seen, and Sally's descriptions, she didn't need to ask who the tall man standing there was.

"Little Joe!" cried Clarence, and immediately placed himself between Sally and the gun in Little Joe's steady hand.

"So, we meet again, Stockly," said Little Joe, with an evil smile, speaking only to Sally, and ignoring the others.

"You can call me by my mother's maiden name, like everybody else does," answered Sally. "It's Keenan."

"I know what it is," said Little Joe.

For a moment there was what looked like a flash of lightning behind his eyes. Then it passed, and he fell back into his condescending air. "Very clever, Keenan," he continued. "You hit the nail right on the head. I planted those men outside the window of the hospital the day that you found out your "secret." It was a back-up plan, in case you ever got away. I know your love for adventure. I figured you wouldn't be able to resist such an exciting invitation. Well, I was right."

"Little Joe, you are a no good, filthy, contemptible liar," Clarence blazed out.

"A criminal maybe," answered Little Joe, "but in this case I have not lied. You found the thing you came looking for. My young apprentice's identity you know."

Christine looked wonderingly at Sally, trying to think what Little Joe meant.

"We do?" she asked, her curiosity getting the better of her fear.

"Oh yes," said Little Joe, "though it has been a long time since I've had him by my side in a caper. Hasn't it Skinny?"

He smiled a cruel smile at Skinny, who blanched at the mention of his name. He looked over at Christine, and nodded wearily, in answer to Little Joe.

"Skinny!" cried Christine, and Becky's eyes grew wide. To their surprise, Clarence and Sally did not seem shocked. Clarence stood, looking at his feet, and Sally looked at Skinny, with a sad and resigned expression.

"Is that the only reason you're here?" she finally asked, turning to Little Joe. "To gloat over Skinny's downfall before his friends?"

"Of course not," said Little Joe, "and you know what else I'm here for."

"Yes we do," said Clarence, with an edge to his voice that the others hadn't heard before, "but it won't happen." He pulled Sally back, and put his arm protectively round her. "You'll reach her only over my dead body."

Little Joe shrugged. "One of you or two, it makes no difference to me," he said, "though I admire your chivalry."

"Somebody has to stay loyal to her," said Clarence, glancing at Skinny, "and I will be, to the death!"

Sally looked up at him, and smiled. Clarence felt he had been more than rewarded for his courage.

"And they won't go down alone! If the Company of Secret Kids is to end here, then my life has no more purpose! Kill me, too!"

They all turned towards Christine, standing straight and tall, the fire of love and loyalty shining in her eyes. Her head was held high, but for the first time in her life it was not for useless pride. She still had a terrible crush on Skinny, but now another purpose had entered her life. Sally nodded at Christine and gave her with a grateful smile.

"No!" cried Skinny suddenly, staring at Christine with pleading eyes. Christine looked back at him, and wondered at his sudden apparent feelings for her. Her heart gave a great leap at the thought that he just might return the affection she felt for him, but then her sense of loyalty and love mastered her own desires. She turned her head away from Skinny, and stood beside Sally with a determined air. Skinny looked down at his feet, his face the picture of misery.

"And you'll have to kill me too!" cried Becky staunchly, though her little legs were shaking under her.

Little Joe stared hard at them for a few moments. His face was set in hard lines, his brow furrowed in thought. Though she was very frightened, and expecting to die within the next few seconds, Christine couldn't help noticing that Little Joe was a very handsome man. His cold blue eyes were now surveying the five children with a steely stare. Skinny still stood motionless, staring at the ground as though his grief had taken all the life out of him.

Little Joe suddenly seemed to be hit by an idea. He looked up the track in front of them.

"Walk that way," he said, pointing down the track with his gun, in the direction away from town.

Sally and Clarence turned and began walking. Christine and Becky followed. Skinny stood, irresolute, until Little Joe grabbed him roughly by the arm and pulled him close.

"What's wrong with you?" he hissed, thrusting another gun into Skinny's lifeless hand. "Don't you try and back out now, or I promise you," his voice turned to a menacing growl, "I promise you, I'll make you pay."

Skinny shuddered, and his grip tightened around the gun. A few paces ahead of them, Christine and Becky stood, holding hands, and giving each other reassuring looks. In front of them, Sally walked with her head held high in the first proud gesture the others had ever seen her use. Clarence stood next to her, wearing a new mature and determined look.

"Sally, you got any ideas?" he finally whispered.

Sally looked at him, but made no reply.

"I suppose, if I rushed him, unexpectedly, I could get his gun, and you girls could head for the trees on the sides of the track."

Sally shook her head. "There's still Skinny," she said softly. Clarence wasn't sure if she meant her remark to remind him of the other danger, or to suggest another way out.

"What do you mean?" he asked.

"I mean never say die till you have to, and never give up on a friend."

"And if he doesn't come through, what then?"

"Then we will have done all we could, and given him a chance."

Clarence nodded.

They walked for a few moments in silence, getting further down the track. The snow drifts on the sides of the track were getting so deep, that they soon had to walk single file on the track. Clarence was in the lead, and he was first to see what Little Joe had been aiming for.

Only a few feet in front of him, there stretched out before him a canyon, with a thin trestle-work bridge spanning it. The entire width of the bridge was train track, now made slippery and shining in the damp night air.

Clarence turned and looked at Sally. He had stopped at the edge of the bridge, but already could see the long deadly drop below, and his stomach was turning.

Little Joe and Skinny had fallen behind a little bit, once the snow drifts had made escape nearly impossible. Now they rejoined the others, their guns still in hand.

Christine and Becky took one look at the bridge and the drop beneath it, and began to feel dizzy. Becky began to cry, and tried to hide it.

"Well, that bridge looks mighty high to me," said Little Joe with mock apprehension, "and to think that the midnight express will be along here in about a minute and a half!"

Then he laughed; a dry hacking laugh. It sounded more like a cough.

It seemed a strange laugh for a man so young, but at the moment none of the Company was paying much attention to details.

"Now, Skinny," he said, glancing back over his shoulder toward town, "before that train gets here, how about you jog on down to the other side of this little ditch, and stay there so these fine kids don't try to leave that way."

Skinny slowly started across the bridge, acting like he was walking in his sleep. Christine was afraid he might tumble off the bridge, for he was reeling like a drunk, his gun held loose in his hand. She held her breath until he safely reached the other side, where he turned around and faced them, his gun pointed at the middle of the bridge.

"Now be sure to get out of the way of the train, Skinny!" hollered Little Joe. "I'm looking forward to working with you again, and I don't want you hurt!"

Skinny seemed to nod in answer, though the moonlight was fading and the night was getting darker. Suddenly, faint and far away, they heard a train whistle.

"Well, that's your train!" said Little Joe, and he gave Sally a shove. She stepped forward onto the bridge, with a dignified and regal air. Clarence and the girls followed. Sally led them to the center of the bridge. There she stopped. She continued to face Skinny, and did not turn around in the direction from which the train would come.

Clarence turned to Little Joe, and thought he could faintly hear the sound of the approaching train. Little Joe climbed up onto a drift, safely out of the way, but covering them with his gun, alert and ready. It seemed to Sally that Little Joe was aiming his gun at Christine, and not at her. Then another train whistle rent the silent air.

As if its shocking noise finally woke them to the reality of what was coming, the two girls panicked at the same time.

Becky began sobbing, and Christine looked about wildly for an escape.

"Clarence!" she cried, "do you think we could climb down the side of this bridge?"

Clarence looked over the edge dubiously.

"Somebody get a ladder!" cried Becky, almost mad with fright.

"Sally, do something!" cried Christine, who still had the feeling that Sally could wiggle her way out of any desperate situation.

But now Sally stood motionless, staring at Skinny, only a few yards away from her, with a look as though she would bore into his soul with her gaze. He was still staring blankly at the ground, and would not raise his eyes.

The clattering sound of the train was now clear and distinct, only a few miles away. It would soon come into view, and then all would be lost.

Clarence turned to Sally, in an agony of pity for Becky and Christine, and yet unable to help them.

"Sally, it's too late!" he cried, glancing at Skinny.

It seemed Sally hadn't heard him. Her gaze was more intense on Skinny every minute, her fists clenched, her teeth clenched, every muscle in her body set for a sprint, as if with pure will power she was willing Skinny to do something.

Then, just when Christine was considering leaping from the bridge, in a last, desperate attempt at escape, Skinny looked up.

His eyes met Sally's.

She whispered his name.

A light came into his unseeing eyes, and his mouth tightened into a determined line. He shook his long hair back from his face. Christine had never seen him look so handsome. A noble light shone from his face, and though it was shadowed by remorse, his bearing was proud and confident. He was the real Skinny once again. He gripped the gun in his hand so tight that his knuckles showed white.

He raised the weapon in his no longer shaking hand, and pointed it at Little Joe. His finger pulled the trigger. The sound echoed in the canyon below them as the report of the pistol cracked and hovered on the dense night air. They turned, all except Sally, and saw Little Joe fall backwards with a cry, and roll down the opposite side of the snow bank. He lay motionless in the shelter of the trees on the other side.

"Come on!" yelled Skinny, tossing the gun aside. Sally suddenly sprang into action. She grabbed Christine by the hand, and flew down the track towards him, passing her record speed in the fastest sprint of her life. Clarence scooped Becky into his arms and followed close at her heels.

As they came close to reaching solid ground again, Sally let go of Christine's hand, and Christine, who had been practically dragged the whole way by the determined Sally, slipped on the wet metal, and with a shriek almost fell off the bridge. Sally spun round immediately, but Skinny was quicker. As she slipped from the rails, Christine felt his hand round her waist, and was pulled back to safety.

Clarence and Becky reached the edge of the bridge just as the train swung into view around the corner. As it roared across the bridge at a terrifying rate, Skinny swung Becky and Christine up on a snow drift, and out of the train's way. He turned to Sally, and offered her a hand up, but she scrambled up the hard packed snow by herself, giving him a defiant glance as she gained the top. Clarence and Skinny leaped off the tracks just a few seconds before the train came rattling by. The immense noise and bulk of the thing jarred them all as it passed, speeding by, totally oblivious of the five bedraggled children who so nearly escaped its threatening jaws.

When it was gone, the silence was deafening. Now that the danger was passed, they all realized with a shock how slim their chances had been. Finally, Skinny looked up at Sally and Clarence, guilt and remorse written all over his face.

"I ... I don't know what to say," he murmured. "I wouldn't blame you at all if you chucked me off the edge of that bridge and had done with me. You see, there's something you just don't understand. But, I'm sorry."

Clarence sighed, and looked at Sally, leaving the decision up to her. Sally looked at Skinny for a long moment, and finally said slowly, "There certainly is a lot to say to a guy who you thought was your friend, but then betrays you and leaves you to die."

Skinny looked down, crushed and defeated. Clarence looked again at Sally, but said nothing.

"But," said Sally, in a tone that made Skinny look up again, "there is also a lot to say to a guy who you thought was going to kill you, and then turns around and saves your life. I don't know about the rest of you, but I say that everybody makes mistakes, and that those mistakes shouldn't break up the Company of Secret Kids. Shake hands, Skinny."

Christine breathed a sigh of relief, Clarence laughed shakily and Becky began to cry, from joy or relief she could not tell. Skinny looked at Sally, and his face read volumes of gratitude. She gave him a slow smile, and her eyes shone moist in the moonlight.

Their hands met.

Chapter 11

Christine's Brother

The next day they read in the newspaper that Little Joe had been found by the police, only a few hours after midnight, shot in the leg, but in no other way injured. Authorities said that if they hadn't been tipped off by an anonymous phone call, Little Joe would have frozen to death long before they found him in such an out of the way place. He was in police custody.

Only the Company of Secret Kids could have shed some light on the mysterious phone call. Having been forbidden by Skinny, once again leader of the Company, to directly aid Little Joe, Sally had to be satisfied with living out the rule "Love Thine Enemies" in the safest method possible.

With the fear of Little Joe out of the way, the Company of Secret Kids spent the rest of their days in New York, "living it up," as Sally put it. On the fateful night, after they had alerted the police where to find Little Joe, they returned to the best part of town and celebrated the fact that they were all still alive by practically buying out the nearest ice cream shop. During the course of their celebrating there was much hand-shaking and hugging all round and a good deal of crying on the part of Christine. Clarence was praised for his loyalty, Sally for her trust in human nature, Skinny for making her trust worthwhile, Christine for her courage in standing by her friends, and Becky received many a slap on the back for her remark about the ladder. No one felt it necessary to spoil the festivities by asking Skinny the many questions about Little Joe that were in the back of all their minds.

That night, or in the wee hours of the morning, as they settled into bed, the three girls talked about the events of the night, and fought their battles o'er again, until Becky dropped off to sleep, and Christine and Sally were left snickering in the dark, under the blankets of the bed they shared.

"Sally, weren't you scared?" asked Christine as she snuggled down, rejoicing in the wearing of warm, dry pajamas.

"Yes, for a minute there, when I thought Skinny might faint," she answered.

"Did you know he would turn back to our side the whole time?" asked Christine.

"I had a feeling," said Sally, and was then interrupted by an enormous yawn.

"He looked so handsome when he finally decided to save us," said Christine.

"Did he?" asked Sally sleepily.

"Sally, aren't you listening?"

"Sorry, Chris, but if I yawn again, my head'll split open,"

"His long hair streaming in the wind like that, and his cold blue eyes with such a shivery glare when he shot Little Joe," said Christine, ignoring Sally's answer.

"It was good aim," murmured Sally, "I'm glad he didn't try to hurt him too badly. Good old Skinny."

"Sally," said Christine after a minute, trying to sound careless, "do you remember that night when we were on the plateau in Africa, and I asked you whether or not you thought Skinny was handsome, and then he showed up behind us and you never got a chance to answer? Why don't you tell me now, do you think Skinny is handsome?"

Sally made no reply. Her peaceful breathing and closed eyes told Christine that Sally was off in the land of nod, and that her question would again have to wait for another time.

In the boys' room down the hall, Clarence was stretched out on the bed, his feet on the pillows and his chin in his hands at the foot, in one of his favorite positions, deep in thought. Skinny had donned his pajamas, and was now crawling around on all fours, hunting for his slippers.

"Well, it sure has been a big day," Clarence said finally.

There came an answering grunt from underneath Skinny's bed, followed by the sound of a head smacked against the bed rail, and a groan.

"Skinny, you're not listening to me."

"Yeah, I am," said Skinny, emerging red faced and tousled from under his bed, "I'm just trying to find my slippers."

"What do you need slippers for if you're going to bed?"

"I thought I'd go down the hall and make sure the girls' door is locked. Since Little Joe is put away they might be getting lax about their security. I just want to double check. New York is a rough town, you know."

"Yeah, I'm finding that out," said Clarence. "Well, anyway it's nice to see you back as fearless leader of the Company. When you were battling with your conscience and Sally was in charge, she came by to see if our door was locked."

"She did?" asked Skinny coming out of the closet, still slipperless.

"Yeah," he looked off into space dreamily. "Man, she's quite a girl, don't you think so?" Clarence cupped his chin in his hands again, thinking of Sally's staunch bravery and unquenchable spirit.

"Well, I guess I'll just go without them," said Skinny. "After all, it's just down the hall, and I don't think I'll catch a cold."

"Don't you think so, Skinny?" repeated Clarence, still dreamily.

"Not if I keep them warm when I get back," answered Skinny as he opened the door.

"Not your feet, dummy," said Clarence, "I was talking about Sally."

"You were?" said Skinny, turning around on the threshold, "what did you say?"

"I asked you if you thought Sally was quite a girl."

Skinny smiled, shrugged and went out. As he sauntered down the hall, his confident, cocky self once again, he stopped for a moment and considered Clarence's question again.

He thought of Sally as she stood, fearless, on the bridge, slim and white, her dark curls framing her animated face, her cheeks made rosy by the cold, her eyes shining with passion. For a moment he stood in silent thought. Then he shook himself, smiled, and shrugged again.

* * *

The next morning at breakfast, the Company held an informal council meeting. They all had questions for Skinny, and they had to lay out their plans for the future.

"First of all, I think we deserve to hear the true story of Skinny's life," said Clarence, as they finished demolishing the hotel's supply of provisions.

"Okay, just wait till I've finished my toast," replied Skinny.

"Oh, by the way, Sally," said Christine, "I meant to ask you, why did Little Joe call you Stockly when he first saw you?"

"That was my father's last name. Little Joe seems to like to call me that, because he's trying to kill me in revenge of something my father did to him. I suppose he calls me that to remind himself why he hates me."

"Well, at least he's been put away for the time being," said Skinny. "And now I'll give you another version of my life story."

"Another version?" asked Sally. "We want the true one."

Skinny grinned, and started his story.

"Well, my parents died when I was about seven, and after that I had to lone it. We had lived in New York, and I had nowhere else to go, so I stayed living in our old home. At least it was paid off, and they left enough money to last a little while. After a while, I thought in my innocence that I would have to get a job or something if I wanted to survive. It's not easy getting a job at the age of seven, even in New York.

"When the going got tough, I decided to try my hand at a little pocket picking. Shop-lifting and purse snatching is a pretty big business in New York, since there's an abundance of unsuspecting tourists. I lived the semi- criminal lifestyle for quite a while, and discovered I had quite a knack for swiping wallets, and I was pretty agile when it came to getting away."

"A regular Billy the Kid," said Sally.

"Well," continued Skinny, "that life was going pretty well for me, and who knows where I'd be today, if I hadn't accidentally tried to swipe Little Joe's wallet once. Being a crook himself, Little Joe trusts no one, and is always on his guard. He caught me red-handed.

"At first I thought I'd get dragged off to jail, until I realized who Little Joe was. Then I really got scared. He was already a well known gangster back then, and I thought I was a goner. Luckily for me, Little Joe had a different idea. He noticed that I was pretty slick at swiping wallets, and made great getaways, so he told me that in payment for not turning me in, or killing me on the spot, I would join his gang, and work as a petty thief and decoy on odd jobs."

"So you weren't ever a pop star?" asked Christine.

She was ignored by all.

"That sounds dangerous," breathed Becky.

"It was no picnic," agreed Skinny, "but after a little while, it got better. Little Joe and his gang kind of got to like me, in their own way. As I got older, my fame started to spread in New York. I was known as 'Little Joe's Little Friend.' By the time I was twelve, I was successful, happy, and very dishonest. Then, one night when I had just turned thirteen, me and Little Joe got in a fight."

"Little Joe and I, Skinny," corrected Christine.

"Shhh," hissed Sally, who was listening intently, "what did you and Joe fight about, Skinny?"

"Oh, I can't remember now, and it doesn't matter. What does matter is that he beat the tar out of me over it. That was when I decided to run away. I planned my escape and waited for an opportunity for a long time. Finally my chance came. We had done a bank job, and something got messed up in the planning. Little Joe and his men made it away in the getaway car, but because the chase was so hot, they didn't wait for me. The cops showed up almost instantly, but I jumped a fence and they didn't notice me. I had a feeling Little Joe would go to one of his out of town hideouts until the heat was off, and since I was left alone, I left New York."

"Where'd you get the funds?" asked Clarence.

"Oh, I carried a good sum wherever I went, and that night I had helped empty the safe, so I was loaded. It was the chance of a lifetime.

"I had no idea where I was going, but I left New York and went out West. When I reached Kansas, I found a nice little boarding house, in a tiny town near the border. I settled down, got an honest job, became good friends with the widow who owned the house, and lived happily for a while. I made a few friends in town, and that was how I ended up coming to England. One of my chums had a cousin who went to--"

He broke off, and blushed.

"Go on, Skinny," said Sally.

"Well, that's really the end," he said with a shrug. "My friend said that England was a nice place, and I decided to go there. Then I met you guys."

"But I thought," began Becky with a bewildered expression, "I thought you said you came--"

"And I want to apologize to you all," interrupted Skinny, giving Becky a slight kick under the table, which she alone noticed, "for lying to you about being a famous rock star. I guess I just thought you wouldn't want to go around with a criminal."

"That's okay, Skinny," said Clarence.

"We know you've changed since then," said Christine.

"Yes, though that little bit of acting on the bridge last night was just a tad sneaky," said Sally with a grin.

"Now tell us what happened with you and Little Joe the other night," said Clarence.

"Well, after I sent you all back here, I went into Flannigan's, which I remembered was one of Little Joe's favorite haunts, he being the son of an Irishman and all. It was there that I confronted him."

"Oh, Skinny, you must have been scared," breathed Christine.

"Actually, I was more terrified," admitted Skinny with a grin. "But I knew I'd have to face him again sooner or later. He knew me, though I imagine I'd changed a good deal since I was thirteen. I think he was glad to see me. He bought me a drink, said there were no hard feelings about me running off. He told me I was welcome back to the gang. I could tell he had been drinking too much, and let me tell you I was not looking forward to telling him I was against him.

"I finally screwed up my nerves, and told him that I wasn't coming back to the gang, and that he should leave off Sally."

"What did he do?" asked Sally.

"He stood up real quietly, and told his men to wait inside. Then he took me by the arm, led me outside, and made it very clear to me that I was to join him again, or die. I held firm for a while, but like I said, he was drunk, and not master of even himself. I let him rough me around, and pound me into the snow, and use some language on me that I wouldn't like to repeat. But finally, just to save my skin, I told him I'd help him - I'm sorry."

Skinny's story did not seem complete to Sally, but she gave him a reassuring grin.

"Then you came back to the hotel, and we know the rest," said Clarence, rescuing Skinny from further painful memories.

"Well, I'm glad it's over, and we're all back to normal," said Christine.

Becky had been sitting silent during Skinny's narration, ever since he had interrupted her and now she sat staring at him with a baby pout. He smiled at her when no one else was looking, and winked. She wondered what she had missed, but she decided to keep her mouth shut for the time being, to avoid getting kicked under the table again.

Sally had noticed the slip she had almost made, and gave it some thought as Skinny had continued. She had also noticed his apparent reticence to explain the cause of the fight between him and Little Joe, which had forced him to run away in the first place. She supposed all the mysteries would be cleared up eventually, and she knew she couldn't rush Skinny, so she too held her peace.

"Well," said Skinny after a moment, "I suppose we should start making our plans for what we're to do next."

"I say we stay here for another week or too," said Sally, "and by then it will be February, and we can head for Manchester to find Christine's brother."

"So we're really going to do that?" asked Skinny dubiously.

"Of course! We can't leave the little kid to rot in that screwy professor's house, can we?" asked Sally.

"Why are you so against finding my brother, Skinny?" asked Christine.

"Oh, I'm not," said Skinny, "I just hope there really is someone there to find."

"There will be," said Sally, giving Skinny a sidelong glance, "and the true identity of Christine's brother will soon be known to all of us. I can feel it."

* * *

About a month later, the wild, daring, trouble-causing Company of Secret Kids descended on the town of Manchester.

Being back in the town where they had all met more than half a year before brought back many memories. It made the members of the Company realize how lucky they had been, if luck you could call it, to have found each other at such a perfect time.

Though they were obligated to stay in a hotel, they spent as much time as possible around St. Joseph's Convent, reliving the first days of the company, and reviving old friendships they had made with the Sisters, who were delighted to see them.

Through all the happy days, Skinny had remained leader of the Company, and was once again his bold and confident self. Though it seemed that he had left all his shadowy past secrets back in New York, Clarence still noticed some oddities about him.

On the day they had arrived in Manchester, for instance, Clarence had seen Skinny talking earnestly to a railway attendant, who kept pointing at Christine and beaming at Skinny. Clarence assumed that Skinny had met the man on his first trip there, but he wondered what Christine had to do with it. He wondered, but he kept silent.

Then came the day, about the tenth of February, when the Company decided to force the issue with the Professor the next evening. They prepared themselves to do combat and rescue Christine's brother or die in the attempt.

They went downtown the next day, and found the address of the Professor's house, following the directions into a gloomy looking row of houses.

From a hiding place across the street, they got a good look at it. It was a forbidding, three story mansion sort of a place, perfect for a mad scientist. All around the house and yard was a huge fence, rusty, but still sturdy enough. There were spikes lining the top, and on the gate there were chains, and one huge padlock. The bars were too close together for even Becky to slip through, and the boys weren't sure they could scale its great height.

Skinny gave the others strict orders to remain where they were, and then cautiously made his way across the street. It was a damp, overcast day, and a heavy fog lay over the street. Beyond the Professor's house there was a large park; a big grassy hill covered with trees. The shelter of these trees was only a few yards away from the Professor's gate, and it had been previously arranged that if anything went wrong, and they were discovered, they would run for the woods, and there re-group.

As the four reminded themselves of these plans, Skinny reached the fence. He crept along it till he was facing the side of the house, where a slim alley ran between the fence and the wall surrounding the house next door. Skinny peeked carefully through the fence, and stared at something inside. Then he looked across the street and motioned for the others to come.

When they were all crouched down in the alley, Skinny pointed through the bars and whispered, "that must be the laboratory."

He was looking at a small, squat building behind the main house. It had two small chimneys, one of which was smoking. There were only two windows, and from their position, they couldn't see in to them, except that there was a flash or two of a dim light coming from them every few seconds.

"Let's go have a closer look," said Sally, rising to her feet and starting to scramble up the fence.

"Wait!" hissed Skinny, reaching up and pulling her down. "Let's not be rash."

"How about you and me hop the fence and take a closer look?" suggested Clarence.

"That's a good idea, Clare, come on," said Sally.

"He was talking to me," said Skinny, once again pulling Sally back to earth.

"Well, let's have at it then," said Clarence.

"You girls stay here," commanded Skinny.

The two boys reached up to the bar that ran across the top of the fence, and with much pulling, scrambling, shushing, and slipping, they finally managed to reach the ground on the other side. By then the girls were covered in flakes of red rust which the boys had dislodged from the metal, and the heavy fog made it stick to them, making their skin glow with an unearthly orangeish hue.

Skinny and Clarence crept towards the laboratory on hands and knees.

After what seemed an awfully long time, they reached the building and knelt under one of the windows.

"Should we risk a look in?" whispered Clarence.

"Yes, but it has to be fast. If we were spotted, I'm not sure how quickly we could make it over that fence."

"Who should look in?"

"You, you've got a better knack for taking things in at a glance."

"Thanks," said Clarence, and after a moment's pause, to get his breath and brace himself, he stood up, took one very brief look in the window, and ducked down again.

"Anybody see you?" asked Skinny.

Clarence shook his head. "There's a lot of test tubes and stuff," he whispered, "all lined up on some long tables, and at each end of the room there is a fireplace."

"Is the Professor in there?"

"Yes. He had his back to me, and was bending over some papers. And also, there was a little door in the corner of the room, with three or four stairs leading down to it, and a big lock on it. That must be the basement where he keeps Christine's brother."

"Yeah," said Skinny, in a doubtful voice. His mind appeared to be on something else.

"And now the two most important things," continued Clarence, "are that he had a gun in a holster, and there was a big shotgun near the door, and ..."

"That settles it," interrupted Skinny.

"What?"

"We're not going to mess with this Professor. He's dangerous."

"But what about Christine's brother?"

Skinny looked at Clarence for a long moment. He was thinking so hard he could almost feel his brain throbbing in his head.

"There's something I've got to tell you about Christine's brother," he said quietly, "and what I have to tell you is ... is something I should have told you all long before."

Clarence leaned closer, for Skinny was hardly speaking audibly.

"And I have to tell you now, or we'll all be in danger for nothing. We won't find Christine's brother in there."

"But I saw him!" said Clarence, wondering what Skinny could possibly be getting at.

Skinny opened his mouth to continue with what he had been saying, when he suddenly stopped. His mouth stayed open, and he looked at Clarence with an astonished expression.

"What did you just say?" he asked, his eyebrows twisting themselves into one of the positions of astonishment that only Skinny could perform.

"That I saw Christine's brother in there," said Clarence, "that's what I was trying to tell you when you interrupted me."

Skinny didn't reply; his mouth was still open in astonishment.

"I was going to say that I saw a little boy with blond hair, dressed pretty shabbily, tending one of the fires in there."

"Maybe he's the Professor's hired boy," suggested Skinny dazedly.

"If it is, then he's pretty rough on his hired help," said Clarence. "That kid looked half starved, and he had a chain round one of his ankles, which was attached to a hook in the wall."

"That does sound suspicious," admitted Skinny, "but I've still got a very good reason to believe that that is not Christine's brother."

"Well, wait with it until we've rescued the kid," said Clarence.

"Okay," said Skinny, seeming relieved, "and I guess we might as well rescue him, whoever he is. The girls are all keyed up for an adventure."

"Right, now come on."

They crawled back to the fence, and through the bars they told the girls what they had seen. Of the three girls, Sally alone noticed Skinny's dazed expression and baffled look.

Christine didn't notice anything unusual about him, though she thought he looked handsomer than usual, for the damp air had made his hair wet, and his blondish locks looked dark against his pale face and gray blue eyes. Once he had turned back to their side, after that awful night on the bridge, Christine had developed a mad crush on Skinny all over again.

She was contemplating how his pointy nose and bony jaw made him look as if his face was carved from stone, when he suddenly turned to her and asked if she was ready to execute the plan. She blushed, as she realized that she had been so wrapped up in the contemplation of his face that she had forgotten to listen to what he and Sally and Clarence were so earnestly discussing.

"What do I do again?" she asked.

"You wait right here with Becky," said Sally, "and Clarence and Skinny will go get the kid while I keep the Professor occupied."

"Are you sure you want to be the decoy, Sally?" asked Skinny. "It might be safer for one of us boys."

"Not a chance," said Sally, with a mischievous grin, "I've got an idea."

"Well, okay," said Skinny, forgetting that he had previously been arguing that it was dangerous. "Now, Clarence, from what you saw of him, do you suppose that little kid could slip through these bars?"

Clarence considered a moment. "I think so. He was pretty skinny. If he couldn't though, it'd be pretty easy to throw him over the top, if there was someone on this side to catch him."

"Do you girls think you could do it?" Skinny asked. Christine nodded, though she wasn't sure herself.

"Well, then let's go for it!" cried Sally, and before they could stop her, she darted down the alley way, and disappeared around the front side of the house.

Skinny stared after her in exasperation.

"Here we go," he said. "Good luck, girls."

For a moment his eyes met Christine's and she thought his glance was strangely affectionate.

Skinny turned and crawled back toward the window with Clarence. They waited, and began to wonder if something had gone wrong with Sally. Then they heard, from deep inside the house, the sound of a doorbell ringing frantically. It sounded as if someone wanted to pull the ringer down. The boys smiled at each other, recognizing Sally's obtrusive manner of getting attention.

Then they both crouched up, and looked in. The Professor was looking in the direction of the house with a surprised and almost frightened look. It did sound as though whoever was at the door was someone vicious. He hurriedly pulled a huge key ring from his pocket, filled with countless keys. He ran to the boy at the wood box, unchained his ankle, and pulled him down the steps to the little door.

"Now, watch which key he uses," said Skinny, standing up a little more to get a better view.

"Can you see?" asked Clarence, as he watched the Professor open the door, shove the kid in, and slam it again.

"I think it was a pretty big key, more copper-colored than the others."

Suddenly the Professor spun round, and for a moment was facing them. Skinny ducked back down and pulled Clarence with him. They waited for a long moment, wondering whether or not they had been seen.

The Professor stood for a moment, wondering if he really had seen a face at the window, or if it was his elderly eyes playing tricks on him. He would have gone to find out, but just then the doorbell rang again with such vigor that there came the sound of a bell hitting the ground with a clang, and the ringing stopped.

The Professor turned toward the door, forgetting all about the face at the window, straightened his spectacles on his nose, and went out.

"Perfect," said Skinny, rising slowly to his feet, "he left the …"

Suddenly the Professor came back in, and the boys slipped out of sight just in time. The Professor hurried to the table, snatched up the key ring which he had forgotten, and left again.

"Darn!" said Skinny, as they came up again, and saw what had happened. "That was too easy. We had the key ring right there, and now the old idiot took it with him!"

"We'll just have to find a way to get it from him," said Clarence.

Meanwhile, Sally was getting impatient. At first she had been afraid that she might be too slow, for it took her some time to climb over the fence, though she did it quicker and more gracefully than Skinny and Clarence had. Once she was over, she had rung the bell as hard as she could, non-stop for what seemed an eternity. Finally, she gave it one vigorous yank, lifting her feet off the ground and swinging from the bell rope. From inside she heard the sound of the bell dropping from a great height, and then the bell rope slithered down from its fastenings, and slid through her hands. She sighed heavily, wondering whether the Professor could be as deaf as all that. She tied the bell rope round her waist with the air of a conqueror.

Since the bell was out of commission, she began to knock. The great oak front door boomed when she struck it, but after hammering at it for a minute, her fist became numb. She removed one of her shoes, and began banging on the door with it. When no sign of life came from within, she began to get really annoyed.

She went down the front steps a little way, and ran up as fast as she could, hurling her whole slender self against the door. She bounced back like a rubber ball, landing on her back, and the door looked no different than before. She got to her feet with a look of utter determination for revenge on that stupid mass of wood. She decided she would make one more endeavor. This time she went all the way down the front steps, and down to the gate. Then, with one shoe on, and the other one in her hand, she stuck out her lower lip, put on her most determined expression, scraped the ground behind her with her feet, like a bull set for the charge, and then, she charged.

All the energy in her little body propelled her up the steps with a speed even Skinny might have envied. As fate would have it, the Professor had just reached his door, and being a bit frightened of what was making such a tremendous racket on the other side, he opened the door suddenly, and half hid behind it.

For a moment he saw what looked like a little orange and blue streak of lightning before his face, and then heard a commotion in his broom closet. He looked out the door, and saw nothing out of the ordinary, except for some small flakes of orange rust on the doorstep. Then he turned and looked toward his closet.

The closet had a small door that swung very easily on its hinges, either in or out, and that door was in a direct line with the front door. He now realized, that whatever that thing was that had come streaking through his door, was now loose, in his closet.

He shut the front door, and very cautiously started creeping toward the closet. There was a lot of bumping and banging coming from within, and the poor old man hadn't the foggiest idea what sort of creature he had in his closet.

He was just a few feet away from the door, when it was suddenly, violently, flung open. The Professor leaped back in terror, shielding his face from what was inside. When he finally dared look, he beheld: feet.

He looked again, to make sure he wasn't hallucinating. There, kicking madly, at about waist level, were two feet. One was shod and the other wasn't. The owner of the feet was apparently face down in a large pile of oddments that the Professor kept in his closet. He stepped a little closer, and might have even dared to touch to the flying feet, but suddenly, they stopped waving about, returned to their rightful place on the floor, and the rest of the strange creature emerged from the wreckage.

The Professor once again recoiled in terror. His fear was well based this time, for the thing that emerged was enough to make anyone a bit nervous.

It wasn't very tall, and was slim. Its arms and face were an orange tinge, and the eyes were bright blue. Its hair was very mussed, and standing out in every direction, as though it had been electrified. Around its slim waist, doubled several times, was the Professor's very own beautiful bell rope. Around its neck was a large coil of copper wire, which it had acquired when it came in sudden contact with the contents of the broom closet. In its right hand it held menacingly, a shoe.

"Boy, that was unexpected," said the creature, and started laughing. The Professor backed up against the wall, shaking like a leaf. Sally pulled the coil of wire off her neck, and tossed it back into the closet. She smoothed her hair back, and wiped some of the orange rust off her face. The Professor felt less afraid, but was still cautious. Sally glanced around at the inside of the house. Everything was very old, very gloomy, and very scientific. There was a stair case to her right, and what appeared to be a kitchen door to her left. She glanced around till she noticed the Professor, backed up against a small table near the front door.

"Hi," said Sally, with one of her winning smiles, "I'm Sally Keenan, are you the Professor?"

She approached, holding out her hand, in friendly fashion. The Professor looked at the hand suspiciously. It still had the shoe in it.

"Oh, sorry," said Sally, and tried to restore her shoe to its rightful place, hopping about on one foot, trying to keep her balance. "You see, your bell broke, and I was using my shoe to knock. Your door is a bit rough on the bare hand."

The Professor nodded, watching her closely as she hopped about, wondering vaguely if this was some form of distracting the prey before the spring of the predator.

Outside, Clarence and Skinny had given the girls by the fence a report of what was happening, and then they began to creep closer to the house itself, somehow hoping to obtain another glimpse of the key ring.

"I hope we did the right thing in sending Sally in there alone," whispered Skinny. "After all, we don't know how dangerous that Professor is."

"Sally can take care of herself," answered Clarence confidently. "She's quite a girl."

"Yeah, but what if she does something rash?" asked Skinny, cracking his knuckles as he did when he was nervous.

"Shhh," said Clarence. "If the Professor heard you cracking your knuckles, it wouldn't matter what Sally does in there."

"You're whispering is just as loud," said Skinny shoving his hands in his pockets. Visions of Sally, backed up against a wall, terrified of the unknown malice of the Professor, sprang before his mind.

While Skinny was working himself into a tizzy outside the back door, the Professor was backed against his own wall, with Sally vainly trying to put him at his ease.

"So you're a Professor of science, right?" she asked, after an awkward silence. "Well, I've always been interested in bombs, and explosions and stuff like that ... Chemistry, I suppose that's the sort of thing, though I never had a good head for all that math."

Slowly, the Professor stepped toward her. He was beginning to suspect this thing of being a mere child, and now his embarrassment at his cowardice was mastering his fear. He had also just remembered the gun he wore round his waist.

"Oh, by the way, here's your bell rope," said Sally, as she untied it. "I thought you might want it back, it's very pretty."

She looked up to find herself covered by an ancient looking pistol, held by an aged hand which was desperately trying to stop shaking.

"Hey, what ... " began Sally, but broke off, seeing the look of suspicion and contempt in the Professor eyes.

"You've trespassed on the wrong ground, you 'ave," said the Professor stonily. "I'm a dangerous man, I am, and I don't want no little nosy kid spoiling months of work with 'er stupid questions."

"Well, I just passing through," said Sally.

"And now you're gonna leave, right quick," said the Professor.

"Okay, okay, don't get excited," said Sally, backing towards the closet, and thinking as hard as she could all the while.

"I ain't excited," said the Professor, gathering courage as Sally retreated, "but you better be clear out that door within the next few seconds if ya knows what's good for ya. An insane scientist some say I am, and an insane chap is a dangerous thing sometimes."

His words gave Sally a sudden inspiration. A wild thought shot through her head. She decided to test her acting abilities, and prayed a quick prayer that her scheme would work. Suddenly she stopped retreating, and stiffened. She raised her eyebrows and gave him an unearthly glare. The Professor stopped in his tracks, halted by her strange look.

"Insane?" said Sally softly. "Insane you say? Let me tell you that you don't know what it is like to be insane."

She took a step forward, and went up on her tiptoes, trying to look menacing. The Professor stepped back.

"I have been called insane many a time before," growled Sally, with an awful grin she had mastered just to scare Christine.

"Now see here, miss," said the Professor, turning and beginning to inch toward the kitchen. "If you come one step closer, I'll be forced to take drastic measures, I will."

Sally threw back her head and laughed. That laugh had once been named "Sally's crazy laugh" by Becky. Sally did admit it was unnerving, and it served its purpose on the Professor. He turned and fled, dropping his gun in his haste to get away.

Sally started in hot pursuit, snatching up the gun as she went. She paused before the kitchen door, whence the Professor had gone, and glanced at the gun. It was not loaded. She grinned, and slipped it in her pocket.

When she entered the kitchen, there was no sign of the Professor. The other door out of the kitchen was swinging back and forth, as though someone had just bolted through it at a great speed. Sally ran her hands through her hair, to add to the crazy effect, licked her lips, and sped after him.

On the other side of the door, she found herself in a butler's pantry. Through that, she ran into a dark dining room, through the library and past the study. After a few more rooms, she found herself back by the front door, having made it through the entire circle of the house. She was standing panting at the foot of the huge staircase, looking about, wondering where the old man could have gone off to so fast. She was just about to check the front door, when she heard a door slam upstairs.

Sally leapt up the stairs, two at a time, and slid to a stop on the shiny wood floor of the upstairs hall. She paused and surveyed her surroundings. There were several doors around her, leading to different bedrooms, and one into a large bathroom. Next to one room which appeared to be a study, library, or dining room all in one, there was a little door, about three feet off the ground, with a tiny knob at the bottom for sliding the door up. Sally went over to it, and slid the little door up. Inside, there appeared to be nothing but a large box, hung from above by ropes. After a moment, Sally recognized the strange thing from the many books she had read about murders and things in old English mansions.

"Wow, a real dumb waiter! I've always wanted to ride one of these things!"

She examined the ropes more closely, promising herself to test it out if the occasion should arise. Reluctantly, she tore herself away from the fascinating thing, and turned to examine the rest of the upstairs. She stepped into the large room, furnished with a tea table, several book cases, a large desk, and a glass door leading out onto a balcony.

She went through the door, and stood on the balcony, staring out at the world beneath her. She was now facing the back of the house, and the balcony was almost overhanging the small laboratory. She leaned out over the fence around the edge, to see what part of the house was directly under her. She saw the back door which she had noticed from the inside, while going through the kitchen, and next to it, two crouching shapes.

"Hey, boys!" she called softly, rattling the metal rail to attract their attention.

Clarence glanced up, and his eyes opened wide. He tapped Skinny.

"Shhh," growled Skinny, "I'm trying to get a glimpse of Sally."

"Try looking up," grinned Clarence.

"What?" Skinny looked where Clarence pointed, and his jaw dropped.

"Sally!" he cried, and the two of them began carefully crawling toward the balcony.

"You needn't be so cautious," whispered Sally, "the Professor's up here."

"Sally, be careful," said Skinny, getting to his feet. "He's armed."

"You mean with this?" asked Sally, pulling the gun from her pocket. "I wouldn't worry, it ain't loaded."

Clarence laughed. "Sally, you're a wonder!"

Sally bowed.

"Hey, Miss Wonder," said Skinny, glancing nervously towards the back door. "If you're such a magician, see if you can get your hands on the Professor's key ring."

"What does it look like?"

"It's big and has a lot of keys," said Clarence. "They're old and ancient looking."

"So is everything else in the house," said Sally, "but I'll look for it. When I get it, I'll drop it off this balcony to you. Stick around, and don't get hit by flying keys."

Before Skinny had time to remind her once more to be careful, Sally disappeared back inside. She now went in search of the Professor himself. She tried all the bedrooms, and found them empty, except for the last one down the hall. It had the biggest door, and was obviously meant for the master of the house. This she found locked.

"The old buzzard must have barricaded himself in and the key ring with him," she muttered, wondering how she could possibly break through a door of that strength.

"When brawn fails, brains must prevail," she thought, and sat down just outside the door, buried her face in her hands, and started thinking. After a moment, she leapt to her feet, and snapped her fingers.

She leaned up against the Professor's door, and in as loud a voice as she could make without attracting Skinny and Clarence's attention, she hollered, "Okay Sam, he's locked in. You can clean out the valuables down there. I'll see if there's anything up here worth bringing along!"

She sprang back, into the bathroom, a split second before the Professor's door flew open. He came rushing out, his long white hair streaming behind him, and went clattering down the stairs, yelling for the police.

Sally slipped in his open door, and made a quick survey of his room. There was a huge bed with a canopy at one end of the room, and a wardrobe at the other. Sally wondered where to look for the keys, for there was a dresser in the corner as well, and she didn't know how much time she had before the police actually did show up.

She checked quickly under the pillows of the bed, and the pockets of the clothes in the wardrobe. Then, before she attacked the dresser, she went to the door to see why everything was so quiet.

There, standing at the top of the stairs, was the Professor. He was staring at her with a steely glare. Sally grinned sheepishly.

"There ain't nobody in this 'ouse but you an' me, missy," he growled, "an' I don't know why you're 'ere, but you're leaving right now."

From his waist coat pocket, he pulled a tiny automatic gun. Sally didn't wait to see if it was loaded. With a spring and a bound, she got into the room with the balcony, and slammed the door behind her. She stayed leaning up against it as she found the lock, and turned it. A second later, she heard the Professor rattling the locked knob.

"Blast, where did I put me bloody key ring?" she heard his voice through the door, and pressed her ear to the keyhole, hoping to get some information.

"Let's see. I needed them to get into the whiskey cupboard," muttered the Professor, providentially thinking out loud, "'cause I needed something to settle me nerves when I came up 'ere with that little she-devil on me 'eels."

Sally glanced around the room, for she didn't remember a cupboard in any other bedroom. She got up, and began examining the room. Then she heard his voice outside again, and pasted her ear back to the keyhole.

"Drat it, then, the keys are in there," she heard him say. "Well, I'll 'ave to go an' get the other set."

She heard the sounds of footsteps descending the stairs. Then she turned, and looked about the room. "At least I know they're in here somewhere," she thought. "Now I've just got to find it before he gets back."

She ran to the bookshelves, and started running her hands across the books, hoping for a clue. Along one of the top shelves, her finger hit a book that was sticking out further than the others. She grabbed it and pulled. To her amazement, six or seven books came with it, all attached to each other, and she saw that they weren't books at all, just the bindings, backed by a wooden door. Inside, there was a wooden cupboard door, and in the keyhole, at last, the key ring!

She pulled it out victoriously, and ran to the balcony. As she reached it, she heard a key rattling in the lock of the door, heralding the reappearance of the Professor.

"Skinny!" she called, and dropped the keys. Clarence made a flying leap from the back door, and caught them in the air.

"Good work, Sally!" called Skinny. "Come on down!"

"I'm on my way!" returned Sally, and she flew back to the door. She flattened herself against it, just in time. The Professor swung the door open, and Sally went with it. He entered the room gun first, and headed for the balcony. Sally came out from behind the door, slipped out of the room, and ran for the dumb waiter, with a mischievous smirk. As she sat down on the tray, she turned back and realized that the Professor would see Clarence and Skinny if he reached the balcony.

She grabbed the rope, and braced herself for the ride down, then, just before she let go, she gave a shrill whistle. The Professor turned just in time, and watched in horrified amazement as she let go, and sailed down with a blood-curdling whoop.

He ran to the dumb waiter and looked down. There was a square patch of light below where the dumb waiter door opened into the kitchen. For a moment he saw Sally, as she slipped out, and whipped out of sight. Her disappearance was followed by the slam of the back door, and Sally's favorite war-cry, "Erin Go Bragh!"

Then, being satisfied that the horrid thing had left his house in peace, the poor, ruffled Professor fled back to the sanctuary of his room, bolted the door, and remained there till tea time.

As soon as the keys had been dropped, Clarence and Skinny headed for the lab. Clarence remained outside the door as a lookout, while Skinny entered with the keys and began testing them on the basement door.

Finally, one fit and the door opened. Skinny reached in and pulled the boy out, explaining his situation in a few words. As they started for the door, there rang out upon the silence of the house, a shrill, chilling, yell. The boy started in terror, and began to run back to the basement, but Skinny, (who had recognized the voice as Sally's), pulled him on, and they joined Clarence and ran for the fence just as Sally reached the door.

Christine and Becky had been waiting impatiently. From their hiding spot, they could see the balcony, but hadn't been able to hear what Sally and the boys were talking about, and the suspense had almost killed them. Christine began to feel a slight tinge of jealousy towards Sally rekindling. Why did Skinny depend on her so much, and spend so much time with her? She wondered about it. If only she could have read Skinny's thoughts during the past hour, she would have found that Skinny was barely thinking about Sally, so wrapped up was he in his thoughts of Christine, but for much different reasons than she imagined.

Christine's ponderings were cut short, for Skinny had reached the fence, and found that the boy was thin enough to slip through the bars. Christine helped him through, trying to hurry, and at the same time trying to get a good look at her younger brother. She vaguely noticed that Becky wasn't being much help, just leaning up against the fence, staring at the boy with a dazed expression, but at the moment she was too busy wondering how Skinny and Clarence were to make it over the fence in time to take notice of anything else.

Just then Sally reached the fence, looking wild and free and far too beautiful, thought Christine, enviously.

"Hey, I'm not sure, but the nutcase may have called the cops, and they should be here by now if he did," panted Sally.

"Okay, then Christine and Becky, take the kid and head for the park," ordered Skinny.

"What about you?" asked Christine, as she stood up and took her brother by the hand.

"We're coming, now move!"

They ran down the alley way, Becky still looking dazed, the boy looking scared, and Christine wishing with all her heart she could stay with Skinny.

"Okay, Sally," said Skinny, when the three were out of sight, "go on over."

"No, if he comes back out here, I ain't leaving you two alone with him, you first."

"Darn you, Sally," cried Skinny, "you're enough to drive a fellow mad with all your noble ideals, now git!"

Sally opened her mouth to protest, but Skinny picked her up and fairly threw her over the fence. She picked herself up on the other side with a malignant look. Clarence scrambled over after her, and Skinny came last. As he reached the ground, they set off after the others.

The park was only a few yards away, and they soon reached the shelter of the trees. Becky and the boy were sitting on a bench together, down the other side of the hill, but Christine was waiting for them just inside the trees. When they reached her, she threw her arms around Skinny.

"Oh, Skinny," she cried passionately, "I was so worried about you!"

"Yeah, he really could have killed himself sitting outside that door," said Sally sympathetically, "whereas I was just as safe as a daisy inside with that armed lunatic."

Christine gave Sally a withering glance, and kept her arms around Skinny. As if to compensate for her unappreciative attitude, Clarence put his arm around Sally.

"Oh, stop that," laughed Sally, shaking herself free. "Come on, let's go meet Christine's brother!"

She pulled Clarence after her, and charged down the hill, but not before Christine noticed that, as she made her remark about the brother, Sally gave Skinny a sly glance. Christine also noticed that Skinny had blanched, and was seeming troubled.

"Skinny dear, what's wrong?" she asked, thankful of an excuse to be sympathetic.

At her use of the word 'dear', Skinny seemed to wince again. He looked hard at Christine for a moment, and then pulled her arms from around his neck.

"Christine," he said, making a great effort to sound normal, "Christine, there's something I've got to tell you about your brother."

Christine cocked her head, unconsciously imitating Sally. "What's the matter with my brother, Skinny?"

"Come on," said Skinny, "let's get away from the others. They needn't hear us."

This was fine with Christine, who was rejoicing in some time alone with Skinny, even if he was acting peculiar. They walked along the outskirts of the trees for a little way, till the sounds of the others' excited voices faded. Then they walked down the hill into the park, and found a bench, quite secluded. Christine was puzzled, but she made no protests or inquiries, lest she destroy the beautiful moment they were sharing.

"Christine," said Skinny again, once they were settled on the bench and had sat for a moment in silence, "Christine there's something I've got to tell you."

"You already said that," said Christine quietly.

"Well, it won't be easy for me to tell you, and it won't be easy for you to hear."

Christine looked hard at him. This sounded ominous.

"Skinny, what in the world is troubling you?" she asked, beginning to feel a bit frightened. For a split second, she wondered if he had joined Little Joe again, and was planning to murder her, but the sadness and love which shown from his melancholy face dispelled these thoughts from her mind.

"I know I should have told you this sooner," said Skinny, looking down at his lap, and speaking fast, "for I believe, and now please remember, I'm just supposing ... " here he looked up at her, and the pain in his face was so deep, that she placed her hand on his, and smiled encouragingly.

"Christine, do you ... what do you think of me?" he finally asked.

Christine thought for a moment, and decided that this was the time to be perfectly honest. "Skinny, I love you more than any other person in the world."

Skinny nodded, and looked down again. "I thought so," he whispered.

"What's so terrible about that?" asked Christine.

"Well, what's so terrible is, that I love you," answered Skinny, and Christine felt as if she could have flown away with happiness. But Skinny continued, "but not in that way. You must forget that sort of love."

"Why?" asked Christine. "Oh, Skinny, if we both love each other, why can't we just consider ourselves engaged --"

"No!" cried Skinny, standing up very quickly. "No, we can't do that! Don't think like that, or what I'm trying to say will be all the more hard."

Christine made no reply. She sat motionless, staring up at him with eyes full of tears. Skinny looked down at her and sighed. He put his arm around her again and spoke softly.

"Christine, you're only a little girl, you shouldn't be thinking such grown-up thoughts yet."

"But I love you," whispered Christine, and she buried her face on his shoulder and cried. Skinny gently patted her hand.

"Now, before the others start to worry about us, I really have to tell you what I have to say. You ready to hear it?"

Christine sat up and nodded, wiping her tear-stained face and runny nose with her sleeve, letting all the dignity she was so proud of fall off like a cloak, leaving only a little weeping child, who was, in truth, much more pleasing to behold.

"Christine," said Skinny, "the truth is that the boy we just rescued is not your brother. He can't be."

"Why?" asked Christine.

"Because," here Skinny paused, and took a deep breath, "because, I am."

Chapter 12

The Company Parts

Christine sat still for a moment, too stunned to move. Skinny looked at her for a while, and planted a gentle kiss on her brow. Then he stood up.

"Shall we go and join the others?" he asked after deliberating over what to say.

Christine shook her head.

"Why didn't you tell me before?" she finally asked in a choked whisper.

"I know I should have," said Skinny, leaning dejectedly on a tree, and playing with its bark, "and now I'm sorry I didn't, but there were reasons, which still haven't all together disappeared. And I wanted to get to know you first, you know, I haven't seen you in person since you were four years old."

"Who am I, then?" asked Christine. "You've knocked my world right out from under me."

"Your name is Christine Conklin, and you were born in New York."

"Then I'm an American?" she asked in her gentle British accent.

"Yes. You were born to Luke and Christine Conklin about three years after me. They died within a few months of each other when you were almost three. Do you remember them at all?"

Christine shook her head again, too bewildered to try to remember. "We didn't have any living relatives that I knew of, except one aunt who lived in London," Skinny continued, "and since that seemed very far away, I tried to support you as best I could. That was why I started along my crooked path. Then there was the day I met Little Joe. In the story I told the rest of the guys, I left out the fact that, after a while of being with Little Joe, I figured I couldn't hang on to you, and really be part of the gang at the same time.

"So, after proving myself worthy of being a crook under Joe's command, I asked him if I could have leave to go to England, to leave you with our aunt, telling him that I could be a much better asset to him, without having an extra mouth to feed. Reluctantly, Joe let me go. Before we left, he made me swear to come straight back, without you, and not breathe a word of being in cahoots with him. He made it very clear to me what he would do to me if ever I broke my word, and let me tell you, he had me scared. But what scared me the most is that he threatened to harm you if I did not obey completely. His connections are far reaching."

Christine was beginning to understand.

"When we finally got to England, on a plane flight financed by Little Joe himself, I discovered that our elderly aunt had passed away, and she had no relatives in London. I knew I couldn't go back to New York with you, or Joe would cut my throat, and you would be in serious danger. So I decided to enroll you in a place I found in the heart of London. I instructed the president of the school to give you every comfort possible, and said I would send him a check regularly. I also told him never to tell you that you had a brother, because I didn't want you to know about me, since I was going to be a criminal from there on.

"I managed to send in the payments so you could stay in school, 'cause Little Joe gave me a reasonable share of our profit, for a kid my age. As you got older, I found it harder and harder to keep my eye on you. I learned a few facts, like what you were starting to look like, from the Dean of the school, but he didn't seem to like you much, and his descriptions weren't much help. I also learned that you were developing a somewhat proud disposition. From what I heard of you, I figured you were pretty much like me.

"Going back to New York City with you was a mistake. Little Joe threatened to harm you if I didn't cooperate with him, just as he did years ago. You didn't notice it, but that night on the railroad tracks, he had his gun pointed straight at you, not at Sally."

Christine sat, staring at the ground, only half listening to Skinny. Her mind was reeling in circles, and she couldn't get her emotions straight. Skinny had paused for a moment, and looked at her. Christine at last noticed that they did have the same color eyes, and almost the same color hair, and even the shapes of their faces were similar. She wondered why she hadn't seen it before.

"When I left Joe's gang," continued Skinny, "I still kept my eye on you. I got a job in Kansas just to keep you fed and clothed, but I was growing uneasy about you. I figured it was my duty as your only living relative and guardian, to come find you, and claim you. I knew it'd be a big shock to you, finding out you had a brother all of a sudden, and being taken away from everything you knew. It was a delicate situation, and I really didn't know how to handle it.

"I wondered about it for a long time, and asked the advice of the widow I was boarding with. She said I should go to you and tell you the truth. She's a great lady. She was pretty young for a widow, and very beautiful. I still keep in touch with her, and I've written to her about you since I've really gotten to know you. Anyway, I was still debating about my course of action, when, a guy I knew in Kansas, who had a cousin at your school, told me about you getting kicked out. I realized I hadn't sent the money for you in a while, and I figured that they had used this as an excuse to boot you out. I had to find you right then and there, so I said goodbye to the widow, and came out here as fast as I could. I traced you as far as Manchester, and met you in the convent. I hadn't seen you since you were three, and I must admit that when I first saw you, I thought you were the prettiest girl I'd ever seen."

Christine smiled softly, flattered by such a compliment from Skinny, but even as she smiled, she realized that her reasons for liking Skinny were all changed. She now had a reason to really love him, but in a different way. It was a much more permanent and holy type of love; the love of brother and sister. She wondered how she could have been so silly as to have a crush on him, and her cheeks grew rosy with shame and embarrassment as she thought of it all.

Then her embarrassment turned to anger; anger at Skinny for leading her along in her silly daydreams, laughing at her behind her back, (so she thought), and never telling her until she had made a complete fool of herself in front of the whole company, and leaving her broken-hearted in the ruins of her dreams.

"You understand everything, don't you Christine?" asked Skinny, misunderstanding her dazed look.

"Oh yes," said Christine quietly, "I understand."

"Good," smiled Skinny, "then let's go tell the others that ..."

"I understand that you're a cruel, brutal, detestable, conceited, wretch!" blazed Christine, springing to her feet, her eyes ablaze, her whole body racked with passion.

Skinny stepped back, as though he had been struck.

"How could you lead me along like that, encouraging me to fall in love with all your idiotic, disgusting, charm, knowing you'd eventually have to tell me the truth! I shudder to think what you think of me now, a silly, juvenile, boy-crazy baby most likely! Well, I'll have you know that I've never loved a boy before I loved you, and I doubt I'll ever love again. I bet you like the thought of me, never having a life's love, just because you wanted to see how ridiculous I could be! I can't stand to even look at you!"

She paused for a moment, trying to get her breath, still quivering with anger. After the pause, in which they stared at each other silently, Christine composed herself into her dignified air again. She smoothed back her disheveled hair, and adjusted her skirt. Then she turned back to Skinny, and said in a voice coated with ice, "Goodbye, Skinny Conklin, you won't be seeing me again."

She turned and fled without looking back. Skinny stood in silent dismay, watching helplessly at her wish to disappear from his life. He couldn't give chase. He knew his sister by now, and knew that reasoning wouldn't work at this juncture. She needed to be alone.

He slowly sunk back onto the bench, and buried his face in his hands. He realized now that he had been foolish to wait so long to tell her. In truth, he hadn't really noticed that Christine thought she was in love with him until just now. He had realized it too late.

He wondered what she would do. He supposed she'd wander around the park until she had cooled off. Then he began to wonder if she'd do something drastic. He'd heard about the fury of a woman scorned. He tried to think like Christine. Her heart was broken, or so she thought, so she didn't really care what she did, unless it was to show Skinny that she didn't care for him.

She might run off to the South Seas, or even turn herself into the police for kidnapping the Professor's hired boy. He then wondered why he had to have such a passionate, touchy, emotional sister. He subconsciously realized that if Sally had been in her place, she probably would have been overjoyed to find she had a brother, and think Skinny a great jokester for keeping it from her. Sally wouldn't be in any way sad, because she wouldn't have had a crush on him in the first place. Sally was the type that didn't fall in love. She considered life one big game, and whether she won or lost didn't matter to her, it was just about playing the game well and honorably, and having a lot of fun.

Skinny wondered if he wished Christine were more like Sally. He decided he didn't. Christine had to be herself, just like he had to be himself, and Sally couldn't possibly be anyone but Sally.

Skinny supposed he'd better go after Christine soon. Though he couldn't reason with her, he could still keep an eye on her, and make sure she stayed out of trouble. He wondered how he could possibly ...

"Freeze!" said a deep, croaky voice behind him, and he felt something like the muzzle of a gun in the pit of his back. "This is Little Joe, I've got you covered."

"Hey, Sally," said Skinny, turning round on the bench to face her. She was wearing her 'hood' face, in which she stuck out her bottom lip, and she had her forefinger sticking out to form a gun.

"What's up?" she asked, bending over and leaning her elbows on the back of the bench.

"I've lost her, Sally," said Skinny, "she's gone beyond my reach, and I'm left alone."

Sally straightened up and gazed off into the distance, at Christine wandering among the trees on the far side of the park.

"That's beyond your reach?"

"Her heart has been broken, Sally. And I can't mend it."

"Well if you two aren't the perfect example of fools, I don't know who is," laughed Sally. "Imagine all this fuss over a teenage girl's silly crush. And you take it so seriously!"

"Sally, go away!" said Skinny, "you don't even know why she's upset. It's the sort of thing you wouldn't understand. You're not that kind of girl."

Sally stared at him in silence.

"I ... I guess I'm sorry, Sally," said Skinny after a long pause, "I've just had a rough time of it."

"That's okay," said Sally, her smile returning. "After all, you're right. I'm not boy-crazy, nor do I want to fall in love. I ain't romantic at all, just plain boring."

At this Skinny laughed, in spite of his troubles. "You, boring? Sally Keenan, there are thousands of adjectives I could use to describe you, and not all of them complimentary, but 'boring' is definitely not one of them. Sometimes you come up with the strangest things."

"Well, whether I'm boring or not," said Sally, "I don't think you should make such a huge thing out of nothing. Christine will get over it."

"No, she'll hold on to this anger and regret for a long, long time, if I know her. You see Sally it's a lot different than you think. I haven't jilted her. I told her something that I should have told all of you a while ago."

"Skinny, don't go through the whole dramatic routine again, I know you're her brother."

Skinny looked at her in amazement. "How did you know?"

"Oh, different things made it clear. I keep my eyes open. I knew you and Becky had a secret which involved Christine. And don't you realize how much the two of you look alike? And you never seemed to notice when she started making goo-goo eyes at you, which was dumb of you, and well, everything adds up."

Skinny nodded. He was too befuddled by all the events of the past hour to really listen. He felt amused, ashamed, confused, guilty, and impatient.

"Now, come on back to the rest of us," said Sally laying her hand gently on his bowed head, "Christine will come back on her own."

Skinny stood up, and looked off in the direction Christine had gone. She was now out of sight. He sighed, and turned to go with Sally.

"Hey, did you hear the news?" asked Sally as they made their way back up the hill, "that kid you rescued is actually one of Becky's friends from the orphanage."

"What?"

"Yeah, he's the one who promised to marry her, his name's Jack. Apparently the Baron arranged for the Professor to keep him. Pretty funny how things work out, isn't it?"

Skinny nodded again. His mind was reeling like a whirlpool. Sally's voice was making his head hurt. He wondered if he was going crazy.

"Sally, I've got to get out of here," he said, running his fingers through his long hair.

"I figured you'd want to," answered Sally quietly.

"Well, I've got to. I can't go after Christine now, it'll only make things worse. Explain it to Becky and Clarence, and tell Clarence he's been the best buddy I've ever had. So long, Sally."

He held out his hand and Sally took it. "Best of luck to you, Skinny. Look us up if you're ever in a jam."

He turned, and headed in the direction of the still quiet Professor's house.

"Skinny, where will you go?" Sally called after him.

Skinny turned around and shrugged. "Anywhere, everywhere. Maybe nowhere. Good-bye."

* * *

About two weeks later, Christine, looking a bit paler and a good deal older, kicked open the door of her hotel room, struggling with several unruly grocery bags and a hat box. She set the bags on the night stand, gathered the things she had dropped, and then threw herself face down on the bed, and began to cry. She had done a lot of crying since the Company parted ways. Now more than ever she wished for Sally's reassuring smiles, and undignified ways. The money she had had with her when she ran off was almost spent. She had been very thrifty, and gone hungry several times, but still the money was running out. The hotel bill was what had mostly depleted it, though the rates in the little Manchester hotel to which she had moved were very good.

Having finished her cry, she stood up, blew her nose, and began to see about dinner. She opened the rather beat-up hat box she had entered with, and pulled out half a grilled cheese sandwich. On the first day she had been separated from the others, she had found the hat box in a garbage can outside a fancy clothing store. It was slightly scuffed, and no longer wanted, so she followed her 'Sallyish' instincts, and took it home. It now doubled as her purse and doggy bag when she ate out, for she had quickly learned not to waste a single morsel of food. She liked the impression people got of her when she went about with it, for it appeared that she had just come from a high class store, and was flaunting her purchase.

Now she emptied out of it all the valuables she'd collected within the past few days, among them the remaining money she possessed, just a little under ten pounds.

She stared at the coins in her hand for a moment, and wondered how far they would get her. She wondered how hard it would be for a fifteen-year old girl to get a job in Manchester. She supposed the only way to find out was to go looking for one.

She slipped the almost-ten-pounds into her pocket, and fixed her hair in the small bathroom mirror, trying to do it in a certain way so she'd look older. Finally having to be satisfied with a lop-sided bun, she locked her room, and went to take her chances with the outside world.

She walked around the town, looking for a nice place to ask for a job, until her feet felt ready to fall off. Finally, as she was just about to turn back and return to the hotel, she stopped in front of the Manchester Zoo, which she had passed many a time, and always wanted to look into. Now she noticed a large sign was hooked to the gate, with big red letters that read, "Help Wanted." She wondered what sort of job one would get at a zoo.

"Well, can't hurt to try," she said to herself, as she approached the ticket booth.

"How much for a ticket?" she asked, silently praying that the nice man who sold them would be satisfied with the little she had.

"Ten pounds," came the dreaded reply.

"Well, I'm here to see about that help wanted sign, so does that give me a discount?"

"'ow much of a discount did you 'ave in mind, little lady?" asked the man, whose heart had already gone out to her pitiful looks and manner.

"How about a little under ten pounds, and a Hail Mary offered for you?" asked Christine, desperately trying to imitate Sally's methods as closely as possible.

"That's more than enough," said the man kindly. "In fact, how 'bout two 'ail Mary's, you keep your money, and we'll call it h'even."

Christine thanked him profusely, and skipped inside. She figured she'd have a look around first.

For a very pleasant hour, she chattered with monkeys, studied the seals, and stared at giraffes till her neck got stiff. Then she came to a large cage, with many people in front of it. She squeezed through the crowd, till she came right up to the cage bars.

Inside there was a shallow pool, and some flat rocks lining the bottom of the cage. And in the pool, all on top of each other and disorganized, were about six or seven, bumpy black crocodiles. Christine had never seen a live crocodile before, and the sight of them made her feel quite sick. She looked at the plaque in front of the cage which read "African Crocodiles, newly imported."

She decided then and there, that she didn't want to have anything else to do with crocodiles, for just the sight of them and their terrible jaws made her blood run cold. She glanced at them one more time in disgust, and as she did so, her eyes opened wide with amazement.

In the pool, one of the crocodiles had just surfaced, and was crawling up the bank. He was by far the biggest of them and his huge bulk and awful teeth would have made anyone look twice. However, it was not the size or grandeur of the beast that Christine was staring at so incredulously. In fact, she was beginning to feel a bit faint. She had glimpsed something as the thing had come out of the water, and she desperately needed to see it again.

"Come on, you brute, turn 'round," she whispered, standing up on tip-toe.

As if he had heard her, the great beast slowly began to turn. After what seemed an age to the impatient Christine, its horny head came into view, and as it did, her heart seemed to stop beating.

There, in the center of what might be called the thing's forehead, was an intricate yellow mark.

Clarence left the airport with a sigh. He had just seen Becky and Jack off on a plane to Paris, where Jack had a few family friends, and where they'd be safe from the Professor.

Now he was alone in Manchester, except for Christine, and he had no idea where she was. When the Company had split up that awful February day, he and Sally had made an agreement that they would do their best to get the Company back together again. Sally had insisted on going after Skinny, saying she had more chance of catching up with him than with Christine. Clarence had reluctantly agreed, secretly wondering how in the world he was going to reason with the unreasonable Christine.

But he had agreed, and Sally had left for New York, where they learned Skinny had gone, and now with Becky gone, he was left alone.

He felt worried when he thought of being alone in a strange country with Christine. He had never really made an opinion of Christine, she had just been there, and that was it. Everyone else in the Company he had great feeling for; Skinny he admired and imitated even though he sometimes didn't understand him, Becky he thought was cute and abstract, and Sally he worshiped for her bravery and nerve.

He had thought a lot about Christine in the days since they had parted. He had been staying with Jack and Becky, who weren't much fun since they were so little, and so wrapped up in each other, and spoke mostly French or German.

Clarence had come to the conclusion that Christine was pretty similar to her brother. She was hard to read, though a good deal more emotional and dramatic than Skinny. And she was the kind of girl that needed to be looked after. She wasn't like Sally, who could take care of herself through any kind of trouble. Christine needed someone to depend on, and Clarence began to like the idea that he was that someone for the time being.

Here his ponderings were cut short by a cabman asking him if he wanted the use of his services. Clarence accepted, feeling angry with himself for standing around and daydreaming instead of trying to find Christine.

"I guess I'm in the same boat Skinny was in last July, when he set out for Manchester to find his kid sister. Now I'm looking for her."

He asked to be let off at an area populated by hotels, and at the first one he saw, he inquired if Christine was staying there. The young clerk remembered that a girl fitting her description had come in about two weeks before, and asked how much the rooms were. She had left when she heard the price, looking discouraged.

"I wouldn't have remembered her for so long," said the clerk with a grin, "except that it struck me how depressed she looked, and how pretty at the same time. If she's your girl, then congratulations, pal."

Clarence left feeling even more confused. It had never occurred to him that Christine was pretty. He thought about it for a minute, and decided that she was, in reality, a pretty good looking girl. He wondered about what the clerk had said about her being 'his' girl. The thought of that made his heart beat faster, though he didn't know why.

He next began to traverse the hotels that weren't as high-class, judging by the amount of money he thought Christine had with her. As he kept asking around for her, Clarence began to wonder why he hadn't noticed Christine before. Those that he met that had seen her always described her as a "pretty little thing" and he began to think so himself. Then he began to wonder if perhaps the reason he had never thought much of Christine, was because she had never noticed him. All wrapped up with love of Skinny and jealousy towards Sally, she'd hardly ever noticed the slim, black haired, brown eyed, freckled faced boy that she had been with for so long.

Then Clarence thought of her proud, regal air and her scorn of pretty much everything that he was interested in. She thought herself too high and mighty for the likes of him.

He was now walking along dejectedly, not asking anybody about her anymore, hardly noticing where he was. Then suddenly, a voice broke into his thoughts.

"Laddie, is your name by any chance Clarence?"

Clarence looked up. He was slightly surprised to find himself in front of the Manchester Zoo. A man had just come out of a ticket booth nearby, and was standing in front of him.

"Yes, my name's Clarence, what do you want?"

"Well!" said the little man, beaming with joy, "well, ain't it a small world after all! I'm so glad you've come, and you look just like she said you would."

"She?" cried Clarence. "Who was she?"

"A little miss that went by the name of Christine," said the man, "and she was a pretty thing, too. She told me to keep an eye out for you, and I 'ave, just as good as you please."

To his surprise and gratitude, Clarence leaped into the air, and knocked his heels together with a whoop.

"Well, I see you know who I'm talking of," grinned the man, "or else you've just 'ad some sort of attack."

Clarence laughed. "Tell me!" he said, "where is Christine?"

"She left here in a great hurry about ten minutes ago, to look for you, and said she was headed for the hotel on James Street."

"James Street, got it," said Clarence, and shot off at a dead run, leaving the ticket officer feeling very helpful and happy.

As he ran along at full speed, Clarence's mind was working faster than his legs. He wondered why Christine had been at the zoo, and how she'd had the money to get in for a pleasure excursion, if she was staying at a cheap little hotel.

Then, a sudden thought struck him, and the impact of it was so hard that he came to a total stop, right in the middle of the sidewalk.

"She wanted me," he said aloud, as though to assure himself that it was true. "She wanted me, not Skinny, or Sally, or anybody else. She doesn't know the others have left, and if it is really important, she might have asked for Skinny, but no! She wants me!"

He leapt into the air again, wondering why he felt so joyously happy. He flew down James Street at break neck speed, and slid to a stop in front of the hotel, just as Christine entered the door to the stairway.

"Hey, Chris!" he shouted, barreling in the door and through the lobby, "hey Chris, I've come for you!"

The stair doors flew open, as Christine bounded back down the steps. "Clarence!"

Her voice was high and shrill, and edged with all the care and worry she had been living with. Her voice shook a little too, as though she was fighting back tears.

They met in the middle of the lobby, and before he could fully realize what he was doing, Clarence had thrown his arms around her. To his amazement Christine made no protest. She buried her face on his shoulder, and began to cry and laugh at the same time. They hurried over to the stairs, and sat down on the bottom step, closing the door behind them.

"Now," he said, "suppose you tell me what this is all about."

"Oh, Clarence," said Christine with a shuddering sigh, and a quivering lip, "I've missed you so much."

Clarence blushed. "Well, why did you run off then?"

"You know why."

Clarence nodded. When he had been told, he saw for the first time, how much Skinny and Christine looked like each other. Even the way they were sad was similar.

"Why can't you just forgive Skinny, and be happy he's your brother, and find someone else to like the other way?" he suggested, though he knew before the words were out of his mouth that he made her feel silly.

"I will never fall in love again," said Christine, staring straight ahead, stolidly.

Clarence sighed. "Well, what did you want to see me about?" he asked.

Christine's face suddenly became animated again, as the memory of her discovery came back to her.

"Oh, Clarence!" she cried, "you'll never believe what's happened! I was at the zoo today, and there are some new crocodiles that have just been imported. And one of them, has the treasure mark on it!"

Clarence leapt to his feet. "Holy Mackerel!" he cried, "come on, let's go!"

A few minutes later, the ticket agent happily admitted two very excited children into the zoo, and, despite many earnest protests, received more than enough money from Clarence to compensate for Christine's lack.

"Now, Christine," said Clarence as they ran towards the cage, "you're sure it's the right crocodile?"

"Oh, Clarence, how many crocodiles go around with intricate yellow marks on their heads?"

Clarence laughed. When they reached the cage, he affirmed that it was the right animal, and the two of them hugged, and whooped, and cried, and laughed, until a few people in the crowd were considering calling the authorities.

After some hasty planning, they decided to return to the hotel, and there decide in secrecy what to do.

"Too bad we can't see the mark clearly enough from here outside the cage," Clarence remarked as they walked away.

* * *

Skinny emptied his glass in one swig, and sat staring at the empty cup. His thoughts were far away, and jumbled together. His brain couldn't function properly. He glanced at his watch and found it was almost one o'clock in the morning.

He was seated at a booth in a tiny bar, in the heart of the New York slums. There were no windows in the bar, and in the wee hours of the morning, it was not heavily populated.

Skinny had been in the same position, in the same booth, for hours.

He was desperately trying to sort out his mixed up feelings. He was annoyed with his sister for being so flighty, and at the same time he felt sorry for her, and guilty about making her so upset. He thought about Sally's light-hearted view of the situation, and wondered if they were really handling it the best way. He knew Sally made light of everything, even death, and yet this time she could be right.

For a moment his thoughts rested on Sally. That crazy, bizarre, happy, funny Sally. She certainly was food for thought. Then he wondered again, as he had so many countless times in the last few weeks, what he should do about Christine. He could go back to England, and beg her to stay with him, and they could settle down. Then he wondered where they would settle down, whether or not she was still in England, and what to do about the other members of the Company.

If they did set up housekeeping together, what sort of job could he get to keep Christine provided for? And how would he find her if he went back and found that she had left England? His head ached from all the wondering.

He buried his face in his hands, resting his elbows on the table, and tried to stop thinking.

"Look, buddy, why don't you go back to the chick you're brooding over, and make up, or if that's out, find yourself another one?" said a voice above him. Skinny looked up at the waiter, who was looking very sympathetic while energetically chewing gum.

"Thanks, but I'm okay," said Skinny, though he knew only too well that he wasn't.

"Well, just remember, my advice," shrugged the waiter, "and cheer up."

Skinny nodded, paid his bill, and stood up. As he started toward the door, he noticed for the first time, a small figure wearing a trench coat, seated at a corner table. The person was wearing a hat, pulled down low over the eyes, and the coat collar was turned up so Skinny couldn't see the face. He supposed the stranger must have come in while he was deep in thought. As he made his way past the tables toward the exit, he could feel the eyes of the stranger following him. At the door he turned round, and made eye contact, not liking the idea of being watched. For a second he saw the flash of clear blue eyes, then the stranger turned and the face was concealed again.

When Skinny had left, the waiter approached the mysterious figure. "Can I get you anything?" he asked, bending down, trying to make sure that there really was a human inside the coat.

"I'll have Sarsaparilla," came a croaking voice from deep within, "and a little information about that kid who just left."

Skinny made his way from the bar, pulling his jacket closer about his shoulders. The night air was biting, and a deep, penetrating fog hung close about him, sinking into his hair and clothes, and chilling him to the bone.

He walked slowly down the alleys, not really knowing or caring where he was going, not even noticing that he was gradually heading into the worst parts of New York.

Once he thought he heard footsteps following him, but when he stopped to listen, the noise of them ceased. Then his weariness and sorrow began affecting him, so that his eyes played tricks with the moonlight, and his ears heard unearthly sounds. For a while he heard a light patter of feet behind him again, and they sounded strangely familiar, though he couldn't quite place where he'd heard them before. Then they were replaced by the sound of heavier feet, like those of a grown man. Then these too passed out of hearing.

When he turned around once, he thought he glimpsed a light figure dash into the shadows, and he fancied he heard the whisper of a coat rubbed against a wall. He put his hand to his throbbing head, trying to think straight.

His head cleared a little. He suddenly began to wonder if he was really being followed, and if so, by how many and for what purpose. He remembered what it was like, being a crook on the scent of a rich victim. He wondered if he was now on the other side of the spectrum, and hoped that whoever it was behind him was as nervous and truly gentle as he had been long ago.

He turned again, and then began to walk faster. Almost immediately, he heard the steps behind him start again, quicker this time. For a moment he heard heavy footsteps, and then he fancied he caught again the light patter of other feet. Were there two of them?

Finally he decided to stop fleeing, and fight. He was coming up on the sharp corner of an old building, along which ran a thin alley. The roof of the building was long and low, and for a moment he considered climbing up and making an attack on his pursuer from above, but from the sound of the steps behind him, he doubted he'd be able to get up before he was caught.

Leaving himself in plain view, he swerved aside, and went behind the jutting wall, leaving the impression that he had turned into the small alley. Once out of sight, he flattened himself against the wall, and waited for whatever was coming. He realized that his footsteps had stopped suddenly, and if his pursuer was alert, his stop would undoubtedly be noticed. However, the approaching steps continued towards him, and he held his breath, waiting to spring.

His right hand clenched into a fist, and he raised it up, so he'd get the stranger on the top of the head, and be able to bear him down. Then, as he always had to do, he screwed himself up mentally to deliver the blow. But the blow never fell. The footsteps stopped only a few feet away. Skinny waited for a moment, holding his breath. Finally, after what seemed an impossibly long time, he cautiously peeked around the corner. For a moment he saw an awful face, not an inch away from his own, and then felt a dull pain in his head. He looked at the ground, and it suddenly flew up to meet him, and hit his brow with a staggering force. The whole world swam and reeled before his eyes. He felt something sticky running down his face, and his temples throbbed so loudly he almost didn't hear a voice say,

"Stupid kid, I taught you everything you know."

Skinny got a whiff of a strong, and yet somehow faded cologne, and with it the scent of cigarettes. He would know that smell anywhere. Many a time it had haunted his dreams, and now it was here to haunt even his waking hours, and transform them into a nightmare without hope of an awakening.

"Little Joe," he thought, all hope fading within him. "I'm a goner."

"Well, my pretty companion," growled Little Joe, "I see you've returned. You must have thought this town pretty safe, once I was put away, and that thanks to you. That little devil Keenan once said I didn't like traitors. She was right, and now you're gonna pay."

Skinny didn't struggle. Now his perception and thinking were clear again, indeed, clearer than usual. Though he was fully aware of the deadliness of his situation, he was hardly listening to Little Joe. His mind was far away, repeating acts of Faith, Hope, Love and most earnestly, an Act of Contrition. He was grateful now to Sally, for so earnestly instructing him in matters of faith.

When he had made himself as ready as he could for death, he began to think of the other members of the Company. He hoped they would think of him fondly, once he was gone, and he wished he had made things right with Christine.

Then he thought of Sally's words, "if ever you're in a jam, don't forget to look us up." It was almost the last thing he had heard her say. Now he wished he could hear her again, talking nonsense as she usually did, or hatching one of her bizarre plots.

He wasn't really afraid of death. He had known pain before, and was at heart a brave lad. He hoped his Maker would have mercy on him for all his mistakes and failures throughout his life. Sally had spoken endlessly on the subject of God's mercy to repentant sinners, and now he tried to recall every word she had uttered.

As these thoughts flew through his head in much less time than it takes to write down, Little Joe had made a few more gloating remarks, as well as a summary of his escape from prison, to which Skinny paid little heed.

Then, behind Little Joe's head, he thought for a moment he glimpsed a dark figure balancing precariously on the ridge of the roof of the old building, high above him. He figured his thinking and sight were going batty, for he could tell that the cut on his forehead was deep, and the loss of blood was beginning to make his head swim again.

Then he heard a sound that made him feel slightly sick. Little Joe had whipped out his switchblade. For one dreadful moment, Skinny felt terribly scared. He'd never died before. He shut his eyes, and stopped himself from thinking. His fear was gone. He would accept his fate as bravely as Sally would.

He lay still, waiting, for what seemed a century. Since his eyes were closed, his other senses were sharpened, his hearing clear and distinct. He noticed that Little Joe's breathing was slightly strained, and every few minutes he started coughing. After a moment, he thought he heard a vague scraping noise far above him, higher than Little Joe, and slowly getting louder. It was the sound of someone sneaking along, and having trouble keeping quiet. He wondered if it could be a rodent of some kind creeping along the roof tops, for once he heard the sound of a sliding shingle.

Then suddenly, he heard a cry. It was high, piercing, and utterly wild. He felt it was the cry of some wild beast before it pounces, and yet at the same time, it seemed familiar to him. Almost at the same instant the cry rent the foggy air, he heard a muttered curse of surprise and anger from Little Joe, followed by a sickening thud. He felt Little Joe's weight fall across him limply, stifling him.

Then, just as he slipped from consciousness, he felt the weight pushed off him, and heard an urgent little voice hissing in his ear.

"Skinny, this is the last mile, you've got to get up and come with me. Just get out of this alley, and then you can collapse."

He vaguely felt two arms grasp his shoulders, and with difficulty, pull him to his feet. When he opened his eyes, he found he was leaning on a small figure with a hat pulled down low over the eyes, and he recognized it as the stranger from the bar, though the trench coat was gone and the hat was muddy and smashed, and fell down over the figure's eyes, so the person had to tilt their head back to see.

"Here, Skinny, just lean on me and try to make your feet move," said the stranger, and as he heard the voice, Skinny realized with joyous surprise that his wish had been granted.

"Sally, how did you--?" asked Skinny dazedly, trying to speak through a lip which he discovered was swollen and bloody.

"Hold it down till we get out of here, I'll tell you the story later."

"I'm not sure how far I can go," said Skinny, putting a hand to his bloody head. "I'm not exactly as fresh as you, Sal."

"Well, we've got to clear out of here," answered Sally, "though I landed on him good, and his head hit the street pretty hard, I'm not sure how long Little Joe will be out."

"Okay, let's try."

"Right, never say die," said Sally.

She let Skinny lean on her as best she could, and together they struggled along the alley.

Sally led him to a main street, and after they had put about two painful blocks between them and Little Joe, Sally let Skinny sink to the ground in front of a well lighted store.

"Okay, now let's see what's wrong with you," said Sally cheerfully, as she sunk down beside him. She pulled his bangs out of his eyes gingerly and surveyed his face.

"Well, you certainly are dented," observed Sally, "but I think you'll glue back together pretty easy. Now wait here, while I go and see about help."

Skinny made no answer. Sally made sure he was still alive, just fainted, and giving him a friendly pat on the head, she skipped off down the street, and into the gloomy midnight world.

Chapter 13

Different Paths of Adventure

"Shhh! Do you want everybody in the city to hear us?" hissed Clarence.

"Shhh, yourself," retorted Christine sulkily, as she made her way carefully down the inside of the fence.

She was almost done scaling the fence of the zoo. It was a difficult task in the dark, and both were laden with cumbersome things. Christine was swathed in a hotel blanket and sheets, and was tangled in a heavy coil of rope. Clarence had a large camera tied around his neck, and was carrying a metal pole. He had already made it over, and stood at the bottom giving Christine directions.

"Here, throw me the rope," he said in a loud whisper.

Christine turned her head, let go of the fence with one hand, and shook the arm that had the rope coiled about it. The rope slithered down to Clarence. Christine then moved one of her feet, and tried to find a lower hole in the chain-link fence. The sheets got in her way, and since she was still only holding on with one hand, she lost her balance, let go, and came tumbling down with a shriek, landing blankets, sheets, and all on top of Clarence.

"Okay, now let's move fast," said Clarence as they picked themselves up. "You okay?"

"If it weren't for these blankets, I wouldn't be," she moaned, rubbing an elbow.

"Come on, we have only five hours till sunrise."

They slowly made their way through the aisles of cages, until at last they stood before the oppressive cage that housed the crocodiles.

"I wonder if zoos have night watchmen," Christine mumbled.

Inside, all was quiet. The night breeze was stirring the dark waters of the pool, and they lapped quietly against the stone. The moon was reflected on the surface, and by its dim light they could see the huge dark shapes that lay in and around the water. The whole scene was eerie and full of foreboding. Christine unconsciously inched closer to Clarence, for through all her blankets she still felt a chill running up and down her back.

"Are you sure you want to go through with this, Clare?" she asked quietly, after they had both stood and stared at the cage in silence.

"Of course," answered Clarence, though his tone had traces of doubt. "Once we get the treasure sign on camera, all our troubles will be over."

"Why can't we just take a picture of him when the zoo is open?"

"They would never let me get as close as I intend to get."

"Well, let's get it over with then," said Christine, untangling all the blankets.

"Wait, we may not need the sheets," said Clarence, as he pulled the camera from round his neck.

"Can you make out which is the right one?" he asked, straining his eyes in the dark.

"No. Get out the flashlight."

Clarence pulled the light from his pocket, and shined its dim glow in the cage. He rested it on each of the beasts' heads for a moment, while Christine stood on tiptoe and anxiously scanned their foreheads.

"There he is!" she cried, as Clarence shone his light into the bright eyes of the crocodile, who lay sprawled on the banks, with his head facing them and his long tail resting in the lapping waters.

"Okay, now we just need to get him to come closer to the bars to get a picture."

"I don't want that awful thing to get any closer," shuddered Christine, "but if we have to, how do you suppose we can get it to come over?"

Clarence considered this problem for a moment. "I suppose we should attract him with something he'll want."

"What do crocodiles eat?" asked Christine. "I mean, besides you." Clarence gave her a sidelong glance, and knelt down, squeezing an arm through the bars.

"What are you doing!?" cried Christine, watching in horror as the great beast turned towards them, and surveyed them lazily through his slanted eyes.

"I think you hit upon a good idea," said Clarence, "that crocodile has gotten his teeth into me before, and maybe the thought of doing it again will attract him. Look, it's working!"

He was right. The great beast slowly began lumbering up the bank towards Clarence's freckled arm with its zigzagging scars that ran from shoulder to wrist, from their last encounter. Christine held her breath, watching the terrible thing approach, and not daring to make a sound.

Though it seemed clumsy and lazy as it lay still, now the crocodile moved with surprising speed. Christine waited for Clarence to draw his arm back to safety, but he didn't.

"Clarence, pull it back!" she cried, when the thing's horny head was only a few feet away.

"We've got to get it close enough," said Clarence through clenched teeth.

They watched as the beast drew nearer and nearer. Then suddenly, it opened its great jaws, revealing countless jagged teeth. Christine gasped in horror at the sight. Clarence gritted his teeth, and held his arm steady.

The beast sprang. Clarence pulled his arm back, but the joint of his elbow got caught in the bars. He twisted his arm and pulled free as the terrible teeth grazed his hand. Christine gave a little shriek. Clarence threw himself backwards, and landed on his back. Two of his fingers were scraped, and bled a little. He was pale, and seemed to tremble slightly, but he gave Christine a reassuring glance, and wiped the blood away on his shirt.

"Quick, the camera!" he cried, springing to his feet.

Christine shook herself, and snatched up the camera, aiming its lens at the mark. Clarence held his breath as she twisted the lens, and leaned as close to the bars as she dared.

"It's too dark, get the light!"

Clarence got the flashlight as fast as he could, and shone it at the crocodile's head, but before Christine could flash the picture, the crocodile turned away with amazing agility, leaving nothing but its tail for Christine to photograph.

"Oh, brother!" Clarence sat down dejectedly. Christine slid to the ground next to him, laying the camera aside, and cupping her chin in her hands.

"Well, now what do we do?" she asked, hoping he wouldn't suggest another bait attempt.

"We need to attract him again."

Christine sighed. "Do you really want to lose an arm?"

"No, let's not try it that way again. These bars are too close together."

"Then what do you suggest?"

Clarence's brow furrowed. He was silent for a moment. "I'm going in."

Christine looked up in disbelief and terror.

"No!" she cried, leaping to her feet. "You'll be killed, for sure!"

"Not if I'm quick enough," answered Clarence, rising also, "and once I am in there, I'll be able to follow him around till I get the picture."

"But what if something happens? I wouldn't go in there for anything in the world, and if you get hurt, what would I do?"

"I'll be careful. It's the only way."

"We should have just told the authorities."

"It's a *secret* treasure, Christine."

Christine stood undecided for a moment. She wondered whether Clarence would go against her wishes. He probably would. Her opinion wouldn't change his mind. She decided that she might as well go along with it.

"Well, okay," she sighed, "but you'll have to be fast."

Clarence sighed with relief. "I'm so glad you agree, Chris. I wouldn't do it if you really didn't want me to."

Christine blushed. "Really?" she asked. "You'd sacrifice the treasure, just to make me feel better? Why?"

"Cause you're a swell friend," answered Clarence, "now let's get moving."

He hurriedly grabbed the camera and ran around the perimeter of the cage. He stopped at the back of it, which was right up against a short wall and some shrubbery. He looked up at the sides of the cage, and estimated them to be about ten feet tall. The bars along the roof of the cage were much wider than the ones surrounding it, almost two feet apart, it seemed. He figured he could get up on the wall on the outside, and swing himself in easily enough. Getting out would be harder. The rock formation inside the cage was higher toward one corner, and Clarence figured that he could stand on it and jump to reach the bars, when he needed to get out, provided he wasn't being chased too closely by a ferocious crocodile.

"Looks pretty high," murmured Christine, who had followed him around the cage, still laden with blankets.

"I can make it," answered Clarence, trying to imitate Skinny's cocky manner.

"Well, here are the sheets, what do you need them for?"

"I hope to use them on the crocodile if it attacks. A sheet thrown over his head or shoved in his mouth or wrapped around his snout should slow him down."

"Oh," said Christine, feeling all the more inadequate to be Clarence's assistant.

"Now, I have to find the easiest way to get in."

"How about the rope?" asked Christine, "it's still over on the other side."

"The rope!" cried Clarence, slapping his hand to his head, "I'd forgotten it! Christine, you're a wonder. I'm so glad you're here."

Christine blushed happily. "I'll go get it," she offered. Clarence, who hadn't for one moment forgotten the rope which he had so carefully packed, smiled after her.

When she returned with it he slung it over his head, and slipped an arm through the coil. He then instructed Christine on how to hand him the camera once he was in, by slipping it through the bars where she stood. When everything was ready, he vaulted onto the wall, and looked down at Christine.

"Clarence, you... you will be careful?" she whispered.

Clarence looked down into her eyes and smiled. He nodded slightly, and without a word, leaned over, and pulled himself onto the bars of the roof.

For a moment he looked down. Christine was shining the flashlight in the cage so he could see, but her eyes followed his every move. Slowly, he crawled from bar to bar, holding with sweaty hands to the slippery metal. Finally, he was directly above the place where the one large rock, almost more like a boulder, made the highest point in the cage. Clarence carefully slipped the rope off his arm, and tied it fast to the bar. When he was certain his knot was tight, he got a firm hold on the loose end, and holding his breath, slipped off the bars. He swung gracefully down, and landed with hardly a sound. The crocodiles were all splayed out on top of each other in the corner near the pool. Clarence started down towards them on tip-toe. He was only a few feet away from them, when he heard a low hiss behind him. He spun round, and saw that the one he was after; the biggest of them all, had been lying in the shadow of the boulder, and was now sneaking up on him.

Christine, who had been shining the light on the crowd of them in the corner, gave a gasp, and directed the flashlight at the approaching beast.

Clarence was now trapped between the largest of the crocodiles, and the whole pack of them. There was no safe way to reach the boulder and the rope. He stood silent for a long moment, keeping his eyes on the big fellow, and listening with all his ears for sounds from the others. Finally, when he could stand the suspense no longer, he began inching towards Christine.

"Get the camera!" he hissed, "and have the sheets ready."

Christine nodded, and pulled the camera from around her neck. As she did so, the glare of the flashlight left the crocodile's face for a moment, and in that briefest moment, he charged.

Clarence had taken his eyes off him to grab the camera, and Christine was first to see the gaping jaws and yellow teeth charging him. She screamed, a high shrill scream, lined with terror. Clarence turned just as the beast reached him, and his face went a sickly white. He sprang aside, and the horrible teeth only made contact with his ankle. Still, the gash was deep, and his stocking was soon stained. He had the wits to spring up on the boulder, out of the thing's reach. There he sat still, his hand pressed to his ankle, and his face growing paler by the second.

Christine stood stunned for a moment. She felt as if she wasn't really awake. This wasn't happening, and she wasn't even there. Her vision became blurry, and for a moment she wondered if she was going to faint.

She had always thought that fainting was a romantic thing that only cultured ladies could do, and she'd wished someday she would, too. Now she knew that fainting was an awful thing you did when the world was falling in around you.

"Christine," said Clarence, and something in his voice brought her back to reality. She suddenly realized the horror of the situation.

Clarence was fading fast. In a few minutes he might slip from the rocks, and then everything would be over. Christine had to act. She wondered what to do. She figured she'd have to go in and save him.

Finally, after a long time of being hidden, the hero in Christine awoke. She hardly noticed it once it was there. She didn't feel any braver, she just knew what she had to do, and she intended to do it. Everything was as clear as day now, and she actually felt better and more alive than usual.

"Clarence, hold still," she said, with an air of authority that made her look very much like Skinny, "I'm coming."

Clarence glanced at her in surprise, but protests, he knew, were useless. He was wondering how much longer his strength would last. He looked at his ankle. The fabric of his stocking was ripped and stained red. His ankle and foot were throbbing, and a numb feeling was spreading towards his knee. Below him, the crocodile lay, waiting to finish him off, as soon as he gave way.

"No!" cried Clarence at it, his voice shaky and desperately fierce. "No, you won't be my death, you won't!"

Christine glanced at him as she scrambled over the shrubs and onto the wall, once again wrapped in sheets.

"Good grief, he's going crazy," she thought, "he's talking to the crocodile."

She stood up on the wall, and leaned forward until she grasped the sides of the cage. Then, with much scrambling, panting, kicking, and muttering, she and the sheets gained the top. She lay on her stomach, looking through the bars at Clarence and his enemy.

"Clare, just hold on another minute!" she cried, "I'm on my way down."

She crawled over to Clarence's rope, and took the end of it. Then she had to maneuver herself into a position where she could slip through the bars. In the process, she got her foot caught in the sheets, lost her hold on the rope, and slipped through the bars with a yelp. She landed on the rocks next to Clarence, and rolled off. Clarence gave a cry, for the crocodile's interest in him had suddenly been diverted by easier game. It started towards Christine, who was still tangled in the sheets.

"Chris, run!" he cried, and leapt off the rocks towards her. As he hit the ground, a groan escaped him. A stabbing pain ran from his right foot all the way up his leg. He realized he could do next to nothing to help Christine, unless by letting the crocodile eat him instead of her.

Christine, on the other hand, was quite in control. As she had rolled off the rocks, she had decided that the time had come to make a decision; either die like the corny Christine of the past, or act fast and bravely as Sally would.

She chose the latter as she hit the ground. Now the horrible beast, the mere sight of which had before made her sick, was charging her, with murder in its eyes. She sprang to her feet, just as Clarence hit the ground.

The crocodile stopped for a split second, as if trying to decide which of them to attack first. Christine took the opportunity, and in one swift movement, loosed herself from the sheets, and while the crocodile was still contemplating Clarence, threw the sheets over its head. Before the thing could realize what had happened, she grabbed the hem of the sheet, and doubled it around his head two more times.

Pulling the flashlight out of her pocket, she gave it a deafening blow on the head, aiming for its eyes.

"Quick, Clare," she screamed, "the blanket!"

Clarence turned and grabbed the blanket which lay on the rocks. It was a heavy quilt, and Clarence could hardly lift it in his weak state. Christine snatched it from him, and succeeded in wrapping it round the crocodile's head several times. Now the beast lay still, except for its tail, which flicked back and forth perilously in the edge of the dark water.

"Chris, be careful!" cried Clarence.

"Wait, we've got to finish this in one fell swoop," said Christine. She tried not to notice Clarence's pale face and stained stocking, for she needed to be calm a little longer.

"Hand me the camera."

Clarence pulled the camera from around his neck. He seemed dazed now, and was slowly leaning down towards the ground. Christine took the camera, and looked down at the crocodile.

"Here goes nothing," she muttered. She hung the camera strap round her neck, set her teeth, and turned to the animal again. This time she approached its back. She had wrapped the blankets and sheets only around its eyes and jaws, and left an opening for the tip of its snout. Now, she wished she'd tied the bonds tighter, for she wondered how long they would hold the thing still. She quickly adjusted the lens. The crocodile was slowly retreating backwards into the pool, wagging its head, and Christine's feet were wet.

"It's now or never," she thought, and reaching up, she pushed the sheets a little way down the brute's forehead. She shuddered at its slimy flesh. But as soon as the mark was visible, she snapped the picture. Almost at that same instant, the thing threw itself backwards. Christine was knocked off her feet, and into the water. She held the camera above her head, and prayed that it stayed dry. The pool was actually only a few feet deep, and she had wriggled out almost before the crocodile was in. She stood panting on the banks for a moment, while the crocodile slid down into the pool, and as the insanity and courage that she had just displayed began to sink in, she felt a bit faint.

"I wonder what Sally would think of me now," she murmured, half laughing, half crying.

She heard a slight thump behind her, and the thought of Clarence shot back into her racing mind. She spun round, and was just in time to see him slide to the ground, and lie still, his eyes closed as in death, at the base of the boulder.

"Oh, Clare!" she cried, the tears starting in her eyes. She ran to him, and looked at his pale face, searching for signs of life. She looked at his swollen ankle, and shuddered.

"Clare, Clare," she pleaded, "you've got to come to and get out of here!"

She dragged, or pushed, or pulled, she was never quite sure how she did it, but she got Clarence back on the boulder, where he began to move his head about.

Then she began to wonder about a good bandage. She spied the sheets, which now lay in the dark water. She supposed the water wasn't very clean, but the sheets would have to do. She crept back down to the water, trying not to attract the crocodiles' attention, and when she reached it, she gently pulled out one of the sheets.

Dashing back to the boulder, she began wringing it out, and ripping it into a few large pieces. She carefully and tightly wrapped Clarence's ankle. She didn't remove his sock, for she knew that if she got too close a look at the gash, she'd probably be sick, and once the whole area was bandaged, it seemed to be a good enough job.

She was just wrapping the last strip of sheet around it and tying it tight to ensure that the bandage stayed on, when Clarence groaned.

Christine looked up, her heart in her mouth. Clarence's face was not half as pale as it had been, and after a few more minutes, he opened his eyes, and pushed himself up on his elbows.

"Hey, Chris, what's going on?"

Christine let out a squeal, and threw her arms round his neck. Clarence blushed, and tried to sit up. Christine helped him, and showed him the bandage.

"That's great," said Clarence, gently touching the wraps, "you've stopped the flow of blood, and I already feel better."

"Great," said Christine, "then let's get out of here."

Once they had managed to get outside the cage, Clarence appeared in no hurry to go get help for his ankle. He sat down, resting against the bars of the cage, while Christine hurriedly gathered the belongings that they'd been able to hold onto.

"Okay," she panted, as she coiled the rope around her arm, "we just need to get out of here, and put you in bed, and then tomorrow we can get this picture developed, and then we can fly to wherever we have to go next and find the treasure. Okay? Now, come on."

"Not yet, Chris," Clarence murmured.

Christine looked at him, puzzled. His face was strangely agitated.

"Chris," he said, "what you just did was the bravest thing I ever saw."

She blushed rosily, and he looked seriously into her eyes. "I think there's no one like you in the world," he said suddenly.

Christine stood staring at him silently, too surprised to speak.

"Chris, I know you think you could never fall in love again," he went on, "but don't you think you could love someone, like me?"

She blinked. She was still struggling with many emotions; fear, anger, panic, and now he was asking her if she loved him. She thought about it for a moment. Of course she loved him, just like she loved all the members of the Company. They were the only family she'd ever known.

But she knew what Clarence really meant. She had convinced herself in the past two weeks that she would live her life without love. All the drama and romance had never gotten her anywhere. But now she wondered about it. A simple kid was asking her if she loved him, and she was a simple girl who didn't know what to say.

Then she realized. All along, when Skinny, her faithful brother, had been the hero, Clarence had always been in the background, yet a hero all the same. She thought of his quiet, thoughtful ways, and his sense of loyalty and honor. Now, for the first time in her life she didn't mind the fact that she wasn't anyone important. She was important enough to him and that was all that mattered.

"Oh, Clare," she whispered. She slowly sunk onto the pavement beside him, and he took her shivering hand in his. His heart was thumping madly, his ankle was throbbing and there was a ringing in his ears, but he was infinitely happy all the same.

The moon, which had gone behind some clouds while Christine had been silent, suddenly shone forth again, and its splendor gleamed down on a certain Manchester zoo, where a handsome young man with a bandaged foot, and a pretty young girl, all dripping wet, were perched outside a cage crowded with crocodiles, and gazing up at the lovely moon, with hearts full to bursting.

* * *

Skinny could feel the warm sun on his face, as he rolled over in bed. He didn't really want to get up. His head hurt, and the bed was beautifully soft and warm. He decided he'd stay asleep a while longer. Then suddenly, into the stillness of his peaceful dreams, there came a familiar voice, breaking into his thoughts with a rude abruptness, and yet not really unpleasant. The voice was far away, and was singing. He could make out the words, "And hurrah, me boys for freedom, 'tis the rising of the moon!" The voice was young and beautiful, though it had a wild tint to it, and was too loud.

The singing drew nearer, and then he heard a loud, violent banging on his door. Slowly, reluctantly, he opened his eyes. As he gained full consciousness, he sighed, and rubbed the long sandy hair out of his eyes. As his hand passed over his forehead, he felt a clean white starched bandage. The spot was sore, and he winced. With that, all the horrid memories of the night before rushed back to him. He sat up in bed with a suddenness that made his head ache.

He glanced around, and found that he was in a small, but nice hotel room. It looked so similar to the ones he had been in before, that he half expected to see Clarence sprawled in the other bed. It however, was empty, and the other members of the Company were miles and miles away. Then he recalled another thing about the night before, which would explain the loud singing, and chattering outside, and the unceasing tattoo being beat on his door. He wasn't alone.

"Hey, you sleepy knuckle-head, wake up!" cried a voice outside his door, followed almost instantly by another rousing chorus of *The Rising Of The Moon*. Skinny put his hand to his throbbing head.

"All right, all right," he hollered back, "keep it down, Sally, I'm coming."

Five minutes later he opened the door, fully dressed, and Sally, who had been leaning against it, fell in.

"Well, little Miss Peaceful," he said, pulling her to her feet, "and to what do I owe the honor of your visit?"

"It was high time you got up," retorted Sally, "you've slept longer than anyone I ever heard of."

"What time is it?"

"Five o'clock."

"Five o'clock?" cried Skinny, "in the morning?"

"No, you ding-bat, in the evening," answered the irreverent Sally. "I had you put in that bed last night at four, and you've slept the whole day away."

"Wow," said Skinny, rubbing his head, "what happened after you fell on Joe like a ton of bricks? And how did you get there in the first place?"

"Well, when the Company broke up, I came out here after you. I tracked you down, and last night I found you in that second-rate bar."

She flopped down in a chair. "I had heard that Little Joe had busted out of prison, and I knew that he knew you were here, so I figured there'd be trouble. When I went to follow you, Little Joe appeared. He was in between you and me, which turned out to be good, since I could keep an eye on both of you. He nailed you, and was about to do something worse, so I ditched my trench coat, which cost a pretty penny, and climbed up the fire escape onto the roof of that building. I fell on him before he ever knew I was there.

"I went and got a hospital to come pick you up. You weren't in too bad shape, and they let you go after about half an hour. I've got a room down the hall, and I've been exploring, and sitting around, and just about going crazy waiting for you to wake up. There, does that answer your question?"

"Yeah, but now I've got another one," said Skinny. "I'm starved, how about breakfast?"

"You mean dinner."

"Right, where is it?"

"It's wherever we can afford to go," said Sally. "We're on a budget now, without Clarence funding us."

Skinny sighed. "I'll pay."

Around seven o'clock that same night, Sally pushed back her plate, and sighed.

"Good chow, don't you think?" she asked.

Skinny nodded.

They had found a little out of the way restaurant that had a live band, and a dance floor, and during dinner, they had caught each other up on the news they had missed. For the moment, the fear of Little Joe went out of their minds. They felt relatively safe in the crowded place.

Sally told him what she knew of the other company member's doings and Skinny told Sally the true story of his and Christine's childhood, most of which Sally had already guessed.

"This widow, whom you lived with in Kansas," said Sally, after a pause, "what did she look like?"

"Why do you ask?"

"Because you've spoken so highly of her that I want to know what she was like."

Skinny thought for a moment. "She was slim, and had dark hair. She didn't smile a whole lot, but when she did, it was worth the wait."

Sally shut her eyes, and smiled, imaging the kindly widow. "How old was she?"

"Pretty young, late thirties I think."

"Do you still keep in touch with her?"

Skinny grinned. "I've written to her about everything the Company has done," he said, "from Africa to New York, from the snowy Alps to foggy England. She's written back too, and she says you sound like an interesting character. She wants me to send her a picture of us all."

Sally smiled. She liked to hear about this woman. Skinny rarely talked about her, but when he did, he seemed more innocent, as though his behavior reflected how she treated him.

"So, we need to work out what we're going to do next," she said, "and since Little Joe is still at large, the first thing to do is go to Confession."

Skinny nodded. Sally always went to Confession when there was a chance she would die in the near future. Though he hadn't been observant of it then, she had gone before that awful night on the train tracks and in the village before they went into the Alps.

Skinny didn't argue with her, and often tried to imitate her in these matters, for he firmly believed that there was a connection between her devout faith, and her heroic courage, fantastic brainstorms, and amazing good luck.

"Okay; and second, we need to find a more secluded hotel," said Sally. "Last night I took you to the first one I saw, but Little Joe will probably look for us in all the nearby ones."

"And what do we have planned for the future?" asked Skinny, "I mean, will we find the other Company members, or just stay here, or what?"

"Well, we have to stay here until we hear from the others, 'cause I don't know where they are," said Sally, "and don't you think staying here, with Little Joe on our trail, is a pretty good way to spend Lent?"

"Well, it is quite a penance. I'd forgotten it was Lent," said Skinny, feeling slightly guilty.

Sally grinned. "Maybe since you forgot, your sacrifices have been made for you. If you reckon it out, Ash Wednesday was the day we left New York for Manchester, remember Becky sneezed the whole flight because the ashes had slipped off her forehead and down to her nose. So if that was the beginning of Lent, then we've only about two weeks left, and then there's Holy Week."

"I wonder where we'll be at Easter," murmured Skinny, "or if we'll even be alive."

Just then, the band struck up a popular new swing dance tune, and a few shy couples wandered onto the dance floor.

"Does it really matter whether we're still alive, just as long as we're ready when it's time to go?" asked Sally.

Skinny nodded.

"You want to dance?" he asked, glancing at the gleaming floor, and tapping his feet to the beat.

Sally's face lit up. She slid from her seat, and took his hand. Their table was at the edge of the dance floor.

They stepped into the middle of the floor with more courage than the other couples. After the swing, the band played a waltz. Skinny slipped his arm around Sally's waist, and she laid her hand on his shoulder. It was strange. They had been so close for the past eight or nine months, planning together, fighting together, almost dying together, and yet now, with something as simple as a dance, they both felt a bit shy.

"What's wrong with you, Skinny?" he asked himself under his breath, "She's still Sally. The only time you've ever been scared of her was that night on the train tracks, and that's all past. She's your friend, nothing more."

Sally was thinking her own thoughts, but she didn't mutter them under her breath; they were far too private for that. After a moment, they fell into step with each other, and the timidity melted away. They began to move more freely around the floor, and the other couples couldn't help but stop and watch them, they made such a charming, and yet contrasting pair.

Sally had a slender grace about her, with her short dark hair, and lightly freckled cheeks, impish nose and clear sparkling blue eyes. Her lips were so red that they gave the impression of lipstick, though Skinny knew it was caused by being chapped.

Skinny, too was an interesting person to study. A tall, slim lad, with waving sandy hair falling almost to his shoulders, his deep gray blue eyes were more sober than Sally's, and possessed a slightly dangerous glint. His pointed nose, and bony jaw; all his chiseled features were the perfect contrast to Sally's more rounded, mischievous look. Skinny could have been described as "devilishly handsome," though his smiles betrayed an innocence and beauty that neither age nor bad company had dispelled.

The leader of the band glanced at his musicians and smiled. Their handsome, dark faces were all grinning at the couple in the center of the floor. The leader turned to his microphone and in a low, melodious voice that only an African-American could boast of, he started in on a popular love song, slowing the dance beat slightly.

Skinny and Sally were completely oblivious of the change, and of all the attention they were attracting. They were looking at each other, and the rest of the world was remote and far away. Slowly the other couples resumed dancing, while the band winked and grinned, thinking on the glory of young love.

Although he was having a pleasant time, there was nothing in Skinny's mind that involved love. He was trying to analyze his feelings. A strange sensation came over him as he met Sally's eyes. It was the first time since he had known her that he didn't feel a pang of guilt when he met her pure, fearless gaze. He wondered why he felt shaky. Slowly, he pulled Sally closer to him, and the gaze was broken. He glanced out over her head, at the shining floor, and wondered where his life was going. He was content, for the present, but he wondered what the future might bring.

Sally's thoughts were more centered on the present. All she could see was his shoulder, directly in front of her, and she moved by trusting his guiding arms. She could see the tear in his dress shirt, which he had come by while wrestling with Clarence after a dinner in Switzerland. It seemed to stand for all the good times they had been through together. Her thoughts, had Skinny known them, would have cleared up the conflict and confusion within him, though they would have surprised him greatly. She glanced up at him, and smiled.

* * *

Christine watched in amazement as the plane glided down onto the runway. Everything looked so strange. There were big, smooth barked palm trees lining the air field, and the sky was immensely blue, and cloudless.

"It sure is different than England," she muttered, "and Africa, and America."

"Yup," answered Clarence. "No place like Trinidad."

Christine sat back in her seat, now that the excitement of landing was over, and closed her eyes. The past week and a half had been almost insane. She needed some time to think it all out.

That night, that wonderful, terrible night when they had taken the picture, seemed like years ago. At the hospital, Clarence's injury turned out to be minor, although it had bled very badly. Once he was properly bandaged, they returned to the hotel. The next morning, they had the picture developed, and to their extreme joy, it turned out that the one Christine had taken was clear and light enough. Christine smiled as she remembered how they had hugged, hopped up and down, and squealed with delight in the film store, not minding the attention they had attracted.

After that, they had decided to pack up and come to Trinidad, and from there try to get some information about coconuts with yellow marks on them, which were last seen on the little island called Tobago. Christine wasn't sure how Clarence was intending to find them, but she figured he had a plan. Now she always trusted in his genius ideas.

It was a long shot, considering Tobago exported many coconuts, but they just had to try.

Once they had collected their scanty luggage, and were standing outside the airport, Christine asked Clarence what his first move was.

"Well, for now we should go drop off our stuff at the hotel," he said, while trying to attract the attention of a cab driver, "and from there we can start planning."

Christine began to wonder if he even had a plan at all, but she let him put her bags in the cab and got in. As they pulled onto the main streets, she was surprised to see traffic driving on the left side of the road.

While gazing out the window at the sunny day outside, Clarence decided it was time to come up with a plan. He had always supposed that if he should ever find the crocodile and see the mark again, that he would return to Tobago, and go back to the place where he had left the coconuts. Now he realized that he had never really expected to find the crocodile again, for it seemed next to impossible to locate one certain coconut, which he wasn't even sure still existed. The coconuts with the marks could have been shipped out long before, and sold. Maybe someone else had found the treasure, and was living off it happily.

"Man, is this a wild goose-chase," he muttered to himself. "The only way we could find that treasure now is by Divine intervention. Dear God, please help us!" He wondered if God wanted him to care about it overly much.

His prayer was interrupted by a gasp that was more like a scream from Christine. They were at a red light, and the car was stopped. He turned toward her, and was just in time to see her slip out her door, and dash off through the stopped traffic.

"Chris!" he cried, sliding across the seats, out the door, and after her. "Wait! What's wrong?" He signaled to the cab driver to wait.

Suddenly, a few cars ahead of him, Christine stopped, stood on tiptoe for a moment, straining to see something over the traffic, and then turned, and sped back towards him.

"Quick, back to the cab!" she cried, grabbing his hand and pulling him along. She pushed him in, sat down beside him, and turning to the perplexed cabman she cried, "follow that big produce truck!"

Clarence looked at her in amazement. She turned to him and laughed at his befuddled expression.

"Clarence, I know you think I've gone crazy, but you've just go to hear me out. I was just sitting here, and started praying that we might find the treasure soon, so that we could get back to Skinny and Sally and everybody. Then, I suddenly looked up, and I saw a big truck, with no roof, and only some fences around its sides and inside there were all sorts of coconuts with yellow markings on them!"

Clarence looked at her in silence, his mouth open. "I'll never doubt the power of prayer again," he murmured. Christine laughed.

"It's just too fantastic," he said aloud, and then suddenly he realized the urgency of their situation. "Driver, if you catch up with that truck, you'll be paid as you never have been before!"

The driver made a u-turn on two wheels, and careened down the street whence the truck had gone. Christine and Clarence knocked heads, as they leaned forward to look out the front window, and it hurt like anything, but neither noticed. After a tense moment or two, the truck came into view. Clarence saw it was a standard produce truck, piled high with wooden crates all containing coconuts, probably on its way to some open-air market.

Once they got behind it, the cab once again began to observe the basic laws of driving, and they tailed the truck successfully for about half an hour. Finally, when they thought they would burst if they had to wait any longer, the truck left the city, and drove for a few minutes on a remote country road.

It pulled onto a large field, covered with straw and dotted with many tents. It drove around the back of the tents to what seemed to be a make-shift loading dock.

The cab driver tried to follow but was held back by a man with a shiny badge who said no unauthorized vehicles were allowed past him. Clarence told the driver to park, and he and Christine got out.

"What should we do now?" asked Christine, blinking in the bright sunlight.

"Let's go into the market place, and try to find a booth selling coconuts. Maybe they'll have them."

Christine nodded, and they plunged into the crowd. The market was like a small city. Everyone was smashed together, buying, selling, jabbering, bargaining, and arguing. There was a booth for practically everything known to man; fruits, vegetables, meat, cheese, wine, clothes, jewelry, toys, knives, furniture, pottery, religious articles, and even a few of the smaller exotic animals.

Christine was tempted to stop several times, her attention caught by beautiful shawls or skirts, or huge pieces of jewelry, or even some strange tropical fruit, that looked as though it might spring up at any moment and bite her.

Clarence stolidly avoided the throwing knives and chattering monkeys in their wicker cages, and kept himself and Christine on their course. After making their way down several rows of booths, Christine saw a booth piled high with coconuts and other fruits. There was an old man behind a pyramid of them, bickering with a lady over the price of a bag of mangoes.

Christine turned and pulled Clarence out of a crowd of ladies, and pointed the stand out to him. Clarence looked at the dwindling pile of coconuts, and supposed that the man would restock pretty soon.

"Let's just wait around and watch," he said.

He pulled the legendary photograph from his pocket, and looked at it intently. He tried to memorize the mark, and stared at it so hard that he could see it with his eyes closed.

"Here, you keep it when we move in, so my hands can be free," he said, handing the photo to Christine.

"Look, he's getting more coconuts!" cried Christine, slipping the picture in her pocket.

The man had turned, and was filling the skirt of his dirty apron with coconuts which he pulled from a large wooden crate. They recognized the crate as being the same kind that was in the truck they had followed.

They saw the man glance at one of the coconuts, then look at it more closely. After a moment he looked at certain other ones, shrugged, and continued working.

"He must have seen the marks," said Clarence, "maybe he'll think they're some sort of brand marking. Come on."

They made their way over to the booth, and scrutinized the fruit for some time, trying to look like they knew what they were doing. The man gave them some curious looks. Two American teenagers so interested in his stand was a little strange, but he dismissed his suspicions and left them alone, for he had other customers to attend to.

"Should we get some mangoes for Sally?" asked Christine, while scanning the many yellow marks. "You know how crazy she is about them."

Clarence smiled, for he liked to be reminded of Sally. Anything that connected them with the other members of the Company was dear to them now. They hadn't realized how close they had all become until they had been separated. Clarence supposed …

"Clare, is that it?" asked Christine excitedly. She pulled the photo out of her pocket, and pointed towards a coconut near the top of the new pyramid. Clarence snatched the photo from her, scrutinized it for a second, and then looked hard at the coconut.

The mark was slightly scuffed and obscured from its trip, but to all outward appearances, it appeared to be the same one. Then suddenly, Clarence had a flash of recognition. A thought returned to him, having been lost by the mental effects of his fever so long ago, and he remembered that The Coconut had been odd, for it was slightly more oval shaped than most of its kind, and more resembled a football.

"That's It!" he cried, forgetting in his excitement to be inconspicuous. Christine gave a squeal, but as they pushed through the crowd which had closed in around them again, Clarence saw an old native woman pick up the priceless coconut and carelessly toss it in her big canvas shopping bag. Then she turned, paid the man, and shuffled off.

Clarence turned to tell Christine, but she was already ducking through the crowds, in hot pursuit of the woman. Clarence was about to start after her, but then went back, snatched up another coconut, tossed a dollar at the man, and followed Christine.

* * *

Skinny stood up. He was beginning to discover that he was bored. He had stayed inside all day, and was getting antsy.

While they remained in New York, Sally and Skinny had worked out a plan that only one of them would go out at a time, and only when absolutely necessary. Nothing had been heard about Little Joe since the night of the attack, but they still weren't taking any chances. Sally had gone out today for groceries, as she had for the past week or two. Skinny paced restlessly around the room while she was out, praying and worrying in turns, and listening for sounds of her return.

He glanced at his watch for the twentieth time, and discovered it was almost three o' clock. He paced over to his bed, and sat down on it. A moment later, he stood up, and paced into the bathroom. There was nothing to do. All the interesting things, such as books, or a deck of cards were over in Sally's room, where they spent most of their time.

After wearily looking at himself in the mirror for a moment, Skinny decided he would sit back down at the small table. He shut off the bathroom light, and started across the floor again. As he passed the door, he stopped. He gazed at it for a moment.

Suddenly, the door flew open, and Sally flew in. She ran into Skinny head on.

"Sally, what's wrong?" cried Skinny, half expecting to see Little Joe come tearing in after her. Sally wrestled herself off of him, and got to her feet. In her hand were a torn envelope and a letter, written in what looked like a child's handwriting.

"He's got her!" cried Sally, pulling Skinny roughly to his feet.

"What? Who's got who?" asked Skinny, pulling the letter out of her hands and looking at it.

"The Baron, he's got Becky," said Sally. "This is a letter from her friend, Jack. He says that Becky was kidnapped by the Baron, on Palm Sunday night. That was two days ago."

Skinny's face set in hard lines. "You said they're in Paris?"

Sally nodded, and as she watched Skinny's face, a slow grin crept over her face. "I'll go pack."

Skinny gave her an appreciative glance, as if saying thanks to her for being able to read his mind. He hurried towards the closet, snatching up his suitcase on his way and tossing it onto the bed. Sally turned and left for her own room, where she hurriedly threw her belongings, few of which were clothes, into her bags, humming happily to herself.

"Finally," she thought, "after two long weeks, we're finally going back into an adventure."

* * *

Christine dodged and ducked through the crowd, trying to be as nimble and light as Sally always was, and feeling more than ever the clumsy side that she had always regretted. She didn't glance back to see if Clarence was behind her, for she knew she must not let the old woman out of her sight for one moment. Even as it was, she could barely keep up with the old thing, who apparently was a seasoned shopper in such crowded market places, and knew how to maneuver.

Then, to Christine's great joy, the old woman stopped to inspect a brilliant array of colorful scarves. Christine squeezed past a crowd of people, and came up beside the woman. As she reached her, she wondered what she had intended to do next. She couldn't steal the coconut, which the woman had rightfully bought with money that was probably pretty dear to her, and she didn't even know whether or not the woman spoke English.

She finally decided not to speak to the woman, but just keep an eye on her, when Clarence sprang up beside her, bearing another coconut.

He approached the woman, and tentatively asked if she spoke English. To his great relief, she did. He explained to her, in the simplest terms possible, that he wanted to trade coconuts, because he liked the funny shape of the one she had bought.

The woman considered for a moment, looked carefully at Clarence's coconut, turning it over in her wrinkly hands, and then she pulled the fateful coconut out of her bag and shook it. It rattled. Christine and Clarence caught their breath, wondering if she would guess their secret and claim the treasure for herself, but to their relief, she simply shrugged, and made the exchange. Clarence thanked her profusely, and before the old woman could change her mind, he pulled Christine back into the crowd.

"Could we look at the jewelry for sale now, Clare?" asked Christine, her attention once more caught by the gaudy display, as they headed back towards the parking areas.

Clarence glanced at Christine, then at the coconut, and laughed. "Chris, darling; wonderful, fantastic Chris, we can look at more jewelry than you can stand, and anything you like is yours. Money is no object."

Clarence regularly forgot that he was already rich.

Christine looked at the coconut, and then up at Clarence.

"Do you know what this means, Chris?" he asked. She nodded, though the reality hadn't really sunk into her yet.

"Does it mean we can go find Skinny and Sally and all, and go live happily ever after in your house in California?"

For answer, Clarence threw his arms around Christine, still clutching the coconut in his right hand, and lifted her off the ground with a whoop.

Chapter 14

The Road to Paris

Sally and Skinny arrived in Paris on a sunny Wednesday morning. They had flown all night, and even Sally was drooping. They collected their luggage in the same routine way that they had so many times before, and headed out into the sunlight outside the airport.

The traffic of Paris looked pretty much the same as it did everywhere else, and Skinny sighed as they joined the throng of waiting travelers. His quieter side disliked having to fight for a cab, while his natural leadership qualities made him frustrated when he couldn't be in command.

Sally usually didn't mind the cab searching that they were doing so often, for she enjoyed seeing which cabman she could attract first. But today she was tired and seemed a bit distracted, so Skinny figured he'd have to do it alone. He was just beginning to elbow his way through the crowd, when a man in the fancy green uniform of a porter for one of the finer hotels approached him, and bowed.

"Excuse me, Mr. American," he said with a thick French accent. "I was told to look for you and the young mademoiselle. Your car is waiting."

"What?" asked Skinny, looking at Sally, who shrugged.

"I think you have the wrong couple, Sir."

"You are mademoiselle Sally, and monsieur called Skinny?"

"Yeah, but …"

The porter smiled and nodded, motioning them towards a fancy car, with "Le Hotel Magnifique" stamped on its sides around some sort of insignia.

"I thought you said we were going to stay in a second rate place," murmured Sally, as the porter took her bags and put them in the fancy car's trunk.

"We were," answered Skinny. He was quite bewildered, and knew he couldn't get a full explanation from the porter's limited vocabulary. Still, he was glad to get a ride without a hassle, so he let himself be helped into the car, and once inside, fell into a brown study.

As they drove along the streets, Sally looked out the windows curiously, wanting to see as much of this new city as possible. She noticed that they were definitely heading in the nicer direction of town, as the hotels kept getting bigger and grander.

"Hey, Mister driver," she asked, "who arranged for us to get picked up, and where exactly are we going?"

The man furrowed his brow in thought, trying to follow Sally's rapid talk. "Ride was arranged by friend."

"Our friend?"

"Oui. Yours. He say you know him, but say we not to tell you until later. Surprise."

Sally shrugged. "Maybe Clarence has found the treasure, and wants to live it up, and surprise us," she said to Skinny.

"I don't know," said Skinny hesitatingly, "wouldn't Clarence have written us if he'd found the treasure? There's something funny going on."

"Well, whoever it is that arranged this, he doesn't mind spending money on us in Paris."

They rode in silence until they reached the hotel, whereupon Sally's jaw dropped, and Skinny ran his fingers threw his hair, and cracked his knuckles at an amazing rate.

"Man, this place is really high class," he muttered as they climbed out. Sally didn't answer. All she could do was stare upwards, and whistle occasionally.

When their bags were unloaded, the driver bowed very politely to both of them, kissed Sally's hand, and drove off. Skinny looked at Sally, who was staring at the hand that had been kissed with some perturbation, as though she didn't know what to do with it. She looked up at him, then up at the stories and stories of the ornate building before them, and shrugged.

"I guess we go in," she said.

Before Skinny could respond, several bell boys, all in immaculate uniforms with shining gold buttons, came rushing out the door. They all clamored in French for the honor of taking their luggage.

Skinny cleared up the argument, and let them take everything but Sally's small bag, in which she kept her most prized small articles, among them, her pocketknives and her diary.

Then, with some apprehension, Skinny and Sally went through the revolving door, and stood, spellbound in the lobby. It was the richest, biggest, grandest place either of them had ever seen.

"Holy cow," murmured Sally, unable to say more.

"I really don't think this is right," said Skinny. "But come on." They hurried down the marble steps, across acres of beautiful carpeting, and over to the colossal front desk. It was taller than Sally, and even Skinny had to stand on his tip-toes to look reasonable.

"Hi, my name is Skinny Conklin, or Mark Conklin, or Skinny Smith, I'm not sure," he said awkwardly. Sally muffled a laugh. She was too short to see the clerk's face, but she could imagine it.

"What I mean is I don't know what name we're registered under, because I didn't make our reservation."

The man stared down at him from his lofty height, and sniffed. "Young boy, I don't think you are in the right place. Au revoir."

"Yeah, I thought we were in the wrong place, too," said Skinny, "but the guy who drove us here said that someone had paid for us, and wanted it to be a surprise."

A light of recognition came into the man's eyes. "What you did say your name was?" he asked.

"Skinny Conklin, or Skinny —"

"Ah, oui, and the mademoiselle," he leaned over the desk to get a look at Sally, who grinned, "she is Sally Keenan?"

"Yes, that's me," said Sally, "but can't you tell us who arranged all this?"

"Oui, that I can," said the clerk, rummaging through the papers on the mammoth desk.

"He said his name could be revealed once you were here. He said to tell you his name as, 'Black Hawk'. Odd name, but he said you would recognize it. He also said that you would know why he is here, and what business he has with Miss Sally."

Sally, indeed, did seem to recognize the name. Her sleepy, somewhat bloodshot eyes popped open. She looked at her nose for one long moment, while the slow beginnings of a smile seemed to play about her lips, and then, with a grace and beauty that Christine would have envied, she fell backwards, and with a small thud, lay spread across the richly patterned carpet.

The clerk, who couldn't see her even when she was standing up, now had to slide himself on top of his desk, and looked down at the unconscious girl in some confusion. He looked questioningly at Skinny, who seemed lost in thought.

"Excuse me," faltered the clerk, "I wonder if … " Skinny suddenly glanced down and saw Sally.

"Hey, Sal!" he cried, and he knelt down and picked her up. There was still the slightest hint of a smile around her lips, but she now lay in Skinny's arms in a dead faint. "We should get out of here!"

He shook her. Sally was immovable.

"Do you want me to call an ambulance?" the clerk asked.

Skinny thought for a moment. Both he and Sally were exhausted from the overnight flight. They hadn't slept a wink.

He shook his head. "No, she'll be okay in a minute. Could you just tell us her room number?" he asked, trying to dig into his pocket for a tip for the clerk, and still keep Sally in his arms.

The clerk handed him the key, accepted the tip gratefully, and directed him towards the elevator.

"Oh," said Skinny, as he started towards the ornate elevator doors, "and could we have another room, preferably next to hers, or down the hall, for me?"

The Frenchman nodded, and started back towards his desk. "Put it on Black Hawk's bill," Skinny called after him.

He entered the elevator with the bellboy and their luggage cart, and tried to look casual, despite his unconscious companion. They were taken up to the thirteenth floor, and showed to a room at the end of the hall.

"Great, a dead end," muttered Skinny as they stopped outside the door.

"Hey, bellboy?" Skinny asked

"Oui?"

"Could you give the clerk a message from me, please?"

The boy nodded, but didn't really seem to understand. "Oh, brother, you don't seem to speak English."

The boy nodded happily, and taking that to be the message he was to deliver, he started off.

"Hey, hey, wait!" called Skinny, "here, I'll write it down. That clerk seems pretty good with English."

He checked in his pockets for any scrap pieces of paper, and realized that he would have to set Sally down. He tried propping her against the wall, but she immediately slid to the floor.

"Ugh, Sally, why do you have to make everything so difficult?" asked Skinny, picking her up again. "Hey, bellboy, come here," he beckoned.

The sturdy bellboy came over, and was surprised to have Sally plopped in his arms. "Hold her," explained Skinny shortly.

He pulled out his suitcase, and opened it, looking for a piece of paper. The bellboy watched in perplexed silence, while Skinny searched through his different baggage articles, but to no avail. Finally, when Skinny was wondering whether or not it would be decent, under the circumstances, to look through Sally's suitcase, the bellboy suddenly tapped him on the shoulder, and handed him a notebook and a pencil.

"Where'd that come from?" asked the exasperated Skinny. The bellboy pointed at the pocket in Sally's jacket.

"Oh," said Skinny, and took the notebook. The cover read, "Story ideas taken from my own personal adventures, by Sally Keenan."

"Golly, I think it's her diary," muttered Skinny. He quickly flipped to the back of the book, ignoring all the writing as best he could, and ripped out a blank page. Then with the stubby pencil he wrote, "Would appreciate it if you didn't tell Black Hawk that we've arrived. We want to surprise him. Thanks."

He folded the note, took Sally from the bellboy, and handed him the note.

"Deliver this to the clerk at the front desk, and be quick about it!"

The boy, who was already quite in awe of Skinny, ran all the way down the hall, only stopping at the elevator entrance to doff his cap. Skinny smiled to himself, and made a mental note to tip the lad before they left.

Then he looked at all the disorganized luggage that lay on and around the cart outside the door. His clothes, and other belongings were strewn every which way, and as he looked wearily at the mess, another thought struck him.

"Oh, brother," he moaned, "where'd I put the key?"

Just then, Sally sighed. Skinny held his breath, praying that she would wake up. Slowly her eyes opened. She looked up at him, and then around at her surroundings. She put her hand to her brow and shut her eyes for a moment. Then, seeming revived, she opened them again. She looked up at Skinny, and suddenly blushed.

"Skinny, put me down," she said, a bit flustered, "I don't need your help."

Skinny obeyed, though with a slight reluctance. He felt rather shunned, and wondered bitterly just how far Sally would have gotten without his help. He set her on her feet with more energy than was necessary, and steadied her firmly.

Sally didn't understand his gruffness, for she was still flustered and confused, and slightly embarrassed.

"Where are we?" she asked, rubbing the top of her nose, as she always did when she was confused.

"On the thirteenth floor," answered Skinny curtly, "waiting for Black Hawk to show up, and cut us to ribbons, as he surely will."

Sally paled again, and unconsciously leaned up against Skinny. "Oh," she said, in a small voice that made Skinny feel guilty.

"I'm sorry Sal," he said, gently patting her head, "but I've had a trying morning. I guess I can't complain though, after all, you're the one that, well that ..."

"That Black Hawk wants to kill," Sally finished for him.

They stood in silence for a few moments, each thinking their own thoughts.

"How soon do you think he'll come?" asked Sally finally.

"Huh? Oh, Black Hawk," said Skinny. "Well, don't feel too down in the mouth Sally. I figure we'll make it look like we've checked in, and then we'll slip out the back stairs, that is, when you feel up to it. I've asked the clerk not to let Black Hawk know we're here yet."

Sally rubbed her forehead. She had to smile when she heard of Skinny's troubles in finding paper to write his note on.

"Oh, and Sally," said Skinny uncomfortably, "I took the paper from your diary, but I didn't see anything. Honest."

Sally smiled. "All you would have read is the hard to believe adventures of five kids, who all had something to hide when they met each other. I was seriously considering sending our story into a publisher when we were in New York, but I've decided to wait until we see how it all turns out."

She sighed. "It wouldn't make a very good book if the heroes all died in the end, but that does seem to be a possibility."

Skinny nodded.

"So what do we do now?" asked Sally, "I mean, it's not that I'm a complainer or anything, but I'd like to live a little longer. And also, I don't want to be a bad judge of human nature, but I think that Black Hawk, whom I've heard is superstitious, didn't put us on the thirteenth floor as a gesture of health and long life."

"That's what I thought," answered Skinny, "I'll just re-pack my things, and we can get out of here, and go find another hotel. Perhaps Black Hawk will temporarily be fooled."

They fixed Skinny's things, and started down the hall. Sally had been surprisingly quiet, and seemed to be concentrating very hard on something.

"A penny for your thoughts?" said Skinny, as they started the long climb down the stairs, avoiding the elevator.

"Well," began Sally, stopping on a landing, "I was just trying to figure out exactly what we're up against. Now, as far as I know, Black Hawk didn't know who we were. Though he somehow knew about Clarence and the treasure, he most likely wouldn't know our names. Now he does. So I think he must have met up with somebody that does know us. On our travels we haven't met many people that would just go blabbing our names and addresses to a guy who looked as creepy as Black Hawk. Unless, of course, that person wanted to kill us also, for reasons of his own.

"Now, if my calculations are correct, there is a rich Baron in the Swiss Alps, an absent-minded professor in England, and a powerful gangster in New York that all have us on their list. So what we must assume is that Black Hawk has teamed up with one of our other enemies. One, or more. And that is a kind of disturbing thought."

Skinny had listened in silence, leaning against the stair rail, his face a mixture of amusement and concern.

"You mean, you think all our enemies are ganging up against us?"

"Perhaps, it's 'The Company of Villains' versus 'The Company of Secret Kids,'" she said.

Skinny smiled, though he was troubled.

"Well, we have the disadvantage of being disbanded at the moment," muttered Skinny. "Of course, if all our enemies are joined, then it's four against five."

"Right," said Sally, "Little Joe for you, Black Hawk for Clarence, the Professor for Christine, the Baron for Becky, and they all try to kill me in their spare time."

"Well, we don't know yet if that's really the case. Black Hawk could be alone."

"But we aren't sure," said Sally, her face setting in grim lines. "In fact, the kidnapping of Becky, which we can thank the Baron for, might have just been a trap, set for us. And it worked, because here we are."

"Well, for the time being I say the best thing to do, is go find another place to hide in, and prepare for war," said Skinny.

That night, settled in her small but nice room, Sally sat and looked out her large window at the enchanting world of Paris. In her hands was a well- loved, travel-worn copy of *Harry Dee* by Father Finn, S.J. She was at the best part, when the heroes set out to rescue the passengers of a sinking yacht, but just now she wasn't reading.

Aside from the fact that she had read the book many times before, her attention was now attracted by the mystery and adventure that seemed to hover over the city outside. For her safety, Skinny had ordered her to remain in her room, while he went out to explore, and now her impatience was getting the better of her.

She stood up, and went over to the window. She could see directly down, and into the street. She noticed a figure huddled in the shadows at the end of the alley which was behind the hotel.

From her height on the tenth floor, Sally couldn't make out what the person looked like, for the shadows were deep and the light played tricks on her. All she could see was the red glow of a cigarette. Though it could be any employee out for a quick smoke behind the building, or a homeless person wanting shelter, for some reason Sally felt herself go tense when she looked at the figure. She got the distinct feeling that this person was waiting for someone, and with no good intention. And though he was far away and heavily shadowed, Sally almost felt she recognized him.

Then, as she watched, into the alley came a figure she did recognize. With his slightly arrogant swagger, his head held high and long hair thrown back, Skinny didn't look exactly timid as he walked unknowingly toward the person at the corner.

When Skinny was about a yard away from the stranger, he suddenly stopped dead in his tracks, looked hard at the shadowy figure for a few moments, and then turned tail and fled.

It was a hopeless flight, for his pursuer had been expecting such a reaction, and was prepared for a sprint. Before Skinny got half way back down the alley, his assailant had reached him. Sally watched helplessly as Skinny was caught from behind, and brought heavily to the ground, with the stranger on top. Sally knew the scenario only too well. As soon as he had left the sheltering shadows, she had recognized the man. He was tall and well built. His black hair was unruly, and he appeared shabbily dressed.

"So Little Joe is here," muttered Sally, clenching her fists, and leaning against the window panes to steady herself. "They've all come to get us."

She stood, frozen in the dreadful reality, for what seemed an eternity. Then suddenly, it returned to her that Skinny was down in that alley below her, in the clutches of a murderous man, who had more than once made attempts on his life.

"What am I standing here for?" she cried to herself, and spun away from the window. She smashed her feet into her shoes, flung herself into her coat and ripped the sheets off the bed. She would tie them into knots in the elevator and use them on Little Joe. Before she headed for the door, she ran back to the window and looked out one last time.

To her utter amazement, she saw Skinny standing up, leaning against the wall, seeming quite at ease. Little Joe was next to him, and if one hadn't known better, it would seem that they were just two friends having a friendly chat. Sally wondered if Little Joe had a gun at his back, but if he did, Skinny was cooperating surprisingly well. She waited in silence, watching every move Little Joe made, and ready to spring to Skinny's assistance at a moment's notice.

Finally, Little Joe slunk off down the alley, and Skinny turned and went the other way. Before he went around the corner, Little Joe turned and called something to Skinny. Skinny nodded.

Suddenly, Sally had the suspicion that Skinny might have joined up with Little Joe again, and her heart sank. This time, if Skinny should prove disloyal, she would be on her own, without Clarence, or Christine, or even Becky to stand by her.

She figured that, if the encounter had been something important, Skinny would come by her room and tell her. On the other hand, if he really had succumbed to Little Joe, then anything he said to her might be a trap.

She sat down dejectedly on her bed, which was stripped clean, the sheets piled messily by the door. She had nothing to do but think depressing thoughts. She waited for almost an hour, but Skinny never appeared. She wondered if he was in the hotel or not. Finally, she got up, returned the sheets to the bed, and placed a chair in front of the door.

"Look at me," she muttered, as she checked the lock. "I'm scared of getting murdered in my bed by my own friend."

Everything in her mind told her to be on the watch, and not trust Skinny. Yet all the feelings of her heart urged her to believe in his noble nature, as she had before.

As she fell asleep that night, lying on the disheveled bed, she mulled over in her mind all the coming possibilities and she came to the decision that, no matter how reckless it was, she would bring the truth out into the open the next morning.

Her mind was made up, and she was no longer troubled. But despite her peace of mind, the moon shone in the window, and glistened on the tears that dropped onto her pillow.

* * *

Christine and Clarence spent most of that wonderful day enjoying the marketplace of Trinidad. Christine bought several pieces of jewelry, Clarence got a beautiful hunting knife, and they spent much time deliberating over the best mangoes, which they would bring back to Sally, since they had decided that although she would love a pet monkey, it would be too hard to transport.

Once when they were in sight of the parking lot, Clarence had seen a rather beat-up rental car wheeling around the parked cars slowly, as though waiting for someone to come out of the market.

"Hey, Chris," he said, quietly grabbing her arm and pulling her to a stop, "have you ever seen that car before?"

She followed his gaze and her eyes grew wide. She nodded and gulped. "It was at the airport, and then I saw it behind us while we were driving to the hotel. I thought whoever it was must have been staying at the same place we were."

"Yeah, I thought that too, but the question is, why?" Clarence looked at her and then back at the car which was slowly pulling into a parking place.

"Oh, Clarence," breathed Christine, gripping him tighter, "do you think it's somebody from the enemy and they're here to ..."

Clarence nodded so that she did not have to finish. "It's a safe bet."

"Then what are we going to do?"

Clarence looked around. The marketplace was thinning out as the heat of the day grew. "If only there was big a crowd like when we first got here," he muttered.

"Clare, look!" cried Christine, pointing toward the car.

Clarence looked and saw the old man in the white lab coat and large spectacles that he had seen once before in Manchester.

"Well, that's the professor, all right," he said, standing on tip toe, "but it looks like he's alone."

As Clarence finished speaking, all four doors of the car opened at the same time, and men came out of each one. They were big gruff looking characters, all wearing dark sunglasses. They grouped around the tiny professor and stared at the marketplace menacingly.

"Well, I was wrong," said Clarence.

"What are we going to do?" asked Christine again, this time a little shriller and shakier.

Clarence glanced around. "Come on!" He pulled her none too gently back through the booths, dodging and ducking through the crowd. It was much easier to maneuver now. Once Clarence glanced back and saw one of the professor's men heading after them.

"Hurry, he's seen us!" he hissed.

They made a sharp turn down a small aisle. They stayed as close as possible to the other shoppers and tried to mingle with them. Suddenly as they reached the middle of an aisle, Christine stopped with a gasp.

"Look, another one!" she said.

At the end of the aisle, scanning the crowd with the eye of an expert tracker was another of the men, wearing the telltale sunglasses. The two spun around at the same time, and saw yet another grisly looking man starting towards them.

Clarence reached into their bulging shopping bag and produced the coconut. He shoved it into Christine's hands. "Here, you'd better make a run for it. Try to keep the coconut hidden. Make for the cab. I'll try to draw them off."

"Clare, be careful, they're armed."

"Don't worry," said Clarence. "If they know about the treasure, they might not know we have it yet, and might want to get me alive. Now move!"

He gave her a shove that started her toward yet another clothing booth. She slipped in, and stepped behind a primitive clothing rack, that stood up against the back of the booth and ducked down so her head couldn't be seen. She noticed that the walls of the booth were constructed from a heavy canvas, held together by metal poles. She knelt down and lifted the canvas that made up the back wall. There was about a foot of space between the slack fabric and the dusty ground.

Slipping the coconut under her sweater, Christine half crawled, half rolled under the canvas, and standing up, found herself in a thin passageway that ran between the booths, and was filled with supplies and broken items. She crawled under a large truck filled with pottery, and ran out of the passage. She was now at the very edge of the crowded parking lot. Scanning the cars anxiously, she found the cab they had taken and ran towards it.

As she drew near it, she could see Clarence wasn't inside, and her heart sank. Still holding the coconut, she turned back towards the market and waited for a few moments in anxious suspense. She was just about to go back, when she saw an old woman, wearing many shawls and a heavy veil around her head, suddenly come dashing out from between the booths. After bumping into the Professor and knocking him to the ground, she came tearing toward Christine. For a split second Christine was terrified that something had happened to Clarence, and this was the bearer of the bad news, but just then, the woman's veil flew off, revealing the dark head and flashing eyes of a handsome teenage boy. By the time he'd reached the cab, Clarence had wiggled out of his makeshift skirt, shawl, and headpiece and screeched to a halt before her in his own clothes.

Before the Professor and his men had realized that the strange old woman who had so athletically smashed through their ranks, had really been their prey escaping the trap, Christine and Clarence were already in their cab, speeding their way back to the airport.

* * *

Skinny slowly slid into consciousness with the impression that something was wrong. There was an odd feeling in his bones, a sort of stiffness that he wasn't awake enough to analyze. As he became more conscious, and tried to stretch, he became sure that there was something amiss.

He opened his eyes to see bright sunlight streaming through his windows, and next to his window, seated cross-legged, and deep in a book, was Sally. Skinny automatically tried to sit up, and found one ankle was tied to the bed post.

"What the ...?" he looked at his hands, which were bound together at the wrists.

"Sally, what's the idea?" he asked, wondering what sort of prank she was trying to play on him.

Sally looked up from her book and smiled brightly. "Good morning Skinny. You certainly are a sound sleeper."

"Good morning?!" asked Skinny. "Why am I all tied up? What's happened?"

"Now Skinny, just go back to sleep," answered Sally, returning to her book. "I'm at a good part."

"Sally Keenan!" cried Skinny, "just you get up and tell me what this is all about, or I'm going to get mad!"

"It won't make no difference whether you get mad or not, you won't be able to get out of bed either way."

Skinny opened his mouth, and shut it again. Sally looked levelly at him for a moment, and Skinny got the feeling she was trying to read his thoughts.

"You really don't have any idea why I tied you up, do you?" she asked at length.

"*You* tied me up?" cried Skinny. "Why, Sally the only answer that I can think of is that either you were sleepwalking, or you had a mild attack of temporary insanity."

Sally smiled, and to Skinny's utter confusion, she seemed greatly relieved.

"Well, that's good," she said, "either you're the greatest actor I've ever met, or you're telling me the truth. I must admit you seem genuinely baffled."

She shut her book, and put on a military look. "Now, we need to talk." Skinny figured there was no way to get himself unbound unless he tolerated Sally's ramblings.

"Now, the first thing I want to know is, why did Little Joe let you go last night?"

It suddenly dawned on Skinny what this was all about.

"Oh, Sally ... " he said, and realized how alone and helpless she must have felt through the long night.

"What does 'Oh Sally,' mean?" she asked suspiciously, and licked her lips, the clear sign to him that she was nervous.

"I know why you have me all done up, Sal, but I want to make it clear to you that there is no truth behind your suspicions. Last night Little Joe let me go, only because he is sure he can kill me another time. I haven't gone back to his side. I know because of what you must have seen last night, that this might be hard to believe, but you just have to trust me on this one."

Sally looked at him. She looked in his eyes, trusting herself to be a good judge of human nature, and one of the few who were immune to Skinny's bewitching charm.

"Okay," she said, after a long moment of silence, "I trust you."

She got up, and started undoing the knots. "You know, this is a pretty good way of keeping you quiet, when I want to talk to you. I should remember it," she winked, and pulled him up.

"Beware, little girl, or I'll try it on you," returned Skinny, glad for her signal that everything was back to normal.

"But now, I really do have a right to know what all that was about with Little Joe last night."

"Well that is an interesting story," said Skinny, "and maybe you can help me figure it out. As you probably saw, I was walking down the alley, to get into the hotel by the back way, when I saw Little Joe. He got me down, and I was sure it was all over. I didn't think he'd stop to gloat, because of what had happened last time. Man, I was glad we'd gone to Confession recently.

"Anyhow, I was expecting the worst, and was really surprised when Little Joe asked me, right off the cuff, where Christine and Clarence were. I hadn't been expecting that, so I told him honestly that I didn't know. He said I was lying, so I decided I might as well prove him right. I told him that in actuality, Christine and Clarence had gone back to Africa to find the crocodile. I hoped that would make Black Hawk go there, and leave Paris. I just hope that Clarence and Chris aren't really there."

"Well, keep going," said Sally, "why didn't he kill you once he had that information?"

"That was what was so strange. After I'd told him that, he looked at me real hard for a second, and then, he stood up, and told me to get up. I was so surprised to be alive, that for a minute I couldn't move. He pulled me up, and told me it was a rotten shame that he couldn't kill me right then and there, but he had reasons not to. I didn't ask him what sort of reasons. I didn't want to gamble with my own life.

"Then, he asked me whether or not I wanted to defect back to his side. I gave him a flat refusal. I figured that after that, he would finish me off, but he still didn't. He just nodded, and rubbed his left leg. I think he was sore from where I shot him last time.

"It was as if he really didn't want me to switch to his side. It almost seemed as though he had been told to ask me that, and told to hold me up ... as if it wasn't his idea, and his heart wasn't really in it.

"Then he told me to get lost, but also mentioned that sometime soon he would get to finish both you and me off, and not to be fooled by his mercy on this occasion. Then he just let me go, and snuck off, and hollered just before he turned the corner that I'd better watch out, because someday soon he was going to get me."

Sally listened with furrowed brow. "Sounds fishy," she said, "as if now Little Joe is taking orders from someone else. Someone powerful, like Black Hawk."

Skinny nodded. "I thought the same thing. Little Joe did seem to be on edge, as if something was annoying him. If I know him, taking orders from someone else would be just the thing to get him in a bad mood. Also, he was coughing the whole time. He had a cigarette, but every time he blew out smoke it came out in fast little clouds. He was hacking like someone with pneumonia."

Sally didn't pay much attention to this, though she thought it commendable that Skinny seemed concerned about the health of a man who wanted him dead. "Well, I guess we'll just have to wait for them to make the first move," she shrugged.

"Yeah, we're just here to rescue Becky," said Skinny. "Hey, you know, we have to think about how we're going to pull that rescue off."

"I have thought about it, but we can't do anything until we hear from her friend Jack. I don't know the address of his friends here, and he is the only person who could give us a lead. I've written to him, but all I have is a post office box address. My letter told him we've arrived, and where we're staying, so all we can do is wait for him to contact us."

"Okay, then what are we doing today?"

"Well, it's Holy Thursday, and I figure we can catch a pretty good Mass here in Paris."

"They won't look for us there. And after that?"

"I hadn't really planned on anything."

"Good," said Skinny, "because I had some ideas."

"Like what?"

"Well, we don't exactly know how much longer we're going to be free, so I thought we could call today a holiday, and just do whatever we want."

"Sort of a 'last meal' concept," grinned Sally, "only instead of food, it's having fun. Okay, but we need to stay alive for Becky's sake."

Chapter 15

A River Rescue

"It was great wasn't it?" said Sally, as they stood on the steps of the beautiful church where they had attended the Chrism Mass.

Skinny nodded. In the past he hadn't really paid much attention to the celebrations that surrounded the Passion and Resurrection of Jesus, but now Sally's enthusiasm was spreading over him. The terror and glory that were involved in the Easter Triduum were fascinating him, and the renewal of the priest's vocations had been touching.

"So where do we go from here?" asked Sally, looking out at the busy street before them.

"Anywhere you like," said Skinny. "This day is for doing things we've always wanted to do, before it's too late. They'll never dream we would go sightseeing, and we're safer in big crowds."

"Okay, then let's ... " began Sally, but suddenly her face changed. Her carefree, somewhat bored expression vanished, and in its place, the wild, brave, happy look came over her that she exhibited when she smelled danger.

"Come on, I know what we'll do today," she said, leaping down the steps three at a time.

"What?" asked Skinny, sensing that something was wrong, and an adventure lay ahead.

"We're going to rescue Becky," said Sally, and shot off across the street.

Skinny followed her as best he could, though Sally zipped down the street and ran through traffic with a speed and agility that made it hard for him to keep up.

Finally, she came to a screeching halt at a curb, and flagged down a passing taxi. Before it had even halted, she was inside, and though Skinny couldn't tell whether she had gone through the door or the window, he managed to get in also. Sally, in a frenzied mixture between French, English, and the language Becky called "Sally Talk," instructed the driver where to go.

After making two sharp turns, and running a red light, Sally let out a whoop that almost made the driver wreck.

"There it is!" she cried, pointing to a dented white cargo van that was a few cars ahead of them.

"Now cabby, just tail, I mean follow that white van. Doesn't it look like it's been used as a getaway car in some rough jobs? But don't let it look like you're following them. You know, drive slowly, but don't lose 'em!"

The driver, who had always prided himself on his fine English speaking skills, nodded, and prayed that the young lady in his precious cab wouldn't request anything more, until he'd had time to digest his latest instructions. Whenever they got too close to the van, Sally flattened herself and Skinny down on the seat, and told the driver to let them get a further lead.

"Sally what's up?" asked Skinny, as he ducked down when they pulled onto a thoroughfare directly behind the van.

"I'll tell you what's up. When we were standing on the front steps, I saw that van go by, and in the passenger seat, was the Baron. Either it's him or it's his evil twin."

"Do you think Becky's in there?" asked Skinny.

"No, I know she is. You didn't let me finish. As the van passed, I got a look in the back window. I saw a hand fly up and hit it, like someone was trying to smash it from the inside, but the hand was so tiny, it didn't even dent the glass. Then, there was a larger hand which pulled the little one down, and then for a fleeting second, I saw Becky's face. It looked as though there was a struggle going on in the back, and for a minute, she'd gotten free."

"Well, let's just see where this van is going," said Skinny, slowly sitting up.

They were slowly heading out of the main body of Paris. From what Skinny knew of their whereabouts, the church they had gone to was relatively on the edge of the most populated part of the city, and a short drive would get them out into the countryside.

"Well, we're heading out to more rural country, so either the Company of Villains has a base, or he's taking Becky out into the country for some other reason."

Sally glanced at Skinny, her face grim. He knew what she was thinking. They sat in silence for some time, as they followed the van out into the beautiful French countryside.

"Hey Sal," said Skinny, who had been considering all the possibilities that lay ahead very carefully, "since this whole kidnapping of Becky could be just a trap set for you and me, why couldn't this drive, and what lies at the end of it, just be to catch us?"

"It is a possibility, but we can't risk Becky's life, just to save our own. Maybe the Baron is just sick of Becky, and wants to kill her off, or maybe it's time for the trap to spring shut."

"Spring shut, on us."

"Not if we're fast enough."

Skinny glanced out the window, and found that the van had turned off the main road, and was heading down a steep dirt road.

"Looks like we're heading towards that river that we've been passing by," said Skinny.

Sally looked out, and then looked at him. "So that's it. They send her down the river, then wait downstream for us to jump in and save her. When we three come out, they grab us all. Pretty slick."

"And hard to get around. I don't see any way we could ..."

"Well, I do," Sally smiled mischievously. "All you need to do, is drop me off a little way downstream of where they stop, and then you go on. I'll find myself a good spot, relatively far away from them, but still within sight and hearing range. Then, I'll chuck myself in the water, and make a whopper of a racket. They're sure to come after me, and I'll be in before they have a chance to do anything to Becky. Then, you'll go get her."

"But they'll leave someone to watch Becky for sure."

"But not more than you and the cabby can't handle."

Skinny considered the plan. "One more slight hitch. How will you get out alive?"

Sally sobered. "I hadn't thought about that."

"No, you usually don't. But luckily, I've thought of something."

"Really?"

"You're not the only member of this company that has brains, you know," said Skinny dryly, "but here's my thought. You take a hat, or scarf, or something along with you when, as you put it, you have 'chucked yourself in.' Then, once I've rescued Becky, you'll be a good way downstream, and you take off the hat. Take a good breath, and go under. Swim off, and leave the hat or scarf floating away. Hopefully, if you're far enough away when you do it, the Baron will think that it's you, and keep up the chase. Then you swim back up to where I'll be waiting with Becky and the cab."

"Skinny, you general, you ain't such a dingbat after all!" cried Sally, instantly intrigued by the daring idea. "Why, I'd be a goner if it weren't for you."

Skinny smiled, for though he wasn't usually one to react to flattery, praise about strategy from Sally was a gratifying thing.

"Now Sally, one thing," he said, as they made their way along the windy road. "You need to promise me you'll be careful. I got carried away just now and didn't realize how dangerous your venture is. Anything could happen in a river in the spring. The current will be strong, and the water will be really cold. You might be shot at by the Baron's men, though that's a bit unlikely. And even if they don't shoot at you, the river is full of dangers too. You could hit your head on a rock, or get carried far downstream, or run into a floating log or something ..."

"Oh, stop," said Sally, "you know, this won't be the first time I've ever been in a river before. It's just like the rivers back home. I don't know why you have to be such a mother hen whenever I get to do something fun."

"Also," continued Skinny, ignoring her interruption, "it won't be any small feat to swim all the way past the Baron and his men, who might be spread out all along the river."

"Right, but I can do it, all of it," Sally grinned, and glanced out the window. They were driving along the top of a ridge. At the edge of the road, there was a steep cliff, dotted with trees and shrubs, and some large rocks. At the bottom of the hill was the swirling water. It seemed deep even by the banks, and was frothing and bubbling its way downstream with a satisfying roar. Its usual size and strength was magnified by the melted snows that ran down to it from the hills all round. Sally looked at it, and smiled.

Then the driver cried, "Is stop!" and slammed down on his brakes. At a speed which made Skinny's stomach turn, he backed up, heading straight for the hill's sharp edge.

Just in time, they silently slid to a halt. Skinny sat up in his seat, and looked ahead. They were at the top of a deep dell, that spread out before them, and through which the road cut. The white van had descended into the valley, and was turning down what seemed almost a driveway that went straight to the water's edge. It was obviously a previously arranged spot.

Then Skinny realized how ingenious it was of the cabman to stop where they were. They had a good view of the white van, through the long, low branches of some trees that clustered together on the roadside, but unless someone was purposely looking for them, they could never be seen from the Baron's standpoint.

"Okay, now before they spread out," said Skinny, opening his door as quietly as possible, "Sally, you need to get out, and get a good way downstream. Make sure you're downstream from all the men when you 'fall in.'"

"Check! Now let's go!"

Before Skinny could finish his instructions, Sally was out of the car, and heading down towards the water.

"Sally, wait!" he caught up to her, and pulled her to a stop. "One more thing you need to remember. When you swim back up, stop here, provided this place isn't guarded, and we'll pick you up, and take off."

"Right! Then how do I know when to jump in?"

"Get in as soon as you get far enough away; we're not sure how much time they'll give us before they throw Becky in, if that's their plan. Oh, and here, take the hat."

Skinny crept back to the cab, and after a moment, came back with the cabman's hat.

"It's the only thing we have with us that will do, and I promised to buy him a new one."

Sally shrugged. "Okay, but I'll look mighty silly in a hat that big." She put it on, and it slid down over her eyes and ears.

Skinny grinned. "Perfect. Now the trick will be keeping it on while you swim."

"Oh, wait!" cried Sally, and ran back to cab. She returned with a long, vibrant, red scarf.

"Wow, where'd you get that?"

"I carry it with me in my purse, along with my pocketknives and pepper spray. I figured someday I'd need it as a distress flag. Well, now is the day."

"With all that stuff in your purse, where do you keep your lipstick?" teased Skinny, who secretly admired Sally for her indifference towards what she called 'female war-paint.'

Sally rolled her eyes, and put the cabby's hat back on. She tilted it back on her head so she could see, and then put the red scarf over it, and tied it firmly beneath her chin.

"How do I look?"

"Like a ridiculous little girl wearing a cabby's hat, with a distress flag tied around it."

"Thanks, but as long as I'm noticeable, I'm happy."

"Sally, you'd be noticeable in anything," laughed Skinny, as he turned back to the cab. "Now get moving."

Sally nodded, and started down the slope. In between two trees, she stopped and turned around. She saw Skinny standing outside the cab, watching her. For some reason, she felt a bit unsure of herself, and his presence was helpful. He smiled at her, and made the 'thumbs up' sign. She nodded again, and saluted with two fingers. As she made her way through the trees, and over the large, slippery rocks, she whispered her Act of Contrition, and keyed herself up for the coming adventure.

"I wonder if I'll make it," she thought, almost carelessly.

She was almost at the water's edge now, and though the sun was shining brightly, she could already tell that the water would be icy. She glanced down the river, and then up it. She could see vaguely, a group of maybe ten or twelve men, and could easily recognize the Baron. He was still dressed finely, his red cape flowing around him in the wind, his shining sword hanging at his belt.

She could also see that one of the men was holding something small and struggling. It appeared that Becky had a blindfold on, and was well tied up. Sally's usually dormant temper suddenly awoke, as it almost only did when she saw a defenseless creature in distress.

"Hold on, Becky," she whispered to herself, "we're on the way."

She scrambled onto the largest rock around, which jutted out above the water. One last time she glanced around, but resisted the urge to look back up at Skinny, for fear he would think she was scared.

"Okay, Guardian Angel, I'm putting my life in your hands. Again."

As she prayed, she looked down at the beautiful, and yet deadly water splashing beneath her. "If it is my time to go, let me to Christ's bosom fly, but if it ain't, then I know I don't have anything to worry about. Take care of all the rest of the Company. They're good kids. Whoopee!"

With a spring that resembled that of a great cat's, she flew into the air. Skinny, who had been watching her hesitation with much concern, caught his breath. In the air, she rolled herself into a ball, and did a perfect summersault. She landed with hardly a splash to be heard, above the roaring of the water.

"Drat, they're not going to hear her," thought Skinny, with sinking heart.

Then, out upon the rhythmic sounds of nature, there pierced a rousing yell.

"Sarsaparilla, Soda Water,
Ginger-ale, and Pop,
We're the Company of Secret Kids,
We're always on the top! Whoopee!"

Skinny smiled to himself. "What am I worried about?" he thought, "that Sally can handle anything."

He now saw her bright red head, bobbing up and down as she treaded the romping water. There seemed to be a connection between the river and Sally. It was something about the rambunctious, reckless, joyous energy, that romped and played in both of them. It appeared that the happy-go-lucky stream had found a playmate.

But for all the gaiety that glowed from her, Skinny knew Sally well enough to tell that the voice was shriller, and it cracked a bit. Her face also, was turning pale, and Skinny could only imagine how cold the water was.

Sally's war cry had accomplished its purpose, however. The Baron had turned an incredulous face immediately, and seeing the bobbing red head, gave a yell, and set off down the bank, followed by his men.

The man holding Becky stood undecided for a moment, pondering whether to go or stay. The Baron glanced back at him, and shouted something. The man lifted Becky up, and started towards the van.

"Come on, quick," cried Skinny, and started down the hill at a dead, but quiet run. The cabby followed him, trying as best he could to imitate Skinny's stealthy, swift way of moving.

As he ran, Skinny watched the man coming toward the van. He was looking down at his feet. Skinny stopped behind a tree, and waited for the cabby to catch up. When he did, the Baron's man was at the back door of the van. He pulled the keys from his pocket, and fumbled with them for a moment. Skinny figured he would have to put Becky down to unlock the doors, and when he did, they would jump on him.

But suddenly, too quickly for Skinny to act, the man clicked in the key, made a strange movement with it, swung the door open, tossed Becky in, and slammed the door shut. The lock clicked, and the man hurried off to follow the Baron.

"Darn!" cried Skinny, as they crept from their hiding spot.

"Darn?" asked the cabby.

Skinny nodded gloomily. "Let's see if we can get the door open." He crept towards the van, the cabby close at his heels. When he reached the rear door, he rattled it for a moment, but it held fast. He looked hard at the keyhole, for something about it seemed amiss. There were small tick marks lining the outside of the lock, and, though they were very small, he could see numbers above the marks.

"It looks like it's a strange sort of lock," he muttered, more to himself than to the cabby, "it's almost like a safe. There seem to be tumblers inside, but you put in the combination with the key. That's why when the guy put the key in, he wiggled it around in a weird way, instead of just turning it. It must be the Baron's own invention. I've never seen anything like it before."

"Becky," he called softly, trying to make himself heard through the closed windows, and yet not attract attention. "Becky!"

He thought he heard a muffled cry from inside, but with the roaring of the water, and Sally's yapping chatter, he couldn't be sure. Sally now was hollering war cries, shouting the choruses of patriotic Irish songs, and every once in a while varying her performance with 'Whoopees' and 'Yahoos.'

"It's no use," Skinny told the cabby, after pressing his ear to the door, "she can't hear us, and if she could, she wouldn't be able to answer."

"We help you leetle girl," the cabby told the van. He looked dejected, seeing that was the general mood. He pondered the problem, watching Skinny's face closely. Suddenly, Skinny's face lit up.

"I've got it!" he cried, snapping his fingers, "come on."

They ran back to the cab, and at Skinny's command, the cabby opened the trunk. Inside were articles that passengers had left behind in the cab, and Skinny was impressed and overjoyed by the assortment.

He found a coil of rope, which the cabby kept for maintenance uses, and also a light purple shawl left behind by an absent-minded flapper. Then, he removed his jacket, and rolled it and the other clothing articles from the trunk, well in the shawl. Then, over the whole thing, he wrapped the rope, finishing by tying his tie over the top half of the bundle to resemble a blindfold.

"There, it doesn't really look like Becky, but it's worth a shot."

The cabby, who had caught onto the idea, nodded, and grinned. As he had been preparing the phony Becky, and explaining his plan to the cabby, Skinny had been listening intently to Sally's voice. He could still hear it, but it was steadily growing farther. Sally was drifting further downstream.

"Okay, let's do this fast, I don't want Sally to have to swim too far back."

"Let's shoot!" said the cabby, proud of himself for picking up Skinny's slang. Skinny smiled, and nodded.

The cabby leapt in the cab, and drove a short way back up the hill. He was now on a line with the Baron and his men, who were slipping and sliding about on the rocks in their hot pursuit of the small figure in the bobbing red cap, treading water only a few yards ahead of them. The Baron had his gun at his side, but apparently was under the same orders as Little Joe, and would not kill anyone that day.

Skinny, when the cabby had driven away, crept back to the trees that were a few feet from the Baron's van, and there crouched in total silence, except for the cracking of his knuckles. From where he was, he could hear Sally's voice getting a little breathy, as though she were losing her wind. From the glimpses he had caught of her face through the trees as he had crept back down the hill, Skinny had noticed rather worriedly that Sally's usually rosy face was now a striking white.

He waited impatiently for sounds of the cabby executing his part of the plan. After what seemed a very long time, he finally heard what he'd been waiting for.

Almost at the top of the hill, the cabby had parked, and was now hopping up and down in front of his cab, and yelling at the top of his voice, while in his arms, he held the dummy that was supposed to be Becky. The Baron and his men immediately turned and saw him, and several of them started up the hill towards him.

Sally, who saw what was going on, recognized the thing the cabby was holding as a dummy, and guessed Skinny's plan. She realized that their plan would fail if too many of the Baron's men attacked them at once.

"Hey, Skinny, Clarence, Christine!" she yelled, directing her face and voice towards the opposite bank, "quick, run, the Baron is coming!"

The Baron heard the names of her companions, and saw the direction in which she was shouting, and luckily for Skinny and the cabby, he fell for Sally's trick.

He turned, and looked hard at the cabby's bundle. His brow furrowed, and he seemed to be considering his strategy. Then he shouted something in German to his men.

Immediately, two of them broke off from the rest, one heading up the hill towards the cabby, the other racing back towards the van and Skinny.

The rest of the men followed the Baron, who now renewed his pursuit of Sally with more vigor. Two of his men crossed the river by deep wading and swimming, and climbed out and began searching the tree covered slope that went up from the opposite bank.

Skinny meanwhile, waited with bated breath for the Baron's man to reach the van. He saw the cabby leap in the cab, taking the bundle with him, and drive slowly backwards, up the hill. Almost as soon as he had started the car, one of the Baron's men reached the road, and started running towards it.

The cabby locked the doors and drove away, but slowly enough so that the man didn't give up the chase to go help Skinny's adversary.

Skinny watched him as he followed the cab around the corner at the top of the hill, and was lost from sight. Then Skinny saw the other man, heading for the van. In his hand he held the key, and now Skinny could see it was a strange key, made to fit the combination lock.

Even if Skinny could get the key from him, he could never figure out the combination in the limited time he had, and he was slightly glad he didn't have to take the keys by force, for his enemy was a good sized man, and his face had a ruthless glint.

Skinny watched as he reached the van and went to the back door. He put the keys in the lock, and slowly repeated the strange turning movements. Skinny eased himself to his feet. As the man opened the door, and stuck his head in, Skinny hurled himself forward. For a moment it seemed that everything stood still. Skinny knew how close a call it was, and that the lives of Becky and Sally, and even his own, were hanging in the balance of that moment.

He sprang as the man, who had looked in and seen Becky lying huddled in a corner, pulled his head out the door, and prepared to shut it. As he did, Skinny suddenly seized him from behind, and pulled him backwards in an old alley gang mugging trick, that Skinny had almost forgotten.

"Complements of Little Joe," he hissed, and with a swift kick, sent the man spinning back towards the van door. As he did so, he suddenly realized that this could be a bad move. If the man hit the slightly opened door, it would shut, and automatically lock.

Skinny leapt forward again, this time to save his opponent from his fall, but before he even moved, he knew it was hopeless. Then, beyond all hope, there appeared in the doorway, a tiny foot. The man hit the door and it swung shut, but was stopped.

Skinny heard a small "Ouch!" from inside, and with a rush of love for Becky, he leapt on the man again, who was now leaning up against the door, trying to get his breath. This time, however, he saw Skinny's attack coming, and braced himself.

Skinny pulled him up, and away from the door, but was then hurled backward. His enemy was taking the offensive. Skinny landed on his back, slightly winded, but jumped back up, and saw the man heading for the door.

Skinny threw himself upon him, and bore him to the ground. For a moment it seemed that things were going his way, but the man underneath him suddenly twisted around, and before Skinny could recover, the man was on top of him.

"Becky!" yelled Skinny, struggling fiercely, "Becky, get out!"

His opponent quickly silenced his cries with a rap on the jaw. Skinny felt blood in his mouth, but was too excited to notice. He couldn't see the door, so he didn't know whether or not Becky had heard him, or could carry out his command, but he read his aggressor's face, for he too was watching for Becky.

Then suddenly, the man's face grew intent, and desperate. He aimed a blow at Skinny, which got him between the eyes, and made him see stars. The man sprang up.

Skinny had just the wits about him to roll over, and grab the man's ankle as he leapt over him. The man was in midair, and Skinny's grip was tight. The man fell to the ground with a thud. Skinny, as he had rolled over, had seen what had made the man move. Becky had rolled herself out the door, and onto the ground. She was well bound, but she had somehow managed to remove the blindfold. She was now rolling herself under the van, and out of the man's reach. Skinny also noticed that the back door was now pushed wide open. This presented a solution to Skinny's problem of fighting the stronger man.

With a graceful spring, he rocketed himself over the sprawled form of the man, letting his ankle go, and pushing off of him at the same time. As soon as he was over him, the man got up, slower, and less gracefully than Skinny, but with sufficient speed.

Skinny planted himself firmly before the open door, and letting his hands drop to his sides, presented a tempting target. The man growled something derogatory at him in German; he heard Becky gasp in shock from under the van; and then, the man leaped.

It was the pay-off punch. Into that plunge the villain put all his strength and fury. He expected a futile resistance attempt from Skinny, which he thought he could easily crush.

To his surprise and dismay, however, just before he hit Skinny, the graceful youth stepped aside. The man's forceful spring had nothing to collide with, and he sailed into the van quite beautifully, and smacked himself onto the floor. Almost before he was in, Skinny had swung the door shut, and rattled it to make sure it was locked.

"Quick, Becky," he called, leaning up against the door, "do you know if there's any way to unlock the back doors from the inside?"

"No, there isn't," answered Becky, rolling out from under the van, "believe me, I tried. Once you're in, you can't get out, even if you have the keys."

"Great," said Skinny, "come on!"

He scooped her up, ropes and all, and started up the hill at a run. He turned the corner just as the cabby came screeching around it.

"Hey, how's it going?" asked Skinny, opening the back door, and tossing Becky in, "where's the guy that was after you?"

"Back up at main road," answered the cabby, "him thinking I up there too. But I come back to you, monsieur."

"Great, now wait here, and be ready to take off at a moment's notice. I'm going to get Sally."

He ran to the top of the slope, and looked down. The Baron and his men were well ahead of him, and just a little beyond their reach, Sally was still treading and bobbing in the splashing water. She was floating down the river backwards, facing the Baron and Skinny.

He stood there in silence for a moment, wondering how he was supposed to get Sally's attention without setting the Baron and all his men on his trail. Thankfully though, Sally had been waiting for him. She glanced up, and saw him.

He made the 'thumb's up' sign. Almost imperceptibly, she nodded, and he almost thought he saw her salute again.

He watched as she spun round, and suddenly swam downstream with a speed that surprised the Baron and his men. They quickly doubled their speed as well, but Sally still had a good lead. Then suddenly, Skinny realized that the bobbing cap was now on its own.

Sally had been staying under water as she swam downstream, and even he, who was expecting the trick, wasn't sure when she had let it go. He looked in the swirling water, trying to catch a glimpse of her, but there wasn't a sign.

The Baron and his men kept up their pursuit of the hat and scarf, and since it was floating away very quickly, it seemed that it would be a while before they caught up to it and realized their mistake.

Skinny glanced down and saw that Becky, who had untied herself with the help of the cabby, was standing beside him, anxiously scanning the choppy waters.

"If she's swimming back up this way, then why don't we see her, Skinny?" she asked.

Skinny didn't answer. He was thinking the same thoughts. Becky slipped her hand in his, and he gripped it hard.

"Don't worry," said Becky, looking up at him confidently. "Sally is a hero, and heroes can't die."

Skinny nodded. "Sally is a hero," he repeated to himself, "and heroes can't ..."

Suddenly panic took him. "Come on!" he yelled, dashing down the slope, still clutching Becky's hand. They reached the water's edge, and stood looking out at it, in silent despair. The Baron and his men were turning a bend in the river, and were disappearing from sight.

Skinny didn't dare call out, but the silence and the noise were driving him mad. Becky's eyes were wet, and she breathed hard from the run, in little panting sobs. Suddenly, her sob turned into a gasp of joy, and she hiccupped.

"Look!"

Skinny turned to where she pointed, upstream. There, floating down on her back, with her hands behind her head, and an impish grin on her face, was Sally. Skinny started breathing again, and Becky laughed aloud. Slowly, Sally paddled over to them, taking her time, and looking very pleased.

When the first wave of joyous relief passed, Skinny felt annoyed. Sally had probably seen them on the bank, and decided to give them a scare.

"She thinks she's so funny," thought Skinny bitterly, "but I could have done it in my sleep."

In truth, he was almost disappointed. At the water's edge, he had been picturing himself seeing the unconscious form of Sally drifting away, and diving in and rescuing her fearlessly. He thought of how Becky described Sally as a 'hero.'

Deep down, he wished she wasn't such a hero, so he might have a chance at heroism himself. He remembered her words when she had come out of her faint at the hotel: "Put me down Skinny, I don't need your help."

"No," he muttered to himself, as he watched her pull herself out of the water, and climb nimbly over the rocks towards them. "No, she doesn't need my help. She never will."

When Sally leapt off the rocks, and came towards them, Becky ran to her, and threw herself into Sally's arms.

"Hey, toothless one!" cried Sally, giving her a wet bear hug. "Man, did we have a time rescuing you!"

"Come on, we'd better go," said Skinny, and pried Becky off Sally. He took Becky's hand, and grabbed Sally's arm, to pull her along. As he touched her, he started, for her skin was ice cold. He glanced at her face, and saw that her lips were a bluish-purple, and her teeth were chattering. They started up the hill, and he didn't mention it, for he was still feeling the pangs of jealousy, and figured she'd warm up soon enough.

"Sally, I was worried about you," said Becky.

"Aw, you don't ought to," shivered Sally with a grin. "After all, never say die."

Suddenly, she started coughing. It was a wet, hacking cough, that racked her whole body. The sound slightly reminded Skinny of Little Joe. It worried him.

Sally's wet curls shook, and she came to a stop, with a choking sigh. Skinny realized it was time to put aside all minor annoyances.

"Here Sal, let's hurry up to the car," he said, and without giving her time to protest, picked her up, and started up the hill. To his surprise and concern, she made no objections. When they reached the cab, they piled in, on top of all Becky's ropes, and the wraps of the fake Becky. The cabby, who had been waiting impatiently, hit the gas as Skinny closed his door, and careened around in a circle, and back up to the main road.

On the road back to Paris, Becky helped Skinny unwrap the Becky dummy, and bundle Sally, who was seated between them, in all the clothes and wraps. The cabby handed back to them a small glass of brandy, which he kept only for health purposes, after which Sally livened up a good deal.

"Golly, I don't know what happened to me," she laughed once she was warmer. "I just froze up."

"You had a reason to," said Skinny, "that water must have been murder."

"It was okay, but now tell me about your side of the rescue, it sounds terrific."

Skinny started on a modest explanation of the story, to which Becky and the cabby added many facts, which made Skinny turn red, and feel quite grateful to them.

Sally listened, spellbound, and when the narration was done, gave Skinny quite his share of praise.

They made plans to return to the hotel, gather their things and quickly move to another place to stay. Sally suggested they look up the Sisters of St. Joseph's house in Paris.

When they arrived back at the hotel, Skinny paid the cabby the usual fee for driving two persons out into the country and back, plus what he felt was adequate for assisting a rescue attempt, placing one's own life in jeopardy, and offering the best support and advice Skinny had heard since he had left Clarence more than a month before.

The cabby was very reluctant to accept Skinny's generous pay, and would not admit that he had earned it, no matter what Skinny said. Finally, they came to an agreement that the cabby would accept the money, provided that during their stay in Paris, the Company use only his cab, free of charge.

Skinny took his card, which read "Marcel Dubois," and listed his station's phone number. They in turn told him to look for them at the convent. Then, with many thanks showered upon him, the very content cabby left the three bedraggled, beat-up, and happy children at the door of their hotel, and went home to contemplate one of the most exciting days of his life.

Chapter 16

Preparing for Battle

"Okay, you medieval pirate," hissed Little Joe, pounding his fist on the table. "All this threatening and trap-setting is very nice, but so far we don't have anything to show for it, and I don't like working that way."

Black Hawk made no reply. He was watching Little Joe pace, slowly turning his massive head to keep his beady eyes on the younger man.

"Patience," he said at length, "patience."

"Yeah, well this river caper isn't too hopeful either," growled Little Joe, "and if you want my opinion, that Baron couldn't catch Keenan if she came right up to him and bit him."

He sat down dejectedly on the couch, and scratched his long, wavy hair.

They were in Black Hawk's room at Le Magnifique, the grandest suite available. Little Joe felt a bit out of place in the grand room, and wished he could get back to his own room in a lower class hotel on the other side of Paris.

Black Hawk in general made him uneasy. His men were far too military and yet unruly at the same time. Little Joe's gangster ways, and his few slick followers, were beginning to seem not so terrifying after all.

Suddenly, the Baron swept in the door, his crimson cape flowing behind him, his tall boots wet and muddy. He was panting, and looked disconcerted. Outside, they could hear his men hurrying down the hall towards his room.

The Baron leaned up against the door, and stared at the floor. He glanced up at the gigantic Black Hawk, seated at the room's large, round table, with a glass of brandy before him, and then to Little Joe's hunched form, staring at him levelly.

"Well?" barked Black Hawk. Little Joe eased himself to his feet, hands in pockets, and gave the Baron a mocking look.

"No," said the Baron, who didn't feel like explaining his failure, and wasn't sure his English was good enough to make Little Joe understand. He had been studying English ever since the Company had escaped from him before, and was far better, but still was baffled by much of Little Joe's lingo.

"What happened?" asked Little Joe.

"They got away." He sauntered over to the table, and poured himself a glass of brandy.

"Who? Who got away?" demanded Little Joe. "Did you let the kid get away, too?"

The Baron nodded. "Becky is gone, too."

"How?" asked Black Hawk ominously.

"Rescued by Keenan."

"Great!" scoffed Little Joe. "Just great. You really fixed things, didn't you? Not only do we not have Keenan or Conklin, but now we don't have that Swiss brat to catch 'em with! Maybe you'd better turn in, your Lordliness, before you sink us completely."

"You peasant!" the Baron spat. "You little worm! How many times has Keenan escaped you? It was a good trick. We followed Keenan all the way down river. She stopped at the rocks near a bridge after a long time, and we thought she was drowned. We went in, but what we chased was only her hat, and she is gone. We went back to van, but the only one inside was my man, Hans. He was locked in by the one that must be your boy, Conklin. Becky, and the other two escaped in a cab. You say I failed, well I say, next time, you be the one to try! Little worm!"

Little Joe sprang at the Baron with a hiss, but Black Hawk stopped him with a sharp command.

"Sit!" cried the old pirate, slapping the table. The Baron, who had drawn his small dagger, sheathed it again, and sat down. Little Joe violently kicked a stool over to the table, and slumped onto it, on the other side of Black Hawk.

"We must stay together," breathed Black Hawk, slowly turning his eyes from one to the other. "If we fight, all is lost. And do not fret,

Wolfgang." He gave the Baron a sidelong glance. "The venture today, I did not expect success."

"What?" cried Little Joe, "then why the ..."

"Because!" barked Black Hawk, silencing Little Joe with a stern glance. "Though they have retrieved their comrade Becky, it is little harm to us, and they will gain confidence. Foolish confidence that will be their ruin. We are still waiting for the other two."

"I don't care about them," muttered Little Joe.

"Well, we do," retorted the Baron loftily.

"And I have a way," continued Black Hawk, "a plan that will not fail. This one, I will lead."

"And so what is this master plan?" asked Little Joe. "I say we should just ..."

He stopped speaking and started coughing. The other two waited, for they were now used to such interruptions from Little Joe. His face turned pale, and his whole body shook. Sometimes it seemed he was choking, but the fits always passed.

He was clutching the table now, so hard that his knuckles turned white as marble. After a moment, Black Hawk reached behind him with his mammoth arm, and gave him a slap on the back with a giant, ring covered hand. The blow knocked Little Joe off his stool, and under the table with a thud, but the coughing stopped.

"Please continue," said the Baron smugly, as Little Joe crawled back into his seat.

"No," said Black Hawk. "Listen to me."

He motioned them to lean in, and lowered his voice. There was no one else in the room, but the air of secrecy and malice held in check was so contagious, that the other two began to sense a mounting threat. They listened respectfully.

"I have a monster in the water," said Black Hawk, his eyes lighting with a cruel flame.

Little Joe and the Baron looked at each other in confusion, both wondering if the other had understood the strange remark.

"A monster," continued Black Hawk, "that I caught on my travels. I will have it put in the water of a tank that I have purchased. A pool."

"What are you talking about; sewers?" asked Little Joe.

"Aye, the sewers, the trapped water. In Paris many old sewers exist. The water can't get out, and neither will the monster."

"Wait a second," said Little Joe, "are you trying to tell me that you carry a sea monster around with you, in your pockets maybe?"

"No," hissed Black Hawk, "no, not in my pockets. In great crate, lowered into sea. Men of mine will bring it when I say. It is grand thing to behold."

"And what does this monster look like?" asked Little Joe wearily, who was beginning to believe he was talking to a lunatic.

"Slimy, and wet, very wet. It is not very big, but with many arms. Sea monster."

"You say it is not very big?" asked the Baron.

Black Hawk nodded. "Not as big as fabled monsters, from the years of my fathers, but still, it would not fit in this room."

The Baron glanced around the spacious room, and gulped.

"Do you mean, something like an octopus?" asked Little Joe.

"Many names, pweza mcubwa, octopus, yes, one of them. Yet, it is not full grown. Baby."

"A baby octopus? You've got a baby octopus?" Little Joe's mind was racing with possibilities, all of which made him feel slightly sick.

"We place in trapped water, and he won't get out. Then, we lure the little devil and her friends to him, and he finish them. All but one. We keep the one who knows of treasure."

"You mean, Clarence?" asked Little Joe, who had vaguely heard of the treasure, and didn't believe a word of it.

"Yes. He will be useful, back in Africa. We use him when we need, then we finish him too."

"Sounds sort of cruel to me," admitted Little Joe, having to voice his thoughts, though he didn't like stating his real opinions in front of the Baron. "I mean, why can't we just fill them with lead, and have done with it? I remember hearing somewhere, that Keenan's mother had a phobia of sea creatures. Keenan might feel the same way. Besides, it would be so much quicker to just shoot them."

"No," Black Hawk smiled a terrible smile. "We will have sport. Keenan dies by the monster. It is decided."

"Oh my, goodness, gracious, me!" said a voice. "It all sounds very gruesome and awful indeed, my dear fellows, if you want my opinion."

They all turned, and looked at the newcomer.

Standing at the door, in a trench coat and battered hat, with an ancient umbrella in his hand, was a thin, old man. His spectacles were crooked, and his expression was one of horror and bewilderment.

"Who are you?" asked Little Joe, not even bothering to draw his gun. The man looked at him blankly for a moment.

"Ah yes, me," he said at length, his face brightening, "I am Professor Rafflesnort, from Manchester, England."

"Rafflesnort?" asked Little Joe with the beginnings of a smile. "Sounds like something you people would eat along with fish stew."

"Why, what a charming fellow!" cried the Professor, rushing forward and taking the unprepared Little Joe's hand. "I see we're going to hit it off, all right, mate. And you, dear Wolfgang Baron Von Stut, so awfully pleasant to see you, too!"

"*Baron* Wolfgang Von Schtut," corrected the Baron, rising and clicking his heels together formally.

The Professor took his hand, and wrung it cordially.

"Of course, me fine fellow, I'd forgotten. So many blasted things going on in me 'ead nowadays, I just don't seem to be able to keep things straight anymore."

"And who is this, that interrupts our highly secret meeting?" growled Black Hawk viciously. The Professor backed away, as the great man heaved himself to his feet.

"Terribly sorry, my grand fellow," he stammered, "didn't know at all. Didn't hear a thing, I swear!"

"Black Hawk is pirate and feared in many countries!" thundered the giant, "and does not need the alliance of such as you! I have heard Baron speak of you, and say you will join us. You will have to be greater, or I will finish *you!*"

"Of course, of course," stammered the terrified Professor. "What an honor, your 'ighness!"

"Now Black Hawk, please be seated," said the Baron. "I wish to hear what this idiot has to say."

Black Hawk turned sullenly and plopped down again, making his chair creak and whine under him. The Professor timidly sat down next to the Baron, looking like he might faint at any moment.

"Well, shan't I be introduced?" he asked, glancing towards Little Joe.

"Oh, yeah," said Little Joe, offering him a hand. "The name's Little Joe, New York gangster."

"Don't be frightened," drawled the Baron slyly, "he's never been convicted. Too soft-hearted."

Little Joe shot him a fiery glance but held his peace, seeing the deadly glint in Black Hawk's face.

"Now," said the Baron, "suppose you tell us how the capture of the other two children went."

"You captured them?" cried Black Hawk.

The Baron looked at him smugly. "I sent my friend the Professor after them," he smiled, "and now you see what has come of it. Tell us, Rafflesnort, tell us how you did it."

The Professor looked nervously from the Baron to Black Hawk, and from Little Joe back to the Baron.

"Well," he began, fiddling with the handle of his umbrella, "well, it didn't go quite as I expected."

The Baron's face clouded.

"What happened?" he asked sternly.

The Professor smiled sheepishly. "Really, my dear friends, you must admit that I am merely a scientist, not a regular murderer like master Little Joseph, or a pirate like his worship, Black Hawk, or kidnapper like your fine self."

The Baron buried his face in his hands. "You didn't get them?" he asked.

The Professor nodded gloomily. "Terribly sorry," he murmured.

"I will rephrase my question," said the Baron. "How did you not capture them?"

"Well, it was all quite difficult, my dear fellow. I followed them, just as you had advised, and they went all the way to Trinidad; beastly little country; and my men and I followed them to a great open air market, and started closing in on the little blighters."

"And?" asked Little Joe, beginning to be interested, "and what happened? Did Conklin's miserable sister give you the slip, or did you just let them leave because you felt sorry for them?"

"Well, they are rather a handsome pair," admitted the Professor, "I think they are rather fond of each other, in fact I saw ..."

"Go on with the kidnapping story," snapped the Baron.

"Oh yes, of course," stammered the Professor. "So, we started closing in on them, and I thought we had them for sure, but then, out of nowhere, they disappeared! Then a little old woman with bright black eyes knocked me down and I had to go back to the hotel for tea."

"Where did they go?" asked the Baron.

"I'm sure I don't know, but when we went after them, all we could find was; nothing, only an old woman who took up a blasted amount of time by trying to sell us a shawl."

"She tried to sell you a shawl?" asked Little Joe.

"Not the same woman who knocked me down ..." The Professor fell silent.

"At least we've got more men to add to our array," said the Baron. "I know that the hoodlums that old Rafflesnort has are fine men."

"I still say," hissed Black Hawk, "that he is an old idiot, and we don't need--"

"No, the one who knocked me down was taller," cried the Professor, slapping his forehead, "I almost thought she was wearing trousers under her skirt! She was just as bad as that little girl I found in my closet a month ago ..."

Black Hawk suddenly heaved himself to his feet, glaring at the old man, with eyes that seemed to shoot flame. "How dare to interrupt me!" he roared.

The Professor stood up, and backed over to the wall. "Terribly sorry," he whined, "didn't think first!"

"You will think before you ever do such a thing again!" bellowed the giant, taking a stride towards him.

"Merciful 'eavens, oh me 'ead!" cried the old man, shaking like a leaf. "Dear Baron, do say something before he chops me into ribbons with his awful looking sword!"

The Baron sprang forward and shouted his explanation to Black Hawk; shouted because there was no other way to be heard over Black Hawk's booming and the Professor's high jabbering.

Little Joe started to cough violently again, though no one heard him, and all the Professor's burly, and the Baron's mostly wet, men came running in to see if their masters were in danger, and immediately added themselves to the chaos.

* * *

"I wonder what the Company of Villains is doing tonight," said Sally, gazing out the window at the quiet garden.

"Arguing with each other," said Becky happily. "That's almost all they did while I was there. The Baron talked about the Professor, and told them how smart he was. Black Hawk blows up every once in a while, and the rest of the time he just sits and fumes. Little Joe does most of the talking; and coughing."

They were in Sally's room, waiting for Skinny, who was getting dressed. It was the night of Holy Saturday, and Skinny had offered to take the girls out to a fancy dinner, to celebrate the eve of Easter.

Back on Holy Thursday, when the cabby had left them, the three children had spent the rest of the day at their hotel, keeping Sally warm. She had developed a slight sneeze, but was still not pleased with the idea of staying in bed all day. Skinny was still wary of attacks from the enemy, and didn't even let the girls go down to the lobby to play in the revolving door.

Also, Becky had notified her friend Jack, with whom she had been staying, that she was safe, and would come by to see him as soon as she got the chance.

The next day, Good Friday, they had quietly moved in with the Sisters. The Sisters of Saint Joseph had a house in Paris. It was right in the heart of the downtown district and was very ancient. Mother Superior had heard about the Company of Secret Kids at the General Chapter meeting. The Superiors of both the Manchester house and the New York house had discussed them. She decided to make them welcome.

"I prefer staying here," Sally said, when they had been installed in a little guest house outside the sister's dormitory that was used for pilgrims. "I've had enough of hotels for the rest of my life."

Skinny agreed. "It does have a better feel to it."

"It feels like home to me," Sally said. "You may have learned everything you know from Little Joe, but I learned everything I know from the Sisters."

There was a beautiful service in their old church, after which the Secret Kids immediately returned to their rooms. That Good Friday they had spent in the correct mood. Sally had decided that lounging around their rooms, with nothing to do, was the best way to observe the day. If Sally hadn't been inspired by that thought, and the rosary she led them all in, she would not have been able to obey Skinny's safety order all through the long, dreary day.

The next day, however, Sally and Becky had refused to be kept confined, while the beautiful, adventurous city of Paris was out there.

Skinny had decided that waiting for an attack was almost worse than an attack itself, and partly because he was going crazy from cabin fever himself, he granted their ardent, and even violent requests, and promised to take them out to dinner in the downtown district.

When she heard that a formal evening was ahead, Becky absolutely demanded that the girls go out and buy appropriate clothing. Sally couldn't care less, and actually had many things she would rather do than go clothes shopping, but she loved Becky, and was touched by her scrupulous attention to her appearance. Sally tried valiantly to keep the focus of the shop's staff and the grandest articles for Becky, but somehow the main attraction was always herself, and Becky glowed in the joy of seeing Sally being appreciated.

During the stops at the many shops, where always the same routine ensued; the staff all being struck by Sally's wild uncensored beauty, of which she was totally oblivious; Skinny waited outside, and kept a watchful eye out for enemies. He guessed they wouldn't hunt them down in a dress shop.

Whenever he glanced in, he saw Becky ordering around all the clerks, in her adorable little French dialect.

Skinny actually thought it a great joke to see Sally made so much of, for he knew her disdain of such things, which was getting less and less concealed as the day wore on.

He made not a few playful remarks, as they sauntered down the streets, heavily laden with clothes boxes, to all of which Sally gave him a scathing, yet good-humored reply, or if she was close enough, a swift kick in the shins. Most of the time, her aim for the kicks was not always as good as it could be, because her vision and flexibility were encumbered by the pyramid of boxes she herself was carrying.

Finally, when they were passing a large trash bin in an alley, Sally came to a halt, set her boxes down, and without telling the others what her motives were, she scrambled up the side, and leaned over into the dumpster, heels flying to keep her balanced.

Skinny had pulled her down, and asked her just what idiotic thing she thought she was trying to do. She had told him to mind his own darned business, and scrambled back up. The second time, she emerged with an empty trash bag, that seemed somewhat clean. Then, she had opened all her boxes, there on the main street, and emptied the clothes into the bag. At first Becky was shocked and mortified, but her arms were tired, too, and after a quick summary on the stupidities of boxes that large for clothes that small, Sally won them over, and they emptied their boxes into the bag, and rejoiced to be rid of the hassle.

Upon their return home, Sally had started in on the changes she wanted to make to her outfit. She had been much annoyed and disgusted by the fashions that young women of her age were supposed to wear in Paris, and the first alteration she made was to pin up the top of the dress Becky had chosen for her, to make the neck line higher than it had been.

Next, she vetoed the matching hat, and nothing Becky could say would change her mind. Finally, Becky removed the wreath of roses that adorned the crown of the hat, and convinced Sally to wear at least it in her hair.

Sally consented, and moved onto the alteration of the shoes. They were made of a lovely satin material and were the make of small dancing slippers, but had spindly little heels beneath them that Sally thought absurd. She bet Becky that the heels would come off if she did anything that she was likely to do, like a handspring, or a sharp turn, or a tap dance.

To prove her point, she took them to the door of the guest house, hooked the heel of the shoe over the knob, and yanked. The stick-like heel popped off.

Sally showed Becky triumphantly, and then realized with much satisfaction, that the shoes were now wearable in her opinion, and even Becky had to admit they looked prettier.

Sally quickly knocked the heel off the other slipper, and the heels joined the unlucky hat in the wastebasket.

As a finishing touch, Sally used the scissors in her pocket knife to remove the starchy lace that stuck far out from the sleeves and the hem of the dress. She replaced it with a little fringe of soft, white lace that had been started by her mother years before, and lately finished by Christine. Sally wasn't the sewing type.

At last, when she was satisfied with what she called the "Outfit of the Insane," Becky admitted that she looked wonderful. Sally shrugged, and said that as long as it was decent, and she could run around in it, she didn't care what it looked like.

Now she was standing by the window, fiddling with the roses on her head, and musing about the evening her enemies had before them.

"I wonder if they've gone to any nice French restaurants while they've been here," she said, thinking about Becky's earlier remarks, and wondering if Black Hawk was the type that would start a food fight if he got mad at the dinner table.

"Maybe, but they didn't take me with them when I was their prisoner," answered Becky. "Hey, Sally, button me up."

Sally turned to her, and began the tedious task of buttoning up the countless little pearl buttons that lined the back of Becky's dress.

Becky was wearing a soft pink dress, the same fairy-like pattern and light breathy fabric as Sally's, and the color perfectly set off her deep brown eyes and hair. She had followed Sally's example in raising the collar, and wearing only the roses on her head. Finally, she even deigned to remove the heels from her shoes, and now the two girls matched almost perfectly.

Becky's dress was accented with pearls, and Sally's with diamonds. She had them as buttons down the back, and a line of the sparkling, star-like ones ran along the waist as a slim belt, and were sewn onto the neckline.

"Hey, Beck, tonight are you going to try all the strange French foods?"

"I once tried escargot. Snails! Bleh!"

Sally laughed. "Yeah, but over in New York I've eaten octopus at a Japanese restaurant, and I'll eat any kind of fruit or vegetable on earth, so I might as well add snails and frog legs to my list."

"I don't know," said Becky, "do you think Skinny will try all that?"

"If I dare him to, which I will," said Sally smugly.

There was a knock at their door, and Sally hurriedly finished buttoning Becky, and ran to answer it. She opened the door to Skinny, and stood still and stared at him for a moment.

He was all in black, from head to toe, with his hair combed down slick. His black shirt was only his undershirt with a hole in it, but over it he was wearing a shining, black, satin jacket. It was tailored to fit him tightly, which made him look more muscular. He also looked taller, and stronger, and his pale face seemed stern and noble. His gray blue eyes shone with a light that could turn at a moment's notice from a joyful, winsome sparkle to a wild, dangerous flash. Sally almost felt frightened of him for a moment. He was standing tall and silent, staring at her, and not saying a word.

He didn't say a word, because he temporarily couldn't. He had come whistling from his own room in his usual bold manner, and knocked on their door totally unprepared for what would answer. Sally didn't know it, and if she had she wouldn't have cared, but her appearance on that night was enough to catch anyone's eye.

She looked more like a fairy princess than a real girl. Her graceful movements and lithe figure had always given her such a look, but tonight the gown brought her beauty to life. The blue dress, just the color of her delft blue eyes, fell loosely about her, in gentle ripples. The diamonds reflected the shine in her radiant face, as the light danced on them, and the small roses in her hair contrasted well with the dark curls that hung round her face. The bodice of the dress was plain, and yet somehow all the more beautiful for that reason. The skirt came flowing out of the belt like a waterfall, and fell down in waves to the lace edging that rippled around about three inches above Sally's ankles. The small, blue slippers were light and airy, and were adorned with one rose each, the soft edges of the petals tinged by just a touch of scarlet. The scarlet was the match for her beautifully shaped lips that gleamed thin and bright in the light.

"Hey, Sally," murmured Skinny, "you ready for dinner?"

Sally nodded, and laughed. That silvery, somewhat shy, and very familiar laugh put Skinny back at his ease. This lovely creature was still the same wild, charmingly bizarre Sally.

"Then let's go," he grinned. "Hey Becky, you coming?"

Becky ran to the door, with Sally's purse, and stopped short. "Wow, don't you look snazzy!"

"I was just thinking the same thing about you, lovely lady," laughed Skinny, bending down and kissing her hand. Becky giggled, and embarrassedly wiped the kiss from her hand, but not when Skinny was looking, for fear she would hurt his feelings.

Sally took her purse from Becky, and looked through it. "Hey, Beck, where's my white pocketknife?"

"Oh, I was using it to cut the roses from my hat, I'll get it."

"Why do you need pocketknives?" asked Skinny patiently.

"You never know when you might," Sally answered knowingly. "I might need to cut roses off a hat."

"Well, come on," said Skinny, as Becky returned with the knife, "it's not every kid my age who can boast of taking two girls as pretty as you two out to dinner at the same time, so let's go!"

The dinner was wonderful. Skinny treated them to a beautiful restaurant, and they enjoyed the fine food to the utmost, even the stranger things, which Becky finally consented to try. They had gone to dinner early, and the sun was still up as they ate dessert.

"You know, Becky," said Sally, as she endeavored to make her small metal dessert spoon stick to her nose, "I think the only reason you say you don't like vegetables, is so you'll have room to eat your dessert, and ours too."

Becky looked up from Skinny's half-eaten éclair that he had let her finish, glanced at Sally with a superior air, and sniffed.

"You know, technically, we shouldn't even be eating dessert," said Skinny, after giving Becky an appreciative grin for her dignified ways. "At least, I shouldn't. I gave sweets up for Lent."

"Me too, but it's Saturday night," objected Becky, and started eating faster.

"Well," said Sally, "my mother always said that you can substitute Lenten sacrifices for other kinds of sacrifices, provided that the sacrifices you sacrifice for the original sacrifices are sacrifices that are worth substituting, because they really are sacrificial sacrifices. Does that make sense?"

"No," grinned Skinny. "But I know what you mean. I was taught, by you Sal, that if you really need to, you can treat sundown on Saturday as if it were already Sunday, and you can break your fast. But Sally, you never told us what your sacrifice is that you will sacrifice for the sacrifice you're sacrificing."

"Not bad, but I said it better," said Sally. "But what I meant was, that the way we're being hounded by the Company of Villains is a lot more of a sacrifice for me, than it would be to go without dessert tonight, so I offer that up."

"Right, so you can stop being so scared, Becky," laughed Skinny, "and finish my éclair at a reasonable pace. You get it?"

"All expect the sacrifice part," answered Becky solemnly, and returned her attention to her plate.

Skinny laughed. "Well, I guess I'll pay this monumental check, and we can get out of here."

"How about we go to a movie?" suggested Sally. "It's early yet. The sun is only starting to go down."

"Does that mean it doesn't qualify as Sunday yet?" asked Becky anxiously.

"Sure, for little folks like you," said Skinny, tousling her hair, roses and all.

"So can we go to a movie?" persisted Sally.

"It'd be in French, you knucklehead."

"Oh yes," Sally slumped down in her seat, "drat."

"How about we go see the Eiffel Tower?" suggested Becky. "It's real pretty at night."

"I guess so, but ... " Sally stopped midway in her sentence, and sat up.

"What's wrong?" Skinny followed her gaze, out the large window in the front of the restaurant.

"Out there, on the curb," said Sally, the familiar light of adventure kindling in her eyes. "The gang's all here."

Skinny looked, and saw Black Hawk, in his full strange dress, carefully conferring with the familiar slouching figure of Little Joe, and the crimson-cloaked Baron. Near them, but obviously excluded from the curbside strategy meeting, was a smaller figure in a white lab coat, happily watching the passing traffic, and absently hopping from one foot to the other.

"You're right," muttered Skinny, "and where they are, their men can't be far behind."

"We move now," said Sally authoritatively. "Skinny, take Becky over to the entrance, and both of you stay there, out of sight from the street."

"Where are you going?" asked Skinny, helping Becky into the jacket she had brought along.

"Well, it's a safe bet they know we're in here, or they wouldn't be watching this place like a pack of vultures. We've got to attack them on all fronts, and give them multiple things to go for. Then they can't gang up on us."

"Okay, but you can bet that the majority of them will go for you," said Skinny, "I'll get Becky to safety, and come help you."

"Right, let's say we meet at the Eiffel Tower in case we get separated."

Skinny nodded, and they stood up, as inconspicuously as possible. Sally glanced towards the kitchen door, and grinned. Skinny guessed her plan, and even he had to smile. As Becky started for the door, he took Sally by the arm, and looked hard at her.

"You be careful, Kid," he said, using his name for her that he saved for serious occasions. Sally nodded, and started off towards the kitchen door. Skinny watched her for a moment, wondering why he felt shaky. She looked so unreal tonight, he almost feared she might disappear into whatever wild, and yet beautiful world she came from. At the door of the kitchen, she turned, grinned mischievously at him, and winked.

Skinny winked back, and turned away, following Becky to the door. Sally stood on tip-toe, and looked into the round windows of the kitchen doors.

"Well, here goes nothing," she muttered to herself, and then smashed through the doors.

She let out a wild whoop as she dodged through the kitchen, making her swift way to the back service entrance. The French cooks turned and stared at her in amazement and bewilderment. When she reached the back door, Sally slammed through it, letting out another shriek, and making as much noise as possible. It didn't really matter whether she did or not, for the villains at the corner were watching the door closely, and would have seen her no matter what, but Sally always felt that her style needed to be fairly obvious during an adventure.

The Baron was the first to cross the street, stealthily loosening his sword in its sheath as he ran. Sally shot away from him, down the alley, passed a produce truck, and ran off onto the main street. As she stopped at the curb, Black Hawk came thundering around it, and charged towards her. She sprang into the traffic, and frantically, yet gracefully came through it to the other side of the street. Black Hawk didn't attempt to follow her, for his great bulk was not skilled at dodging and ducking.

Sally had counted on this fact, and believed her escape finished, when, out of the alley beside Black Hawk, Little Joe emerged. Black Hawk gave a grunt, and pointed at Sally. Sally turned and fled. She knew Little Joe could be as agile as a cat. She wasn't staying to take chances with him. She heard him behind her, as he made his way through the traffic and reached the curb. The busy, bustling city of Paris did not notice a thing.

Sally started off, down another alley. His feet pounded behind her, and she could hear him gaining on her. Though her mind was keen on strategy, Sally knew that in a direct chase, she hadn't a chance against the slick, New York hood.

"He'll know all my ideas," she thought, wishing she was being pursued by any one of the other villains. She hastily thought through all her techniques in the art of escaping, and decided to try one that seemed terribly unoriginal.

It came to her from one of her favorite books, in which the hero used the trick to escape from a bully. As she put the plan into effect, she recalled truthfully, that in the story, by a chance of ill luck, the hero actually didn't escape, but she supposed that made for a better plot.

"Well, maybe I'll be luckier than old Tom Playfair," she muttered, "and if I'm not, I'm in a lot more trouble than he was."

She was approaching the end of the long, thin alley. At the entrance of it, just before the street, there was a lamppost. It was metal and shining in the light of the low sun. Sally slowed just the slightest bit, for Little Joe was almost upon her already. She let him get only a few feet away, and then with a final sprint, she dashed out of the alley, grabbed hold of the lamppost with her right hand, pivoted around it like a flash of blue lightning, and dashed back down the alley, whence she had come.

It was a beautiful move, and executed wonderfully well. If anyone else had been on her tail, she would have gained a lead that would have ended the chase. Unfortunately, her pursuer had used the same trick many times before, and had even been expecting it. Almost at the same moment as Sally let go of the post and shot off down the alley, Little Joe grabbed hold of it, performed the same move, with more speed than Sally had mustered, and took out after her at half the distance that he had been before.

She wasn't half way down the deserted alley, when Sally felt a strong hand grip her shoulder, and with amazing strength, was spun round. Little Joe threw one arm around her shoulders, and slipped the other under her knees, and swooped her into his arms. He kept right on running, not changing his speed at all, heading back toward the place Black Hawk was waiting, while Sally kicked and struggled.

"Well, it didn't work for Tom Playfair, either," he heard her mutter. She didn't say anything else, for though she was always ready with a good one-liner for any occasion, she thought, awkwardly, that she couldn't really say anything to Little Joe, who was probably at that very moment wishing he didn't have to obey Black Hawk's orders, and could kill her on the spot.

In truth, Little Joe's thoughts were a little more in Sally's favor than she supposed.

He was keeping on with his pace, and holding onto her with unexpected difficulty. Sally was kicking, wiggling, and struggling far more than he had thought she could. He secretly wondered how much further he could go, bearing such a wildcat of a girl, and was thankful that the area they had chosen to meet was deserted.

Then, as he reached the end of the alley on the other side, several things happened at once. Sally gave a tremendous wiggle, got herself turned around, and bit his shoulder.

Little Joe gave a muffled shout, that turned to a gasping curse, as a short figure in white suddenly shot out in front of him. He tripped over it.

He heard a groan, with a Cockney tinge to it, as he landed on top of the person, and on top of Sally, and as he hit the ground with a thump, something landed on him with tremendous force.

"Quick Sal!" he heard a whisper above him.

There was another wiggle from underneath him, and he heard the familiar sound of Skinny's voice and the swish of Sally's dress as Skinny helped her up.

"Only a blasted Irishman could have made that 'eavy a landing," came a voice as Skinny sped away, pulling Sally by the hand.

Little Joe rolled off him, and sat up, shaking the stars out of his eyes. "Actually, with Conklin and Keenan in the dog-pile, that makes three Irish Americans that landed on ... " He stopped, and looked at the Professor, who was carefully rubbing his forehead.

"How did you know I was of Irish descent?" asked Little Joe, sitting wearily against the brick wall of the building.

"The Baron told me. He said you were full of low Irish pranks."

"Now see here," growled Little Joe, "I ain't saying I'm a saint, but you can tell your Baron that any low trick I know I learned in New

York. And filthy New York is not part of my heritage. My heritage is the one thing in the world that I've still got to be proud of!"

"Bless my soul," said the Professor, "but you do all behave alike!"

"What?" Little Joe stood up, and pulled the Professor up after him, "who?"

"The way you all three talk, and act, and even the way you get angry is rather similar. Is this an Irish trait?"

Little Joe groaned, and rubbed the shoulder that Sally had bitten. "Perhaps all Irishmen look alike to you? You are a nutcase."

"Well, you needn't get touchy about it, sir," retorted the Professor, "I mean, I 'aven't mentioned even one thing about Ireland belonging to Great Britain."

"And you better not!" cried Little Joe. "Because if you do, then suddenly Keenan and Conklin will be on my side, and you'll have to reckon with us!"

"Do calm down, my dear Little Joseph," said the Professor, patting him comfortingly on the back. "I didn't mean a thing by it. Now, have you by any chance seen my spectacles?"

"They're on your head," said Little Joe wearily. "Now, I'm going after Conklin and Keenan, because I think, though they've got an awful lead, that Keenan was hurt when I fell on her. That should slow them down a good deal."

He shot off down the road again, and hollered back to the Professor to go back to Black Hawk and receive orders.

Quite a few blocks ahead of him, Skinny was dragging Sally down another alley toward a main street, and listening intently for sounds of oncoming danger.

"Skinny, slow down," said Sally.

"Are you okay?" asked Skinny, still holding her hand.

"Little Joe is actually a lot lighter than I thought he'd be," said Sally. "But did you hear that crack the old Professor made about the Irish? I was glad you were pulling me, or I would have gone right back and had it out with him."

"You might like to know that Little Joe takes his patriotism seriously too. If the British half of the Professor prevailed against his chicken half, you and Little Joe might be fighting for the same cause, the honor of our heritage."

"Erin Go Bragh!" cried Sally, and with a fresh sprint, they came out onto the main street.

"We've got to split up here," said Skinny, pulling her behind an empty truck for a hiding place. "I hope Joe thinks you're hurt, so he'll believe we're together and moving slow."

"So we separate and move fast," finished Sally.

"Right. Now when you left, I put Becky in a cab, and she's on her way to Jack's friend's house, where she'll be safe for the time being. I saw the Professor standing to the side of that alley, as if he were waiting for someone, so I snuck up behind him, and waited, too. I heard Joe coming down the alley at a dead run, and it sounded like he was carrying something like a wild banshee, so I figured it was you. Just before he came out of the alley, I gave the Professor a shove, and then the three of you landed on each other, and I gave Little Joe a bonus smack on the head."

"Great operation!" cried Sally, "if we could pull a few more stunts like that, this night might end in our favor."

"Well, for now, it needs to end in our flight." Skinny pointed to the curb near them. "Now, there's a cab waiting for you on the corner, compliments of me. You can take it wherever you want. Meet you at the Tower. I'm going off to lone it. Now move!"

Sally made for the cab, and threw herself in. Out of the window she saw Skinny cross the street, and dash off down a darker street. Sally told the driver to take her down the road that passed by the restaurant where they'd eaten, so she could see if the Company of Villains was still there.

When they drove by, the curb was deserted, and so was the back alley behind the restaurant. Satisfied with the thought that the villains were at a loss as to where their prey went, Sally told the driver to head for the Eiffel Tower.

Skinny ran down the street, pounding the cement with a rather joyous excitement to be on the run again. He was experienced at street chasing, and didn't feel very out of practice. Then suddenly, as he passed a sidewalk café, its windows turned rosy by the light of the setting sun, Skinny heard a familiar voice. He ducked under a table with a long trailing table-cloth, just in time.

"They've got to be around here, somewhere!" he heard the Baron snarl.

"Well, I just hope you have a chance to come eye to eye with Keenan," answered Little Joe, panting. "She's a wild girl. She bit me like a wolf, and she whoops like a hyena!"

"If you can't handle one of your own kind," drawled the Baron, "then maybe I'd better take over."

"What is with that nationality bit and you people?" asked Little Joe. "I don't need to be reminded by you idiots every few seconds that Keenan is Irish, too. I know it!"

"Yes, but the irony is irresistible," laughed the Baron.

"I just hope you get a chance to see that untamable thing in action. Now come on!"

Their footsteps retreated. Skinny waited for a moment, and then emerged from his hiding spot. He could see the Baron and Little Joe making their way down the street. One was striding tall and proud, the other slouching and skulking.

Skinny started at an easy pace, heading in the opposite direction. He mused on what they had said, and smiled. He was glad that the enemy considered Sally an "untamable thing." It gave him a thrill, to think that he was so close to one that even Little Joe was wary of.

"But am I so close?" he asked himself, after considering it for a moment. He agreed, Sally was like an untamed force. And he couldn't say that he knew something that would tame her.

He would have liked to think that he could, but he knew it wasn't so. No one he knew could keep Sally's unmatchable spirit in check. He wondered how she would end up.

It struck him that, maybe before that night was over, she might be gone. Killed or destroyed by any one of the many men that wanted her dead.

Somehow, he couldn't imagine Sally as being the sort of person who could die. Her life had been in danger many times, but she had always made it through. He wondered what he really thought of her, and, more practically, if she could make it through the night that lay ahead, full of perils and unknown adventure.

Chapter 17

The Night of Their Lives

The regal Eiffel Tower gleamed beautifully in the setting sun. It was practically deserted. As Skinny jogged across the grassy park that surrounded its base, he felt as though he were shrinking. Nothing and no one could feel impressive around such a structure. He thought with some satisfaction that even Black Hawk would be insignificant next to it.

He got on one of the elevators, and rode up, feeling majestic and alone, slowly being lifted into the air, suspended between earth and sky, with nothing familiar to cling to. As the doors opened on the first floor, he leaned out, but saw no one. He and Sally hadn't made any arrangements about where on the great tower to meet, but he figured she had beat him there. He checked the second platform, but without success.

As he started up for the third floor, he began to feel slightly nervous. He had never really been bothered by heights, but the lonely feeling of floating on air was growing on him, and making him uneasy. He began to feel annoyed with Sally, for he figured her adventurous nature would have compelled her to go straight to the very top, and though he didn't like to admit it, he didn't relish the idea of being that high up, especially with the unpredictable Sally.

Then, on the third platform, the elevator doors opened, and he saw her.

She was facing the setting sun, leaning against the railing, with her back to him. He hadn't noticed before, what a spectacular sunset it was. There were large clouds in ornate and breathtaking shapes of great height and grandeur, surrounding the fiery ball, and they were turned all shades of rose, violet, scarlet, orange, red, and deep blue. The sun had been hiding behind them, afraid to show itself one last time, in the majestic beauty of its passing.

Now, just as the doors opened before him, it revealed itself, in a splendor and wonder that took his breath away. Silhouetted against the passionate beauty of the dying day, was the slight figure in the light blue dress. The soft breeze, that grew stronger here, above the clouds, stirred her dark hair gently, tossing it playfully, and made her skirt ripple like a sea before a storm, the diamonds studded on it glinting in the rosy glow. The roses on her dark and waving hair were still fresh and light, though the carefully pinned wreath had slid just the slightest bit off center from her wild evening. She was so lithe, so surreal in that magical setting, that stepping out of the elevator noiselessly, Skinny dared not make a sound, for fear of marring the beauty of the moment.

Though he was silent, Sally turned her head just the slightest bit, and saw him. The sunset was reflected in her sparkling eyes shining from within her lively face, with cheeks touched by just a tinge of rosy blush, the proof of the life burning within, and her ruby lips parted ever so slightly, as she smiled welcome to him.

Skinny came forward slowly, his mind and heart racing, but not in unison. He came to her, and stood, leaning against the rail, standing tall and proud. His blond hair tossed back over his black shirt, his features curving themselves into only the slightest possibility of an answering smile. Sally turned back to the sunset, and sighed.

"Too good to last," she whispered.

Her words pierced Skinny to the heart. She was right. The wonder, and the mystery of that beautiful moment would soon be gone forever, and they would face the terrible night that lay ahead. He knew Sally was speaking of the sunset; that it would fade into the deepness and darkness of the night, but to him, her words meant more. He thought of her, a young, beautiful thing, with so much to live for. And he thought that she was so pretty tonight, that she too, seemed far too good to last. Maybe this night was her last. If it was, he was going to make this moment one they would never forget.

Slowly, almost imperceptibly, he slid his arm around her. She laid her head on his shoulder, and sighed again. Together they stared out into the sunset. Skinny felt a thrill go through him, as Sally glanced up, and their eyes met. Hers were moist, and he suddenly found that his were too. Then, a tear escaped her long, black lashes, and slid down her cheek, like a piece of living glass. The light caught it and made it glow. Skinny again let the shadow of a smile flit across his face, and she caught it. Then, she turned back to the scene that spread before them, but already the light was fading, and the whole scene falling into a deep purple shadow, that boded the oncoming of the night.

The moment was over.

As it ended, the two heard a small click behind them; the sound of an elevator door shutting. They spun round at the same time, and saw Little Joe before them, gun in hand. His handsome face seemed strained, as though he were trying to suppress his cough, but he held the gun steady.

Still with his arm around Sally's shoulders, Skinny turned to the elevator on the opposite end of the platform. He knew that to run would be useless. Little Joe would gun them down before they'd moved two steps, if killing them was his immediate purpose. If he was still under orders to keep them alive, then he might just be here to watch them, and escape was possible.

Skinny glanced at Sally. She was staring at the gun, but slowly, her eyes met his. She tightened her grip on his hand, which she had grabbed as they turned around. She slowly looked over Little Joe's shoulder, at the elevator behind him, and then over at the one opposite to them. Skinny got the idea. He was beginning to like how they could read each other's minds. He nodded, but only with his eyes.

Then suddenly, before Little Joe could suspect something was coming, Sally darted off towards the farther elevator, while Skinny ran straight for Little Joe, and shoved past him. Apparently, Little Joe was still under Black Hawk's orders, for he did not fire. Instead of grabbing Skinny, who was but inches away from him, he dashed across the platform, and reached for Sally, just as the elevator doors shut between them. Skinny saw that she was safe, and pushed the button that closed his doors. He wasn't sure which floor Sally was going to, but he headed for the bottom.

As the doors opened before him at the base of the structure, he saw the Baron, the Professor, and several of their men standing on the grass. When they saw Skinny, they dashed forward. He quickly pushed the button, and went speeding back up. He stopped at each floor, to try and locate Sally, but saw no one, not Sally or Little Joe.

Finally, when he came to the very top platform, he found what he had been looking for.

Both of them.

They came zooming past his door, heading for the opposite elevator. Little Joe still had his gun, but it was pointing downwards. Skinny leapt out of the elevator, as Sally landed in the other one and pushed the button.

The doors shut just as Little Joe reached them. He turned, and ran for the other elevator, brushing past Skinny as though he didn't exist. As he entered it, and turned to press the button, the other doors rolled open again, and Sally re-appeared. Skinny ran toward her, and tried to catch the doors before they shut again. But as he did so, he heard a slightly surprising sound. It was the sound of a gunshot.

He turned and saw the elevator doors close on Little Joe. The villain had seen Sally reemerge onto the platform, for his doors were not yet shut. In that moment, his face had changed. His look, which had lately been so hassled and annoyed, became independent once again. As the doors shut before him, Skinny saw him holding his gun steady, pointing it at them.

Sally was standing still, looking at the doors that had just closed on the gangster. Skinny turned back to their elevator, wondering how fast Little Joe could get back. He turned to find Sally standing in the exact same position on the platform that she had been. He wondered if the gunshot had frightened her, or maybe it had gone so close to her that she was still recovering from shock, or maybe, maybe...

As he thought; or tried not to think; the worst thought that had ever occurred to him, he realized that it was true. Sally slowly began to sink towards the ground. It was such a graceful movement, that she made hardly a sound as she hit the floor. Skinny stood still, frozen in the terrible realization of the truth. Little Joe had finally hit his mark.

Skinny flew forward, and threw himself on his knees at her side. He rolled her over, and pulled her into his arms. The fabric of her left shoulder was ripped, the lovely blue material darkening with a small, yet terrible, crimson stain. The wreath of roses had fallen off her head, and lay desolately on the floor. Her long lashes had curtained the flashing eyes, and the rosy hue of her cheeks had faded into darkness like the sunset.

"No," said Skinny, looking down pleadingly into her face, holding his breath, listening for any sign of life. He couldn't believe how a person could be so very alive one moment, and the next moment...

Her words, the last she had spoken to him came back to him; "too good to last."

He nodded. "Too good to last," he whispered, brushing aside a stray black curl that had fallen over her cheek. He wondered. How did he feel about Sally?

All his thoughts took only a split second to pass through his mind. She was a great strategist, and had guts the likes of which he had never seen. She was beautiful, he had always thought that, but until now, he had never thought that mattered much to him. She was fun, wild, and untamable. She was Sally. Did he love her?

Suddenly, memories flashed before his eyes, visions of her in all the glory of the greatest moments that he'd witnessed. He saw her grin welcoming him, in a wild, impish way that first day at the convent; he saw her as she dealt him a blow with her braces in Africa that knocked the daylights of him. He saw her leaping and cavorting around in the forest, with all Black Hawk's men after her, and saw her swaying, and falling from her saddle as they made their escape. He saw her remorseful expression as she asked his forgiveness for her rash deeds, and saw her as she laughed and chattered on their way to Switzerland. He saw her plowing her way through the snow of the Alps, as she tried to find them a way, and her flushed and rosy cheeks as she fought bravely in the famous 'Snow Battle,' and, later that night, face aglow by firelight, he saw her as she sang her favorite Christmas carols, and then dropped off into a peaceful sleep.

Then he saw her graceful, fantastic dance preformed for the Baron, that had saved his and Clarence's lives. He saw her as she broke the mallet on the gong, starting the avalanche, and as she fled to the door, ducking and dodging, the forever present smile still upon her lips. Next he saw her as she looked hard and long at him, in the hotel in New York, trying to help him make the decision to be loyal, and yet letting him make the choice on his own. Then, her fiery eyes, and heavy breathing, caused by the passion inside her, as she pulled him back to their side on the slick bridge in the moonlight.

From there, he saw her, covered in orange flakes of dust, one shoe on, the other off, hair rumpled to create the maddest image, tearing about a fine, old, English home, looking for the key ring, and then, having found it, fulfilling a life-long dream of riding down a dumb-waiter. He saw her, comforting and silent, as he battled with himself after Christine had walked out of his life.

Then, he saw the slim figure in the trench coat, dragging him along the night sidewalks of New York, and taking such care for his safety and comfort. Next, he saw her on the dance floor, in his arms, and the look of content that shone from her face as they danced. He thought of her faint as she heard the news that Black Hawk had come for her, and her modest embarrassment when she awoke. He thought of her as she paddled slowly towards him and Becky in the river, and how she had turned blue on the way home. He thought of the stoic way she bore the long, lonely, Good Friday, and then of her face as she'd opened the door to him, that very night at the convent.

Last to his tear filled eyes, came the vision of her celestial beauty as she'd turned to him, the sunset behind her, and he knew, no matter how old he lived to be, that that image of her would never fade into darkness, as had the reality. He opened his eyes, and saw yet another sight of her, this one more dreamlike than all the blessed memories. It was the sight of her lying cold and still, the rosy hue gone, the shining eyes closed.

Only a moment had elapsed.

"Sal," he whispered.

He pulled her up, and with breathless reverence, kissed the white forehead. "Sally, you nutty kid, I didn't know it till this moment, but now, whether or not you can hear me, I love you."

He almost expected, like some fairytale, or modern movie that Sally so disdained, that she would wake, impractically, at the sound of his voice, and the touch of his lips on her brow. But no fairytale ending awaited him. She made no sound, and took no breath, her face was still.

Behind him, he vaguely heard the elevator doors open. He could hear their footsteps, as the enemies stalked towards him. There was no one else around. The place was deserted.

Obviously, they expected him to make a struggle, for they kept their distance. He glanced up, and saw the Baron, the Professor, and Little Joe before him, backed by about ten of their men. The Professor was standing well behind the Baron, and though he had a rusty gun in his hand, he was shaking like a leaf. The Baron looked at Skinny levelly, his sword drawn in one hand, his pistol in the other. He too, seemed to be waiting for Skinny's attack, and was a bit ill at ease.

It was Little Joe's face that struck Skinny most. As they had approached, Little Joe had taken in the whole scene at a glance. The young man, still merely a boy, kneeling despairing and broken, holding in his arms the lifeless body of the beautiful maiden he loved. Little Joe had seen such moonlit scenes before, and he did not like the memory. He alone of the villains was not waiting for a fight. He alone knew the feelings in the mind of a young man in love, when his dreams lay in ruin at his feet.

"What do we do?" asked the Baron quietly, turning to Little Joe for direction.

Little Joe looked up, and around at their surroundings. "Let's chuck them over the edge," he answered.

"But the monster of Black Hawk," protested the Baron, "you do not want to go against his orders."

"I'll do what I want!" shouted Little Joe, taking a step toward the Baron, which made that dignitary and the Professor behind him shrink back.

Little Joe looked down at Skinny, who was once again gazing into Sally's face, oblivious of anything else that was going on around him.

"I'll do what I want," repeated Little Joe, this time in a quiet, menacing, snarl. "That old insane pirate couldn't get any sport out of Keenan now. We might as well end this, and we can all go back to our own countries. Black Hawk isn't here yet, and we can finish these two off before he shows up. Besides, Keenan is too far gone for any monster fighting."

"All right, I'll go along with you," said the Baron, "but you must take the responsibility when Black Hawk gets angry."

"Right, sure," Little Joe nodded, "now bring those two over to this edge."

He walked to the rail, which was covered by a thick chain link fence, to prevent tourists from endangering themselves. He shook the fence roughly. It was loose. He turned back to the others, who were still standing motionless, staring down at Skinny with some perturbation.

"Go on!" cried Little Joe, "he won't fight. As far as he cares, he's already dead. Haven't any of you ever been in love before?"

Without answering his last question, the Baron barked an order to the men, and they strode towards Skinny. The Professor held his breath, and shut his eyes as they reached him, but Skinny made no resistance. The men pulled him roughly from the floor, and one took Sally into his own arms, and slung her limp form over his shoulder like a sack of potatoes.

Skinny cried out, and sprang toward her, but was roughly pulled back. Now that the men were more certain that he wouldn't hurt them, they began to enjoy their role as captors, for they soon forgot that Skinny had submitted. They acted as though they had vanquished him by their own cunning and bravery. This delusion spread to the Baron too, for once Skinny was held fast, he came over to him and laughed in his face.

Skinny made no response, and stood with bowed head, his grief too great for tears. The Baron gave a snort of disgust, and struck Skinny an open blow on his unprotected face. Except for the slight tightening of jaw muscles, Skinny made no sign to show that he had even felt the heavy blow.

"Hey, stop that, you devil!" shouted Little Joe, springing forward.

He shoved aside the men holding Skinny, and grabbing him by the chin, looked hard at his stern, handsome face. Skinny did not meet his eyes.

Little Joe let his chin go with a jerk, after an almost affectionate, and definitely proud glance at the boy he practically considered his son.

"You cursed idiot!" he blazed, turning to the Baron. "Isn't it enough that we've killed his girl? We don't need to abuse him as though he's our rightfully captured prisoner. You have no heart!"

The Baron looked at Little Joe in surprise. The Professor seemed touched.

Little Joe looked down, slightly embarrassed at seeming so soft in front of his peers.

"All right," he growled, "I know what you're thinking, and it ain't true! This kid was once a friend of mine, and he's got guts and wits about him that you, or any of you others could only dream of. I'm sad to think he's not working with me anymore. But I won't see him mistreated! He's going to his death in a brave and commendable way, and we should respect him. Now come on, let's get it over with."

They dragged Skinny over to the edge. Skinny did not resist, but was not helpful. He was a dead weight, wrapped in his own grief, and wondering over Little Joe's sudden burst of honor.

"Hey," snapped Little Joe, nodding his head towards the Baron. "You come here, and see if you can get through some of this chain-link with that toy sword of yours."

The Baron strode forward sulkily. He looked at the thick wire that made the fence, and then glanced doubtfully at his sword. He barked an order to the biggest of his men, and the man lumbered to him, and took the sword. He looked at the fence, and then at Little Joe, and shook his head.

"No cut," he said in a German accent.

Little Joe sighed.

"Let's just shoot them," said the Baron.

Little Joe backed Skinny up to the fence, and pulled a length of string from his pocket. He put Skinny's hands behind his back, and tied them to the fence, but in a surprisingly loose and gentle knot. The man who still held Sally looked questioningly at Little Joe.

"We might as well shoot her again, just to make sure she stays dead," said the Baron.

At this, there was a hiss from Skinny. He lurched forward, and the loose knot came undone. He sprang at the Baron, who drew his sword, and leaped back with a cry.

"You pitiless dog!" cried Skinny, but before he could take another step, all ten of the men landed on him, covered his mouth, and stifled his cry.

Little Joe chuckled at the Baron's white face.

The Baron flushed in anger and embarrassment.

"Tie him again!" he shrieked. "Tie him down, and I'll run him through!"

"Yeah, you'll fight with him as much as you please, when he's helpless and can't hurt you," scoffed Little Joe. "You make me sick."

The Baron ignored him, for he was ordering his men, in a voice shaking with passion, to bind Skinny again. This time, the knots were none too loose, and once Skinny was bound, and Little Joe looking the other way, the Baron gave him another blow across the face.

Skinny felt blood in his mouth, and shook his head to keep the stars out of it, but did not cry out, and remained standing tall. Sally lay in a heap on the floor.

Little Joe drew his gun, and looked hard at it for a moment. Then he glanced at the bound Skinny, and sighed. Skinny faced him fearlessly. His lip was bleeding. His cheeks were still stained from his tears of grief, but he stood straight and tall, looking defiantly from Little Joe to the Baron.

"You haven't changed, kid," muttered Little Joe. "I will admit you're the bravest man I ever saw. You go with my respect, and envy."

He raised the gun, and Skinny's expression did not change. Little Joe looked down the barrel at his courageous, shining eyes, and then dropped his hand with a sigh.

"I can't," he muttered.

"Then I will," said the Baron, glad to have the chance to show his men that he wasn't a coward. He raised his gun.

Skinny faced him with the same defiance and courage.

For a moment the Baron seemed to hesitate.

The Professor was now hiding behind Little Joe, and had his eyes shut tight.

Little Joe remained looking at Skinny, his fists and teeth tightly clenched.

"Gentlemen," said the Baron, after a long, silent pause, "let us celebrate the coming end of our enemies."

"He's just stalling," thought Little Joe, "he don't want to kill him either."

"In just a moment," continued the Baron, "you will see the end of the most dastardly member of The Company of Secret Kids. They are finished!"

"Not yet!"

A strong, youthful voice had sent up echoes behind them. Skinny glanced up, and for a split second, he felt truly happy.

Standing tall and proud, (in fact now almost as tall as Skinny), Clarence was the picture of glory. His dark glittering eyes were filled with anger, his dark head was tossed back, and the expression on his face was far more fearsome than the gun in his hands.

Beside him, her eyes alight with love and pride was a beautiful girl that Skinny hardly recognized. Christine was wearing a beautiful green dress with gold buttons that accented her blond hair. Her expression was firm and fearless, and she looked a good deal younger and less complicated than she had before.

Becky and her comrade Jack stood beside them, and behind them were ten or twelve armed gendarmes, scowling blackly at the villains.

"I wouldn't say it is the end of the Company of Secret Kids," cried Clarence, "until you are certain. We stick together, and that's why you can't defeat us."

"Besides," said Christine, glancing with a joyous smirk at something behind Skinny, "you didn't get your facts right about our company."

She tossed her head in Skinny's direction. "He's the greatest brother in the world, and I'll love him to the death, but he's not the most dastardly threat that we have in our ranks."

"That's right, I am!"

Skinny turned towards the voice and it seemed that the whole world was lit suddenly with a dazzling light, and deafening music began to play inside his heart.

Sally was standing, without aid, though her hand clasped her shoulder. Her eyes were once again lit, and as their eyes met, she winked.

Skinny gave a gasp, and for a few moments felt terribly afraid that he would cry. Sally's eyes were moist, and Christine wept openly.

"Never say die," whispered Sally.

Skinny nodded.

"Come on!" cried Little Joe, and started for the elevator.

The Baron, the Professor, and their men hurried to follow him. They reached the elevator just as Clarence barked an order to the gendarmes.

Though it was close, the villains' door shut in time. The gendarmes, not wanting to shoot them, but to arrest them, went rushing to the other elevator. Several ran for the lengthy stairs. Becky's friend Jack discreetly went with them, leaving only the Company together once again.

The five children stood silent for a moment, without a movement or a word. They were so glad to be together again, that speaking didn't seem necessary. At last Clarence strode forward, pulling out his jackknife, and cut Skinny's bonds.

"Shake, best of friends," he said, holding out his hand. Skinny took it, and then threw his arms around Clarence.

Christine and Becky ran forward, and took Sally's hands. Sally gave them her habitual smile, though she was still pale, and winced as Becky grabbed her left hand.

"Here, Sal needs help," said Clarence, after he and Skinny had given each other a long, understanding glance.

Clarence picked Sally up quite easily, and started for the elevator. Becky picked up Sally's wreath of roses, and returned it to her. Skinny turned to Christine, and smiled. She laughed, though she was still crying, and then she threw herself into his arms.

"Oh, Skinny!" she cried. His grasp tightened around her shoulders, and for one long awaited instant, he held his baby sister in his arms once again.

"Chris," he whispered into her lovely blond locks, "have you forgiven me?"

Christine laughed through her tears. "Forgive you for being my brother? Oh Skinny, it's me that needs to be forgiven by you, for being such a silly, babyish brat."

"Hey, I hate to break up the family reunion," said Clarence, who was leaning against the elevator doors, with Sally in his arms, "but this kid ain't in the greatest shape."

Skinny hurried forward, and took Sally. Now that she was conscious and herself again, he felt slightly shy.

"Oh, I'm okay," said Sally with a brave grin, "I don't even know why I fainted."

Clarence inspected her shoulder, and nodded. "Not that bad. The bullet only grazed you, but you should still get some medical attention."

As the five happy children rode down in the elevator, they spoke quickly and briefly of the finding of the treasure. Christine told of Clarence's great courage in the alligator cage, and he in return, talked of the valor of Christine so that that young miss blushed to the tips of her ears.

"And just about half an hour ago," said Clarence, "we got a phone call, saying that we needed to get to the Eiffel Tower immediately, and take some cops with us, because you guys were in trouble."

"Who called?" asked Sally

"An anonymous woman."

"What!" came from Skinny.

"Who is this person?" asked Sally.

"We have no idea."

"Well, it's a good thing you did show up," said Skinny, "or we might not be here now."

Christine and Clarence, while talking, did much blushing and smiling, and it was apparent to the others that something special was going on between them. Skinny and Sally were incredulous with joy at the news of the found treasure.

At the base of the Eiffel Tower, they found the park almost deserted. No sign of the villains was to be found. Gendarmes were on patrol in force. Clarence decided that the first thing they should do was get Sally 'put back together again' as she put it, so they headed for the closest hospital.

As they drove down a side street, Skinny suddenly ordered the cabby to stop.

"What's up?" asked Clarence, following Skinny's gaze and staring into the deep night outside.

"Nothing," said Skinny, as he opened his door and got out, "keep on for that hospital, and get Sally some help. I'm going to check something."

Without another word, he turned and ran off. "I wonder where he's going this time," muttered Christine. Sally was silent, whether in pain from her wound or wrapped deep in thought, the others could not tell.

Skinny jogged down the street at an easy pace glancing down every alley he passed. As he was turning down a small residential street, he heard a car horn behind him. He turned, and saw a cab driving towards him. He waited, and as it pulled up beside him, he recognized the driver as Marcel Dubois.

"Oh, hi," said Skinny. "What are you doing?"

"Looking for you," answered the cabby, "I saw you riding around in another cab, and I'm quite disgusted with you. After all, I am an old friend of yours." He shook his head mournfully, and gave Skinny one of the most reproving looks he had ever come across.

"Sorry," murmured Skinny, "it was an emergency."

"Well, you don't need to worry anymore," said the cabby, brightening, "I told my boss man that I would be busy all night with some very important customers, so I am at your disposal."

"How did you know we would be out all night?" asked Skinny, but already he could guess the answer.

"I got a phone call from a lady, very pretty voice," said the man, "and she said that you needed help. She said she was a friend. I hope I have not done wrong."

"Nope, this is great," cried Skinny, "in fact, I'll employ your services right now. Can you take me to the airport?"

"You are leaving?" the cabby's face fell.

"No, I'm going there on a suspicion that I'll meet someone."

"But your other friends, the lovely sister and handsome friend of yours, I already received them. They are here."

"I know, but I bet that this mysterious woman that's been helping us will be coming here too, to see how everything turns out, and I would like to find her, if that's possible."

"I understand, and I will find her, or die trying," said the cabman solemnly.

Skinny grinned, and got in.

Chapter 18

The Monster

The Professor covered his ears with his hands, shut his eyes, and ducked. His head ached from all the yelling that had been going on. He didn't like the place they were gathered in now.

It was Little Joe's hotel room, and a very shabby place indeed. As the night wore on, he began to feel less and less like he really belonged with the villains.

In the first place, he was terrified of all of them, except maybe Little Joseph, and he was also having a dreadful time trying to stay mean. He kept catching himself sympathizing with the children.

He had to admit that the young hoodlum called Keenan, and the handsome young man they called Skinny made a lovely pair, and that the boy was a very gallant, admirable chap. He had also never been able to dislike the other two, for they were a beautiful couple as well, and thoroughly charming to be around, with such gracious manners

These reflections were suddenly cut short, when Little Joe landed with a crash on the floor at the Professor's feet. His clothes were dirtier and more torn than usual, and his cough had grown decidedly worse.

After they had fled the Tower, the villains had split up, and Little Joe and the Professor had gone to the flea bag hotel, in the hopes of gaining some time away from the Baron and Black Hawk, whom they were both beginning to hate.

They had hardly arrived however, when the Baron had appeared, bringing with him a furious Black Hawk. The Baron was a tattletale, through and through, and was very glad to have an opportunity to make Little Joe look bad in front of Black Hawk. Just then he had been, very happily indeed, giving Black Hawk a detailed account of Little Joe's disobedience. He elaborated beautifully, especially on Little Joe's mercy toward Skinny, and how he had deliberately chosen to go against Black Hawk's orders.

The result had been that Little Joe now lay coughing and cursing at the Professor's feet, after Black Hawk had picked him up, shaken him, and thrown him across the room. As Little Joe pulled himself up again, he gave the Baron a look that gleamed with revenge. The Baron backed up, for even he hadn't expected Black Hawk to be that violent, and was wondering what would happen if his tattling got him into trouble as well.

"Now," roared Black Hawk. He strode forward, and dealt Little Joe a savage blow that knocked him to the ground again. "Now you obey me! Those children will die tonight, and you will make that happen! Get up, you scum!"

Little Joe stood up again, rubbing his jaw, and coughing. He was shaking with passion. Muttered curses escaped his clenched teeth as he stood before the pirate.

"I don't like your style," he hissed. "All this sport, this cruelty. It doesn't seem fair. After all, what have those kids really ever done to us?"

"You see!" cried the Baron, "that's treasonous talk if I've ever heard it!"

Black Hawk looked down at Little Joe, and smiled, a terrible, cruel smile. "My ways are not your ways, peasant," he drawled, "but you will learn to respect me." He turned, and stalked out of the room, slamming the door so that the place shook.

The Baron turned to Little Joe, who had sunk down into a chair, and smiled. "Well, now how do you feel about those little brats?" he asked.

A wild light lit Little Joe's eyes. "You," he growled, "you would like to see that old elephant kill me, wouldn't you?" He stood up, and took a step toward the Baron.

The Baron turned pale, swooped out the door, and was heard clattering down the hall after Black Hawk. Little Joe sunk down again, and buried his handsome, battered face in his hands. The Professor stood up, and timidly put a hand on his shoulder.

"Maybe we aren't supposed to do this, old chap," he muttered. "Everything is going so badly. Do you really want to kill those children?"

Little Joe made no answer. The Professor gently patted his black hair in a comforting way. At last, Little Joe looked up, with an understanding glance.

"You know," Joe said, "Black Hawk just said that I would come to respect him. I'll tell you something; that, no matter what happens tonight, one thing will always stay the same. No matter how powerful and strong Black Hawk is, I will never have the respect for him that I have for Skinny Conklin."

The Professor nodded. "I've wondered if it is prudent to stay with these chaps or not," he murmured.

"Well, I'm staying with them, and I still intend to get Keenan at least," said Little Joe, "but if you do leave us, and join the other side, you will have more guts than I've got."

Skinny arrived at the hospital quite keyed up. He'd made an amazing discovery in the past hour, and though he was bursting with it, he'd been instructed to keep his secret from his friends for just a little longer. He stopped at the bottom of the steps that led to the emergency entrance, and looked up at the building. He wondered how it had gone in there, and if Sally was really okay.

A sudden fear crept over him that her burst of life had been passing, and he might find himself thrown back into the nightmare he had lived in for those few dreadful minutes on the Eiffel Tower; the nightmare of a world without Sally.

Suddenly, above him, the hospital doors flew open, and Sally bounded down the steps with a whoop. She leapt off the fourth step, and landed on top of him so they both hit the grass with a thud.

"Hiya Skinny!" she cried, smacking him on the back with her right hand, and pushing herself up off his shoulder. He got to his feet with a laugh, trying not to let Sally see how relieved and overjoyed he really was. As he got up, he grabbed her by the arm, and looked into her eyes. She paused, and stared back at him with a slightly perplexed smile.

"What's the matter with you?" she asked, after the silence had become awkward.

Skinny laughed, and looked down.

"Nothing, just making sure they put you back together again good enough." He looked at the secure bandage that wound itself around her shoulder, and over her neck. He nodded approvingly at it, to prove his point.

"Yeah, it's okay," said Sally, touching her shoulder gingerly. "At first they were just going to wrap me up so I'd have to stay in bed all night, but I told them I needed to be mobile, so they rigged this thing up. It'll hold through a summersault at least, I tested it."

Skinny laughed again, and affectionately rumpled her curls. Clarence, Christine and Becky appeared at the door, and clattered down the steps.

"There you are!" cried Clarence, looking at Sally with an exasperated smile. "You got pretty far this time."

"Do you know," said Christine to Skinny, with mock horror, "that this young renegade made, in total, five unsuccessful escape attempts from that place? As soon as they had bandaged her up, she was bound and determined to leave."

"Yeah, now let's get out of here," said Sally, "I've had enough of hospitals, and doctors who think I need to be in bed."

"Well, you've been officially dismissed, so we can go," said Clarence, "I'll go call a cab."

"I'm afraid there's only one cab in Paris that we are allowed to use, Clare," said Skinny. "He's parked over there, and if you make one move toward someone else's cab, he's likely to have you arrested for heartbreaking. Come on."

"Right," said Clarence.

"So, where are we going now?" asked Christine, as the five of them piled into the cab, much to the joy of Marcel Dubois.

"We're going to get Sally some rest," said Skinny, turning to Sally, "and now, you obey orders."

"Can we go pick up Jack?" asked Becky. "He's probably gone back to his friend's house, and I told him we'd come by if we had the time."

"Okay, give Marcel the address, and we'll go pick him up," said Skinny.

"It's nice not to be on the run for a moment," sighed Christine, leaning back in her seat as they started down the dark streets. "I'm glad we're not being followed."

"Oh, yes we are," said Clarence, from the front seat, where he sat next to the cabby. Clarence had been staring intently out the window.

"What?" Skinny stiffened, and automatically put his arm around Sally, who was sitting next to him. She looked up at him in surprise, and he hurriedly pulled his arm back.

"Yep, the whole gang just came out of that hotel," said Clarence, pointing at a shabby place a little ways up the broad street. "I wonder if they figured we'd go to the hospital and had someone watching."

Skinny leaned forward, and saw Black Hawk and the Baron, with several of their men, getting into a beautiful black car, while just a little way behind them, Little Joe and the Professor were heading towards a dented little rental car.

"Looks like they're splitting up," said Skinny.

"We should do the same," said Clarence. "Cabby, turn us around, and get us down away from that hotel."

"You think we should foot it, Clare?" asked Skinny, as they made a fast u-turn. "They've come to recognize Marcel's cab."

"They probably won't think we'll do that, so let's. We'll leave Becky with Dubois, I'll take a turn with do-or-die Sal, and you Conklins can go together."

"Okay, we get out at this next intersection, and you and Sally get out a block after," ordered Skinny, "just try to stay out of sight, and head back to the convent. Can you make it, Sally?"

She nodded.

The cabby pulled to a halt at the corner, and Skinny and Christine slipped out.

"Good bye, see you soon," said Christine, giving Clarence a shy, but dazzling smile.

Skinny glanced at Sally, and let a hint of a smile flit across his face. Sally responded with a grin.

"Hey," Skinny said leaning down towards her, out of Clarence's earshot, "take care of yourself."

Sally nodded and then turned away with a sudden blush. Skinny took his sister's hand, and they started down a side street. The cabby drove on for about a block.

"Do you think this is a good place?" asked Clarence, as they rolled to a stop at the entrance of a thin alley.

"Sure," Sally got out, and looked around. "No sign of them."

Clarence instructed the cabby to head for the convent in a round about way, since he would be acting as the decoy. Once he'd dropped Becky off, he was to get to a phone in case they needed him. As he departed, Clarence turned, and found Sally half way down the alley, waiting impatiently.

"I hope this is a good idea," murmured Clarence as he joined her.

"Sure, they'll never think we would get out of the cab."

They ran down the alley, and came out onto the street at the other end of it. Slowly passing by, was a long, black car. Sally screeched to a halt, pulling Clarence back. They turned to run, but before they had taken a step, they heard a shout behind them, and the slam of a car door.

"Quick!" hissed Clarence, and they shot off.

"Split," ordered Sally as they reached the end of the alley. Clarence nodded, and veered off to the left, while Sally ran off down the street to the right. She could hear shouting in the alley, which sounded as though the Baron and the men were after them on foot, while Black Hawk took the car around the block, screeching and skidding around the corner.

Sally ran down the sidewalk, her injured shoulder pounding, and headed in the direction of the villains' hotel. She hoped Little Joe and the Professor had already departed, or she would really have a problem.

"Skinny!" cried Christine. She grabbed her brother's arm, and pointed. A beat-up car was heading for them, and in the driver's seat sat Little Joe.

"Down that street, quick!"

Christine dashed off, following his direction, while Skinny kept on a straight course. As he had hoped, Little Joe went after him. Skinny knew how easy it would have been to shoot him down from the car, but apparently that was still forbidden. Then suddenly, as he passed the villains' hotel, out of the revolving door flew Sally.

"Hey, what are you doing here?" she asked as she fell into stride with him and they sped off.

"Get lost," breathed Skinny, "I've got Joe on my tail."

Sally nodded, and turned suddenly to the right. She turned down a small street, and found herself facing Black Hawk's car, with him staring grimly at her from behind the wheel.

Sally stood still for a moment, waiting for him to make a move, but he didn't. He simply sat, and stared at her. The streets were otherwise deserted.

Sally turned, and fled back the way she'd come. She came back onto the main street just as Little Joe drove past.

Skinny had glimpsed what had happened as he ran past, and now was greatly puzzled. As soon as Sally had returned to the main street, he'd heard the sound of a car suddenly thrown into action, and Black Hawk came reeling after her.

But as the chase continued, Skinny noticed a definite pattern. If ever he, or any of the other kids, tried to run to the right, toward the heart of the city, they were stopped, but not molested. The villains would just plant themselves, and wait for them to turn around, then they would give chase. It began to occur to Skinny that they were being driven somewhere specific, as though there was a previously arranged spot to which they were headed.

Sally noticed this pattern too, though she wasn't as concerned. She had been running down a side street, temporarily not being pursued, when suddenly, the walls opened up, and she found herself in a sort of courtyard, with alleys running into it from every side.

In the center of the courtyard, there was a large rift, about ten feet across the top, and at least twelve feet deep. A thin railing ran around its edge, though it was rusty, and chunks of it were missing in places. On one side of the oddly shaped ravine, there was a stone staircase that led down into it. At the bottom, there was a deep body of water, and as she crept closer to its edge, she saw that at each end, down below, there was an opening into a tunnel, into and out of which the water ran.

"Part of some old sewer?" thought Sally to herself. "I've heard about the sewers of Paris."

She looked down into the dark waters below, churning and splashing, shining silver in the moonlight. "Seems odd that the water is so worked up," she muttered aloud, "seems as if it would be still, since there's only a little wind tonight."

Just then, she heard screeching brakes behind her, and knew that she'd been discovered. At the same moment that Black Hawk's headlights turned toward her, and made the courtyard glow, Clarence came dashing out of an alley near her, pursued by Black Hawk's men. Clarence came to a sudden stop. He glanced over at Sally. Before she could think of anything, Little Joe's car pulled up, and then from another alley the Baron's white van.

Sally looked around for a moment, weighing the situation carefully. The cars were already emptying rapidly, though they all kept their headlights shining. Sally figured they would make their move soon, and that now was the time to act.

"Quick, follow me!" she said, in a low voice that only Clarence caught. She darted for the stone staircase leading down into the sewer, expecting at any moment to be gunned down, but to her surprise, no one even gave chase. Clarence was at her heels, but stopped at the top of the staircase.

"You sure this is a good idea?" he asked dubiously, looking down into the dark, swirling water.

"We haven't got any other choice," responded Sally, and took a few steps down. She saw the four villains all running to the rail opposite her, and watching intently. For a fleeting second she knew how the ancient Roman martyrs must have felt, heading into an arena filled with wild beasts, while their enemies looked on, awaiting a good show. Then this sensation passed. After all, she thought, she was escaping them, not obliging them.

As she ran down the steps to the water's churning edge, she heard familiar voices above her. Glancing back she saw Clarence, still at the top of the stairs, and next to him, Skinny and Christine just appearing. Skinny took in the whole situation at a glance, and all at once, the enemies' plan suddenly dawned on him.

Sally waved to them to come down, removed her wreath of roses from her head, laying it carefully on the steps, and then turned to descend into the water.

"Sally, no!" shouted Skinny, shooting down the steps, with Clarence at his heels. "There's something dangerous in there! It's a trap!"

But before his cries had even rent the foggy air, Sally had made a clean dive into the water. It was surprisingly warmer than she'd expected, but also strangely turbulent, as though there was something else in it, that had the strength to churn the waters to a stormy degree.

"Skinny, what's wrong?" asked Clarence.

"I don't know what's wrong exactly," answered Skinny, standing on the bottom steps, so that his shoes were wet. "But I do know that those devils up there have been trying to get us here all night, and I suspect no good to come of this sewer."

"Look!" cried Clarence, "what's that?"

Skinny looked where he pointed, and saw something large and strange, emerging from one of the tunnels. It appeared to be a large snake, though it was somewhat translucent in color, and was apparently sticking to the wall of the tunnel. Christine, who had joined them, let out a little shriek when she saw it.

"What is it, Skinny?" she asked in terror.

Skinny shook his head, and watched the thing intently. After a few seconds, it disappeared under the water. Skinny looked towards Sally, who had turned to face them, and was treading water with her back to the strange thing in the tunnel.

"Look, it's coming out!" cried Clarence. The snake-like thing showed itself briefly again, this time much closer to Sally.

"Either that thing moves really fast," muttered Skinny, "or there's more than one of them. Sally! Come out!"

Sally turned, and looked to him. The water bubbling around her made her unable to hear him, but she saw him gesturing frantically. Christine suddenly screamed, and pointed to something behind Sally. She turned, and saw something purple and bluish, rather like a thick snake, threading its way towards her. She started to swim backwards, her eyes growing large and frightened while the thing approached her steadily.

Skinny slipped off his shoes, preparing to dive in after her, keeping his eyes constantly on the thing in the water. Sally was rapidly swimming towards the stair, but still had about eight feet to go, and the thing was gaining on her.

Then suddenly, Christine let out an ear-piercing scream. In less time than it takes to narrate, another one of the strange things had suddenly appeared, closer to them, and behind the unsuspecting Sally. Not only did it appear, but it lashed out toward her. Clarence gave a shout, and Skinny caught his breath. Sally turned at Christine's scream, and at that same moment, the thing suddenly, with a speed and agility that made the onlookers feel sick, wrapped itself around her waist. Sally did not scream. No cry escaped her lips, yet the silence was almost worse than if she had cried out. Almost as soon as it was wrapped around her, the thing gave a jerk, and Sally disappeared under the dark water. From far above them, Black Hawk let out a cheer.

Skinny dove in.

"Oh, Clarence!" cried Christine, "what is it?"

"They're tentacles," muttered Clarence, more to himself than to her. "It's a giant octopus."

Christine looked at him, horrified and despairing. She turned back to the water, and looked with terrified, and yet spellbound amazement at what was going on.

Skinny had almost reached the spot where Sally had gone down. His eyes constantly scanned the water, looking for some sign of either predator or prey. At last, there was a splash, about six feet away from him, and very near one of the tunnel entrances Sally emerged for a moment. The tentacle had come up, and had looped itself around her, but she was giving it a good fight.

Skinny started towards her.

"No, Conklin!"

Clarence and Christine glanced up, and saw that, though Black Hawk seemed to be thoroughly enjoying himself, his fellow villains seemed anything but well. The Baron was pale, leaning against the rail for support, the Professor had his back turned, and his hands over his ears, and Little Joe was breathing hard, and clutching the railing so hard that it seemed to bend under him. He was watching helplessly, as Skinny swam towards the danger. "Conklin, go back!" he shouted, running his hands through his thick black hair.

Sally was pulled back under, and Skinny stopped for a long moment. There was dead silence around them, a silence that hung in the air and hurt one's ears. For what seemed a hopelessly long time, there was no movement in the water. Skinny silently treaded water, scanning the murky surface for any sign of Sally or the monster, while Clarence, Christine, and the villains above them watched in breathless suspense.

Then suddenly, Sally appeared again with a gasping cry. She was deathly pale, and the force of her struggling was apparently waning. Skinny dove towards her, but was violently hurled backward by a flailing tentacle. He was thrown almost all the way back to the stairs, and had the wind knocked out of him.

Clarence glanced up at the villains, and saw that Little Joe was leaning forward as though he was about to faint. He was watching

Sally intently, his face a sickly color. Then suddenly, his face changed. He looked up at Black Hawk, and his expression grew desperate. He looked back down at Sally, desperately trying to keep her head above water, and fight off the vise-like grip of the octopus, and then at Skinny gasping and foundering in the water, watching in horror and an agony of helplessness as his girl battled for her life.

Clarence tapped Christine, and pointed to Little Joe. They watched him, as he looked from Black Hawk, to the dramatic tableau beneath, and back to the pirate, his breath coming in short coughing gasps, his eyes keen and terrible, his hands and jaw muscles working fiercely.

"He's going to do something," breathed Clarence, "but I don't know what."

"Maybe he's going to help," suggested Christine hopefully, but Clarence shook his head.

"Not him," he muttered, "he's been leading a bad life for too long."

"Look!" cried Christine.

Everything happened at once. Sally went back under, Skinny swam towards her with a yell. Black Hawk let out another cheer, and Christine hid her face on Clarence's shoulder.

Then, it happened.

Something in Little Joe snapped.

"No!" he shouted, and pushed against the rusty metal rail. It gave way, and the old chunks of iron went sailing down into the water. Little Joe sprang back, and tottered for a second on the edge. Just as he regained his balance, Sally reappeared.

Clarence felt his heart go cold, for Sally was no longer struggling. She still appeared to be conscious, but she hung limp. The tentacle was still around her waist, and wound up over her, to loop itself around her shoulder.

"It's too cruel!" came a passionate shout from above. All eyes were suddenly turned to Little Joe.

Before anyone could realize what was happening, Little Joe whipped out his gun, took aim, and fired. The echo of the gunshot rang on the air, and for a moment, everything was quiet.

His bullet hit the thick, slimy tentacle. Sally was jolted slightly, and up rose the stink of wounded octopus. Then, the water began to churn and splash in a turmoil of confusion. The tentacle went limp, and Sally immediately seemed to revive. She wiggled out of its now loose grip, and with a speed that did her credit, plowed through the water toward the stair. Skinny followed her with a splash, and as they reached the foot of the stairs, Sally was dragged out by a rejoicing Christine and Clarence.

"Man, did you see that?" cried Clarence, "what a stroke of luck!"

"Who would have thought that Joe would shoot the octopus?" said Skinny, pulling himself out.

"Sally, are you all right?" asked Christine, taking Sally's shaking hands, and putting an arm around her.

Sally nodded, and managed a grin. "Never say die," she laughed weakly. "Boy, am I tired!"

Skinny smiled wearily. "You certainly have a way of keeping busy, you nutty kid."

Just then they heard a shout from up above.

They looked up, and saw Little Joe dashing back toward his car. Black Hawk was watching him from the railing, and growling like some giant beast about to charge.

The Baron was trying to stay out of Black Hawk's way, and the Professor was creeping over to the edge of the wall, and peering in to catch a glimpse of the octopus, which he was actually very curious about seeing, provided it wasn't killing anyone.

"Well, those guys don't look too happy," said Skinny, "come on, let's get out of here."

They turned and started up the stairs, with Sally still leaning on Christine. About half way up, they suddenly heard a terrible, blood curdling scream, the scream of one utterly terrified. The four children spun around, and saw a sickening sight.

As they had started up the stairs, Black Hawk had let out a bellow, and charged after Little Joe. His huge saber was, as always, strapped in its sheath on his belt. As he turned swiftly around, to give chase, the large saber swooped round, and caught the Professor, still standing on the brink, in the pit of his back. He'd been pushed forward, had smashed through the remains of the already broken railing, and clutching vainly at the slick wall, he had gone hurtling down into the water with a terrible shriek.

Skinny at once started back down the steps to save him, but before he had gotten far he was pushed aside, and Sally streaked by him.

"Sally, no!" he called. "You're already hurt!"

But she dove in, and was making her way toward the thin old man in the lab coat, who was splashing and yelling, and frantically trying to stay above water.

Sally was a great swimmer, and in less than a moment, she'd reached the Professor and told him something that made him stop thrashing. Skinny was already in the water as Sally started back with the old man, and was watching the surface intently, ready to spring at the first sign of danger.

Sally was about half way back with her burden, when Skinny saw what he had feared, a thick, purplish thing emerging from the water.

"Sally!" he called. She turned, and saw the tentacle. She glanced up at Skinny, nodded, and carefully swam away from it. Skinny waded into the water, and swam towards her.

"Here," he said, as he reached her side, "I'll take him, you head for the stairs."

He held out his hands to take the Professor, but at the same moment, felt a tight grip on his ankle. Before he could realize what was happening, he was suddenly pulled under water.

The water was black as pitch, and stank awfully. He'd had his mouth open when he went under, and got a mouthful of filthy water that made his throat burn. The grip on his ankle was tight and deadly, and he could feel the slime of the thing as it touched him.

This time, there was no audience to enjoy the fight. Desperately, he kicked at the tentacle with his free foot, and tried to pull himself back to the surface, longing for a breath of air. He opened his eyes under water for a second, and they immediately began to sting. The lights from above cast only murky shadows in the water, yet for one terrible instant, he glimpsed the terror below. All he could make out was the gigantic shape of the thing, and his heart froze inside him at the thought of its strength.

He struggled madly for a moment, shutting his eyes again just so he'd have the courage to move, and at once the tentacle tightened. He knew he had to get a breath, or everything would be over. He hoped Clarence or Sally wouldn't try to rescue him, for he knew that the beast in the depths could finish them all off in a moment.

"I'm nothing like Sally," he thought sadly, as the world began to grow fuzzy around him, "she stayed under for so long, and even had the guts to get back in, to save one of her enemies. I never even had a chance to tell her the last secret. She'll find out someday, but I won't be around. I'm going to die, and that's all there is to it.

He opened his eyes once more, in a last attempt at life, and saw the dark water around him, but also, two familiar blue slippers and a flowing blue skirt, kicking past above him, and a square of white lab coat.

He was glancing up at this sight, when suddenly he saw another tentacle stretching out towards the slippers. Skinny suddenly realized that, though he would soon be dead, he had one last chance to be a hero. He gave his fettered foot one last violent kick, and the grip gave way. He shot upwards, towards the feet, and grabbed a frantic breath of air. He moved to pull back the tentacle that was after Sally's feet, and knew that it would probably take hold of him, but before he had even had to touch it, it suddenly whirled around to him, as though it had a mind of its own.

He tried to dodge, but the thing wrapped itself around both his legs with deadly speed. Now he had only his arms with which to struggle, and they were weakening, but even in that moment of extreme hopelessness, he felt content to know that at least Sally was safe.

"She may not ever admit it," he thought, "but at least I know that I've saved her once."

He was satisfied. The words of Sally's that he had so often thought of; "Skinny, put me down, I don't need your help," no longer caused him shame.

"I wonder if she'll miss me," he thought, "ain't I a dope to not realize what a great kid she is, until it's too late."

He decided that, one last time, before he gave himself up, he'd try to fight back. He shook his bound legs violently, and reached up with his hands, waving them madly, trying to propel himself upwards. He felt a shock of pain as his right hand struck something hard. For a moment he tried to remember what that feeling was, and what it was that he had hit.

Then, he realized with a flash of unbelieving joy, that he must have hit the stone steps. He reached up again, groping madly, and his hands found their hold. He grasped the cold, hard, wonderfully stable stone, and pulled himself up.

His head emerged, and he drew a gasping breath. The outside air felt cold, and his mouth went dry. With the last strength he could muster, he clutched the step, and pulled himself onto it. The terrible strength that had coiled itself around his legs gave way, and the tentacle slid back into the water.

He opened his eyes, as Clarence grabbed him under the arms and pulled him up.

"Boy, are you okay?" cried Clarence, pounding him on the back.

"Yeah," gasped Skinny, and started coughing. He glanced up, and saw Christine, and Sally a few steps up, each holding one of the Professor's shaking hands. Sally anxiously scanned Skinny's face, and sighed.

"You're okay," she said. It struck Skinny that she said it carelessly. He put aside any wounded feelings quickly however, for Sally then let the Professor's hand go, and came running down the steps. She pulled him to his feet, and looked him over.

"Wow, were you under for a long time!" she cried, giving him a congratulatory slap on the back. "I'd never have lasted that long."

Skinny gave her an appreciative smile for the hard-earned praise. He shook the water out of his ears, and glanced up at the Professor.

Before he could say anything, the Professor came down to greet him with open arms. "My wonderful, wonderful fellow!" he cried. "What a glorious stroke of luck to join forces with you!"

"He's officially one of us now," said Christine, "and I'm glad of it! He's a darling. But please, can't we get away from this horrid sewer?"

"Yeah, come on," Skinny took Clarence's hand to steady himself for a moment, and then ran lightly up the steps. Sally snatched her wreath of roses from the steps, replaced it on her curls, and skipped after him.

"Well," he said as he gained the top with Sally at his heels, "how many times have I told you, young lady, never to go jumping into French sewers in the middle of the night, especially when they are occupied by octopi?"

"Yeah," laughed Clarence, "I hate it when that happens!"

Sally gave them an exasperated grin. "What are you, a Greek scholar?"

Skinny glanced around. Little Joe had taken his car, and sped off into the night. The Baron and Black Hawk, and all their men had split up and taken the other cars. The sewer courtyard was now deserted, and their escape route quite open.

"Maybe you're ready to go back to convent, Sally?" he asked.

She laughed. "Perhaps. But who knows what might happen before this night is over?"

Skinny smiled, and nodded, but his heart was troubled by her words. "You forget you're wounded. Let's head back to the convent," he said, "I just hope we'll get there safely."

"Too bad Becky has the cab," said Christine, as the four children and the old man started through the maze of dark streets.

"You know what I wish?" said Clarence thoughtfully. "I wish we had an army."

"Me, too," smiled Skinny, "but what would you do with yours, and what sort of army?"

"Well, I think all I'd do with it, is use it against our enemies, but as to what sort of army, I've got a theory about that. I want kids."

"Kids?"

"Yeah, and not like us, little kids. Like Becky."

"Why that small?"

"Well, nobody would suspect them for one thing. I mean, if a whole legion of Romans, or Vikings suddenly showed up, I think they'd cause some excitement."

"Yeah, but wouldn't it be great?" cried Sally, picturing herself on a Viking chieftain's horse, or brandishing a Roman spear.

"Sure, but that's not too likely to happen," continued Clarence. "What I want is about fifty to one hundred little kids. No one would expect them to be on the war-path, so we'd have the element of surprise."

"And they'd be small enough to go unnoticed, like hobbits!" said Christine, whom Sally had just introduced to the new epic saga.

"Yes! They could make good escapes, and surprise attacks!" said Clarence. "My only problem is that they wouldn't be that strong when it came to an actual fight."

"Well, that's where we come in," said Skinny. "They can perch themselves in high, strategic, out of reach places, where they can use firearms and stuff, and when it comes to actual fist to fist combat, you and I could take the lead."

They were daydreaming now, as they often did together.

"And don't forget me!" cried Sally, "you wouldn't mind me getting that close to the enemy if there were a hundred little kids backing us up, would you, Skinny?"

He rolled his eyes as if to say, 'when have you ever asked me?'

"Well, even if I say no," Skinny sighed, "you'd still join the fight, so it's okay with me. But now we've run away with ourselves. We haven't got a bunch of little kids at hand."

"Well…" a voice said.

The children turned round, and looked at the smiling Professor.

"What?" asked Sally.

"Don't tell me you've got an army of little kids!" cried Christine.

"No, you do."

"What?" cried Skinny.

"Well, they wouldn't be on my side, if I went to fetch 'em, but they'd love you, mates."

"What are you talking about?" demanded Clarence.

"Well," said the Professor, rubbing his long hands together happily, "you see, when I was given charge over the little chap that you rescued back in Manchester - good old Manchester, how I miss it, and the tea, they haven't got any good tea over here, have you noticed?"

"Never mind the tea, just get on with your explanation!" cried Clarence.

"Oh yes, certainly, what a splendid fellow, now where was I? Ah yes, the children. Well, when my friend, or really used to be friend, the Baron, as I believe you call him, gave me that little blighter to watch, he also told me that there were many other such children he was hiding."

"Of course, Becky's old school mates!" said Sally. "Well, what about them?"

"Well, when I came here, and met up with all the other chaps I've been with, Little Joseph and all of them, the Baron told me that for some reason that I didn't quite catch, the children were hidden here in Paris. I just wondered …"

"Whoopee!" cried Sally, leaping into the air, "what a stroke of luck!"

"Well, Clare," said Skinny, "looks like you'll be getting the army you wanted!"

Clarence nodded, too surprised to speak.

"Well, let's go get them! I've got a battle plan!" cried Sally. "I'm the general, and there ain't nothing that will stop my army!"

"That's a double negative," said Skinny, "and I'm the general. Clare's the colonel. You can be a captain."

"Okay, but let's go get them!"

"Hey, maybe I should go get Becky," suggested Christine, "and her friend Jack."

"You and Clarence do that," said Skinny, "and we'll go with the Professor to get the kids."

"Right! Let's say we meet at the Eiffel Tower once everything is ready," said Clarence. "Now come on!"

He grabbed Christine's hand, and they disappeared off into the night.

"All right," said Skinny, turning to the beaming Professor. "Now take us to the place."

Chapter 19

The Quality of Mercy

"So are you sure you know where Jack's friends live?" asked Christine as they threaded their way through the streets.

"I think so," said Clarence. "I think it's this way."

"Are you sure?" asked Christine dubiously, looking down the darkened street which had no lamps lit.

"Sure, just follow me."

They crept down the street, Christine clinging to Clarence's arm and letting out little shrieks, as mice and other night creatures scuttled around in the darkness before them. When they reached the end of the residential street, they found themselves at a dead-end.

"This isn't right," muttered Clarence.

"No, where are we?" asked Christine, unconsciously edging closer to him, and glancing around anxiously. The cul-de-sac was walled like a courtyard.

"Hey, I think there's an opening over there," said Clarence, looking at the wall before them. He pulled her forward. "Yep, there's a little break in it, a tiny passage about a foot wide. Come on."

Reluctantly, Christine followed him.

Clarence slipped through the passage, or more appropriately, the crack, and Christine did the same. They emerged in a larger courtyard, which had a large opening onto a side street.

"Okay, let's go that way," said Clarence. They ran out, and stopped at the curb.

The street was pretty much deserted at that late hour of the night, and the only light was from one dim lamppost.

"Well, maybe if we go that way we'll come out at ... " Clarence suddenly stopped, and grabbing Christine's arm, pulled her behind him.

"What's wrong?" she asked, peering over his shoulder.

"I hear arguing," he whispered, "and a German accent."

"The Baron?"

They looked, and saw the Baron slowly stride forward into the light, sword drawn, surrounded by his men. At the same time he saw them.

"Make a run for it, I'll try to draw them off."

Christine nodded, though she didn't want to be separated from Clarence. She heard a shout behind her; the Baron giving his men quick and frantic orders. She wondered how many were after her. She was reaching a corner, and quickly decided to turn right. As she reached it, and made her turn, she glanced back the way she'd come.

For a split second, she saw the Baron and all his men, dashing off in the direction Clarence had gone, all yelling and waving their weapons.

"Golly, they're all after Clare," she thought, wondering why he was so important to them. "I suppose I should try to attract at least some of their attention, or they'll get him."

* * *

"This is it?" asked Skinny. He looked dubiously at the little abandoned sidewalk café across the street.

The little place was in shambles. The red canopy that must have once shaded the tables outside its bay window had fallen down, and through the huge rips, they could see the few rusty tables and chairs that remained. The large window was cracked, the glass in the door was missing, and the window boarded up.

"Aye, this is the place," said the Professor. "He took me 'ere, and showed me 'round."

"Okay, then let's go," cried Sally, and darted off across the street. The other two followed. She reached the door, and banged herself against it. It gave way with an ominous squeak. She entered, and glanced around.

There were cobwebs and thick layers of dust over everything, shining creepily in the moonlight. There was broken glass all over the place, and the musty smell of a long forgotten building.

Though it appeared to be undisturbed, Sally noticed that leading into the kitchen were some rather new footprints in the dust.

She went over to the kitchen door just as Skinny and the Professor entered. They quickly followed her through the swinging doors. The kitchen was in no better shape than the outer room. There were only a few broken kitchen utensils lying around, but all the cookware, as well as the larger appliances including stove and refrigerator, were missing.

"Rather drab place, I must say," said the Professor. "But I do wonder if they've left a bit of cooking Sherry around anyplace. That dip in the water has me quite shaken up. I could use a spot of something."

Skinny smiled at the old man, who was now poking around in the various cupboards, and humming to himself. He turned to Sally, and found her staring at a door that occupied a certain corner of the kitchen and which appeared newer than anything else around.

"Do you think the Baron installed that door?" she asked.

He looked at the shining wood which contrasted with the rest of the kitchen, and nodded.

"Probably to prevent escapes."

Skinny looked doubtfully at the solid door. "I wonder how we'll get through it."

"Like this." Sally grinned mischievously, and ran over to the door. Leaning against the wall next to it, there was a tall wooden mallet that almost reached up to Sally's shoulder.

She looked at it thoughtfully. It was padded on top by a thin layer of fabric, and Sally wondered what it would have been useful for in a French kitchen. She figured it would put at least a little dent in the Baron's door.

"Well, okay," she said, and picked up the mallet.

"Sally, wait!" yelled Skinny. He stepped forward at the same time as Sally stepped up to the door, and swung backwards with the mallet for her first hit. Skinny ducked, and the mallet missed him by a hair.

"Sally, stop that!" he cried, quickly stepping aside, and out of her range.

The Professor turned round from his inspection of one of the drawers, and smiled. "No need for that, missy," he said, putting his hand in his pocket and coming forward, "I've got the key. The Baron gave it to ..."

"Hey, watch it!" cried Skinny.

Sally swung the heavy mallet backwards again, the Professor stepped into the danger zone, and Skinny heard a thud.

"Sally!" he cried, reproachfully.

She turned impatiently from the door, looked at the Professor on the floor, and gasped.

"Golly, whoops!" she cried, and bending down, pulled the old man to his feet. "Sorry about that, old chap."

"Not to worry," said the dazed Professor, rubbing the side of his head. "But you don't happen to know where there's a nice bottle of Sherry about, do you?"

Sally shook her head solemnly.

The Professor sighed. "Well then, oh 'ere are those keys you needed." Sally took the keys, and fit one of them into the lock on the door. It swung back silently, revealing pitch blackness inside.

"Let's have a look," said Skinny, peering in. He took one step inside, but his foot found no landing. Open space was before him, and with a muffled shout, he slipped, and slid down a flight of stairs that he hadn't been aware of a moment before.

Sally followed him quite easily, and pulled him up as he came to a thudding stop at the bottom.

"Hello?" she called into the darkness before them. They listened hard, but no answer came.

"Maybe that old Professor was wrong," mused Skinny, rubbing an elbow he had knocked in his rather sudden descent. "Maybe the Baron didn't hide the kids here, or maybe he's moved them since ..."

"Shhh," whispered Sally.

She listened intently for a moment. "There's someone down here."

For a fleeting second, Skinny had a fear that the Professor had brought them there to trap them, and that all their enemies were waiting for them in the shadows.

Then he heard a small whimper from within the darkness.

"Hey, if there's a bunch of scared kids down here, you don't need to be afraid of us!" called Sally, letting her voice soften slightly. "I'm Sally Keenan. I'm a good friend of Becky's, and this big dope with me who just came down your stairs so elegantly is Skinny Conklin. He doesn't bite. At least I've never seen it if he has."

"Thanks," muttered Skinny.

Out of the darkness, they heard some fearful murmurs.

"If you all will trust us," continued Sally, "we're here to rescue you. And if you fight beside us, I think I can guarantee that we can defeat the Baron, and you all can go back to where you belong."

There came a louder murmur, and after a moment's pause, a grubby little boy suddenly appeared on the steps before them.

"Hey!" said Sally, grabbing his hand, and giving it a few strong shakes. "Now, come on, all of you!"

She turned, and skipped up a few steps.

Slowly, the glow of a flashlight appeared, revealing many thin, scared faces.

Skinny grinned at the girl holding the flashlight, and she dropped it. "So, don't you guys want to be free?" he asked.

A few shy heads nodded.

"Then follow us, and we'll finish that Baron for good!" cried Sally, and Skinny could almost hear the Irish anthem as she started in on a speech: "We'll teach him and all his kind that the kids of the world can stand up for themselves too, and that the reign of bullies has ended! He won't soon forget the wrath of the Company of Secret Kids when we fight for the helpless and oppressed! We'll give him a taste of Irish valor, and some Swiss guts too! Give us liberty or give us death! Long live the Company of Secret Kids! Forward! Erin Go Bragh!"

She ran yelling up the steps and out the door, and Skinny was almost trampled by a stampede of little, half-starved patriots, who ran after Sally with a yell that sounded like a miniature wave crashing on the sand. Even Skinny noticed he had goose-bumps. He felt he could have plowed fearlessly into battle for the love of country and freedom.

He picked up the flashlight that had been thrown aside in the stampede, looked quickly in all the corners, to make sure everyone was out, and ran up the steps.

He came out the door just as the unprepared Professor and the heated crowd of kids went smashing through the kitchen doors. Sally, who had leapt out of the way, and stood behind the door, popped out and grabbed his arm.

"Are you with us?" she cried, her eyes flaming with excitement.

It was an unnecessary question, but Skinny looked down and nodded. "To the death!"

Sally grinned, and picked up the mallet that still lay by the door. "Then, let's charge!"

When they reached the street, they found the Professor leaning wearily against a lamppost, while the army of kids was across the street, excitedly hopping up and down and surrounding a cab.

"Hey, maybe that's Becky!" cried Sally. They dashed across the street.

Becky and Jack had popped out of the cab, and were joyously reuniting themselves with all their old schoolmates. Clarence and Christine were nowhere in sight.

Skinny got a report from Marcel Dubois that he had simply taken Becky back to Jack's house, and there they had waited until Jack had arrived home. Once he had arrived, they had come straight to the abandoned café, for Jack had a clue from one of the gendarmes, who told him they suspected the Company of Villains was using the building.

"So you only left Jack's house a little while ago?" asked Skinny anxiously.

The cabby nodded.

Skinny turned to Sally. "That means that Clarence and Chris ran into trouble. I'm going to look for them."

"Right, I'll stay with the army," said Sally, "and maybe get in touch with those gendarmes, too."

"Okay. See you later."

"Skinny wait," Sally called after him as he started off.

She caught up to him, and handed him a white pocketknife. "You asked at the beginning of this crazy night why I need so many pocketknives," she grinned, "well now, take this one. It might be handy. Bye!"

She turned and ran back, and was soon lost in the crowd of chattering children. Skinny smiled after her, and then glanced down at the little knife in his hand. He slipped it into his pocket, and ran off into the night.

* * *

Clarence thought he had a pretty good escape worked out. He figured that none of the Baron's men could squeeze through the crack through which he and Christine had just come, and once he got through it, he'd be safe. He dashed off, and heard a great clamor behind him.

He hoped that most, if not all of the Baron's men, as well as the Baron himself, would go after him, and let Christine alone, and it sounded as if his wish had come true. He reached the crack, slipped through it easily enough, and paused on the other side. It seemed obvious now that the Baron's men would never fit through, so he turned and jogged carelessly down the dirty alley, wondering where Christine was.

He looked as he jogged down the dark street. Christine was not in sight at the corner, nor at the corner of the next block.

Clarence began to feel worried, wondering if perhaps she had turned back to him when she saw him being pursued. He wondered if he should go back and see, but if she was still free, it would be useless to get himself caught.

He was standing at a corner, under the dim light of a lamppost, looking around desolately. Suddenly, he felt a huge hand clapped over his mouth, and his feet were knocked from under him. He immediately began to struggle, but whoever was holding him was a powerful man.

"So now I have the boy that knows of the treasure," said a deep voice in his ear.

He recognized the voice as Black Hawk's and could see the gaudy rings on the hand that covered his mouth. Clarence gave a desperate wiggle, and bit the hand. There was a snarl from above him, and he received a blow on the side of his head that made him go limp. He tried to think clearly, but was on the verge of losing consciousness. Vaguely, he felt his hands pulled behind his back and being tied tightly. Then his forehead hit the cold pavement, and all was quiet.

"Now you'll stay put," said Black Hawk from far above, "and when you wake, your friends shall be dead and you on your way to find the treasure for me. Sleep well, my pretty boy."

Clarence opened his eyes with an effort and saw two huge boots stalking away, accompanied by the sound of clanking jewels and weapons. As Black Hawk turned the corner, and disappeared, Clarence let out a shuddering gasp of pain, which he had kept stifled. He could feel a cut on his forehead, and wondered if it was bleeding. His thoughts were growing vague, and he was terribly worried about Christine, alone in the winding streets with Black Hawk and the Baron on her tail. He twisted his hands around, trying to test the strength of his bonds, and found them tight and biting. He sighed, and fought back a sob of desperation and pain.

"Oh God," he prayed, as the world began to spin around him, "oh God, take care of Chris, and all of them. Please!"

He breathed this heartfelt prayer, and then, after placing the situation in God's hands, his head slipped back to the pavement, and he knew no more.

Only about a block away, Christine was flying down the street. Her mind was filled with guilty thoughts about running to safety while Clarence had to stand alone amongst all their enemies.

"Did I leave his side in that crocodile cage?" she thought.

"No!" she said, digging her heels into the cement as she screeched to a halt. "Will I leave him alone now? No!"

She turned, and charged back the way she had come. Her flight had been thoughtless and wild, and she tried to recognize any landmarks she'd passed, but found herself completely lost. She noticed she'd gradually made her way back into a nicer part of the city, where the streets were better lit.

"Oh, this isn't right," she thought desperately, scanning the streets anxiously with tear misted eyes. "I've got to go back."

She turned back the way she had come, but after several minutes of confused running, she was still completely lost. She finally found an alley that she thought vaguely resembled the one they had gone down before. She crept down it cautiously, keeping a sharp eye out for any small creatures of the rodent variety. She reached a crack and peered through it.

All was still on the other side, and she was about to slip through, when she suddenly heard a sharp voice. She flattened herself against the wall, and held her breath. She could still peek through the crack from her position, and watched in urgent curiosity.

"So the treasure is ours at last," she heard a deep, croaking voice mutter. It was Black Hawk, and his words made her shudder.

"Yes, but what about the other four?" asked another voice that she recognized as the Baron's. "Doubtless they will try to rescue him. Where is he?"

"A block away," said Black Hawk, "bound, and unconscious, behind rubbish. Get your men."

"No, I'll go get him, and have him taken back to the hotel before anyone else can get there. Once he's there, he will never get out."

Christine heard their footsteps retreating, and the Baron's terrible words rang in her ears.

"I've got to find him before that Baron does!" she cried to herself.

She turned, and fled down the alley, not caring if all the rats and mice of the world were scurrying about in it. All she had to go by was Black Hawk's vague directions of "an alley about a block away," and that didn't give her much hope. She hoped the Baron was as confused as she was, and prayed that he might get lost.

After vainly checking about a few of the dirtiest, darkest alleys nearby, Christine went running around a corner at full speed, sensing that time was running out, and ran right into the Baron with a thud.

She glanced up at him, and he looked down at her, both too surprised to do anything at first. Then they mastered themselves at the same time.

Christine gave a little gasp, and turned tail. The Baron gave a shout, and took after her. As she fled blindly down the dark streets Christine's only thought was one of relief. Now that the Baron was after her, he wouldn't be able to take Clarence away, and maybe she could go back and get him, provided she got away.

She could hear his boots pounding on the sidewalk behind her, and the swish of his cape, and the clank of his sword. She could tell by the sounds that he was growing closer.

"I've got to do something fast," she thought, "something smart, like Sally would do."

She tried to remember all the tricks Sally had told her about. Christine had never really cared about them until now. She supposed that if she tried one, she'd probably mess up, and get herself caught. Then, an absurd idea occurred to her. Sally had told her, while at the emergency room, about the Tom Playfair maneuver she had used on Little Joe. Christine remembered her saying that if her pursuer had been any of the other villains, it would have worked. There were no lampposts or telephone poles around, so she decided to do it differently. Her plan was, at the next corner, to turn it, and then spin round, push herself off the Baron who would have followed her around the turn, and get a little more of a lead as she dashed back the way they'd come.

As the corner drew nearer, she keyed herself up, and whispered a prayer. She turned the corner, slid to a graceful and immediate stop, whirled round, and went back. Just as planned, the Baron was coming around the corner full speed. When she ducked passed him, she gave herself a push off of him, and started off again. Everything would have gone smoothly, but as she had pushed off of him, her finger got caught on something metal that was strapped to his belt, and as she started away, she gave her finger a yank, and something heavy had come with her.

She glanced down, and saw that she had her finger caught in the barrel of the Baron's pistol! She quickly put her other hand on it, for the thing was dreadfully heavy. As she ran, she gave a tug and her finger came out with a pop.

Her hands fumbled for a moment with the gun, while the realization of what had happened sunk in. She glanced back, and saw the Baron behind her. He apparently hadn't noticed.

She thought frantically for a moment, and decided that it was time for another of her rare bursts of courage.

They were heading down a long, thin street, the only light coming from the window of a shop, which someone had forgotten to turn off when the place closed. In front of this little patch of light, Christine halted. She did not turn around until she heard the Baron's heavy breathing just inches away, and then, with a fierceness that did her shaking nerves credit, she spun round, and pointed the gun at his chest.

The Baron pulled up short, and stared in disbelief at his own gun, being waved in his face by a mere child, whose countenance had suddenly grown stern and calm. His hand flew to his belt, and clutched at the empty holster.

"Don't move," ordered Christine. "Take another step, and I fire."

The Baron's hand froze on his belt, and he held still.

"Now where's Clarence?" she asked, in as cold and heartless a voice as she could muster.

The tone of her voice must have worked, or perhaps it was the loaded gun covering his heart, for the Baron's face was pale, and his hands shook. In response to Christine's question, he raised a timid finger, and pointed behind her. Christine did not move.

"Okay, I know he's back there," she said, "but what I want you to do, is to take me there, very quickly and quietly, without attracting attention. Now get ahead of me."

The Baron complied in an instant, and Christine stuck the muzzle of the gun in his back. Her finger wasn't even near the trigger, for she feared her shaking hand might accidentally fire the gun, but the Baron couldn't see.

"Now, let's go," she ordered.

They began the long, slow walk back the way they had come so quickly before, the Baron walking first, his hands in the air, and Christine stern and grim behind him.

* * *

"Okay you kids!" shouted Sally, desperately trying to make herself heard above the chatter and at the same time stay on the top of the cab where she had climbed. "You need to quiet down, and I'll give you the battle plan!"

When no change occurred in the melee of young voices, Sally looked exasperatedly down at Marcel Dubois, who was leaning against his cab with an amused expression. When he saw Sally's consternation, he leaned in his window, and gave his horn a vigorous whack.

All the kids who were sitting on the car's hood leapt off with cries of surprise, while the others looked up in annoyance at the cabby for interrupting them.

"Hey kids!" cried Sally, snatching the instant of silence. "It's time we make our move! I have to go find my friends. Marcel here, will be in charge while you wait here - Quietly! When you hear from any member of the Company, telling you that we need help, then the time has come to fight. Okay?"

She was answered by a cheer. Sally waved the mallet, which she still held high above her head, and let out a whoop. Becky elbowed her way through the throng, and came up beside Sally.

"You're leaving?" she asked worriedly.

"I've got to find Skinny, it's been too long since he went to look for Clare and Chris," answered Sally. "Something tells me they're in trouble. You help Marcel keep these kids quiet, and be ready to march into battle at a moment's notice."

"Okay," said Becky, "but Sally, you will be careful, won't you?"

"Never say die!" answered Sally with a wink. She slid off the roof, and with a farewell wave to the little army, jogged off into the night, still armed with the kitchen mallet.

Becky looked after her for a long moment.

"What's wrong?" asked Jack, following her troubled gaze.

"I don't know. I just hope she makes it. She's our leader."

* * *

Skinny anxiously scanned the area where the villains were last seen. He was now about to follow the course that Clarence and Christine had taken, in the faint hope of finding them.

He started from where he'd last seen them, and followed their direction. He wasn't exactly sure how to get to Jack's friend's house, and it occurred to him that Clarence hadn't really known either. After a few minutes of walking, he found himself in the cul-de-sac, with the small crack of a passage as the only exit. He supposed Clarence and Christine had never even come this way, and turned to go back, when his eye was caught by something on the rocky asphalt right near the crack. He went over, and picked it up. It was a white rose petal, like one he had seen on Christine's dress, its edges tinged with just the slightest hint of soft green and gold.

"Chris," he murmured, and stuck the petal in his pocket. "At least I'm on the right track."

He slipped through the crack, and searched the area for a few minutes. The darkness was oppressive, and all the alleys and streets looked similar.

He wondered if Clarence and Christine had merely gotten lost, and were even now safe at Jack's house, or, having found the cab already departed, had perhaps gone on to the café and joined up with Sally.

"Maybe now they're all out endangering themselves by looking for me," he thought. "It has been an awful long time since I left." He looked down the street and sighed. Slowly, he began to walk down it, glancing wearily into all the alleys he passed, hoping for another hint or sign of their presence.

At the entrance to the last alley, he stopped and sighed again. He figured he might as well try to find his own way back, to see if they had been found. As he started on his way again, he glanced back once more, and this time, noticed a forlorn heap that was lying a few feet into the alley, and had a peculiar shape to it. He went back, knelt down, and touched it. It looked like rubbish. It was a body.

Skinny drew back in horror, and got to his feet. He wasn't sure what he should do. Perhaps this was some crime he should not be involved in, or maybe the villains had finally come to murdering each other.

With a shock that was surprisingly fearful, he wondered if he had found Little Joe, or all that Black Hawk had left of him, but the fear soon passed. The form was too small to be the tall figure of his former boss. He slowly knelt down again, and reaching out a reluctant hand, touched the shape.

To his relief, he heard a slight groan. Whoever it was, he was alive. He put out his hand, and gently rolled the shape over. As the face came into the dim light of a far off lamppost, Skinny gave a cry of recognition and dismay. He brushed aside the black hair, revealing the pale face, with the pointed nose and intelligent features that he had grown to know so well.

"Clare!" he cried, pulling the unconscious boy into his arms. He glanced at his hands, and found them bound and chaffed from his struggles. Across the side of his brow, running down to his cheek, there was a cut that was already bruising over and swelling slightly. His face was cold from lying against the wet ground, and his breath came in shuddering gasps, for he appeared to be having some sort of nightmare.

"Clare," said Skinny again, "Clare, best of friends, stay with me." He shook Clarence gently. Skinny held his breath as slowly, the lashes lifted, and the piercing black eyes were revealed. They slowly pulled into focus, as Clarence's brow knit into a confused frown.

"Skinny?" he asked at length, "what happened?"

He tried to sit up, but the cords that bound him pulled him back with a wince. "I can't," he muttered apologetically. "Now I remember. Black Hawk got me from behind. Man, that guy can really pack a powerful punch."

Skinny smiled in answer, appreciating the courageous effort to lighten the situation.

"Here," he said, "let's get you untied."

Clarence rolled over, and Skinny looked hard at the bonds. "Oh brother," he muttered, "I can't untie this."

"You got a knife?"

"No." Skinny suddenly stopped, and snapped his fingers. "No wait, I do!"

He pulled the small white knife out of his pocket, and looked at it with reverence. "How did she know?" he whispered. "If I live to see her once more, I'll never call her crazy again!"

"I'll hold you to that," said Clarence with a weak grin. "Now let's get out of here."

Skinny carefully cut the cords by the dim light, and taking Clarence in his arms, walked out toward the main street.

"Think you can stand up?" he asked as they stopped under a lamppost. The street was deserted.

Clarence nodded, and Skinny let him down, offering him a hand. Clarence held it for a moment, then straightened and let it go with a grateful glance.

"Thanks," he said, running his hands through his hair, and gently fingering his cut.

"It's nothing," said Skinny. "You know, you've gotten so tall, I can hardly even pick you up anymore." Skinny looked at him for a moment. "Yeah," he said, "you're a lot bigger than you were last summer, and you've gotten better looking."

Clarence grinned. Then his face fell.

"Chris!" he said softly, "Skinny, I don't know where she is ... Black Hawk said that when I woke up, all of you would be dead. Do you think that means he already had Chris?"

"No, probably just trying to make you give up," said Skinny confidently, but his heart was troubled.

"Well, we've got to go find her!" cried Clarence, "come on!"

* * *

The Baron stopped half way down a long dark street, and pointed to the last alley opening.

"There," he said. "He's there. Don't shoot."

"Okay," said Christine. "Now walk toward that alley. I still have you covered."

They walked slowly down the alley, where the Baron stopped again. Christine scanned the area anxiously.

"Where is he?" she asked.

The Baron shrugged. "I do not know. Black Hawk said this was the place. Maybe Black Hawk moved him."

"Oh," moaned Christine. Her courage was giving out, and she couldn't keep the tears from her eyes any longer. Her throat was stinging, and her hands began to shake.

The Baron remained still, for the gun was still pointed at him. After a moment, Christine mastered herself again.

"Okay," she said slowly, looking up at him. "You may go."

The Baron looked down in disbelief. "W-what?" he stammered. "Go?"

"Yes," said Christine. "Go."

"But you don't intend to turn me in?" asked the Baron. "Why not!? All those Gendarmes who were here before?"

"I know," said Christine. "I guess it's because, even though you've been beastly to us, I don't want to hurt anybody. I think it just makes you want to hurt us more, and then we want to hurt you more, and on and on, and it won't stop until we're all dead; you and me, and Black Hawk and Clarence and everyone. I don't want it to end like that! Maybe now you'll think better of us. Sally wants to fight, but I don't. I hate fighting. Now, I'm sorry, but I'm going to have to keep your gun. I'll try to return it someday, but for now I need it. Now go, you're free!"

The Baron was silent for some time after this awkward, shakily given speech.

At length he looked up at her again. "But I could just turn and stab you in the back," he protested, in a slightly softened tone. "You are making a great risk for you and your friends."

"Something tells me you won't," returned Christine evenly. "Sally tells me there is good in absolutely everybody. I believe her. She's a saint, and a hero. She once said all she really wants by all this fighting is to have peace. She says that one dream she has is that all you villains and all us heroes would be friends someday. Maybe that could happen. I don't know. Now go!"

The Baron stared at her for a long moment.

Then, to Christine's amazement, he bowed to her, as though she were a princess. He turned, and walked off into the gloom, tall and proud, his cape swirling about him.

Christine looked after him, wondering if she had done the right thing. Then, she suddenly remembered Clarence, and clasping the gun firmly, she set off.

Chapter 20

A Rescue and A Trap

Mallet in hand, fearlessly sniffing out adventure, Sally ran around the deserted high class streets of Paris. She would have attracted a deal of attention to herself if there had been any people about at that hour of the night.

"Drat, where is everybody?" she muttered crossly. "I guess this was a stupid thing to do."

She was standing on a brilliantly lit street, absently swinging her mallet. She turned around, and looked at the shops that were all closed, their large show windows displaying a gaudy array of merchandise.

Sally took a step toward the windows, and inspected the contents of one of the stores. It was a confections store, and though Sally wasn't a sweet-toothed kid by nature, she had a hard time moving away from the attractive assortment.

After entertaining herself in such a way for some time, she came upon a display that really caught her interest. It was some sort of joke shop, and apparently carried every kind of practical joke equipment that had ever been known to man. Sally gazed in wonder at the fantastic assortment of fire- crackers, a commodity for which she had a certain passion.

The elderly proprietor was exiting his store at that ungodly hour. In the window, there was one sort of device Sally had never seen before. She pointed to it questioningly. He indicated that it was a tiny box, filled with powder, that if disturbed once a certain string had been pulled, would ignite a good-sized flame. Sally supposed this was a dangerous plaything, and personally wouldn't have recommended it for average amusement, but it struck her that, in the position the Company was now in, a little surprise defense might be a good idea.

After a bizarre ten minutes within, (involving many words that didn't exactly qualify as being part of any language, English or French), a little bit of bickering about price, and a heated argument about the maturity and prudence of the buyer, she emerged the proud owner of ten of the little magic fire-makers, as she had christened them.

"Now, all I need to do is locate a villain or two," she mused, as she continued through the streets, "and light them on fire."

She skipped down the streets, a bag of the fire-makers on her arm, and her mallet in hand. After a while, without having seen a single sign of either friend or foe, she decided to set a trap with her fire-makers, and try to lure the villains to her.

She deliberated for some time as to where she should set the trap, and finally decided that it should be somewhere away from homes, so she wouldn't set all of Paris on fire. Having made her decision, she looked for an open area.

As she hurried through the streets, she kept a sharp eye out for anyone familiar, still cherishing the hope of finding her comrades alive and together.

In one dark alley, she thought she heard a swish of fabric behind her, and spun round, but saw no one. She wondered if perhaps the Baron was on her tail, but she got no other signs of anyone following her, so she dismissed the thought.

She came upon a large open area, with a big field and the decrepit skeleton of what was once a magnificent old oak tree. It was still standing upright, and made a striking figure against the moonlight. There were no bushes or foliage near. It looked as though the place had already been through a fire.

Sally wondered if maybe it had once been some old farm or home, burned to the ground with all its surroundings, with only the great tree left standing to guard as the sentinel of a destroyed land. It looked completely dead. When Sally got near it, she was amazed at the size of the tree. The yellow moon shone through its leafless branches, creating an eerie effect.

At the base of the tree, Sally stopped. It seemed sacrilegious to disturb the towering tree by setting foot on it. She timidly reached out, and touched the dead bark. It was still smooth, and somehow, when she touched it, Sally got the feeling that the old tree would not object to her intrusion, for she was an honest child, just trying to survive in a world full of evil men with bad intentions, just as the tree had been able to survive the cruel, battering effects that time and the elements had wrought upon it.

"You don't mind do you?" whispered Sally. "I might be silly, but I've always hoped that when we get to heaven, we'll meet you trees. After all, God made you too, and loves you very much, for he dresses you so nicely, especially in the fall. Well, then you certainly won't mind me using you for protection. Thanks."

She reached up, grasped the lowest branch, and pulled herself up, leaving her mallet leaning against the massive trunk. On a thick branch near the bottom, she laid the first fire-maker, and a few branches up, she placed the next one. She worked her way through the branches, climbing higher and higher into the night sky. She talked gaily to the old dry tree, trying to cheer the old thing up a little. First off, she explained what the fire makers were, and who the other members of the company were, and most especially, who the villains were. She told him that, in truth, she would like to have peace between them all, for though they were cruel, she could tell that there was good in them, and she wouldn't have minded being friends.

"Especially Little Joe," she mused, more to herself than to the tree, as she laid the last fire-maker on one of the higher branches. "He really seems like he could be a swell guy. If he wasn't always trying to kill me, I think we could really get to like each other. He sometimes even acts like me, I think."

She stopped for a moment, and thought hard. A strange feeling had just gone through her, as though she had hit upon a mystery that had long been waiting to be discovered. Then the sensation passed, and with a shrug, she started down the tree again. As she passed each of the fire-makers, she pulled the string that made them ready to ignite.

"Okay then," she said, as she swung down to earth again, "thanks a lot, old oak. See you soon!"

She waved a hand to it, picked up her mallet, and skipped off towards the city, gleaming in the light. The tree stood, silently watching her from its great height, still hearing her carefree voice echoing through the long stilled branches, and keeping altogether sacred the secret that she had laid in wait in his boughs.

* * *

"Any sign?" asked Clarence wearily, looking down a long street, and wiping the sweat and dried blood from his forehead and bangs again.

Skinny shook his head, too discouraged to answer. Clarence sighed, and slumped down on the sidewalk.

"Let's take a rest," said Skinny, glancing with concern down at his friend's battered face. "I'm tired."

Clarence didn't respond. He pulled his legs up, hugging them close, and let his head sink down to his knees. Skinny slowly sunk down beside him, and tilted his head back to get a glimpse of the stars. They were faint and far away, but in the darkness of the lonely vacant street, they seemed bright and lovely to him.

He let his eyes shut after a moment, and almost fell asleep. He felt terribly guilty about sitting still and resting while Christine and Sally were somewhere in the dangerous city. But he was so awfully tired, and so discouraged and worried about Clarence, that for the moment, he let his concern for the girls go, and satisfied himself with whispering fervent prayers for them with every breath he took. This was not a wasted effort, in the sight of the One with the real power.

He glanced over at Clarence and sighed. The lad was trembling from the cold, and the bruise on his cheek had begun to turn darker. Skinny edged closer, and gently pulled Clarence from his hunched position, taking his poor head in his own lap. He opened Clarence's collar, and brushed back the dark locks from his brow with the tenderness of a mother toward her child.

Slowly, Skinny also shut his eyes again. They stayed there in silence for some time.

Just two insignificant teenage boys, almost men, that the world had forgotten about, were huddled in a quiet spot in the city. It appeared the heavens had forsaken them. But even in their slumber they both knew better. One staunchly supported his comrade, praying earnestly for all that was dear to them, while the other fought his own desperate battles for consciousness and life.

Skinny woke from an uneasy, restless slumber, and was suddenly hurled back to reality by a rough hand that grabbed him by the collar and dragged him violently to his feet. He opened his eyes with a start, as he felt Clarence's head slip off his lap and hit the ground with a sickening thud.

He found himself held by large arms, and staring Black Hawk full in the face. The gigantic pirate made a satisfied grimace of true malice, displaying his blackened, mostly missing teeth. Skinny was surrounded by four or five of Black Hawk's men; the largest held him captive. None of the other villains were around, but Skinny assumed the Baron would be along soon enough. Black Hawk looked Skinny from top to bottom, and laughed coarsely in his face.

"So, my lovely enemy," he snarled, "your heroic efforts shall end here and now. Your doom has been ordained."

"Again?" thought Skinny vaguely.

Black Hawk stared at Skinny for a long moment, his small dark eyes glinting in rage at the fearless gaze with which Skinny steadily regarded him. Black Hawk's assurance almost seemed to lessen just the slightest bit.

He gave a nod of his head to the man that held Skinny, and the man dropped him to the ground, but kept a tight and merciless grip on his wrist.

"Do what you will, you corrupt bully," said Skinny softly, in a powerful and commanding tone. "But you will never be able to defeat us, and the principles we fight for. You'd best return to your own land now, in honor, before you are forced to do so in shame. You shall not be spared by us, Black Hawk!"

He wasn't quite sure why he was taking such a reckless offensive, for he knew his grave danger, but the speech Sally had given on the steps of the café's basement was still ringing in his ears, and her strong, fearless voice shouted within him to defend the helpless, oppressed and bullied.

Black Hawk let him talk; staring down into his proud face with a scornful look that almost amounted to a cruel sort of pity. When Skinny had finished, he remained tall and proud, his piercing eyes relentlessly boring into the unassailable heart of the pirate.

Black Hawk returned his gaze, and then slowly, like some great, disgusting animal, he turned his large head on its thick neck, and looked down at the slim, attractive form of Clarence, still lying with his face to the stars, his eyes closed, his breast rising and falling gently in the peaceful rhythm of slumber.

Skinny followed his enemy's gaze, and his face changed. The look of cruelty that was reflected in Black Hawk's beady eyes as he looked at the sleeping boy made his heart grow cold.

"No," murmured Skinny, glancing up at Black Hawk, his proud eyes instantly turning humble and pleading, "no, don't."

Black Hawk looked from Clarence's peaceful countenance, to Skinny's changed features, and his smile broadened. He took a step towards Clarence, drawing a long knife from his great belt. Skinny's eyes widened with horror and rage. He wrestled himself free from the man that held him, and charged towards Black Hawk. Immediately he was seized roughly again, and held back, despite his violent struggles.

"No!" he cried, his voice cracking with fear and anger. "No, Black Hawk, please!"

Black Hawk turned and regarded him with a satisfied smile. "Now," he said, "now I will have the sport that was denied me by that she-devil Keenan. She escaped my monster. You will not be so lucky. He!" here he pointed a gnarled finger with a horrid, pointed, yellow nail at Clarence. "He will not be as lucky! Now I shall have sport."

He bent down, grabbed Clarence's collar, and roughly jerked the boy to his feet. Clarence opened his eyes with a shuddering groan, and when he saw his surroundings, their sparkling blackness turned fearful and courageous all at once.

"Black Hawk," cried Skinny desperately, "Black Hawk, he's ill. For the love of God, kill me if you must, but leave him alone!"

Black Hawk smiled again, and gave Clarence a gruff shake. He let him drop, and as he hit the ground, gave him a slap across the mouth. Skinny could see his friend's fists clench as he staggered backwards against the alley wall, but he held his tongue manfully and no tears appeared in his large eyes.

Skinny struggled violently, but to no avail. "Black Hawk!" he cried after a moment of silent desperation, "what of the treasure?"

"He will live enough to serve me yet," answered Black Hawk, "but he shall know after this never to cross my will."

He held his knife aloft, brandishing it over Clarence. Clarence did not flinch, his face did not change. Skinny pulled in a hissing breath.

"Black Hawk, for God's sake!" he whispered desperately.

"For God's sake?" scoffed Black Hawk, lowering his hand. "What good does that do you? How can your God, or your principles help you now? What has your goodness won for you? Your life is ended. Give up. This boy ... " he grabbed Clarence's hair, and jerked his head backward, "this boy is still of use to me, but after I have taught him to respect me, you shall die, and I shall truly have my sport. I hope you will be as brave as you seem when your time arrives. Your God will not help you then, or now!"

He suddenly raised the dagger above Clarence, preparing to strike down upon him. Skinny gave a shout.

He was stifled by Black Hawk's men. They held Skinny down, as their master, with a swift, well-aimed kick, landed his heavy boot in Skinny's stomach. Skinny gave a gasp. He remained only on his feet by the assistance of his enemies, hardly able to draw breath. Now it was Clarence's turn to cry out in pity for his friend and wrath towards his enemy. Black Hawk swung back around to him, brandishing his knife again. Clarence faced him, resolved to prove that he was as courageous as Skinny.

Then suddenly, there was a loud noise quite near them, and one of the men holding Skinny fell to the ground with a yell, clutching at his leg.

Black Hawk turned, momentarily unmastered, and as he did so, another shot rang out on the silence, and another of the men that held Skinny gave a shout and fell forward.

Clarence leapt at the opportunity. While Black Hawk was looking around in bewilderment, to discover the source of his sudden downfall, Clarence suddenly sprang forward, and with both hands, landed all his weight on Black Hawk's arm that held the dagger. He bore it down, and before his huge enemy had realized what had happened, Clarence had wrested it from his grasp, giving himself a cut on his left palm. Once he had the weapon, he backed up against the wall again, holding it in front of him, and staring hard at Black Hawk, trying to anticipate his next move, and wondering who was firing at them.

However, the pirate had scarcely noticed Clarence's attack, for he was anxiously scanning the alleys and streets that surrounded them, fearful that he would be gunned down as fast as his men by the unknown assailant.

When Skinny's captors had fallen, the last two of Black Hawk's men had taken hold of him to prevent escape, but a very gentle hold, fearing that the fate of their companions should fall upon them. They did not have to be rough with Skinny though, for the lad was leaning forward almost on his knees in a swoon, so affected was he by his ill treatment. The extent of his guards task was to keep him on his feet. They seemed to be wavering.

"Black Hawk, retreat and leave your captives, or die!" a voice rang out from above them.

Clarence had been half expecting it to be Sally and her army, but he doubted they could really do much against Black Hawk and his men. When he saw the men fall, stricken down unawares by a gun in the shadows, he knew this could not be an attack from any of his friends. So why would anyone else put themselves into the terrible disfavor of Black Hawk, to try and save two unimportant teenage boys?

Black Hawk looked up in the direction whence the voice came, and his face changed. Above him, perched on the roof of an old building, surrounded by ten or fifteen of his men, all brandishing pistols, was the Baron. His scarlet cape swirled around him in the cold night wind. His dark hair was shining in the moonlight, and his tall, proud figure made a striking picture as he swung himself off the roof, and landed before them.

"Go, Black Hawk!" he ordered coldly. His pistol, and the pistols of four of his men were pointed at the pirate's heart, and in the Baron's eyes shone a new light that Black Hawk did not care to question.

Black Hawk gave a guttural snarl, which appeared to be some sort of command, for his men dropped their weapons, and let Skinny go. Skinny immediately slumped forward, and without a sound, fell prone upon the bodies of his enemies.

Black Hawk glanced back at Clarence, who was still holding the dagger steadily, though his eyes were glued upon Skinny with an anxious look. Black Hawk stared at him contemptuously for a moment, and then with a grunt and an arrogant swagger, he strode out of the alley, his men following close behind him, with cowed expression. As they turned the corner, and disappeared, the Baron turned and looked at Clarence.

"Why?" asked Clarence, after a long pause, "why would you put yourself in danger of Black Hawk's rage, just to save us, your worst enemies?"

The Baron did not answer right away. His eyes dropped down, as though he was ashamed of his courage. Clarence lowered the dagger he held, and took a step forward.

"We don't matter to you," he persisted, "why would you save us? You don't care about us."

"No," said the Baron quietly, "but Christine does."

Clarence's eyes opened wide. "What?"

"Christine cares much about the both of you. I did this for her only."

Clarence opened his mouth to ask the flood of questions coming to his mind, when the Baron looked questioningly from Clarence to Skinny at their feet.

Clarence knelt down, and listened in concern to his quiet breathing. It sounded as though Skinny was choking. Clarence put out a hand and touched Skinny's forehead. When his hand came away, there was blood on Skinny's face. Clarence glanced at his hand and saw his own palm was cut and bleeding from the knife. He hastily wiped his hand on his shirt and looked in slight disgust at the red smear that appeared.

The Baron, who was still standing silent above him, looked down at his plight and curtly pulled his white linen handkerchief from his pocket. Clarence nodded appreciatively, and wrapped the cloth around his hand.

"Skinny?" he asked, bending down to listen to his friend's labored breathing.

Slowly, he pulled Skinny up, and gently patted his face. Skinny opened his eyes, glanced in amazement at Clarence, and then in even greater incredulity at the Baron above them, and started coughing.

"Skinny, here, let me help you up," urged Clarence.

Skinny nodded, and staggered to his feet, leaning heavily on Clarence's arm. "I'm alright," he gasped after a long, tense moment, "I just had the wind knocked out of me."

"Okay, then what do we do now?" asked Clarence.

Skinny glanced down at the men upon whom he had fallen. "We've got to get these guys to a hospital," he said matter-of-factly. Clarence nodded.

Skinny glanced up, and saw the Baron. "Hey," he asked, "why did you save us?"

The Baron was staring down at the men he had shot, apparently pondering Skinny's words. Before answering Skinny, he turned to his men and barked an order in German. They came forward and roughly started pulling the wounded men to their feet. Clarence sprang forward in distress, and the Baron gave another order that made his men suddenly become, though a bit bewildered, much gentler and more considerate in their conduct.

Once they had conveyed the two men to a car that was apparently parked around the corner, the Baron turned to Skinny, and laid his hand on his shoulder.

"To answer your question, boy," he said, speaking slowly, and choosing his words with care, "I saved you because of what you all fight for. You, in your young bodies, have more courage, and honor, and most of all, mercy, towards those you should rightfully hate, than that old pirate has in his whole dirty carcass.

"Mercy is a new thought to me, and it has changed the way I think. Mercy was shown to me only a little while ago, for perhaps the first time. I shall take Black Hawk's men to the nearest hospital myself, and see to their care. You go, and find your girls. They miss you. And tell ... " here the Baron stopped and seemed a bit flustered, "tell that girl Christine that she is a fine miss, and tell Sally Keenan that I wish I could know her better. She's fine too. Good-bye."

He turned, and strode to his car without another word. Skinny and Clarence stood, side by side, and watched the cab disappear into the night gloom.

"Well, that was something," said Clarence at length.

Skinny only nodded.

* * *

Sally turned a corner and ran down another street. She was beginning to get worn out. She'd been dashing down streets and creeping through alleys for almost an hour, searching vainly for some sign of her friends or her enemies. She finally stopped to rest before a dark alley, and leaned up against it wearily, fingering the head of her mallet gently, deep in discouraged thought.

"Whenever I've got something to do," she said aloud after a pause, "that's when either those villains or Becky is so ready and willing to interrupt me. Or whenever I'm about to have a little fun, even if it is sort of reckless, Skinny always shows up in time to stop me. Now, for the first time I want to see them all, and they disappear off the face of the earth!"

She looked around in disgust and exasperation. "Skinny?" she called into the darkness, "Skinny, or Clarence, or anybody? I don't care if any of you villains hear me, 'cause I just need to talk to somebody!"

She waited for a moment, straining her ears for some reply. "Oh, brother," she said at length, and started on her way again, dejectedly dragging her mallet behind her.

"Hey, Sally, what's up?"

Sally whirled round, and looked into the dark alley whence the familiar voice had come. "Skinny? Is that you?"

"Sure, come here."

Sally took one step toward the person in the shadows, when suddenly she recognized the voice. She knew it well, but not as belonging to Skinny. Almost at the same instant she checked herself, there was a stifling noise from the impostor, and then with a choking gasp, a long held in cough broke loose upon the silence, and Little Joe, his tall form racked with violent coughs, stumbled out of the alley.

Sally didn't wait for him to pull his gun or start towards her. She spun round and pounded down the alley as fast as she could. She heard a few more coughs behind her, and then the sound of Little Joe giving chase.

For a few tense minutes, she was running down a straight street, within full sight and reach of Little Joe's gun. She reached the end of it successfully, though, for he seemed to be avoiding opening fire. She figured that her best bet was to make sharp turns, and keep zigzagging through the streets, to avoid getting gunned down from behind.

After a little while, she made a sharp corner turn, and stopped. She suddenly realized that she couldn't hear the footsteps behind her any longer.

Little Joe had stopped. For a moment she considered turning the corner to see the cause of his sudden halt, but she knew it was very probable that he was trying to work the same trick on her that he had played on Skinny in New York. Most likely, if she stuck her head back around the corner, he'd give it a good whack, and finish her off in the blink of an eye.

She waited in silence, holding her breath, for what seemed ages. At last, after listening closely, she decided to risk a quick look. It certainly didn't sound as though Little Joe were near.

Slowly, she stuck her head around the corner, did a double take, and then gaped in surprise at the sight that met her gaze. Almost at the end of the dark street whence they had come, Little Joe was walking, or more, stumbling in the opposite direction. His gun was held loosely in his hand, which hung limp at his side.

Sally instinctively turned the corner and began to follow him. She was desperately curious to see what was wrong with him, and she also knew she had to keep him within sight until she could lure him to the trap she had set in the tree for him.

When he had almost reached the other end of the street, which she expected him to turn in the same lethargic manner, he suddenly glanced back, and saw her.

Sally stopped, ready to turn tail at any moment and run for her life. Little Joe looked hard at her for a moment, and then with a cough that sounded more like a growl and with a look of frenzied hatred, he turned and fled, whizzing around the corner as though the devil was after him. Sally was too surprised to move for a moment. Little Joe was running away from her?

She quickly collected herself though, and ran after him. She turned the corner just in time to see him dash down the next street. Immediately she gave chase, mallet in hand.

"This is crazy," she muttered to herself after a moment, "who's supposed to be chasing whom?"

* * *

Christine took a deep breath and let it out in a long shuddering sigh. She wondered what good it would do to cry anymore. After the Baron had left her, she'd sunk down on the cold, hard ground, laid the gun next to her, and buried her face in her hands in an abandon of grief.

Clarence was gone. Most likely, he was already back at Black Hawk's hotel, with no possible hope of escape or rescue. She knew Clarence was a fighter when he put his mind to it. Most likely, he'd put up a fight that would get him beat up terribly. His captors would be cruel to him, and he'd be lucky if he lived through the night.

Skinny and Sally were far, far away on the other side of the great, unconquerable city. Perhaps they had already found the army of kids that Clarence had wanted. If they had, it wouldn't do much good now. Maybe they'd been caught too, and now she was the only member of the Company left, and it was her duty to try to rescue her friends. Her heart went cold at such a prospect.

"Dear Guardian Angel," she whispered, "please, help us. All of us!" She looked around in despair. "Please, please!" she clasped her hands and shut her eyes tight, praying with more ardor than ever before. "Please, Virgin Mary, and Saint Whatever-Your-Name-Is, that Sally's always praying too, please let me find at least one of my friends!"

She took a breath to continue her prayer, when she heard fast, rather light footsteps approaching at break-neck speed. She glanced up, and saw someone streak past. Though she saw him for only a brief moment, she instantly recognized the tall black haired gangster. It made her recall with slight bewilderment a time when she'd heard Sally say that Little Joe was one of the greatest looking guys she'd ever seen.

Now, she couldn't believe her eyes as he dashed past her. She wondered what he could be in such a hurry for, with no one fleeing before him. Then, just as she had once again composed herself to prayer, she heard another pair of feet, lighter than the first, running towards her. She glanced up again, and saw a streak of blue flash past. She opened her mouth in amazement, but was too surprised to cry out. She heard the footsteps screech to a sudden halt, and then retrace themselves. Sally's head appeared around the corner, and she looked down at Christine in surprise.

"Hi," she said, "what are you doing down there?"

"What are you doing up there?" returned Christine, scrambling to her feet.

"I'm chasing Little Joe," said Sally, swinging her mallet. "Come on, I don't want to lose him."

She turned the corner and ran off. Christine hurried to follow her, her bewilderment steadily growing.

"Wait a second," she said, catching Sally's arm at a corner and pulling her to a stop. "What did you say we were doing?"

"Chasing Little Joe. See?" Sally pointed with her mallet. Christine looked, and saw Little Joe disappearing around the next corner. Sally immediately started after him, dragging Christine along behind her.

"So, what's been happening?" she asked as they ran. Christine opened her mouth to give Sally the bad news about Clarence, but her own grief and horror of the situation overpowered her, and she simply began to cry. Sally looked at her in confusion, and came to a stop.

"Say!" she cried, taking Christine firmly by the shoulders and staring hard at her. "What's all the bawling for? Are either of the boys hurt, or dead?"

For answer Christine let loose another torrent of tears.

"Answer me, you crybaby!" said Sally, paling slightly, and giving Christine a rough shake. Christine was startled by her gruff attitude, and with some difficulty, held her tears in check.

"Well?"

"It's Clarence," she whimpered, "Black Hawk's got him."

Sally's brow furrowed. After a moment of grim thought, she seemed to be brought back to the present by Christine's shaking shoulders. She glanced at her, and found the beautiful young girl staring at her with frightened, tear filled eyes.

"It's okay," said Sally, "we'll get him back. I ... I'm sorry Chris. I didn't mean to bark at you like that. You scared me, that's all. I guess you've had a hard night. Good old Chris."

She pulled her close, and Christine put her head on Sally's shoulder. Christine, at length, straightened up. There were tear stains on the already bloodstained bandage on Sally's shoulder, and her still damp dress was wrinkled and dirty.

"Oh, Sally," said Christine in horror, "I'm sorry, I didn't mean to lean so much on your shoulder." She reached out and gingerly touched the bandage.

Sally grinned, and shrugged. "Well," she sighed, after a last, friendly smile that said more than excess words could, "let's go try to find the boys."

Christine nodded, and wiped her tears away, leaving a dirty smear on her face from her grimy hand. Sally grinned.

"So, where did you last see Clare?" she asked, as they started down the street.

"We split up, and I ran one way," she said, trying to keep her voice steady, "but then I heard Black Hawk tell the Baron that he'd got him. Oh, Sally, do you think we'll ever see him again?"

Sally had suddenly stopped, and was looking back the way they'd come. "Sure," she said, her face lighting with a sudden grin. "Turn around."

Christine turned, and let out a gasp of unbelieving joy. There, walking towards them, though leaning on each other for assistance, were Skinny and Clarence.

Christine gave a squeal of joy, and ran toward them. Clarence hastily let Skinny's arm go, and straightened up. Clarence hurried forward, and caught Christine into his arms. Skinny and Sally, standing each on one side of the rejoicing couple, glanced at each other awkwardly. At last, Skinny grinned at her. Sally returned the formality, though he noticed she seemed a bit reserved.

"Hi, Skinny," she said a last, "how's your night been?"

He shrugged. Sally looked hard at him for a moment. "You've got blood on your face," she said nervously.

"Yeah, but it ain't my blood," confessed Skinny, wiping his cheek with the back of his hand, "that's Clare's. He cut himself a little."

"Oh!"

Suddenly, Sally seemed to remember something, and smacked her forehead. "Skinny, you stay here with these guys. I've got to keep going. See you!"

Before Skinny could reply, she shot off down the street, and turned a corner.

"Chris," said Clarence, looking after Sally, "where's she going?"

"She's chasing Little Joe."

"What?" cried Skinny incredulously.

Christine nodded complacently.

"What's wrong with that kid?" asked Skinny, more to himself than the others.

Clarence shrugged, and smiled. "She's Sally," he answered, "that should explain it."

"Well, come on," cried Skinny, "let's follow her. She'll need help if she's really trying to go after him, even if we have to limp."

He started after Sally as fast as he could go, while Christine and Clarence followed a little more slowly, Christine having to satisfy herself that Clarence wasn't too badly hurt before she'd take a single step.

Soon Skinny was far ahead of them, and close on Sally's heels. As she started down a long street, he caught up to her. Far ahead, he could see the outline of Little Joe's tall, stalwart form, silhouetted against the glow from the lampposts. He'd stopped again for a moment, and was leaning heavily on the wall of a phone booth. Sally slowly came to a halt, glancing a welcome to Skinny.

"Do we keep on?" he asked after a moment. Sally shook her head after some deliberation.

"I take it you've set a trap for our enemies, and you're trying to get him there," said Skinny, "so where is it?"

Sally looked up in surprise. "How'd you know?" she asked.

Skinny smiled, and ignored the question. "Well, if he's not going to run from us anymore, we need to get him to come after us."

"Yeah," agreed Sally, "but he's been acting mighty strange lately. I don't like it."

"He's taken a pretty bad beating from Black Hawk I think," mused Skinny, "both to his body and his pride. He's really not that bad a guy. His morals are mixed up, but overall, his heart's in the right place."

Sally was slightly puzzled by Skinny's words. It appeared to her that Skinny was still very fond, though that wasn't the right way to describe his feelings, more proud, of the grim gangster. Sally had to admit that she too, as she saw more of him, was beginning to be in awe of him, though sometimes she felt it was more pity that she felt for him.

"Well," she said aloud, "I guess we still need to finish off the villains. Now that the Professor is on our side, we have only three to handle."

"Oh, by the way," said Skinny, "you'll never believe what's happened. The Baron is with us. He shot two of Black Hawk's men, and got pretty nasty towards Black Hawk himself. He said Christine had been merciful to him somehow, so that's why he did it. He saved me and Clarence's lives."

Sally stopped short and stared at Skinny with her mouth open. Then a grin spread across her face. "Mine and Clarence's lives, Skinny," she said, hoping that was grammatically correct.

They both laughed.

"Well, anyway," said Skinny, "that leaves only two villains to conquer."

"Yes, I guess I always expected the Baron to come over to our side sooner or later," Sally said. "And as for the Professor, he was never into the evil stuff anyway. It's Black Hawk and Little Joe I've worried about since the beginning, and they're still a problem."

Skinny nodded soberly. "True, and I guess we can safely say that neither of them will be any too easy to change."

"Look! He's moving!" said Sally, pointing to Little Joe. The gangster had turned, and apparently seen them. After a few moments of hesitation, he swung himself around again, and started running away, down into the deep shadows at the other end of the street.

"Come on," said Sally, starting after him at an easy pace. Skinny fell into step beside her.

"There's an outlet into a main part of the city at the end of this street," he said at length, "and a big park, and that bridge that crosses over to the other part of the city. I think it's under construction. What course should we take?"

"Whichever Joe takes," said Sally.

They had almost reached the end of the street, and the phone booth that Little Joe had been leaning against. As they passed it, Sally suddenly stopped.

"Skinny," she said after a moment, "I've got a feeling in my bones that things are coming to a head. How about you call our army?"

Skinny nodded. "You think something's going to happen?"

"Yes, I feel that in a few minutes everything will be over, for better or worse, I don't know! I want Becky and her friends to be here, when that happens. Call them for me, will you?"

Skinny nodded again and Sally took a slip of paper from her pocket. "Here, that's the number. I'm going on."

"Hey," said Skinny, as he slipped inside the telephone booth, "if everything really is coming to an end, for better or for worse, there's something I've got to tell you."

Sally shook her head, and looked down, avoiding his eyes. "No, not yet. I'll see you again."

Skinny shrugged, trying to be careless, though his heart was troubled. "Just keep him in sight, Sal, don't confront him alone!" he called after her.

Without another word she turned and ran off, waving a hand behind her and not looking back once. Skinny looked after her and sighed. Then he remembered her request, and hurriedly shut the door of the booth. He glanced at the paper and the scrawled numbers, and scratched his head.

"Darn you, Sally," he muttered to himself, "why can't you learn to write neatly? Is that a six or a zero?"

Chapter 21

On The Bridge

Sally came out into the main city, blinking in the bright lights. She glanced around hastily, and saw Little Joe just as he fled out of the other end of the long grassy park, and started for the bridge Skinny had spoken of. Sally took out after him.

As she flitted through the trees and little hills, she wondered about the strange feeling that had suddenly settled over her. It was the feeling that something either great or terrible was about to happen. She'd often thought that this was how heroes of old tales of valor and courage felt before a desperate last stand, or perhaps how a marooned sailor felt when he realized he'd discovered a long lost treasure.

"Am I about to discover a treasure?" she asked herself, "or perhaps about to make a last, vain fight?

She could not answer these questions for herself, so she decided just to leave herself in the hands of God, and hope for the best. She came to the foot of the large bridge. It was a massive thing, wide enough to fit four traffic lanes, and a sidewalk on one side.

For safety reasons, there was a chain link fence running up at least eight feet above the concrete wall that ran along the sides. At the moment, there were yellow caution cones and a barricade of yellow safety tape running across the width of its entrance, to keep vehicles off. Sally could see that further ahead, about three feet of the wall and metal fence were missing. Perhaps they had been broken off in some car accident. Because of this, there was no traffic on the bridge, and once on it, she and Little Joe would be virtually cut off from the rest of the world. After a long moment of last minute hesitation, she readjusted the wreath of roses on her head, made the sign of the cross, and slipped under the safety tape; out onto the fateful bridge.

Christine and Clarence hurried down the long, dark street, a feeling of impending doom steadily growing in their hearts.

"Clare," said Christine at length, "do you suppose Little Joe could be working the same trick on Sally that she's trying to work on him?"

Clarence had been expecting the question. It had been worrying him for some time now, as he tried to think out their enemy's actions realistically.

"You mean," he asked, "you think he's trying to lead her into a trap?"

Christine nodded.

"I don't know. At least Skinny is with her."

They ran past a phone booth, and out into a main street. Suddenly, Clarence clutched Christine's arm and pointed. She looked through the huge park that lay ahead of them. The fog was beginning to lift, and they both saw Little Joe run onto the bridge in the far distance.

They glanced worriedly at each other, and then turning back, saw Sally appear on the other side of the park, alone. She ran to the bridge and started across it, disappearing from sight.

"Where's Skinny?" muttered Clarence to himself. Christine turned, and gave a little gasp. She ran back to the phone booth. Clarence followed and saw Skinny.

"She's following Joe alone!" Clarence hollered, banging ferociously on the phone booth door. Skinny glanced up, smiled an absent welcome to them, and slid the door open. His ear was pasted to the phone and a look of silent exasperation had stamped itself upon his features.

"Skinny, Sally's followed Joe onto the bridge!" cried Christine.

"No-no thanks," he said into the phone, holding a hand up to Christine to silence her. "No, I'm not trying to order from your bakery, monsieur."

"What are you doing?" cried Clarence, "this is no time for snacking!"

For answer, Skinny gave Clarence a kick in the shins. "Shut up," he said, and then into the receiver, "No, not you sir. I'm afraid I have the wrong number. Goodbye."

He hung up while the person at the other end was in the middle of a sentence, and looked exasperatedly at a slip of paper in his hand.

"Skinny, listen to us!" said Christine.

"I wonder if it could be an eight?" mused Skinny, staring hard at the paper in his hand.

"What are you talking about?" asked Clarence, leaning over and looking at the numbers.

"I'm trying to get a hold of our army," answered Skinny. "Clare, what would you say that number is there?"

Clarence stared at the number Skinny was pointing at. "It's a nine without a tail."

"Great," said Skinny sarcastically, "I've already called two cafés, one house where a grumpy old man was asleep, and a school, thinking it was a six, a zero, a crossed out five and not even a number."

"Try nine," Clarence said, "and if that doesn't work, come after us on your own. I'm going after Sally."

"Where is she?" asked Skinny, again picking up the receiver, and saying something in broken French to the operator.

"She's on the bridge still following Little Joe," Christine answered. "Are you sure he's not trying to lure her into a trap along with Black Hawk?"

Skinny hesitated. "I don't think so," he said at length, "last we heard Little Joe and Black Hawk weren't exactly on speaking terms, and Joe can hold an amazing grudge. Sally's just watching to see where Joe goes."

"Okay," Clarence started back toward the park. "Chris, you stay here, I'll come back if I can."

Christine nodded, watching him worriedly. As he passed into the trees that lined the closer side of the park, she lost sight of him for a moment.

Then suddenly, she noticed a cab had pulled up only a few feet away from her, and inside there was someone with a hat pulled down low. Christine looked at the person with preoccupied curiosity, still very concerned about Clarence and Sally. Then, as she glanced at the occupant of the cab, the hat was suddenly lifted, and Christine got a glimpse of delft blue eyes.

"Oh Skinny!" she cried, turning and running back to the phone booth.

"What?" called Skinny into the phone, giving Christine a sidelong dirty look for interrupting him. "The Barber Shop??"

Christine laughed in spite of herself. "Skinny, listen to me!" She yanked the receiver from his hands and hung it up.

"Hey!" cried Skinny, "now that barber's going to think I hung up on him! Anyway don't bother me, I'm going to try eight."

"Skinny, look," persisted Christine, pulling his arm forcibly and turning him around. "Look at that woman."

Skinny glanced at the cab, and then suddenly clutched Christine's arm. The light of recognition lit in his eyes, and with a gasp he pulled her forward.

"Come on!" he cried, "Now's our chance!"

As Sally slowly crept past the gaping hole in the wall, which looked like a missing tooth in the well ordered concrete, she shuddered. Beyond the gap, there was nothing but empty space, and a dreadful fall into the black nothingness of the night below. Though fear was the least of her weaknesses, Skinny would liked to have known that Sally had always had a thing about heights. They bothered her. She was usually able to fight the fear, but her feeling of approaching danger was growing so strong that almost everything now made her uneasy.

She hurried past the gap as quickly as she safely could, and then continued on her way, clutching her mallet tightly. There was a slight curve in the long bridge, and as she approached it, Sally slowed down a bit to get a view.

She poised the mallet high above her head, and crept forward cautiously. As she came around the slight bend, she suddenly stopped. There, in the dark shadow ahead that was cast by the few streetlights that lined the bridge, was the looming figure of Little Joe. As he stepped into the light, the pale moon was reflected on the muzzle of his gun. Sally did not move. It appeared that the chase was over.

"Hi," she said at length.

Little Joe nodded in response. His hand was steady, and his eye grim and steely.

"Well," she said, "I guess this is it."

Slowly she swung her mallet down, and its head touched the hard street in a token of submission.

He nodded, and took a step towards her. She did not move.

"You're not afraid?"

"Why should I be?" she returned steadily, "I've been to Mass and confession. I guess I'm only sad for my friends' sake. I promised Skinny I'd see him again."

"He's a good kid, isn't he?" said Little Joe, still in the same even tone.

Sally hesitated. She wondered if Little Joe was trying to get her off her guard, even though she'd made no fight. Little Joe seemed interested in her hesitation.

"Do you love him?" he asked.

Sally was momentarily struck dumb. If Little Joe was trying to get her off her guard, he couldn't have selected a better way. She stared at him in stupefied silence for a moment.

"What does it matter to you?" she asked, slightly annoyed.

"You didn't answer my question," returned Little Joe.

"No, and I'm not going to!" retorted Sally, "Why would you want to know?"

"Because Skinny's the only real friend I've ever had," said Little Joe complacently, "and also because I know he thinks that you're ..."

"Please!" interrupted Sally, "if he hasn't told me himself what he thinks of me, I don't think it's any business of yours to discuss his feelings. Now, have you tracked me down through multiple countries and through many fatal traps just to discuss boys and girls, or did you have something else in mind? Because if not, I'll gladly go away."

Little Joe smiled, almost kindly. "You're a plucky kid, Keenan."

"Thanks, but seriously," she looked at him with piercing eyes, "why all the stalling?"

Little Joe seemed slightly perturbed by her question, and her rebellious gaze.

"No stalling," he answered, "if you must know, I almost think well of you for looking death in the face like you do. A lot like Conklin."

"You couldn't bring yourself to kill him either," retorted Sally evenly.

Little Joe's gaze hardened. "Don't think I ain't man enough to kill you, Keenan. You might think I've softened up a little after seeing me next to that disgusting pirate with all his gruesome schemes. But when it comes down to straight, honest guts, I'm not lacking. I've still got a score to settle between me and you, one that goes back to a crime committed long ago. A real serious crime. You are the price I demand as restitution."

Sally suddenly flushed angrily. "You?" she cried. "You want restitution for a crime? You are a criminal, a murderer. If anyone has a right to hold a death grudge, it's me. You murdered my father!"

A blue spark shot from Little Joe's clear eyes. "Your father was a worse criminal than I could ever hope to be."

Sally's wrath was held in sudden check by the brooding countenance and muttered words.

"What?!" she whispered.

"Your father stole something from me years ago when I was just a teen, and in stealing that treasure of mine, did worse than murder me. He sentenced me to a life of misery and treachery. A living death. A Hell on Earth."

Sally took a step forward. The gun was not aimed at her anymore, for Little Joe's hand was going limp. His eyes were not on Sally now, indeed, they appeared not to see anything but bitter memories.

"What did he steal?" she asked, still whispering.

"Your mother's heart."

The words were spoken so quietly that Sally shouldn't have been able to hear them, but she did. A chill slid down her spine, and she caught her breath.

"What?" she asked at length, hardly daring to breathe in the ominous silence that followed his fateful words.

"Her heart was mine," continued Little Joe in the same brooding, unseeing manner, "and she was glad of it. He was older, years older, and more practiced in the art of treachery. I wasn't even a crook back then, but I'd made a few bad friends. I made a fatal mistake when I lost my head over your mother. I couldn't help it. She was wonderful. She was my whole life for a few heavenly months.

"Then, it hit me that he liked her too. He liked her a lot, though with him it was fleeting and not a very serious matter. It wasn't the true and only love of a young man. I figured I needed to move fast.

"We were both in earnest and ready to spend our whole lives together in happiness, when he came like a shadow of death between us. He stole her heart away on false promises and empty dream castles for a little while, but then she awoke to the reality of him, and told me she really loved me."

Joe began rambling and his voice grew quieter.

"Then, he came and took her by force. She went with him, to save my life from his murderous jealousy, and the day that they were married, my life came to an end. But my troubles weren't even started then. After the wedding, he came to me and forced me into his shady service. I was only a kid, and he liked the way I worked. He trained me in his service, and I did my job well for him. There was one thing though, he was always mad at me for being too soft-hearted. Several times I rejected a theft job because it would hurt the victim, and I never did murder."

Little Joe was slumping down now. Sally stood erect. "He was always on my back for something, suspecting that I hated him. Then, one day he realized it. You were five years old. Maybe I let something slip, but he realized that I loved your mother. That was it. One night he came to me, when nobody else was around and pulled a knife on me. I knew him too well to doubt he'd murder me. I'd seen him do worse before. I didn't really care whether I lived or died, but out of instinct I defended myself. There was a scuffle, I tried to get away, then he fell at my feet. I didn't realize at first what I had unknowingly done, then when I realized ... O my God, have mercy on me!"

He stopped, and wiped the sweat of agony from his deathly pale brow. He was shaking from head to toe with emotion, and even from fear of the awful memory. His face had taken on a much younger look as he relived the days of youth, though at intervals through the narrative he was interrupted by his nagging cough. Sally was listening in silence, her heart in a violent turmoil of emotions.

"It was my first murder," said Little Joe finally, after he had calmed slightly, "and I can say truthfully, my last. I've lied, stolen, cheated, beaten, and sinned, but never since that awful night have I taken a human life. God forgive me, I didn't mean to do it! But, after that, there was no going back. Your mother, of course, took it the wrong way. The scorned advances of a lovesick kid turned murderer was only too clear an accusation. I became what your father had made me into. A while later, I tried to kidnap your mother, and explain. I knew that if only she heard me out, she'd believe me and love me again. But, my men worked the job, and brought your mom back to the hideout when I was gone."

Sally turned her face away to hide the tears that had welled up in her eyes. She knew it must be hard for Little Joe to tell, but she suspected that it was even harder for her to listen to the story of her mother's death.

"By the time I got back," said Little Joe, "it was too late."

Sally choked back a sob.

"She had already escaped."

Sally's head shot up, her eyes opening to their widest, as she drew a gasping, half choking breath.

"What?!" she cried, running forward and touching Little Joe's arm gently. "She's alive?!"

Little Joe looked down at her, as if realizing for the first time in his story that she was there.

"Yes," he faltered, "then she was. I don't know if she is still. She fought my men like a wildcat. She was a lot like you, Sally. When we were in love, I used to say she was untamable, and she really was.

"After she'd gone out of my life of her own free will, I didn't try to follow her. I decided that my place, as far as she was concerned was in the back alleys of New York, living like the rest of the scum. But I swore, as a revenge on the man that had ruined my life, that I would destroy the one thing that had come of that marriage. That one thing was you, Sally."

Sally couldn't speak. Her mind was reeling around madly. She pulled her hand off Little Joe's arm, and looked up at him. He glanced down at her. His tall, now proud form towered above her. They made a striking picture. The tall, slim, dark haired man in his black suit, and the slim, graceful young girl, almost a woman in her fragile blue gown, her dark curls surrounding her tear stained face.

"Little Joe," she whispered at last, and her hand reached out and again gently touched his arm. "Oh, Little Joe!"

She flung herself towards him, and into his arms. He stood silent for a moment, his arms hanging loose, and then, the cruel, hard, worn lines of care fell from his handsome features, and his arms closed around her. As she laid her damp head against his dirty suit, with his strong arms encompassing her in a firm and loving embrace, almost crushed by his sudden, wonderful affection, Sally heard the gun drop from his hands and hit the street with a clank. The token of surrender spelled the final end of the long lasting fight.

The battle was over. The war was won.

Chapter 22

The Biggest Secret

"Clare!"

Clarence turned at the sound of his name. He could see Christine back at the street with Skinny, and now someone else had joined them.

Clarence hesitated for a moment, wondering which course to take. Christine again called his name, and gesticulated for him to come to them. Clarence reluctantly turned and started towards them, giving the bridge one last, worried glance.

As he reached the end of the grass, Skinny came running across the street to meet him.

"Clare, big news! It's The Big Secret," he called, tossing his head in the direction of Christine and the stranger. Clarence followed his gesture, and his face took on surprise and delight as suddenly an incredible realization hit him.

"Skinny, is it possible?" he faltered.

Skinny nodded, a smile flitting across his face. "I'm going back to the phone, and I'm going to try eight, pray that I get the right number this time."

Clarence grinned, gave Skinny a friendly slap on the back, and ran back the way he'd come, still trying to make sense of his muddled emotions, caused by the amazing discovery made but a few moments before.

When Little Joe's arms finally loosed around her, they stood staring at each other in silence.

"Well," said Sally at length, with a shaky laugh, "this night sure didn't turn out like I expected."

Little Joe's face was grave. "Sally, it makes me feel that my life is not worth living to know that up to this moment, all my efforts and thoughts towards you have been evil and vicious. You've every right in the world to take that gun and end my contemptible existence, as someone should have ended it years ago. I'm hardly even a man any more. You are a symbol of all that's beautiful and innocent. I don't even deserve to look at you - you should leave me."

Sally smiled sadly. "You have made some pretty bad mistakes," she admitted, "but God will forgive absolutely anything! If you were ten times as bad as you are, Our Lord would still be glad to forgive you, just as long as you are sorry. Besides, you're not as bad as you think. After all, you've never committed a real murder, and, just between us," she glanced up shyly and grinned, "I always sort of thought that, when it came right down to it, you wouldn't be able to kill me either."

Little Joe reached out, and gently touched her damp curls. "And to think," he muttered, "that you, with all your amazing guts and incredible faith, you could have been my kid. My little girl."

Sally looked up at him and smiled through her misty eyes. "I will be," she whispered, "I am."

Little Joe nodded, and then suddenly, like an omen of ill luck that brought them back to reality, he started coughing. The cough was worse than ever now, it shook his whole body and left a worn and weary mark upon his face.

"Oh, Joe," said Sally, "I forgot, you're sick. We've got to get you out of here. This damp air isn't good for anybody. You're sick!"

With difficulty, Little Joe checked his coughs. "No," he gasped, "it's too late for that now. I will pay for my sins."

"No!" cried Sally, her voice cracking with emotion, "oh, Joe don't talk like that! You'll be better soon."

Little Joe looked down and smiled sadly. "You care?" he asked huskily, "after all I've done to you?"

"Of course!" Sally reached up and brushed his dark locks back from his face. "Of course, and don't worry. You'll be all right."

"You're quite a kid, Keenan," he muttered. His face was gentle, and with the peace that had descended upon him, several extra years of misery were removed from his features, though the pallor and pain inflicted by his illness was growing more pronounced with every labored breath he took.

"Now," said Sally with all the cheerfulness she could muster, "let's go on back down. I'm sure Skinny will be just overjoyed to see you. He thinks a lot of you."

At these words, Little Joe's face relaxed slightly. "Does he?" he asked, "that's good. At least my life isn't a total loss. But ..."

Suddenly he drew in a painful, gasping breath, and collapsed limply. His stormy blue eyes were closed suddenly. His tall form slumped down onto the cold, damp sidewalk and remained still. His tousled hair fell over his brow, the black contrasting strikingly with the white skin.

Sally looked down at him in horror. She bent down and listened closely at the parted lips, and caught, though very faintly, a breath; a choking breath that bespoke the life still harbored within. Gently, Sally stooped and kissed the cold brow.

"I will save you!" she muttered through clenched teeth, "I promise. I might die before this night is over, but before I do, I swear I'll save your life!"

She got to her feet, and with one last, pitying glance at the man lying in the closed street, she turned and with an expression of determination, started back down the bridge, her mind brooding upon her last desperate mission. She ran past the gaping hole in the wall without slowing or flinching. She slipped under the caution tape, ran out and down to the very foot of the bridge, and came to a sudden halt.

She found herself standing in the glaring light of many headlights.

The entire width of the bridge was blocked off with cars and men, all armed. In the center of the menacing array, was the long black car, and in front of it, the massive shape of the pirate, silhouetted against the dazzling light like a shadow of impending destruction.

Sally hesitated for a moment. Her halt had been instinct, not fear. She knew for certain that to go forward was to perish, and yet the urgent pounding in her brave, young heart was reminding her of her mission to aid the dying man behind her. Her actions overcame her own common sense.

"No!" she shouted fiercely, in answer to the light of death that shown in his eyes. "No, Black Hawk, wait! Little Joe is sick, maybe dying! I've got to get a priest for him, then," she wondered if her mind was going awry, but still she followed the dictates of her heart, "then I am yours, without a fight. Just get him help, and ask him to remember, once I'm dead by your filthy hands, that I died for him, because I believed he deserved another chance at life! Please, Black Hawk!"

Black Hawk stood still, staring at Sally coldly, until the silence, broken so piercingly by her fearless, ringing voice, had once again settled over the ominous gathering. Then, slowly, a smile, lined with hate and cruelty creased the dirty wrinkles about the villain's mouth.

"Do you really expect me to believe you?" he growled at length.

"You should," returned Sally defiantly. "Just because you've never done an honest thing in your deceitful life doesn't mean that you can't trust anyone else. I mean what I say and I say only what I mean. Take my offer, or leave it. You won't get a second chance."

Black Hawk flushed angrily, whether from her defiance or her accusations Sally could not tell.

"So," he derided, "you want my choice. I make it. I defy your offer. I curse it, just as I curse you. Your death is nigh. And as for that soft-hearted young idiot you speak of, if he is not dead by the time I finish with you, then I shall have the pleasure of finishing him within the same hour. Prepare yourself, Keenan. You will not be saved this time."

Sally looked steadily at her impressive adversary, her gaze unflinching. It appeared that he was right; even she admitted it.

To charge toward them was suicide, to flee back across the bridge now would gain her only a few more minutes, and if she could get as far as where Little Joe lay without being overtaken, doubtless Black Hawk would kill him where he lay.

Her mind was still ferociously determined upon aiding the man whom she felt was now the closest relation she had in the world, and yet there seemed no possible way to accomplish the mission. For a split second, she was in turmoil, not knowing which course to take. Then, as it always had before, her mind made itself up, as though it didn't need her opinion. Sally had learned to recognize it as the subtle and always present voice of her Guardian Angel. She had long ago trained herself to always obey without hesitation any command or suggestion from this source, but now her heart sank as she thought of its import.

"Give up?" she thought, her heart beating faster, "but I can't give up! I swore to Joe, and besides, I'm Sally Keenan. I guess I've always thought that I would come out all right in the end, and live happily ever after. I had a dream of one day being the heroine of a book, but how can you be the heroine if you give up the fight and die just when you've the chance to be a hero?"

She listened closely to her heart for reasonable answers to these troubling questions, but none came. Time was growing short. If she was going to do something, now was the only chance she'd have.

"All right," she said to the voice within her heart, "all right. You have never failed me before, so I will do as you bid now. Goodbye."

Those that were watching Sally, tense and ready for her next move, were suddenly surprised to see her look up at Black Hawk, her head tossed back proudly in the defiance of a last stand, and start down toward him with steps steady and bold.

"If my fate is ordained," she cried, again ripping the heavy silence unabashed, "then let it be so. You do not have to hunt me down like a criminal. I have no crimes for which to repent. I come to you of my own free will. A person with a guiltless conscience can never be a prisoner, no matter where their body is held. I am not surrendering, Black Hawk, but if my time to meet my God has truly come, and yours is to be the hand that lets me to His bosom fly, then I come without hesitation. Do as you will."

As she slowly approached him, her clear voice ringing proud and strong, Black Hawk almost seemed to shrink and wither before her scathing gaze and matchless courage. A few of the men with him were hastily wiping their eyes with their dirty hands, anxious lest their neighbors think them weak.

At last, Sally stood but a foot away from her greatest enemy. They eyed each other levelly, seeming of the same height and majesty. Then, with a slight start, Black Hawk seemed to be brought back to reality, and the remembrance of who he was.

"So be it," he growled. "You take much pleasure from my victory. You are a wise child. I am a man of war, and thus I know, that, though your life is ended and I have the last stroke, you are victor in the things that matter most."

Silence hung heavy in the air after this surprising speech, delivered in such a tone that only Sally and a very few others caught the muttered words. Sally's heart was calmed. She understood now. Her body did not matter. Her story was over, and she had remained the heroine to the end.

"But!" cried Black Hawk suddenly, the wild light of cruelty and madness unsatisfied kindling anew in his terrible eyes, "but I still have the victory of the flesh, and that victory I will hold to, and be glad of! The Company of Secret Kids is ended! I say again, Keenan, you will not be saved this time!"

He raised his saber aloft. Sally's gaze did not change. Then, as the crowd of surly, filthy men held their breath as one, waiting for the stroke, there rang out upon the silence, yet another voice.

It was clear and loud also, yet with its cry came a chilling fear into the hearts of the men. It was youthful, strong, and terrible to their ears. It seemed to be able to bring destruction in its wake. In Sally's presence they had feared for their souls, now, much more urgent in their minds, they feared for their lives.

"You speak too soon, Black Hawk!" Skinny cried. "It is your doom that awaits! Sally's time has not yet come. But for you and your men, have a care, if you value your wretched skins! Long Live the Company of Secret Kids! Erin Go Bragh!"

And with that a huge roar went up that shook the foundations of the bridge; a hundred voices raised in thundering unison.

Sally looked up in amazement. Her mind had been so occupied with the last turn of her chronicle, that she had not noticed the stealthy approach of her rescue. Now, she looked around in incredulous rapture.

Behind Black Hawk's array, and far outnumbering them, was a veritable army of exultant faces, all grim and determined, and yet at the same time, youthful, joyous and excited to the utmost. There were not only the whole of Becky's friends, as well as the cabby, now beaming from behind a heavy gun, but also a score or more of gendarmes, a touch more serious than the children, yet just as earnest.

As Skinny finished his declaration, all of them, from the smallest child to the tallest gendarme had raised their voices in the rousing war cry that shook the enemy. At the center of the army and pinnacle of grandeur, having noiselessly climbed up the back of Black Hawk's car, and now standing proudly on the roof of it, was Skinny. The effect of his bedraggled, battered appearance was completely lost in the majesty of his angry voice and glittering eyes.

From where he stood, Skinny glanced down at Clarence, standing on the running board of the car, his face alive with righteous anger and the glory of battle. Clarence looked up and nodded.

"Our army is here, and all is well!" he cried up to Skinny, above the din of their comrades.

Skinny nodded with a grin. "It was an eight," he said.

"The army!" cried Sally. For a moment in her extreme joy, she forgot the persistent voice within her, and when she remembered it, her heart seemed full to bursting. She now knew fully that her Guardian Dear was beside her as always, and she could practically hear the pleased voice in her soul saying dryly, "See, I told you so."

As she glanced up at Black Hawk, she was once again defiant and even a little smugly amused. The pirate looked down at her, after having taken in the situation, and his eyes turned cold and desperate. He became livid with the rage of defeat, and yet, he seemed grimly pleased by one last, deadly intention. Sally could easily read his thoughts. His arm was still raised, and the saber glinted in the glare of the lights. Though destruction and humiliation awaited, he could give one final stroke that would forever bitter the triumph of the Company; he could not win now, but he could destroy their leader.

Sally saw the saber descending. She could not move, though time seemed to slow, and everything that happened rolled by with amazing distinction. She briefly hoped that Skinny wouldn't be too saddened by her death, and would know that she had died bravely and grateful to him for his aid.

Then, another thing happened, that made all the adventures and exploits of Sally Keenan seem small and insignificant by comparison. There rang out upon the air, just as the army's war cry subsided, a single gunshot.

At first no one realized what had happened, and then, with a cry that was not unlike the terrible roar of some grotesque animal, Black Hawk dropped his saber, and clutched the hand that had held it. There appeared on the back of his right hand, a deep red wound. Sally winced when she saw it, and then looked around in amazement. As she did so, Black Hawk gave a snarl, and charged for his car.

Clarence leapt back as he came roaring toward it. Those of his men that could move fast enough hastened to get in the other doors, while one stooped and retrieved the saber that had fallen at Sally's feet. Black Hawk himself took the wheel, and after closing the door as well as he could with his injured hand, he slammed the car into reverse.

This proved almost fatal for Skinny, still standing on the roof. He lurched forward, lost his balance, and slid down the hood. As his feet touched the pavement he spun round, looking at Black Hawk through the windshield with a friendly grin.

"Hi, have we met?" Skinny asked.

Black Hawk growled and pulled away, brakes screeching as he turned sharply. The gendarmes looked questioningly at Skinny, whom Clarence had taken by the shoulders and shaken in a good natured manner, for his choice of battle perch. Skinny laughed with his friend, and then glanced at the gendarmes. He shook his head when he saw their guns pointed at the car speeding away.

"Not yet!" he called, "but follow them, and arrest the men still here!" The gendarmes nodded, and several ran to their own vehicles.

Meanwhile, Sally was still scanning the crowd in bewilderment, looking for the face of her deliverer. The aim had been excellent; the shot had obviously not been intended to kill Black Hawk. Sally thought briefly that whoever had saved her must be a person of considerable skill in marksmanship. Black Hawk's men hurried to their cars, but were quickly overpowered by the alert gendarmes.

Sally turned and saw a figure she did not recognize, standing on the running board of a gendarmes' van. The person was dressed in blue, with a light blue veil head covering. Christine stood beside the figure, and had taken the gun from which the saving shot had been fired. It was a rifle.

Christine's face was expectant and radiant. Sally took the expression to mean that there was still something wonderful to come.

As she looked again at the mysterious figure, the rejoicing crowd of police and children hushed. As she gazed at the person, trying to get a closer glimpse through the glaring lights and confusing fog, Sally suddenly saw her look up.

Their gazes met.

Flashing blue eyes danced against the shining eyes of the stranger, and then, Sally's eyes opened wide with an incredulity and joy that had never dazzled her features so radiantly. The stranger was a stranger no more.

"Mama!" she screamed, her voice cracking unsteadily, all the heroism and assurance of her character falling from her, leaving only a little child, running to her mother in her hour of need.

The woman in blue leapt lightly from the car and came flying to meet her. Skinny and Clarence turned, saw the scene unfolding, and then glanced at each other with understanding smiles. Their eyes were swimming. Christine was bawling.

The veil was swept back as she came running toward Sally, revealing a face so like Sally's, that many for a moment thought their eyes were playing tricks on them. Without the extra twenty or so years added to the woman's lovely countenance, it would have been hard to tell them apart.

They met halfway, and Sally was lifted into her mother's arms with the ease of a toddler being carried to bed. For quite some time, Sally's mother held her child close, gently stroking her hair, as the tears of grateful joy coursed down her cheeks.

"My Sally," she whispered fervently, "my little girl."

"Oh Mama," wept Sally, "don't ever let go!"

Skinny gripped Clarence's arm tightly, and turned his face away from the touching scene. He hastily wiped his eyes with his damp and dirty sleeve, and began looking around at the army in a business-like manner, as though trying to decide what to do with it.

Clarence glanced at Skinny, and smiled. "Sort of makes everything seem worth it, doesn't it?"

Skinny nodded, and looked back. "She seems so little," he muttered, "so unsure."

"Yeah," grinned Clarence, "maybe that's what has made her so brave."

"How so?"

"Well, when she thought her mom had died, she figured she had nothing left to live for, so she could always be as brave and reckless as she wanted. Now, she'll need to be cautious, 'cause she has a reason to live again."

"Maybe," said Skinny sadly.

Clarence's words troubled him, though the same thought had occurred to him many times in that fateful night. Skinny had always thought that Sally cared for her friends, too. He wondered if it could be true that she wouldn't have minded dying, and leaving them all heart broken.

He also thought, with sinking heart, that if this theory proved true, now that she was reunited with her mother, perhaps her spirit would subside. It seemed hard to imagine a Sally that wasn't fearless. He didn't like it.

Finally, Sally and her mother loosed themselves from their embrace, and looked hard at each other.

"Well, this really has been a big night for you, my little wildcat," said her mother with a tearful laugh.

"Yes," said Sally, and then she glanced over at Skinny and Clarence. "It's not over yet, either. Where do you suppose Black Hawk has gone?"

Skinny looked up, hopefully.

Sally grinned. "We need to find that old pirate and finish him off for good!" she said.

"Perhaps he'll be taken care of by the authorities," Skinny answered.

"Perhaps we'd better make sure," Sally retorted. "But first I have a lot of questions to ask you." Running back into the center of the circle, she hollered, "somebody needs to follow those Gendarmes and not lose Black Hawk!"

A rousing cheer from the army went up.

"Then pile into what vehicles you can, or follow on foot! Move Now!"

With another war cry to get them going, the army immediately complied.

Christine and Becky came running toward Sally and her mother, and for a moment Sally was smothered by hugs and kisses, and the rather gruff, shy handshakes of the boys.

Sally's mother dazzled them all with a smile quite akin to Sally's. Sheila Keenan was the most beautiful woman any of them had ever seen. Her hair and eyes matched Sally's, though her face was a bit more finely chiseled and the eyes had a deeper look, from all the sadness they had witnessed.

Now Skinny hurried to answer a few of Sally's questions. He tried to give a quick account of how he had figured out, by many long and detailed letters, that the widow he had lived with and loved was indeed Sally's lost mother.

Skinny nodded and smiled as Sally's mother put a loving arm around his shoulders. Sally now was told that Skinny was the one who had saved her mother that night in Little Joe's hideout, when the gangster himself had been away, and his drunken men were on the verge of killing their hostage without his permission. Sheila herself had never seen the skinny thirteen year old, who had fought to defend her tooth and nail against a score of men twice his size. Sally was told later that if Little Joe had not showed up at a critical point of the battle, Skinny would have been killed in that fight. Thus it was that when Sally's mother, just as imaginative and reckless as Sally herself, did succeed in making her escape, only a few moments before Little Joe returned, all suspicion fell on Skinny, as the likely assistant of the runaway. This led to the fight with Little Joe that convinced Skinny he must leave. It was ironic that they had met again in Kansas, and not known each other.

"I was beginning to think that Sheila might come here when I hadn't heard from her for so long. Marcel and I went to the airport. Another cabbie told Marcel a woman fitting her description had arrived, but he didn't know where she'd gone. We went back to the convent and heard that she'd been there and gone through Sally's things."

"And you never told me?" cried Sally.

"I had to be absolutely sure," said Skinny. "And I've had this fear that maybe after you had your mother back, you wouldn't be your old reckless self ever again. I guess that's pretty dumb."

"You thought that all this time I've been trying to get myself killed?" asked Sally. "As if I didn't care about the four of you at all?"

Skinny shrugged and looked at his feet.

"I'll admit that at first my longing for adventure was partly from a hatred of life without Mom," Sally confessed, "but I guess God sent the Company into my life. I mean, once I really got to know you all, I decided that maybe life wasn't so bad after all."

"And now what do you think of it?" asked Sheila Keenan, taking her daughter by the shoulders and scanning her joyful face.

"Why, it's ... it's ..." Sally groped for a word strong enough to convey her unbounded joy. "It's like a Christmas morning, or a summer break that will never end!"

Her mother laughed, and pulled Sally close again. Then she glanced at the other four, shyly watching the reunion, and laughed again.

"Come on, you knuckleheads!" she cried, "don't be shy around me!"

Becky ran forward and buried her face in Sheila's dress. When she looked up, she studied the woman's face, and nodded.

"You are like Sally," she said, "you laugh a lot. I like that."

"So do I," said Skinny, "and it's been a long time since I've enjoyed being called a knucklehead so much!"

"And Clarence," said Sheila, smiling at the tall, lean, solemn-eyed lad, "you are quite a handsome young man." Clarence grinned sheepishly and muttered his thanks incoherently.

Christine was swept into Sheila's arms and welcomed with a warm smile. "So," she said, brushing back the golden locks that had strayed onto Christine's rosy cheeks, "Sally has always wanted a sister. You'll do wonderfully."

Sally laughed and leapt into the air, and then threw herself into a cart-wheel. Skinny and the others watched her patiently, used to such an irreverent exhibition when she was in a joyous mood.

But suddenly, her face changed. A cloud of concern and sudden remembrance flashed across her face, and she came out of her cartwheel with a crash, landing rather unceremoniously on the back of her head. Skinny and Clarence hurried forward to help her up, but she was on her feet before they reached her.

"Oh my gosh!" she cried, "I can't believe I forgot him!"

"Who?" asked everybody in one breath.

Ignoring their earnest inquiries, Sally took her mother's hands, and looked into her face with a seriousness that the others had never seen before.

"Mom," she said earnestly, "I need to know, right now. Do you love Little Joe?"

Her mother returned her gaze steadily. "With all my heart," she answered quietly.

"That's great," she whispered, her eyes once again filling with tears, "because I happen to know that he loves you. You two are a great couple."

"Couple?" asked Skinny, his eyes widening. "Do you mean, you two were in love the whole time?"

"Madly in love," said Sheila. "Oh, Sally, where is he?"

"That's the problem," answered Sally, growing serious once again. "He's back on the bridge, real sick, and fading fast. Mom, if you can stand a few more minutes of separation and suspense, I can too. You go to him. The sight of you is probably the only thing that can pull him through now, and please get him medical attention and a priest, too. I've got to go after Black Hawk and know that this is finished once and for all."

Sheila nodded. "Go and prove yourself," she whispered, "but be careful. I'll take care of Joe, believe me. I've waited for this moment for fifteen years."

Sally smiled impishly as she kissed her mother's cheek, and hurried over to Marcel Dubois, faithfully waiting. The other four followed her.

They found the Professor and the Baron waiting for them in the cab. They had been in the crowd, the Baron armed with his sword and the Professor holding his hands over his ears to keep out the noise.

"Okay, Marcel," said Sally, climbing over Clarence and landing in someone's lap, "if you saw which way the last of the cars went, follow them, and let's hope we can find them!"

Marcel nodded, and the cab lurched into motion. The occupants were tossed out of their seats by the sudden movement, for most of them were precariously perched upon each other's laps.

"Hey, watch it!" said Skinny, rubbing a freshly dented nose that had been caught by a stray elbow.

Marcel muttered his apologies in French, as the boys helped the girls regain their seats. Sally was pulled off the crowded floor by a hand in a white glove. She glanced at it in surprise, not accustomed to seeing such finery around the Company. Following with her eyes the arm attached to the hand, she found herself looking up into the Baron's serious yet polite face.

"Uh, hi!" she said, dazzling him with a friendly smile, "fancy meeting you in a place like this!"

The Baron smiled in spite of himself. "You speak lightly, after such a monumental night."

"Well, if I didn't I'd probably just keel over," shrugged Sally, "and I can't do that yet!"

The Baron looked from her tangled locks to her bandaged shoulder, to her wrinkled and soiled attire, to her battered face, and nodded, mystified.

Sheila Keenan ducked under the caution tape and ran up the bridge with a speed and agility that easily made her Sally's rival in such matters. Her face was serious, yet at the same time bright with anticipation and alive with joy. Her heart pounded madly as she thought of the meeting to come, and yet as she drew nearer the destination, her steps slowed.

She did not know what to expect. She had not seen the man she loved for quite a few years, and wasn't quite sure how she'd feel. She nervously brushed a stray, curling lock of black hair back into the scarf she wore, and kept on.

She saw Little Joe from a few yards away, and her heart seemed to stand still. From what she could see he was unchanged, but that was only the side of a pale cheek and a tangle of dark hair. He lay on his side, hardly seeming to breathe.

She gave a stifled cry and raced forward, throwing herself to her knees beside him. She gently turned his face toward the night sky. With one look, all her doubts were dispelled. The boyish, jocose expression was gone from the face she loved so well, and yet the grim, rugged look that had taken its place was all the more wonderful to her eyes.

"Joe, oh Joe!" she cried, stroking his hair fondly while the tears coursed down her cheeks.

Slowly, as she waited with bated breath, there seemed to be a response from the suffering man. At last, his eyes opened, and the clear blue eyes, so long dimmed by illness and hate, grew bright and youthful as they gazed upon the lovely woman above him.

"Sheila!" he whispered, reaching up to touch her cheek. "Then I have died. I never thought I'd end up in the same place as you, though."

Through her tears, Sheila smiled and let out a sobbing laugh. "No Joe. You are still alive, and I am too. More alive than we've ever been."

Little Joe raised himself on one elbow and stared hard at her. "Really? I'm not dead, and not dreaming?"

She laughed again, and for answer threw her arms around him as he sat up. His arms closed around in a grasp that grew firmer as he realized the wonderful truth and for a moment, neither spoke, so great was their joy.

At last, Little Joe pulled himself to his feet, leaning only slightly on Sheila's support.

"What's happened?" he gasped, again running his fingers through her straying hair, "and how has this miracle come about?"

"Do you remember that night when we spoke about how our love would never cease, and then Stockly started breaking in the door?" she asked.

Little Joe nodded, paling slightly at the awful memory. "Sheila, you've got to believe me," he said suddenly, taking her hands in his and staring earnestly into her eyes, "I did not mean to kill that man. He was coming to take my life."

Sheila nodded. "I know," she said, "I found that out from the authorities a few weeks after I'd escaped."

"So, why didn't you come back?"

"I was told that you'd killed my daughter."

Little Joe winced. "Yes," he muttered, "that night, my men missed Sally in the scuffle, but told me they'd killed her. I believed them myself. But one day one of them confessed because there was an article in the newspaper about a little girl named Sally in a local hospital, who needed to be claimed. I guess you never heard the truth."

"I had gone to hide as far away as I could. Not until I got a letter from Skinny, who was having bizarre adventures with a bunch of kids in Europe, did I begin to imagine she might be alive. After he'd described her in a few more letters, and her exploits in Africa and Switzerland, I began to feel sure that my baby was found."

"Found, but pursued," muttered Little Joe. "I chased her every step of the way."

"You didn't know what you were doing," said Sheila seriously. "But now, as I was saying, just before Stockly broke in and dragged me away, do you remember what we were talking about?

"Yes, I do," said Joe.

"We were talking about getting married ... " she paused while Little Joe took her chin in his hand, and looked lovingly into her eyes, "and I told you when he broke in that someday, help would come to us."

Joe nodded.

"Well," Sheila dimpled prettily, "it has. Look."

Out of her pocket she pulled a small photograph. Little Joe looked at it by the light of the streetlights, and smiled.

It was a snapshot taken in New York, during the Company's happy time there after Little Joe had been arrested. It showed Skinny standing in front of a skyscraper, holding Christine by the shoulders and pushing her out of the way, where she had purposely stationed herself to block his face, while Clarence behind them gave them both "bunny ears." Becky was kneeling between them, big brown eyes fixed upon her nose, cheeks puffed out, and hands pulling her ears out in her notorious "monkey face". In front of the others, suspended in the air, from a dive in front of the camera at the last moment, with her usual smile broadened as she probably let out a whoop, was Sally.

"There," said Sheila, "I told you help would come. The Company of Secret Kids."

"They're some great kids," agreed Little Joe, smiling again at the impromptu picture.

"Oh, Joe," cried Sheila happily. "Nothing is between us now! And we already have five children. The greatest in the world."

Little Joe nodded again, but began to cough. He looked at her as if for the first time. "I still can't believe it," he whispered, "You're mine at last."

Sheila nodded, slipping her arms around him again, and feeling his embrace close about her tightly. "I am yours," she repeated, "for better or for worse, till death do us part."

Chapter 23

The Battle of the Giants

"Okay, Kid," said Skinny as the cab screeched to a stop. "You got us into this, now let's see you finish it!"

Sally nodded, clambered over him, and out the door. The other occupants of the cab quickly followed, filled with premonition and excitement.

They were at the giant dead oak, where Sally had laid her trap. All around were countless cars, forming a large circle around the oak, and filled with assortments of children and gendarmes, shining their headlights towards the tree.

On the way there, Sally had taken control of Marcel's two-way radio system in the cab to instruct her allies. Black Hawk had seen Marcel's cab go by and had followed it, unwittingly ending up just where Sally had wanted him.

"Okay, so what is your plan, Sally?" asked Skinny as he climbed out and stood beside her.

"We've got to get him into that tree. The fire-makers will do the rest."

"And you intend to roast him to death?" asked Skinny patiently.

"Of course not, you chowder-head," she answered calmly. "I intend for him to surrender. Just let him get a little warm, and a little scared. Then, we tell him that we'll let him down if he returns to his own land, and never bothers us again."

"And what if he doesn't give in, and decides to die instead?" asked Skinny.

"Then we rescue him, and think of some other way of defeating him without hurting him too much," said the practical Sally.

"Well, at least you're not too violent with your revenge," smiled Skinny, "though if you get any more civil people might start mistaking you for his mother."

"Oh shut up, and wait here," said Sally, and started for the tree at an easy trot. On the way, she gave the gendarmes a staying gesture. None of them wanted to be shot that night, so they waited. Most assumed it was some private argument.

Skinny looked after her, still wondering what her plan exactly was. Christine and Clarence stood on either side of him, while Becky had been lifted on top of the cab by Marcel, to ensure her being able to see.

"Do you think she'll make it?" asked Clarence quietly, but not quietly enough, for Christine turned and looked fearfully up at Skinny, awaiting his response.

Skinny nodded, and managed a grin. "She's Sally," he said, "and that should answer your question."

Sally walked calmly toward Black Hawk's car. About three feet away from the car door, she stopped. "Okay, you dirty villain," she called. "This is as far as I come. Get out."

Slowly the driver's door opened and Black Hawk heaved himself out. His hand was already well bandaged and his saber once again hung at his side. His look was cold and baleful.

"So, Keenan," he hissed, "you return again to make yet another attempt against me?"

"My only thought is to gain peace for the Company," returned Sally seriously. "If you are already willing to return to your own country, and not bother us anymore, then our hostilities are over. If not, you will be defeated for good. These are my terms. Do you accept?"

Black Hawk stared at her for some time. At last his voice rang out cold and mocking. "Accept your terms?" he scoffed, "as if I would even pay them heed. You forget Keenan, in your fleeting moment of victory, just who you fight. I am Black Hawk. I never surrender."

"Well neither do I!" rejoined Sally. "So it appears our war shall never end."

"I don't know about that," growled Black Hawk. "Now, because you come against me in force, with many greater numbers than I have, you have mastered, by foul means, for the moment. But someday, when your great numbers of brave men are not beside you to instill courage into your fragile heart, then I shall return and the war will end."

Sally flushed angrily, but quickly mastered herself. "So you think it is not fair for me to come against you with greater numbers than you have? Perhaps you have forgotten where you were less than an hour ago, surrounding me with your force! But I will put that aside and comply with your wishes. You will order your men to go to the gendarmes and surrender their weapons, and I will order all those present here, save my fellow Company members and the Baron and the Professor, to leave us and return to the city. Then we will have it out. You against me, till the war is over. Okay?"

Black Hawk smiled contemptuously. "As though you would really have the nerve to face me without your precious army behind you," he said. "I refuse. I will not hand my men over to your pretty police."

"Why not?" asked Sally slyly. "Are you afraid you won't win?"

This tactic worked. Black Hawk's face twitched with ill-concealed anger. He barked an order, and his men emerged from the car. He said something to them, and they, with bewildered and slightly apprehensive expressions, walked to the gendarmes' vans.

"Treat them well," Sally called to the darkly frowning gendarmes. "They still might end up on the winning side. Now go, everybody but the Baron, the Professor, and the Company of Secret Kids."

The gendarmes looked at her hesitantly for a moment, but seeing the determined light in her clear eyes, they finally turned and piled back into the cars, taking every last child with them. They were glad to have Black Hawk's men in custody without a fight. The greatly worried Dubois departed, leaving his cab in Skinny's hands.

Sally and Black Hawk did not move until the last of the cars had driven off to the city, leaving the oak tree a dark and desolate place, but for the shadow of Marcel's cab and the eerie glow of its desolate headlights.

"What does she think she's doing?!" Clarence hissed in Skinny's ear as they watched their whole defense depart into the fog.

"She's got a trap ready," said Skinny confidently. "She has a plan. I hope."

Clarence caught the last two words, which Skinny had muttered under his breath, and they made his throat grow tight and tense.

"What's wrong with her anyway?" asked Christine, making a show of unconcerned irritation, though her voice wobbled unsteadily. "These aren't the days of King Arthur. Duels to the death aren't exactly the normal way of settling fights nowadays. She reads too many books." Suddenly her eyes grew pleading and frightened. "Oh, Skinny, you won't let anything happen to her, will you?"

Skinny looked down at his sister and smiled reassuringly, with still a trace of his customary assurance. But despite his confident manner, for a fleeting moment Clarence hoped he wouldn't pass out.

Meanwhile, within the makeshift arena, bounded by the dim light, Black Hawk made ready. He drew his saber with his unwounded hand. Sally took confident comfort in the knowledge that in her pocket she still had her largest pocketknife, a symbolic resistance to the great pirate's mighty weapon. The pocket knife and the saber were perfect emblems of the two combatants. Black Hawk smiled forbiddingly as he looked down at her, as if amused and almost regretful at her staunch attitude, facing him fearlessly.

Then, with a suddenness that did his great hulk credit, and made the spectating members of the Company draw their breath in sharply, Black Hawk sprang forward, slashing out with his saber. Sally dodged out of harm's way, and then, agile and lithe as a cat, she slipped by Black Hawk, only a few inches away from him, while he was recovering from the vigorous swing, and made for the trunk of the tree.

Black Hawk took after her immediately. Sally veered her course, to make a fast run around his car. As she came around the front, Sally leapt onto the hood, slid over it, and leapt off right at the tree's trunk.

Without even looking back, she caught the lowest branch with a quick spring. She swung onto it easily, carefully avoiding the fire-makers that lined the lowest branches.

Black Hawk came to the base and made another swipe at her still-hanging feet. The very tip of his saber caught her slipper. Skinny saw a thin line of red appear on the side of her foot where it had been grazed. Sally quickly pulled her feet up, glancing at the cut but briefly, and then sprang to her feet, easily balanced on the thick bough. She was now out of Black Hawk's reach, and stopped to look down at him, grinning impishly. She patted her knife in her pocket, as a gesture of self-assurance.

"What's the matter?" she asked sympathetically. "Sorry I left you down there, but you see I just have a passion for climbing trees. I'd try to haul you up, but I don't think this old tree could hold you."

Clarence laughed in spite of himself. Becky slid down the windshield of the cab to be able to see Sally, partly hidden by the dead boughs. Even Christine smiled anxiously.

Sally climbed up another branch, perching herself in the center of the tree.

"So now what are you going to do?" she asked innocently, licking her dry lips.

"End the struggle," answered Black Hawk in a cold, deadly tone. Before anyone realized what was happening, Black Hawk suddenly swung his saber up at her, letting the hilt go as it spun away with great force and speed. It came spinning straight at Sally, skillfully aimed too high for her to jump over it, and still dangerously low to duck.

Sally chose the latter, and with a quick movement, threw herself forward, onto her stomach. The deadly missile whistled by less than an inch from her head, and came crashing through the dead wood till it landed with a clatter on the hard ground. The rest of the Company let their breath out slowly, each silently thinking a prayer of thanksgiving.

Sally, however, was concerned about other matters. As she'd sprawled down in her haste, she had knocked her foot against one of the fire-makers, and the saber, as it crashed through the branches had dislodged three more.

Now they were sputtering dangerously. Black Hawk had gone around the trunk and retrieved his weapon. As he did so, suddenly, not more than a foot away from Sally, the first of the fire-makers sprang into life. Its flame was tall and bright in the night fog, and licked dangerously at the dry wood around it.

As Sally and her enemy gazed at it silently, the other disturbed charges started up too, and soon the lower quarter of the tree was beginning to flame up. The twigs that hung near Sally's hair caught after just seconds, and she leapt aside quickly to avoid getting singed. Beneath her, Black Hawk had watched for a few moments in amazed silence, but now was smiling cruelly, relieved that he would not have to climb the tree to get at her.

Sally quickly took in the situation. She could climb up further to avoid the flames, but the fire was spreading quickly and once caught, the top of the tree would be the worst location she could find. She had only a short while before the whole tree went up in smoke.

She looked down, wondering how good her chances were of getting down alive. Descent would be laborious and dangerous. Sally decided quickly that her safest bet would be to brave the descent from the other side. Black Hawk came around, still grinning. Sally looked around again, the hopelessness of her situation finally descending upon her unquenchable spirit.

She climbed back to the center of the tree, glancing around wildly as the unstoppable fire drew in upon her. For a moment the flames held her mesmerized. It was as though they said, in crackling, hissing voices, that though her spirit was wild and free, and her courage never daunted, her plan had backfired on her, and there was no one to which she could turn.

Then, like a beacon of hope on a sea of terrible flame, the thought rang into her head, as though put there by another source: there was someone to whom she could turn, someone who had been there all along, but had usually been forgotten in the heat of adventure.

All this takes time to tell, but these thoughts shot through her head in only a few seconds.

She spun round, her hair whipping around her desperate, but not yet fearful face.

"Skinny!" she cried, holding out a beseeching hand to him, while the other clutched a still unlighted branch.

"Skinny, help!!"

Clarence glanced up at Skinny, and was amazed to find he actually looked joyful, through his surprise and concern. His face had suddenly lighted, and all the care that had been stamped upon it by their adventures was lifted.

"She needs me!" he shouted as he dashed forward. On his way he held out his hand to the Baron, who instantly passed him his sword.

"What's wrong with him?" asked Christine. "He's proud again, all of the sudden."

Clarence smiled. "I think it comes with being needed," he said, wisely. "It's his moment."

Though his assured attitude had lightened his spirits, and once again made him feel his old confidence, Skinny knew full well what sort of ordeal he faced. He quickly spanned the distance to the tree. Sally saw him coming, and turned pale. Her own suicidal bravery did not bother her, but with his life now at stake, her courage faltered.

As he drew near she saw the proud glitter in his daring eyes, and it finally dawned upon her thoughtless heart that Skinny must have felt she left him in the dust every time she did something heroic.

Yet she knew suddenly that she had always counted upon him to be behind her. It had not occurred to her that he was lost in the praise she received afterward.

In only a few moments, Skinny reached Black Hawk's car. He still had his back to Skinny. For one fleeting instant, Skinny thought that if he could but sneak up behind his enemy, he could strike him down, and there would be no terrible fight. Then, his thoughts took their proper course, and he dismissed such a shabby tactic with a quick resolve.

"Black Hawk!" he cried in a deep voice. "Turn and face me!"

The pirate swung his great frame around, and regarded him coldly. "The deal I made was for single combat," he sneered, "and I surrendered my men on those terms. Yet another of you whimpering idiots has dared to challenge me."

Skinny flung back his proud head. "A man of your stature against a girl? Only you would have accepted such a deal."

"I will dispatch you both!"

"You have not fought me yet," Skinny returned evenly, praying quietly, "the battle is Yours, Lord. Guide me."

Black Hawk gave a snarl, and came charging around his car. Skinny did not move, except to raise his sword, preparing for the first blow.

When the blow came, it practically knocked Skinny to the ground. Black Hawk swung down upon him with a strength that should have cracked his skull. As it was, Skinny warded the powerful blow off with all the strength he could muster.

Skinny was not a weak boy. Despite his slim stature, he was muscular and strong, and as the other children knew, he had the power, when pressed to it, to use skills and tactics he had never displayed for them.

Even so, now he was matched against an adversary almost twice his weight. The browned scarred arms of the seasoned pirate were almost the same diameter as Skinny's legs. As Black Hawk slowly, relentlessly bore Skinny to the ground, his look of satisfaction grew. This fight had been easier than even he had reckoned for. When Skinny was bent almost double, his sword still held above him, he suddenly stopped resisting, and with a swift, dexterous, movement, rolled out of the clinch, and under the car.

Black Hawk, who had not been expecting this sudden turn, sprawled forward onto his face. Skinny quickly pulled himself out on the other side.

Switching the sword to his left hand, he shook his aching right wrist. It gave him a strange tingling sensation.

Now he was on the side of the car that was near the flaming tree, and as Black Hawk lumbered to his feet, Skinny glanced up at Sally. She was still safe, but it wouldn't be much longer, for the flames were spreading fast. She smiled at him, and instead of looking concerned as he usually did when she was in danger, he grinned reassuringly and winked.

He was confident of victory. She laughed, despite her precarious situation, and as Black Hawk came rushing around the back of his car she gave Skinny the "thumbs up" sign.

"Even if I have to be barbecued to see it, and though it does get old on a daily basis," she muttered under her breath, "I must admit I like it better when he's cocky."

Now Black Hawk had come face to face with Skinny, and made another swing at him. Skinny ducked and backed up a few feet, not wishing to match his strength against Black Hawk again too soon, especially while his wrist felt so shaky.

Black Hawk didn't give him much time to recover, and followed up his swing with yet another more vigorous one. Skinny leapt backwards again, but the slightly protruding wheel of Black Hawk's car caught him in the back of his leg, and with a muttered gasp he fell to the ground, and the swing, aimed at his waist, was now coming more toward his neck. He instantly pulled his head back, and the very tip of the saber grazed his collar bone. He felt a numbing pain. With an effort, he swung his legs around and slipped under the car again, in front of the wheels. Black Hawk brought his saber down again as he did so, and Skinny pulled his fingers out of the way just in time. The saber stuck deep into the ground and as Black Hawk tugged it loose Skinny had a chance to reach out and grab his sword from where he had dropped it. When he saw the hand poking out, Black Hawk raised his heavy boot and stamped on it.

"Ow!" cried Skinny, drawing his hand back with alacrity. "Darn you!" he hollered to the heel of the boot that obscured his vision. Now he must really use his left hand; from his numb fingers to his throbbing wrist, his right hand was practically useless. Since Little Joe was strongly left-handed, Skinny's extensive training in all matters had left him practically ambidextrous.

As he slid out from under the car on the far side, Black Hawk wrenched his saber from the hard ground again. Skinny glanced over to Marcel's cab where the others were watching, and saw another car pulling up. Two figures leapt out. One was graceful and attractive, dressed in blue, and supporting the other figure; a tall, stalwart figure of a man, his shaggy black hair falling around his face in disordered locks.

Skinny smiled when he saw them, slightly surprised at his own relief that Little Joe was safe. Becky hurriedly slid off the hood and ran into Sheila Keenan's arms, while Christine and Clarence drew closer to them also, giving them a quick account of the surprising turn of events.

Something in Little Joe's face made Skinny glance behind him, and he ducked barely in time as Black Hawk, who had stealthily crept up behind him, swung again at his head. Skinny tightened his grip on his sword and decided it was time to fight back. Before Black Hawk could raise his saber again, Skinny struck out wildly. Black Hawk, slightly surprised by the sudden retaliation, took a step backwards. Skinny saw a line of red appear on the huge, weather-beaten hand, and realized with a shock that he had scored. He knew he should follow up his lead with another blow, so he swung again, but ridiculously out of range. The sight of Black Hawk's blood, and knowing that he had spilt it, on the whole made him feel a little sick.

Black Hawk took another swing at Skinny, and smiled contemptuously. Skinny retreated a step or two, heading for the back of the car. Black Hawk made a savage rush at him, and Skinny went dashing round the car just in time.

Now it was a deadly game of both tag and hide-and-seek. With the car always in between them, the two combatants ran round, stopped, sized each other up, and started circling again, Skinny always on the defense. How long this fatal game would have gone on no one could tell, had there not been a most inopportune interruption.

Just when Skinny had come around to the side facing away from the tree, there was a terrific cracking noise above him. Skinny turned and watched in amazement as a large limb from high up, flaming and crackling, came crashing through the boughs and twigs, setting things on fire as it came. Sally swung herself out onto a limb nearby to avoid it.

It splintered into hundreds of pieces of ash and charred wood as it hit the main body of the tree. Sally covered her eyes with one hand, shielding them from the flying bits of flaming wood, when suddenly, the limb beneath her began to creak and give way. She glanced down at it, seeing the flames licking at its tip and darkening its dead wood, and barely in time, she leapt off it and into the heart of the tree. Now the flames were licking around her dangerously and she was momentarily hidden from Skinny's view by a cloud of smoke. Through the crackling and roaring of the now huge fire, he could hear her coughing.

"Sally come down!" he cried. "I'll cover you!"

Her dark head appeared through the smoke, and glanced down at him. Her eyes were large, but not frightened. After studying the situation for some moments, Sally suddenly grasped the limb she was balancing on with two hands, and swung herself off it, ready to drop down to safety.

Skinny was waiting for her to drop, when suddenly he was thrust aside violently and Black Hawk came charging by. He went straight for Sally with murder in his eyes, and she hurriedly pulled herself back up onto the limb.

Meanwhile Little Joe and Sheila Keenan were stealthily approaching the combatants. Sheila carried her rifle.

"Let's split up and approach from opposite sides," Sheila suggested.

Little Joe shook his head. "I think Skinny needs to win this battle on his own," he answered. They stopped a few yards away, Sheila keeping a wary eye on the tree.

At that moment, Black Hawk turned upon Skinny, and sent a wide swing towards him, and again the tip of the saber caught him. This time the small gash appeared on his cheek, just below his left eye. Skinny staggered and fell back, hitting the car with a force that temporarily winded him.

"Skinny!" cried Sally from the tree.

Skinny glanced up at her, and her look of concern was so earnest and beautiful that the pain in his head suddenly lessened, and he couldn't keep back a contented smile.

Black Hawk saw the expression, and his look suddenly changed. The saber stopped in midair. He looked up at the lovely girl in the tree, and the dashing boy lying at his feet.

"So," he said, a sneer curling his lip. "You love her."

Skinny's smile died on his face, and he looked up angrily. Sally, from her dangerous perch, shut her agape mouth with a snap, and regarded the pirate with unconcealed surprise and disgust.

"You love her," repeated Black Hawk, this time a bit louder, to ensure that Sally heard him. "Do you really think she feels the same way about you? Can't you see that she's the hero type? You thought you had the chance to be her savior. To take up arms for the defense of your damsel in distress! Well, you have proved to her now that you aren't worthy to follow in her footsteps!"

He laughed mockingly. "You're quite the knight in shining armor! And even if you had won the fight, do you really think she would love you? Look at you! A skinny, impudent, weakling! Lying in despair at the feet of your enemy. A fine object for her fancy. Now what must she think of you, young fool? She could never love you!"

With that Skinny sprang to his feet. As Black Hawk had continued, Skinny's face had grown pale, from loss of blood or rage, Black Hawk could not tell. He had grown stern. A haunted fear had lighted in his eyes as Black Hawk spoke, and with it, the light of mad fury. His hands had closed again over the hilt of his sword, so tightly that the knuckles showed white. As Black Hawk finished his taunt, expecting to finish the fight with a quick slash, he was surprised to face a Skinny, white with rage.

"No!" he cried, and flew at the pirate. Black Hawk had hardly the time to raise his saber in defense before the frenzied young man was upon him. The fire above them was reflected in Skinny's dangerously flashing eyes, and something made Black Hawk retreat with less than dignified speed. His saber easily turned the blows that Skinny dealt him, but there was something in the fury of his assailant's attack that kept him tense and apprehensive.

Skinny dealt blow after passionate blow upon his enemy's strong defenses, his rage seemingly giving him a strength he had not had before.

Black Hawk's parries slowly began to weaken. His retreating steps had taken him closer and closer to the flaming trunk of the tree, and now he could go no further without being backed up against its flame-licked wood.

When Black Hawk glanced back at the trunk of the tree, still warding off the attacker, with a last burst of wrath and long checked strength, Skinny struck such a blow that the saber was whipped from the pirate's grasp. Black Hawk cried out with pain. As his weapon fell with a thud, Skinny's sword immediately took its place, covering his enemy's chest, not an inch away from the grimy, sweaty shirt that covered a malicious heart.

Slowly, Black Hawk raised his small, bird-like eyes. Skinny was panting hard, his young bosom still racked with passion, his eyes sparkling with livid wrath, as he fixed Black Hawk in the most vicious version of the glance that had gained him Company fame and admiration. He flung back his head and shook the blood from his cheek without giving it a thought.

"Sally, come down," Skinny ordered.

She dropped to the ground.

"Well," murmured Black Hawk. "You have won. Any true man of war knows when to admit defeat. Kill me now, but I still say that you are not worthy of that girl. She does not love you."

"Maybe you are right," answered Skinny defiantly, "but, even if everything you say is true, it is still my duty to defend her. At least I can offer my life so she might live. But as for you ... " he regarded his opponent coldly, and Black Hawk stiffened, awaiting the blow. "You say you are a true man of war. Perhaps by your standards you are. But we, the Company of Secret Kids, wage wars slightly differently.

"You are free. I shall not hurt you, nor call the authorities to put you, justly, under lock and key. Your men shall be returned to you, and you shall be free to go wherever you please, but," his eyes flashed brightly again, "if ever you come against us in arms again, your life will be our property, and I shall destroy you. I do not know if these are the terms Sally would have given you, though I believe they are, but I am still the leader of the Company, whether or not I am worthy, and this is my treaty with you. Take my terms. Give me your word that you shall never come against us again."

Black Hawk raised his hand slowly, and intoned in a solemn whisper, "I swear."

Skinny nodded, and slowly lowered his sword. "Go," he said shortly, nodding his head in the direction of Black Hawk's car.

The pirate looked at him, and then down at the saber at his feet. Skinny did not move. Slowly, Black Hawk bent down and retrieved his weapon. Skinny's gaze did not change. His sword was down, resting at his side. Black Hawk's was held at the ready.

They stared hard at each other for a long, dreadful moment, whilst everyone else held their breath. Then, with a shrug that almost seemed akin to a laugh, Black Hawk lumbered to his car, and got in the driver's seat.

He still looked at Skinny, seeming puzzled by the fearless eyes. He started the car, and Skinny stepped aside to give him room to pull out. Then, just before he slammed his door, Black Hawk took his saber and tossed it towards Skinny. It landed at the boy's feet.

Skinny looked up into the pirate's eyes. Black Hawk nodded, and for the first time that anyone had ever seen, he smiled an honest smile. Skinny nodded back with a slow, solemn smile.

Then Black Hawk shut his door, and slowly drove away from the fateful spot. As he passed the cabs where the rest of The Company stood, he raised his hand in salute. Becky waved back, though slightly bewildered.

Skinny, still standing and watching the long black car fade into the night gloom, bowed his battered head, and sighed. The last war was over.

Behind him, Sally came forward, her clothes dark and soiled, her face smeared with ash and dirt. One lock of her waving, black hair was smoldering slightly, and she gave it a quick slap to extinguish it. She looked at Skinny for a moment, smiling a bit shyly, and then looked down quickly.

"That was pretty good, Brother Fat," she said quietly, a grin flitting across her features, and then quickly disappearing. She glanced up again, seeming a bit desperate. Her gaze traveled over his bruised and bloody, yet serene features, and then across the stretch of cold, hard ground to where the others of The Company remained, discreetly leaving themselves out of the way while the two heroes faced each other. Skinny felt his cheeks go hot, and felt a good deal more frightened than he had at any time during the duel.

Suddenly, Sally brightened, and ran past him, without another glance in his direction. She ran, slightly favoring her injured foot straight to her mother and Little Joe, who were standing together.

"You're all right!" she cried joyously, throwing herself into Little Joe's arms. "Thank God! I knew you'd make it! I told you!"

Little Joe nodded, a smile brightening his face. "You too, kid," he answered. "Thank God. You've made it."

Sally nodded, and turned to her mother. Sheila Keenan laughed through her tears, and took Sally into her arms again.

"My little girl!" she whispered. "You're not hurt."

Sally grinned, and turned to Clarence, Christine and Becky. She glanced from them to Little Joe.

"I guess you all have met!" she laughed. Clarence grinned, and nodded. His face was relieved and happy, but an air of concern and pity still lingered. After giving Sally a comradely pat on the back, he broke away from the party, and jogged off toward the tree, where Skinny still stood. Sally glanced after him, but before she could say anything, Christine came forward and threw her arms around Sally.

"Oh Sally!" she cried, "my sister!"

"Right," answered Sally. "Forever."

"What about me?" asked Becky, elbowing her way in between the two girls.

Sally laughed. "Who could forget you, Toothless One?" she cried, hugging Becky. "Your army worked wonders tonight!"

"Yes," assented Becky, her brown eyes glowing with excitement, "and those nice gendarmes said they would tell the important people here in Paris to help them find their relatives!"

"And what about you?" asked Sally. "You aren't about to go back to Switzerland and live with all those shrimps, and leave the Company?"

Becky shook her head emphatically.

"No, Sally," said Sheila Keenan, "she's coming back to California to live with us."

"Us?" asked Sally, looking hopefully at her mother.

"Yes," said her mother, "we're taking Clarence, and the Conklins, and Becky; the whole Company back to California with us to be our family."

"But," faltered Sally, an impish grin appearing on her face, "but how can you adopt them? You need to be married!"

"Oh," said Sheila with a shy smile, "I think that could be arranged."

Sally took Little Joe's hand again. "Golly," she whispered, "I'll have a dad again. Boy, ain't love wonderful?"

Sheila Keenan, who, through the whole course of the conversation, had been glancing behind Sally, now nodded solemnly.

"Yes, Sally," she said, and taking Sally gently by the shoulders, she turned her around to face the flaming tree once again. "Love is wonderful. And speaking of that, I think you've forgotten someone."

Sally looked, and saw the tall, grim young man, leaning a little on Clarence's arm.

"No ma," said Sally, "I've not forgotten. I'm just scared."

"You?" asked Becky, wide-eyed. "I didn't think that was possible."

"Don't worry, Sally," said Christine, "you can do it."

Sally nodded, and raised her hand to her dirty brow as though she might faint. "I'm okay, just a little tired and shaky. And, my shoulder feels sort of stiff."

She took a few steps forward, and then stopped. Christine came forward, and taking her friend's hand, led her back to the tree. Clarence glanced up at them, and said something to Skinny. Skinny looked up. His face was dreadfully pale. The cut on his cheek was nasty looking and his collar was stained red. He was trembling, from passion or nervousness Clarence could not tell, but for all his battered appearance, he held his head proud as always.

When Sally was only about a yard away from the boys, Christine let her go, and Sally, who'd been leaning heavily on her, straightened and licked her lips nervously. Clarence came forward, and taking Christine's hand, they walked back toward the cabs.

"Well," he whispered as they went out of Sally's range of hearing, "This'll be something. A regular battle of the giants."

Sally fell to studying her feet. Skinny looked at the ground. Finally, with a sharply drawn breath, he looked up and stared her squarely in the face. It struck him how haggard and worn she looked. His eyes traveled from the dress she wore, to the slightly smudged face. He took a step toward her, and Sally glanced up, and then quickly lowered her eyes.

"Sally," he said quietly as he drew a bit closer.

"Yes?"

"Sally, you were great tonight," he faltered, trying desperately to regain his cool attitude.

"You, too."

She looked up and their eyes met. They both smiled as they realized how awkwardly they were acting, as if remembering for the first time that night who they were.

"You know," said Skinny, an honest look of concern crossing his relieved features, "I was really worried about you tonight, kid. I thought more than a couple times that you were a goner."

Sally grinned, and shrugged. "Never say die."

Skinny nodded. "No, you never do. Sally," he took another step nearer, preparing himself for the ordeal. "Sally, I've got to tell you something. I've been trying and meaning to tell you all night, but somehow, it never happened."

Sally smiled, though a wild tinge of pink flashed into her pale cheeks as he spoke.

"Sally," said Skinny, resolutely planting his feet apart and facing her boldly, "Sally, we're good friends."

"Yes," assented Sally. "We think good together."

"Yeah," said Skinny, much heartened by her cooperative attitude, "and I think that we do a lot of good when we're together."

"Sure," said Sally, "but Skinny, before you go any further, I've got an apology to make. I'm sorry for always being so proud. I always rush into the limelight, without giving you a chance. You're a lot braver than I am, and you think more before you do something, but usually I've just gone ahead and done it without giving you a chance to be the hero. I'm sorry."

Skinny grew pale again. "That's okay," he murmured.

"And," said Sally, finally getting around to it, "by the way, thanks for saving my life just now. I know I never would have made it if you hadn't been so brave."

Skinny shrugged, trying to be careless. "Well," he said loftily, "That was nothing, just my duty. And it really wasn't so bad, I ..."

He stopped short, and looked at her. "Actually," he said, with a wry grin, "I was scared silly, and didn't have any idea what I was doing."

Sally smiled. "You couldn't have been any more scared than I was," she answered. "Let's shake on that. The two biggest cowards in the world." She held out her hand, and he grasped it with a laugh. They shook hands, and then, for some reason that neither of them could quite understand, they let go suddenly, and rather awkwardly.

"Sally," said Skinny, "you know we're a couple of idiots."

Sally nodded.

"But, before I keel over I have something to say. Sally, I think you're the greatest kid I've ever known."

Sally glanced up hopefully. Skinny appeared to be regaining his confidence.

"And," he said resolutely, "I wouldn't rather have anyone else in the world beside me than you, in an hour of need."

"Skinny?" said Sally, after an ominous pause. "May I tell you the last of my secrets?"

Skinny raised his eyebrows. "There's another one?"

"The last of the Company of Secret Kids."

Skinny grinned. "Shoot."

Sally took a deep breath, and looked him squarely in the eyes. "Skinny," she said quietly, "I fell in love with you the first moment I saw you in the convent in Manchester."

Skinny didn't move. He couldn't. His heart was pounding in his ears so loud he knew he must have heard wrong.

"Not "falling in love" like in all the corny movies," Sally continued, seeing his blank expression, "or like Christine back when she was boy-crazy. It was just that I knew we were a good team, and figured we should be a good team always. Are you mad, or just disgusted?"

She looked hopefully up into his face, trying to assess his emotions. At length, Skinny looked down at her, and she saw his eyes were misty.

"Mad?" he asked in joyous incredulity. "Me? Sally, it's you who should be mad at me, for not seeing until tonight, in those terrible moments on the Eiffel Tower, that the only thing I want in life is you."

"Well, at least we've finally agreed on something," she said with a surprised grin.

Skinny suddenly turned serious. He opened his mouth as if to speak again, then suddenly stepped forward and pulled Sally into his arms. She buried her face on his blood stained shoulder and he could feel her shoulders trembling with emotion.

"Oh, Skinny!" she whispered, "thanks. For everything."

He only nodded, and for a moment held her tight. Then his grip loosed around her, and they began slowly walking away from the fateful spot toward the cabs.

Behind them, when they had gone a good distance away, they heard a tremendous cracking and ripping nose, and quickly turned around.

The great tree went crashing backwards and hit the ground, exploding into a fresh burst of flame.

"Good old tree," said Sally softly. "It's done its task well."

"That's the last stroke," said Skinny. "The war is finally over."

Sally nodded, and after a moment's hesitation, they turned back again, and saw the horizon turn scarlet and rose, heralding the arrival of the sunrise.

"Sally, look," said Skinny, seeing the rosy clouds reflected in her starry eyes. "At the beginning of this night, we watched the sunset together. Then, we didn't know if we would ever see it rise. Happy Easter, Sally."

"Everything is perfect," said Sally, closing her eyes. "Mom and me have found each other, and you will always be with me."

Sally suddenly gave a little gasp and staggered. Skinny steadied her, and then, with a reckless sort of smile, he swooped her into his arms. She looked up at him, half guiltily. He looked at her inquiringly, the words she had spoken only a week before still ringing in his ears.

"Thanks, Skinny," she said, "I ... I guess I do need your help, sometimes."

He only grinned. "Oh, and by the way," he said, after a pause, "It's 'mom and I', not 'mom and me.'"

"Well," said Sheila, "I guess it's time we all head back. You kids could all use some sleep."

"Sleep?" cried Clarence, in mock horror, for the gravity of the situation was beginning to weary even his melancholic disposition. "We're big heroes after tonight. We never sleep!"

"Even heroes sleep," said Sheila Keenan sternly. "If you're going to be my son, you're going to learn to obey me right now. Get in that car." She pointed to Marcel's cab.

"Aw, come on!" said Clarence putting one arm around her and the other one about Christine. "You're not my mom. You're too cute."

"Thanks," said Sheila, "now into the car."

Clarence complied reluctantly, and as he opened the door to Marcel's cab, Sheila gave him a well-aimed kick that sent him sprawling onto the seats.

"Gosh," he muttered as he righted himself, "having a mom will be more interesting than I thought."

Sally and the other girls were ushered into the other cab, laughing. The Professor and the Baron followed them, leaving Little Joe standing with Skinny. Sheila started the car, and looked up at Little Joe. "You'll take care of Skinny?" she asked.

Little Joe nodded. With a quick glance behind her, she looked up at him, and then over at Skinny with concern.

"Don't worry," said Little Joe, "Skinny's the greatest guy in the world. I can handle him."

She looked up at him and smiled. "Second greatest," she corrected.

Sheila drove off toward the sunrise. Clarence stuck a cautious head out of Marcel's cab, and then climbed out, satisfied that the coast was clear.

"God bless them," whispered Sheila, looking into her rear-view mirror at the lone cab with the three tall figures beside it. The girls glanced back, and Sally nodded, her eyes still shining.

"God bless them."

"What a night," cried Clarence.

"Yeah," said Skinny, "Wow!" His voice shook unsteadily as all the emotion of the night rushed to his head. He looked at Little Joe and smiled ecstatically, then suddenly held his hand to his forehead and fell forward in a dead faint.

Little Joe, who had been expecting such a turn of events, caught him before he hit the ground.

"He'll be okay," he told the horrified Clarence as he kicked open the door and laid Skinny in the passenger seat. "Happy Easter, Clarence."

Chapter 24

A Wedding

"Hurry up, Sally!" cried Christine, "you need to help me button!"

"Hold your horses, I'm coming!"

Sally appeared in the doorway of a spacious hotel bathroom, fiddling in consternation with her own score of buttons that lined her back.

"Here's proof that men are smarter than women," she grumbled. "Who thought of putting buttons up the back?"

"Count your blessings," laughed Christine, as she turned Sally around and began unbuttoning all the ones she had done wrong. "At most weddings, the bridesmaids have to wear worse than this!"

"True," assented Sally, "I guess we're lucky that Mom is like me when it comes to all that silly stuff."

"She is a lot like you. She jumps into things. Why, she's arranged her whole wedding in just one week!"

"Well," said Sally, "she's been planning it for the past fifteen years."

"Let's go and wait for her to come out. I want to see her dress," said Christine, and the two girls exited into the parlor of the hotel suite.

"Boy, I can't get over how big and swanky this place is," said Sally, gazing about the room in wonder. They glanced toward the closed door of the private bedroom, behind which Sheila was preparing herself, with Becky's assistance.

It was Divine Mercy Sunday, one week after Easter. The whole Company, new members and old, were in excited preparation. At eleven o'clock that day, just a few hours away, Sheila Keenan and Joseph Sean

O'Donnell, as Little Joe was now called, would finally be joined in the sacrament of Holy Matrimony.

"Joseph Sean O'Donnell!" Becky had cried in horror. "But I thought she was going to marry Little Joe!"

"She is, you bone-head!" Sally had laughed, "that's his name now. Although, I suppose you'll be made to call him Dad."

On Easter Sunday morning, after the Battle of the Giants, Sheila and Joe had sent the entire Company straight to bed. Late in that day, they'd all gone together to Mass. Clarence and Sally were recuperating well and Skinny, although battered, sore and groggy, was almost himself again. That night, after the Easter festivities, Sheila and Joe had taken the more juvenile members of the Company back to the hotel and put them to bed at five o'clock in the evening, much to their disgrace. Their humiliation, however was not long lived, for before the happy couple had even set foot out of the hotel door, all five children, and the Professor were sound asleep.

On Easter Monday they made a visit to the sisters at the convent to thank them, and let them know how the war had turned out. The sisters were delighted with the news and showed interest in every detail of their story with their tears and laughter.

Though many things were talked of during that busy week, the main topic of interest was the coming wedding. Little Joe went to confession, and the rest of the company, Baron and Professor included, joined him. A priest had been consulted, and the long separated couple had been granted permission to be married as soon as possible.

The Company spent the week attending daily Mass with Becky's army, which was temporarily under the care of the Good Sisters. Mass was celebrated in their beautiful and very ancient French cathedral, and it was a great way to start each day.

Skinny and Sheila explained that they had been exchanging letters ever since he left Kansas, as she had a burning desire to hear more of that wild, adventurous girl he had continually been describing. Her suspicions were confirmed finally when he sent her the photograph of the company, taken in New York City. From that time The Company had led her on a bit of a chase as she searched the globe for them, during which Skinny had heard nothing from her. She had made it to Paris on the night they were on the Eiffel tower.

Though their injuries had been a concern to all, Sally, Skinny, and Clarence were all in fine condition by the middle of the happy week. Christine told the boys that Sally had been greatly disturbed when her mother had told her that with proper care the cut on her foot would heal within a week. She had so wanted to show it off a little longer. The understanding Sheila had refrained from applying many of the remedies that would speed the healing of Sally's hard-earned trophy.

Skinny was the most practical of the three, and bravely endured every treatment that could be devised for the speed of his healing. It had to be admitted, though, that when Little Joe told him, backed by the best doctor they could find, that he would bear the scar from Black Hawk's saber for the rest of his life, Skinny had looked more pleased and proud than he would have liked to admit. Sally and Clarence had been deeply jealous when they heard this news, though Clarence was still given much attention for his gashed hand. Sally at last, in view of her injured shoulder had deemed it only fair, and even consented to admit to Skinny that the scar on his collarbone was, in her terminology, "A beaut!"

Sally, Skinny, and Clarence were all in fine condition when the sun rose gloriously on Divine Mercy Sunday. Despite a few bandages that took only a little of the glory away from their festive attire, the three wounded warriors took great pride in their 'battle trophies'.

Once the health of the children had been taken care of, the next most important thing in everyone's minds was the welfare of the ragged Little Joe. Though he assured one and all many times over that his cough was merely a bad cold, Sheila wouldn't rest until he'd been examined and remedied. They learned soon after that had it been left untended any longer, his 'mere cold' would almost definitely have been fatal. The doctor assured the greatly concerned Sheila however, that with good care, proper nourishment and a less harrowing lifestyle, he'd soon be as strong as he'd been fourteen years before.

Black Hawk, along with all his men, had left for Africa, with a solemn promise to never again molest any of the Company or its affiliates. With his departure, the last of the Company's concerns left as well, and the day dawned bright, and fresh and wonderful.

"Hey Chris," said Sally, "do you remember when we were on that plane about to take off for Africa, the first time we'd ever gone anywhere together, and you said that if we were in a book, you just hoped it was a book with a happy ending? What do you think of our story now?"

"It's better than any happy ending I've ever read!" said Christine joyously. "Oh, and Sally," she added, a roguish light coming into her eyes, "Remember that night in Africa, I asked you whether or not you thought Skinny was handsome? Somehow you never got a chance to answer!"

Sally grinned sheepishly. "All I'll say for now is, that your brother ain't such a bad chap after all."

Christine smiled. "And to think it all happened, just because five kids met by chance in Manchester."

"You really think it was chance?" asked Sally, going over and looking out the window at the lovely city, shining in the morning light.

"No," smiled Christine, "I think it was all Sheila's prayers finally paying off."

"That's what me and Mom talked about last night," said Sally. "We stayed up till about two in the morning, talking about mother-daughter things. I was thinking about it all, and came up with a thought. If everything had gone right for Joe and Mom back when they were young, I wouldn't be here, and wouldn't know you, or Skinny, or Clare, or Beck, and everything would be rotten."

"Or at least duller," agreed Christine. "Though maybe a little safer. I wonder if all our adventures are over."

"Are you kidding?" cried Sally. "No matter where you put me, especially when Skinny and Joe are around, the adventures will never end. Besides, Clare said that there are woods near his house, or really, our house. That means there'll be bears and mushrooms and all kinds of things. Plus, the house backs up to a cliff that drops straight down to the ocean. You can have all kinds of fun on a cliff, and the ocean is even better!"

Christine smiled, though she raised an eyebrow in perturbation, unconsciously making herself look very much like Skinny.

"Yep," said Sally, once again turning back toward the city. "Everything is great. I think that if ever I ..."

She began turning back to Christine, and stopped short. There, standing in the doorway of the bedroom, with Becky behind her, proudly holding the train, was the most beautiful bride either of them had ever seen. Christine automatically jumped to her feet, while Sally leaned up against the window for support, gazing open-mouthed at her mother.

Sheila was a lovely sight. Her slightly curling black hair came out of the lovely wedding veil and fell around her gentle face. Her eyes shone with happiness and excitement, and added the striking touch of blue to the snowy whiteness of the dress. For, though it was not customary at a second wedding, Sheila wore white.

Becky, in her gentle pink dress made the sweetest impression of a flower girl that any bride could wish for, though her saucy grin and impish nose gave evidence of her character.

"Holy cow," murmured Sally. "You look swell, Ma. Boy, I can't wait to see Little Joe's face when he sees you!"

Sheila dimpled appreciatively. "Oh, he knows what I look like," she said.

"Come on, Beck," said Sally. "Let's go find Dad."

They skipped out of the room together.

"You look wonderful, Sheila," said Christine, then grinned as Sheila opened her mouth to correct her. "I mean, you look wonderful, Mom." Sheila laughed and hugged her.

"Here," ordered Sally, planting Becky firmly in front of a hotel room door. "You wait here for any of the boys to come out, and I'll go check that courtyard place downstairs."

Becky nodded and pasted her ear to the door. Sally hurried down in the elevator and came out in the lobby just as Little Joe appeared outside the great glass doors of the atrium.

In the center of the hotel there was an open courtyard, which held planter-boxes filled with a glorious array of spring flowers, now lit by the dazzling morning sun.

Little Joe, despite looking infinitely more refined when clean shaven and wearing a new suit, was still his same rugged self. His tall figure looked well as he paced around the courtyard, though he couldn't keep his waving black hair in place no matter how he tried. Sally watched him for a minute with a grin. Then she flung the doors open, and with a whoop flew down the few steps and into his arms for a bear hug.

At the sound of her voice he had turned and caught her as she came skidding to a stop. His arms closed about her in a strong grasp, and he lifted her easily into the air.

"Well, my little wildcat!" he smiled, as he returned her gently to the earth. "You look awful happy."

"And I have reason to!" cried Sally, "It ain't every kid that has to go without a dad for practically her whole life, and then gets one that she's liked all along!"

Little Joe looked hard at her for a moment. When he spoke, his voice was husky. "All along? You've liked me all along? Where does a heart like yours come from?"

"It's all grace," Sally answered. "Sacraments do it all. The Sisters taught me that!"

Little Joe nodded knowingly. "Speaking of which, it won't be long before we'd better get over to the church."

"Are you scared?" asked Sally mischievously.

"No," said Little Joe. "More like terrified."

Sally laughed. "Don't be. Mom's terrific."

"You know," Little Joe said, "she was always so good, just like you. She always used to say that she wouldn't kiss me until our wedding day. Well, I guess that's today, although," his face clouded, "now it isn't her first kiss."

"Though I suppose," said Sally after a pause, "that you've gone around with a lot of fast girls, who go with gangsters. Is that true?"

"I forgot other women existed when I met your mother," said Little Joe seriously. "And after she'd been taken from me, I was satisfied with memories. There's never been anyone else. Except you. I think what I mistook for hate was really love for you all along."

"Yes," said Sally, "a lot of boys do that. When they're mean or rude to a girl, it means they really like her. Not many try to shoot the girl they like, though. You're just the type that overdoes things."

Little Joe smiled ruefully. "Well," he said, seeing something behind Sally, "if I'm going to be your dad now, then any guys that are interested in you are going to have to get by me. Except for my buddy Skinny."

Sally followed his gaze back to the doors, where Skinny and Clarence had just appeared. She blushed.

"Hey, you sentimental reminiscers!" called Clarence, as the two boys saw them and came springing down the steps. "Are you ready? We're leaving for the church! Marcel's cab is waiting outside, and boy, did he deck it out with cans and signs and streamers!"

"Well, we'd better go then," said Sally, taking Little Joe's arm.

He looked down at her and took a deep breath. "Well, here goes nothing."

Skinny smiled and gave him an encouraging pat on the back as they entered the lobby. "Let's hope we'll be that brave when it's our turn," he muttered to Clarence.

"Let's hope we won't have to wait as long as he did!" answered Clarence.

"Come on," said Skinny, pulling him out the doors to the street. "I want to get to the church soon. The best man can't be late, you know."

"Neither can the chap giving the bride away, my good mate," said the Professor, appearing on the curb beside them.

The two boys looked in surprise at the old Englishman. He was wearing a new suit, and from his top hat to his shining shoes, was the picture of grace and elegance. Beside him, now flaunting a new crimson cape and shining sword, was the Baron, looking as dignified and graceful as he always had.

Joe and Sally were deep in conversation next to Marcel's cab.

"Hey, Clare," Skinny said. "Go get the groom, I think Sally's scaring him."

As Clarence sauntered over, Skinny addressed the Baron.

"All Becky's friends are coming to the wedding. Have the French authorities found all their relatives?"

The Baron carefully picked the specks of dust off his sleeve with his white gloves, much to Skinny's amusement. "Everyone has a place to go but one, Becky's little friend Jack."

"Then what will happen to Jack?!"

"I will be adopting him as my son," answered the Baron calmly.

"What?!"

"Yes," said the Baron with a warm smile. "He has a heart of gold."

"Well I'll be switched," muttered Skinny. "I guess after all these festivities, when we head to California, you'll take Jack back to Switzerland. Becky will be blue. You'll have to come and visit us."

"Young Becky is a little dictator," answered the Baron. "And with my Jack they're a pair that won't be refused. We're already scheduled to visit next Christmas, Easter, and several weeks next summer."

Skinny laughed. "Oh, did you hear? The Professor is coming with us for good. He's selling his house and coming to live in California. So it looks as though we won't miss each other too much!"

Less than an hour later, Skinny and Clarence were in the front row of a beautiful church, expectantly awaiting the first strains of the wedding march.

"Are you scared?" whispered Clarence, when Skinny had finished his first prayers and sat down on the pew, cracking his knuckles.

"Not especially, just a little nervous," he whispered back, and ran his fingers through his hair.

Just then, the organ rang forth in a thunderous chorus of the wedding prelude. The door opened upon the pretty, and very proud figure of Becky, who processed toward them with the greatest dignity, tossing her flowers before her with the air of a queen. The boys smiled at each other, and glanced over at Jack, who was blushing like an angry bee beside the Baron.

Next, one in blue, one in green, came Sally and Christine.

Skinny's heart skipped a beat, and he hardly noticed the swift kick that he received from Clarence. The lovely figure in blue, which had seemed so unreal that night on the Eiffel Tower, when backed by the sunset, was now lit gloriously in the colored lights of the morning sun streaming through the stained-glass windows. For Skinny it seemed to make the coming Mass truly perfect. Clarence, gazing in pride at the lovely Christine, after looking sideways at Skinny with a good-natured grin, turned back toward the altar.

Sheila entered the church, her arm linked with that of the Professor's. As every eye turned to the breathtaking bride, up at the altar, Little Joe's filled with tears. Skinny's lips twitched slowly at the sight of it.

Sally glanced across at Skinny, as if thinking of all the joy and adventures that the five children had gone through together, and of all that was to come. He saw her long black eyelashes flick at him, as the glow of the sun, turned into every color of the rainbow by the art of the window, hit her face, and she ended the most amazing chronicle of their lives, with a confidential wink.

The End

Epilogue

As the reader will probably guess, the Company lived happily ever after.

They all went to live in California after the wedding, after fond farewells to Marcel and the Sisters, leaving Paris a good deal emptier than it had been during Easter Week. With them went the Professor.

Clarence returned the stolen diamonds to Scotland Yard before their departure, and was given a sizable reward for their recovery.

Clarence's beautiful home was the perfect settling place for the wild family. The house was a huge affair, styled to resemble a mountain lodge, and was full of enough nooks and crannies to keep the Company exploring its secrets for years on end.

One of the first things Sheila and Joe did to perfect their new home was to buy three rowdy puppies, who instantly became much adored members of the family, and soon grew to quite enormous sizes.

The ocean was accessible from their lofty perch by a secret path that the children soon discovered, and practically every warm summer day found them frolicking on the sands or swimming in the rowdy surf. Every night the lodge was lit by a beautiful sunset over the sea, and from the balconies and patios of their home, the Company could watch the lovely sight that ended each day of their paradisal lives.

Because of its rather out of the way location, the nearest city being a good thirty miles away, not many people were disturbed by the riotous living of what were soon called, "Those crazy O'Donnells!"

The town nearby was always interested when they received an assortment of O'Donnells to do the shopping, or to dine out. These outings always promised to be eventful, and a few became legendary.

When winter arrived, Jack and the Baron came for a visit. There was an unseasonably large snowfall not too far away, and the entire clan had a grand revival of the "Great Snow Battle," though this time the boys were aided by the sharp-shooting Joe O'Donnell, the energetic Jack, and the dignified Baron. The Professor was persuaded to join the girls' team, (though he didn't help much), and everyone agreed that with two Keenan girls on one side, the teams were only fair.

After a year or so, Sheila and Joe presented The Company with a baby brother, who was named Patrick Michael O'Donnell. Sally, having danced all the way down to the hospital cafeteria, upon her brother's arrival, informed the O'Donnell's that their new treasure's nickname was officially 'Coconut.'

And so the golden years passed by quickly and happily, with the girls growing in loveliness, and the boys in strength and courage, until Sally was a beautiful, though still wild lass of nineteen summers. Then, one lovely spring night, when they stood on the cliff, looking out at the most beautiful sunset of their lives, while the dogs romped around them, and a soft breeze made the pines sing above, Skinny formally proposed to Sally, and her consent was happily given.

Edwards Brothers Malloy
Thorofare, NJ USA
November 14, 2014